Murray wheeled on the big kid and shoved him backward against the bar.

"Hey...hey, what gives?!" Dozer said.

"You darkin' idiot," Murray said. "You could've gotten yourself and Knees killed. Because what, you wanted to prove yourself?"

"B-but..." Dozer stuttered. "They were insulting us! What about honor? What about the Codes?"

"Codes don't mean being stupid," Murray replied. "You want to keep going on Pilgrimage, don't you? Instead of getting holed up in some empire rot-chest?"

"Yeah, I do, Coach." Dozer looked down at the ground.

"I understand how it is," Murray said. "I wanted to put that block's head through this bar, bad. But I've figured some things out, though it took me a while. You can't always do what feels right at the time. Sometimes, the fight's not the one in front of you. And for you, the fights are waiting down the Grievar Road."

Praise for
THE COMBAT CODES

"This exciting and ambitious sequel to *The Combat Codes* expands the world and excels in character development.... The precarious ending will leave readers hungry for more."

—*Library Journal*

"Both protagonists are well realized, and Darwin masterfully balances vivid fight scenes with Cego and Solara's character growth, all while neatly setting things up for the trilogy's conclusion. It's a knockout."

—*Publishers Weekly*

"Darwin writes violence with the rhythm and surprise of a well-executed sonnet, wedding the smooth grace of choreography with the unflinching brutality of fists breaking bone. The fights are mesmerizing, layered like fascia, twitching and flexing and propelling the story toward a conclusion that both satisfies and opens the door to the next volume."

—*New York Times*

"With surprising depth and touching relationships, this debut packs a punch and sets up a fascinating foundation for the rest of the series. Great for fans of Will Wight."

—*Library Journal* (starred review)

"Brutal and relentless. *The Combat Codes* is that rare book that fully satisfies me as an action fan."

—Fonda Lee, author of *Jade City*

"A vividly realized tale both focused and sprawling. It's a book about warriors written by a master of the martial arts, and the mastery shows." —Evan Winter, author of *The Rage of Dragons*

"This book kicks ass—literally and literarily!"

—Richard Swan, author of *The Justice of Kings*

"If Mike Tyson wrote a sci-fi novel (and could write like he threw a right hook), it would read a little like *The Combat Codes*. Bare-knuckle brilliance."

—Jackson Ford, author of *The Girl Who Could Move Sh*t with Her Mind*

"*The Combat Codes* is combat as it was meant to be written: raw but elegant, a blend of the poet's wordsmithing and the martial art master's technical expertise. A fantastic reading experience."

—Moses Ose Utomi, author of *The Lies of the Ajungo*

"*The Combat Codes* is a perfectly balanced cocktail of high-octane action, enthralling mystery, and genuine heart. A gritty, fully realized world sets the stage for lovable (and hateable) characters, heart-pounding action, and twists that literally had my jaw dropping."

—M. J. Kuhn, author of *Among Thieves*

"A well-paced sci-fi brimming with action, brutality, thoughtfulness, and heart. From ruthless underworld to storm-harried, glistening academy, every fight is clear and visceral, and I couldn't help but be ensnared by the mystery and tension woven throughout."

—H. M. Long, author of *Hall of Smoke*

By Alexander Darwin

THE COMBAT CODES

The Combat Codes
Grievar's Blood
Blacklight Born

BLACKLIGHT BORN

THE COMBAT CODES: BOOK THREE

ALEXANDER DARWIN

orbitbooks.net

Copyright © 2024 by Alexander Darwin
Excerpt from *Cyberpunk 2077: No Coincidence* copyright © 2023 by CD Projekt S.A.

Cover design by Lauren Panepinto
Cover art by Peter Bollinger
Cover copyright © 2024 by Hachette Book Group, Inc.
Author photograph by Jeanette Fuller

Orbit
Hachette Book Group
1290 Avenue of the Americas
New York, NY 10104
orbitbooks.net

First Edition: December 2024
Simultaneously published in Great Britain by Orbit

Orbit is an imprint of Hachette Book Group.
The Orbit name and logo are registered trademarks of Little, Brown Book Group Limited.

The publisher is not responsible for websites (or their content) that are not owned by the publisher.

The Hachette Speakers Bureau provides a wide range of authors for speaking events. To find out more, go to hachettespeakersbureau.com or email HachetteSpeakers@hbgusa.com.

Orbit books may be purchased in bulk for business, educational, or promotional use. For information, please contact your local bookseller or the Hachette Book Group Special Markets Department at special.markets@hbgusa.com.

Library of Congress Cataloging-in-Publication Data
Names: Darwin, Alexander, author.
Title: Blacklight born / Alexander Darwin.
Description: First edition. | New York : Orbit, 2024. | Series: The Combat Codes book 3
Identifiers: LCCN 2024012934 | ISBN 9780316493574 (trade paperback) |
    ISBN 9780316493703 (ebook)
Subjects: LCGFT: Science fiction. | Novels.
Classification: LCC PS3604.A794 B53 2024 | DDC 813/.6—dc23/eng/20240322
LC record available at https://lccn.loc.gov/2024012934

ISBNs: 9780316493574 (trade paperback), 9780316493703 (ebook)

Printed in the United States of America

LSC-C

Printing 1, 2024

*For Ma and Da, who gave me the confidence
to pursue creativity.*

PART I

CHAPTER I

Return of the Lacklights

A Grievar must stand upon many different grounds. The ground beneath one's feet, to push off of and close the distance to an opponent. The ground of one's ancestors, those who gave their lives in the Circles of the past. The ground of awareness, seeing one's environment for what it truly is. As long as a Grievar keeps their roots planted in the ground, they will not fall.

Passage One, Sixty-Third Precept of the Combat Codes

Thaloo Jakabar ran a hand across his head, feeling for the few wispy hairs that remained. He shifted his considerable weight in the ornate chair to find a comfortable position, before reaching into the desk drawer to pop a wad of gummy chew into his mouth.

Thaloo's face scrunched at the bitter taste, but he swallowed the medicine he'd procured from the clerics' quarters to numb the pain. Of course, taking such medicines didn't abide by the Codes, but Thaloo had long since forgotten those ancient texts that were supposed to guide the Grievar.

After all, where would he be if he'd followed those idiotic prescriptions? To not accumulate wealth? To not seek power? Thaloo scanned his domed bedroom, lavish even by Daimyo standards: intricately carved wooden furniture shipped in from the Jade isle, ceramic vases from the Desovian steppe, a gar-bear-hide rug spread across the floor, elaborate latticework shutters that overlooked his courtyard outside. The rest of Thaloo's cavernside estate was similarly decorated to impress.

Thaloo's beady eyes returned to review the contract set on the desk. Armond Bernatti was desperate. The perfect position for Thaloo to sell to the man. Bernatti was one of many Besaydian lords vying for power in the vacuum that Cantino's assassination had left last year. The lords of the Isles sought to build up their mercenary Grievar teams, and Thaloo had been ready.

He signed the paper with a flourish and sat back in his chair, chuckling, thinking of those who thought the ways of the world were about to change. He laughed at those who thought the so-called Flux rebellion would even make a dent in the Daimyo institutions. They would be squashed like ants, run over by the Daimyo machines of war, and business would proceed as usual.

A sudden thump brought Thaloo's attention to his window. Likely one of his idiot guards messing around in the courtyard again. He employed nearly a dozen high-end mercenaries to protect the estate, and though he vetted them personally, they were young men, prone to the lures of the Underground.

Thaloo slowly lifted himself from the chair and shouted, "Garbar, what was the noise?"

A burly Grievar with cauliflowered ears opened the door to the room immediately. "Yes, sir?"

"The noise," Thaloo repeated. "I heard something from the courtyard. Go to ensure your team is not slagging off again."

"Yes, sir." The man closed the door briskly, and Thaloo sat back at the desk to continue his work.

Another contract, this one from the Ezonian administration. Thaloo scowled at the low offer they'd made for top-scale fighters coming out of his Circle. All this rebellion was accomplishing was making life more difficult for the rest, for folk like Thaloo who had clawed their way up, earned a place on top.

It was the Flux, those zealots, who bit the hand that fed them. Perhaps the Daimyo were right when they said most Grievar had mental limitations, their brains shrunken and unable to think straight. Perhaps it was only a select few like Thaloo who had been blessed to think freely. To understand the way of the world: Everybody wanted something. One just needed to decipher what that something was.

A shout snapped Thaloo's head back to the window.

"Garbar? What in the dark is going on?"

Thaloo stood and moved toward his doorway. "Garbar?"

A bead of sweat formed at the big man's brow as he reached into a desk drawer and closed his fingers around cold metal. He lifted the spectral rod and slowly flipped the switch at the bottom, initiating the weapon's energy cycle.

"Garbar…" Thaloo whispered this time. He listened carefully but heard only the mechs drumming up the cavern in the distance.

Thaloo set himself against the window and lifted the shutters. He craned his head, breathing heavily, to look at the courtyard below. The darkness of the blackshift undulated on the cobbles, made shadows dance across his lush topiary displays.

Though Thaloo's combat abilities had never been sufficient to fight in the Circles, though his hearing was dulled, he still sensed the sudden presence behind him in the room. He grasped the glowing rod and spun around to see a black-cloaked figure standing by his bedpost.

"Who sent you? Lord Tiyano?" Thaloo released the rapid-fire

words like a defense system. It wasn't the first time an assassin had shown up at his doorstep.

"Or perhaps you're of Ezonian employ? Callen was fed up bartering with me, eh?" Thaloo feigned a chuckle as he started to lower the crackling weapon. "Either way, I'll pay better. Far better, enough to let you—"

Thaloo's voice caught as the intruder lifted his cowl.

"You…"

A set of piercing gold eyes stared back at Thaloo.

"Boy…little gold-eyes."

Thaloo clutched the weapon with white knuckles, tried to ignore his heart leaping into his throat.

"I've been looking for you…Cego." Thaloo let the sweetness seep into his voice. *Everybody wants something.*

The boy remained motionless by the bedpost, those golden eyes never leaving Thaloo. Cego was larger than when Thaloo had last seen him. Several years ago, he'd been a scrappy boy fighting for his life in Thaloo's slave Circles. Now, even beneath the cloak, Thaloo could see muscles taut across the boy's wide shoulders.

"You must be good, just as I've heard," Thaloo said. "Did you dispatch my entire team? The rumors from my little birds must be true, then. You defeated the Goliath?"

Cego took a step forward, silent still.

Thaloo knew this boy would take no flattery, no money. He was a true believer. He'd need something else.

"I saw your friend Murray recently." Thaloo changed tactics. "Is that why you're here? Do you seek Murray Pearson?"

Finally, Thaloo saw something flash across the boy's eyes. A small betrayal to the darkness that seemed to wrap around Cego, sucking the light from the surrounding spectral lamps.

"Yes, he was looking for your brother," Thaloo continued. "But Murray didn't look so well at the time, I'll be honest. I was worried about him. Are you worried about him as well, Cego?"

Cego appeared to be fighting some invisible force. He snapped his head to the side, looked to the shadows of the room. Perhaps the boy had been lost to insanity. Thaloo had seen it before, among those Grievar who trained too hard, who had given their minds to the spectral light.

"I can reunite you with Murray, with your brother Sam," Thaloo purred. "I heard he found your brother, he took him from this place, back to your home at the Lyceum."

"That is not my home any longer," Cego spoke without emotion.

"Oh?" Thaloo's eyes glinted. "Is that so? So your home is with your other brother now, the one they call the Slayer. You're with the Flux. If that's the case, I have a proposition for you. If your rebellion has any chance of survival, of success, your brother needs a way to ship supplies up to the front lines without—"

Cego took another menacing step toward Thaloo, silencing him. The slaver grasped the spectral rod harder. But Thaloo was no fighter. Only his words would save him.

"If not something for the Flux..." Thaloo said, slowly backing up. "You care about those in my slave Circles, yes? I remember, you wanted to save that little boy Weep, so long ago, but you couldn't. You seek redemption? Instead of harming me, why not take my money and buy their freedom? Just as Murray Pearson bought yours."

Cego stepped forward again and the lights flickered.

"Wait—" Thaloo's voice broke. "What do you want?"

Cego shook his head. "Nothing."

"How can you want nothing? Even if you are Grievar, there must be something. Power? Friends? Women, men? I can give it all to you...gold-eyes."

Thaloo turned away, as if accepting his fate, but suddenly lunged toward Cego, hissing as he launched his considerable frame forward, spectral rod crackling.

He didn't even see Cego move, but Thaloo felt his chest explode as his active weapon clattered to the floor. The thick rug beneath him immediately caught fire.

Thaloo heaved for air and stared up into those golden eyes.

"I do want something," Cego said, as smoke began to curl behind him.

"Yes…" Thaloo pleaded, sputtering. "Just tell me what you want, it is yours."

"I want to end your life."

*   *   *

"Darkin' Bird."

Murray Pearson shifted uncomfortably in the saddle atop his mount. Maybe it was the back injury he'd sustained years before, or maybe this roc was purposely sloping its long neck toward the road to unbalance Murray.

"Ku, you should probably call his proper name if you want him to ride better," a dark-haired girl said from beside Murray, astride her own, smaller roc. The girl stroked the midnight plumes on her bird's head and pressed a foot against its hindquarters. "Let's go, Akari!" The roc burst forward in a show of speed, and the girl turned back toward Murray and smirked.

"I've given mine a name," Murray muttered. "Let's go, Bird!"

Instead of this prompting his ruffled grey roc to speed up, Murray's mount reared and jolted its head forward, tossing him onto the dusty path. Laughter erupted from Murray's traveling companions, all stopping to witness the burly Grievar's fall.

"How about some darkin' respect?" Murray shouted from the ground. "Four decades your elder, and your professor too. I could have all your Level Three asses held back until you've got grey in your beards."

A lanky boy with a wicked scar crossing his face dismounted his roc to help Murray up with a firm wrist-to-wrist grasp. "We know you won't be doing that, Coach. You'd hate to go all that ways back south to be writing reports to Callen Albright."

Murray accepted the helping hand as familiar pain shot up his back. "You're too sharp for your own good, Knees."

A burly kid, shirtless and thick with muscle, joined Knees beside Murray. "Plus, we know you're having good fun out here with us on Pilgrimage."

"It's because of your fun we're pressing to make the next challenge, Dozer," Murray responded.

"Hold on," Dozer protested. "That girl back in Mirstok was giving me eyes; I'm sure of it."

The dark-haired girl dismounted her black roc and slapped Dozer on the shoulder. "Right, so is that why you ended up with your bit-purse gone, your rations eaten by her friends, and no action to show for it?"

Knees nodded. "Brynn's got a point there."

Dozer's face reddened. "I did have something to show, just not enough time to work it. She even said she'd make me her ma's stew when I come back—"

"Enough idling here," Murray said as he dusted himself off. "If we're to make the Tanri challenge, we need to move now; we're still two days out at this pace. Plus, I need to stop in Wazari Market to resupply."

"Are you sure that's a good idea?" Brynn Mykili asked. "Those harvesters we passed a few hours back said patrols have been constant off the Grievar Road. Spirits be asked, if we were detained, we'd certainly not make the next challenge."

Murray's face darkened. "They find us and they'll see exactly what we're here for: Pilgrimage. It's been Lyceum tradition for the past fifteen decades, even while Kiroth and Ezo have been tearing at each other's throats. A little rebellion shouldn't change nothing."

"Little rebellion?" Knees said incredulously as he deftly leapt onto the back of the large brown roc he shared with Dozer. "From what we heard, this be more than little. They say the Slayer took down the biggest stim depot east of Karstock few days ago."

"I don't want to hear another darkin' word about that one," Murray said. He vainly tried to cajole his grey roc toward him, making a clucking sound. The bird sauntered away, pecking at some worms in the mud. "I've heard this story before, someone stands up and says they'll change the way things have always been. Thinks he'll move against the Daimyo. Want to know the end of that story?"

"What's that?" Dozer said from behind Knees atop their roc.

"They get ground into the dust by the mechs, then folk keep going on about their business," Murray said. He tried to grab at his roc's saddle, only to have the bird scramble out of range again.

"But Silas took down the entire northern front!" Dozer exclaimed. "He united the Ice Tribes behind Bertoth; he's got thousands of Grievar backing him up, and he's got some special powers like—"

"Enough," Murray growled with frustration as he unsuccessfully attempted to grab his roc. "Bird, get back here before I decide we'll be having poultry over the campfire tonight!"

"But they said Silas broke into Arklight. He destroyed a battalion of Enforcers on his way to getting his brother. Cego might be with him!" Dozer protested. Murray shook his head.

"Those are stories, Dozer, the sort that grow like weeds." The old Grievar Knight looked pleadingly at Brynn. "Some help?"

The girl urged her mount forward and pulled up beside Murray's roc. She gently whispered in its ear and stroked its grey feathers. Bird clucked, as if letting out a sigh, before hopping over to Murray to lower its head.

"Thanks," Murray muttered, finally climbing onto the roc and breathing deeply. He turned to Dozer. "And that story about Cego, that's the worst to be repeating. That story will be giving you hope. And that's not what we're out here for. You're here on Pilgrimage. You've got matches to fight across the whole of Kiroth along the Grievar Road. You do good here, you'll be adding to your scores back at the Lyceum as Level Threes, so keep focus."

BLACKLIGHT BORN   11

Dozer quieted down, awkwardly wrapping his big arms around Knees from up on their roc.

"Time to be on our way, Boko," Knees said to his bird as they set pace on the road snaking through the green plains ahead.

"Let's go, Akari!" Brynn yelled.

Murray watched the Jadean shoot past the boys on her sleek black roc, kicking up a cloud of dust behind her. The Kavel Mountain Range sprawled like a pale slumbering giant in the distance, set beneath the cloudless blue sky. Murray shifted uncomfortably from atop his roc. He could have sworn the bird was purposely tilting forward.

"Bird's a fine darkin' name," Murray grumbled as he followed behind in the dust.

*   *   *

Murray was accustomed to the street-stalled markets of the Underground; the clamor of Markspar Row; hawkers screaming at the tops of their lungs in front of their rusted carts, selling imported lightdecks and illicit neurotech. But Wazari Market, the sprawling tent city that sprang up in the Kirothian highlands every summer, made Markspar seem an organized affair. Murray sucked his stomach in as a wooden cart nearly ran him off the path through the market. A trio of rocs pulled the cart at breakneck speed, and the driver screamed back at him in some dialect he couldn't understand. Murray had visited Wazari only once before, during his own Pilgrimage through Kiroth. The giant market sprang up alongside the influx of traveling students. Pilgrims from every nation came through, and the local hawkers did not discriminate as long as you had a full bit-purse.

"Maybe I'll replace you," Murray muttered, thinking of his own rebellious mount, as he passed a tent full of squawking rocs cooped up in cages.

"You want?" A hawker caught Murray eyeing the scrawny birds. "Guarantee you fill bit-purse many times over if you bring one of my roc to the ring! They bred for fighting, like you."

Murray shook his head and pushed on toward the central stalls farther in. Dusk cast the market in a crimson hue, the colorful tent awnings like a field of wildflowers set on the Kirothian plains. One could purchase not only a new mount at Wazari but any sort of wild beast. Murray passed iron cages with pacing gar bears and penned-up wild tuskers from the northern forests. He even saw a hawker pawning a giant boa snake from the Besaydian jungles. As a student, Murray hadn't paid attention to how chaotic Wazari was; he'd probably had his mind on his next fight, or maybe, like Dozer, he had been focused on some blushing highland girl he'd seen at the last village along the Grievar Road. Murray's memory of Wazari was likely as naïve as the rest of his youthful thoughts, right up there with the notion that he'd been fighting for honor, for his nation, for the Codes. He passed a section of purple awnings with the heavily perfumed scent of night flowers wafting from them. A veiled woman draped in silk peered out seductively and waved Murray toward her.

The kids would have enjoyed this, Murray thought. Dozer would likely have tried to steal off for a peek into these courtesan tents. And he could imagine the Jadean girl, Brynn, looking wide-eyed at the assortment of animals. If he'd only come for rations, like he'd told the Whelps, he probably would have brought them into the market.

But that was not why Murray had come to Wazari.

He weaved his way through several stalls selling colorful silk robes and emerged in front of a red tent with a six-fingered-hand symbol on the awning. Murray pushed the thick curtain aside and walked through the dimly lit tent. The goods sold here were not up on display like in the rest of the market, and buyers looked over their shoulders as they took wrapped bundles under their arms. He ducked his head as he passed into a short stall set against the tent's back wall. Murray pulled his cowl back and looked down at a little man in a steel chair wearing a strange pair of bifocals that magnified his eyes.

"Stims or neurotech?" the hawker said nonchalantly as he fiddled with a broken deck.

"Neither," Murray replied.

"Then you're wasting my time," the man responded. "Get out of here."

"Thaloo said I could come to you for something else."

The man looked up from his work, pushing back his chair. "How is that fat bastard doing now?"

"Same as always; he's a piece of shit," Murray replied.

The man nodded. "So, what now did Thaloo say I might be providing you?"

"Information," Murray said. "I'm looking for someone's whereabouts."

"There are many someones who I used to know the whereabouts of," the man responded. "But strangely, my memory is foggy right now."

Murray laid three midnight onyx pieces on the table and waited.

"Ah, yes," the hawker whispered. "I remember where some of these folk are. Who in particular are you looking for?"

"The one known as Silas," Murray said.

The man burst into laughter. "You think I'm crazy?! You want to know where the Slayer is at? I do not have a death wish." Murray sighed. He reached into his pocket and pulled out six more bits and laid them on the table.

"There are Enforcers at all way-stops on the road, and even some patrolling this market, asking the very same question as you," the hawker said.

Murray emptied the rest of his bit-purse onto the table. The man's eyes gleamed, as if he were salivating, but he shook his head as he pushed the pile of onyx back.

"I can't do it. I don't know shit. Why don't you get out of here before you get us both buried?"

Murray didn't back down. "I need to know where Silas is."

The man turned away, grabbing a piece of neurotech off the shelf.

"I told you, I don't know anyone by that name."

Murray reached over the table and grabbed the man by the shoulders. He lifted the little hawker like a doll and wrapped a thick arm around his neck. Murray squeezed for a moment to constrict the man's arteries. "Now, it'll be a few seconds of me squeezing and you'll be out," Murray whispered. "And while you're out, you know what I'm going to do? I'll take all the darkin' stim in this shop and give it out to those hungry-looking Grievar mulling about outside."

The man tried to struggle but could not move an inch. Murray squeezed again, sensing darkness was closing in on the man.

"Wait!" The hawker managed to get the word out, and Murray loosened his grip.

"Last I heard, Slayer had taken a stim production depot to the west," the hawker said.

"I already knew that," Murray growled. He began to ratchet the strangle up again.

"And!" the man yelped. "And there's been word he's close to the capital. Clerics been ending up dead in and around Karstock."

"Are you lying to me?" Murray felt the man's pulse against his arm. "Why in the dark would the Flux leader put himself in the seat of the empire?"

"I swear, I'm telling you the truth," the hawker pleaded. "Let me be."

Murray threw the man back over the table and onto the floor of the little stall. He slid the onyx pile back into his purse, all but one coin that he tossed onto the floor beside the hawker.

"One more question," Murray said. "And I need you to think carefully before you answer."

The man glared back at him with his beady eyes.

"Is the Slayer with anyone else?"

"What do you mean, *with anyone else?*" the hawker yelled. "He's leader of the darkin' Flux; he's got an army of rebels with him!"

"With anyone in particular, though," Murray said. "Someone close by him most of the time."

"Yeah." The hawker stood and dusted himself off. "I heard he's got a kid with him. Some boy that doesn't leave his side."

Murray stared hard at the man before turning and ducking back beneath the low entry.

"And tell Thaloo he owes me!" Murray heard the hawker scream as he went back the way he came.

*   *   *

A yellow moon rose above Wazari Market like a watchful eye as Murray trudged back toward the lodging.

He glanced up at a sign hanging over one of the big tents along the path, a large ram's horn with golden liquid frothing out the top. Murray still had to fight the pull, the urge to walk through the inviting curtains of one of these pop-up liquor stands that sprang from the highland floors every fifty meters like giant weeds.

"Darkin' said I wouldn't; not going to turn back now," Murray whispered through clenched teeth as he produced a small vial from his pocket and downed it.

A man in a ragged cloak with a cowl overhead stumbled from the tent, coughing. Murray stared wide-eyed, held his breath as the man's face caught the moonlight. *Not him.*

Though Murray had looked for Farmer everywhere since his last trip to the Underground, the old master hadn't appeared to him again. Murray was reluctant to even make sense of his last trip Deep in search of Cego's brother Sam. Though he'd found the boy and brought him to the Citadel, put him in Memnon's care, Murray still couldn't make sense of Farmer's role in it all. Somehow, the old master had infiltrated Murray's mind, appearing to him like a ghost. No one else in Lord Maharu's compound had been able to see the old master. Murray still questioned whether he'd been entirely sane or whether Farmer really had been a figment of neurosis, a mirage floating in too many years of ale.

Murray shook his head, attempting to rid himself of the memories as he rounded a corner and eyed a set of wood-framed stalls cast in the moonlight.

"Not sleeping either, eh, Bird?" Murray came to the front of one stall and met the eyes of his rebellious roc. Murray reached out and ruffled the bird's sparse head feathers that covered up a balding spot.

The grey bird squawked back at him, digging its talons into the dirt and tossing its head toward the air.

"What's gotten into you?" Murray murmured. Bird was always an ass to him, but he could see something else in the roc's eyes now. The other mounts were stabled nearby and also shifted uncomfortably when they'd normally be resting at this hour.

Murray's eyes darted to the sprawling circular tent set next to the stables. The Wazari Inn, where the Whelps were holed up for the night before setting back to the Grievar Road in the morning. The tent's thick curtain caught the highland wind, and Murray heard shouting from within.

He strode toward the tent as he heard Dozer's voice clearly.

"Why don't you try and put those clasps on me, see what happens!"

"What've those kids got themselves into," Murray muttered as he pushed the curtain aside.

Dozer stood at the center of the lounge area, several stools tossed to the floor, across from two large Grievar who looked ready to pounce on the boy. Knees stood by his friend's side, jaw clenched and fists curled. A sour-faced hawker behind the bar eyed the situation warily.

"Coach!" Dozer shouted. "Glad you're back here to witness these two scumslaggers getting floored."

One of the men took his eyes off Dozer and turned toward Murray.

"You in charge of these kids?" he asked.

Murray eyed the man. Clearly a merc, maybe ex–empire Knight, with a scar running across his jutting jawline. Both were thick-shouldered, wearing Kirothian reds over mismatched studded leather. Murray's eyes dropped to the merc's belt, where a black rod was holstered, his hand hovering over the weapon as he stared down Dozer.

"Dozer, stand down," Murray said with an even tone. Dozer and Knees could hold their own, but not against a full-grown Grievar, not to mention one packing a spectral weapon. He had no intention of letting a student in his charge end up under wet earth.

"What?" Dozer protested. "These two were the ones that started it. Put hands on Knees for nothing!"

Murray stepped in front of Dozer.

"Maybe you should take your own advice, old-timer," the merc said threateningly. "Stand down so we can bring these boys in."

Murray breathed steadily and fixed his good eye on the merc. He was aware he was older than these two Grievar. But as adrenaline pumped into his veins, he plotted the path he would take to put the two down.

Feint a quick jab, then right high kick to take the armed one out. Take the second one with a double-leg, get some airtime and make sure to crack the man's skull to a table on the way down.

"Don't think I'm going to let you do that," Murray growled.

The merc laughed, turned to his partner. "Hear that, Dross? Maybe we take old-timer in for disobedience too."

The one called Dross ripped his rod free of its holster. A spark lit at the weapon's base and began to crackle along its length.

Murray held his ground but motioned for Dozer and Knees to step back. The two boys didn't move.

Murray would need to go low, maybe a quick ankle pick to get beneath the weapon. Even a touch from the rod would put him down.

But it was too dangerous. Not with these kids who were clearly ready to jump into the fray. They were under Murray's charge. He couldn't lose another.

"Why don't you tell me why you want to bring these kids in?" Murray let his hands hang at his sides. "What've they done, tried to pinch a drink from the bar? I've got the bits and have no problem paying for them."

The merc lowered his weapon slightly. "It's not that, old-timer. These kids fit the bill of people we're looking for. Rebels."

"We already told you we're no rebels," Knees snarled, and held up his arm, displaying the spinning circle tattoo fluxed to his inner wrist. It was dangerous for Ezonians to travel in Kiroth, and Murray had made sure the entire team had the safe-passage flux done before the journey began.

"Kid speaks the truth; they're here for Pilgrimage," Murray said. "Why don't you let them be on their way. They got enough fights on the road ahead."

"We heard that before," the merc said. "Thing is, empire wants to stamp out some rebels right now. That's what they're paying us for. And if we go back to post empty-handed, we don't get paid."

Murray growled. He despised mercs. Grievar, working for the Daimyo as hired bodies. Bouncers for fancy nightclubs, guards for nobles, or bounty hunters looking to root up a growing rebel force, it was all the same.

Murray reached into his pouch and produced two onyx bits, a tiresome habit today. "Now, why don't you go tell your empire lords you've seen no rebels in these parts."

The merc snatched the piece and bit it, handing the other to his grinning partner.

"You did right, old-timer," the man said as he reholstered the rod. "And next time, you better keep an eye on your boys here; something about this ugly one I don't like."

Dozer pushed up against Murray as the mercs left the tent.

"We could've taken 'em," Dozer muttered.

Murray wheeled on the big kid and shoved him backward against the bar.

"Hey...hey, what gives?!" Dozer said.

"You darkin' idiot," Murray said. "You could've gotten yourself and Knees killed. Because what, you wanted to prove yourself?"

"B-but..." Dozer stuttered. "They were insulting us! What about honor? What about the Codes?"

"Codes don't mean being stupid," Murray replied. "You want to keep going on Pilgrimage, don't you? Instead of getting holed up in some empire rot-chest?"

"Yeah, I do, Coach." Dozer looked down at the ground.

"I understand how it is," Murray said. "I wanted to put that block's head through this bar, bad. But I've figured some things out, though it took me a while. You can't always do what feels right at the time. Sometimes, the fight's not the one in front of you. And for you, the fights are waiting down the Grievar Road."

Dozer nodded.

"Go get some sleep," Murray said as the two kids made their way back to their quarters.

Murray eyed the leftover ale set on the bar. The bartender waved his hand invitingly. "Take it; you earned it by preventing this place from getting turned over."

Murray breathed deep, watching the golden bubbles rise and fall in the glass.

He turned away and muttered again, "Sometimes, the fight's not the one in front of you."

CHAPTER 2

Unbalancing Act

One should consider the story of the gar bear hunting the weasel. It is said that the bear resolutely clawed at the weasel's hole until it lacked the strength to even crawl down to the river to sustain its thirst. The weasel waited until the bear died of starvation to emerge from its burrow. The smaller animal feasted upon the giant carcass for the entire winter. Determination must be easily discerned from desperation.

Passage Two, Twenty-Seventh Precept of
the Combat Codes

"Where is everyone?" Knees said, looking up at the vast azure sky above.

"Maybe they saw us and turned scared." Dozer chuckled as he dismounted the roc from behind Knees into the tall Kirothian high grass.

The Whelps had arrived at the center of the triangle-shaped plateau formed by three intersecting rivers. Murray had made sure to map it out the day prior, as the Whelps had already been lost several times, trying to navigate the unfamiliar terrain.

"We're a bit early still, likely," Murray said, trying to halt Bird's movement by yanking on his harness, which only caused the roc to trot in a dizzying circle.

Brynn placed a calming hand on Bird's beak and whispered a few choice Jadean words. The roc stopped in its tracks and lowered its head obediently.

"You got to teach me how to do that," Murray said with a sigh as he dismounted.

"Ku, you just need to be nice," Brynn said as she took to reining in the entire group of rocs.

"I'm plenty nice," Murray grumbled. "Darkin' bird has an attitude…"

Murray's words were overtaken by a growing tremor beneath their feet. There were no storm squalls on the horizon, but a billowing cloud of dust careened toward the Whelps from the north.

"In Venturi, we used to have sandstorms that looked like that," Knees said warily.

"That's no storm, Knees," Murray replied as the distinct forms of riders broke out in front of the dust cloud, sweeping onto the highland grasses. At least fifty rocs charged toward the Whelps.

Murray watched the students to gauge their reactions. Dozer and Knees appeared ready to fight, their fists curled into balls. Brynn made a strange sign toward the sky.

"What should we do?" Dozer yelled, swiveling his head as the roc riders circled the group, whooping alongside their screeching birds.

"Do nothing," Murray said. "This is the Tanri tribe here for your challenge."

It was comforting to Murray that there were still some Grievar who kept to the old ways. The Tanri were just as Murray remembered them, even more than two decades later.

The riders finally stopped circling. Each wore a colorful feathered mask sitting over the forehead, a central slit for the eyes and a hooked beak down over the nose and mouth. The Tanri gazed down silently at the Whelps from atop their birds.

One of the largest and ugliest rocs Murray had ever seen trotted forward from the pack. The giant bird was missing an eye, like Murray, and its deformed beak jutted to the side. Atop it was an equally imposing man wearing a brilliant bird mask, a jumble of plumage shooting from its top.

The man agilely dismounted his roc, sliding off and landing in the high grass. Like the rest of the riders, he wore a leather vest with cutoff sleeves.

The man held Murray's gaze through his mask as he strode forward aggressively.

Murray stood his ground, keeping his hands down by his sides. Even as the man came within Murray's reach, a point that normally would bring his hands high, he suppressed the reaction. He wasn't planning on insulting their host, ruining this opportunity for the Whelps.

The large man stopped an inch away. Murray could smell his sour breath beneath the hooked beak and see the flecks of his bronze eyes inside the mask's slit.

The man clasped a hand behind Murray's head, another action that would normally set Murray's synapses on fire, arm his defenses for an incoming head butt. Instead, Murray responded in kind, reaching behind the crown of the man's head.

Simultaneously, the two slowly brought their skulls together and pressured in. The jagged edge of the mask cut into Murray's forehead. Blood began to trickle down his brow into his eyes.

Finally, the man released the clinch and Murray followed suit, taking a step back.

"It been too long, mighty one." The man spoke the broken Tikretian words in a baritone as he lifted the mask off his head, revealing a round face with red, leathery cheeks, worn by the unending highland sun and harsh winter frosts.

"Indeed it has, Muhai," Murray replied. "You look the same as I last saw you. Ugly as that darkin' bird of yours."

The man named Muhai rocked his head back with laughter. "You too, my friend, ugly still! And old now."

Muhai turned and motioned for the rest of his riders to dismount. They did so gracefully, sliding from their unsaddled birds into the high grass. Murray knew the Tanri had been riding rocs since they could first take steps. They grew up with their birds like brothers.

Many of the men and women removed their bird masks, but several of the smaller ones kept their faces covered.

Muhai walked purposefully to each of the Whelps and performed the same ritual, getting uncomfortably close and pressing his head up against theirs.

"This is way our birds greet and say farewell," Muhai explained. "We bird people, Tanri, do same."

The man ran his hand through Brynn's hair, murmuring as he felt her thick curls. He sniffed Dozer and squeezed his shoulder.

"This one, look strong. Maybe has Tanri blood? Smells a bit different than rest of you city kin."

"What's he mean?" Dozer asked defensively. "He says I smell?"

"It's a compliment; best take it." Murray chuckled. "Muhai is a chieftain of the Tanri tribes."

The Tanri stood among the Whelps, not paying the wide-eyed group much heed as they went straight to work, smiling and laughing as they did so. They unloaded several packs off the backs of their birds.

Muhai spoke to the Whelps to translate the events. "We Tanri must please the sky before we can start challenge."

A stout Tanri boy with a long tuft of black hair hanging down his back smiled as he walked fearlessly toward Knees and Dozer. He nodded and motioned for them to follow. "Help."

The boy brought the Whelps to the side of a plump-looking roc, one that Murray noticed had no rider atop it. The young Tanri pulled a leather pouch from his side and crouched beneath the bird's undercarriage. He reached out and squeezed. Thick milk poured from the roc's teat into the leather skin. When it was full, another boy took the brimming skin and handed the milker another empty container.

"What…what are they doing?" Dozer asked.

"You'll see," Murray said, smiling as he watched.

Several of the younger Tanri came forward when enough liquid was collected, and passed the skins around, each taking a long swig, letting it pour down their face and splash across their leather vests. One handed a skin to Dozer and nodded.

"You—you mean I'm supposed to drink bird piss?" Dozer stuttered.

"It's not piss, you block!" Knees said. "It's milk. That be a mother bird, and she's just given you some of her supply to drink."

"That's even worse than piss!" Dozer yelled, holding the skin up to his nose and giving it a wary sniff.

"Best not insult them, Dozer," Murray said as the Tanri boys eagerly eyed the foreigners.

Dozer breathed deeply and took a swig of the roc milk, closing his eyes as it went down. "Hey, not so bad," he said as he passed the skin to Knees.

Each Whelp took their turn.

Muhai stood next to Murray. "You watch over your children."

"They're not my brood, Muhai," Murray said. "Students. I'm a professor at the Lyceum now."

"Children, students, same," Muhai said. "I see how you watch them."

Murray nodded as the Tanri chief motioned for the Whelps to sit in a circle in the grass. Several of the younger masked Tanri sat alongside them.

One of the tribesmen led a black roc forward into the circle and stood with his hands outstretched. A Tanri boy stood to volunteer and stepped into the circle across from the roc.

The boy shuffled forward cautiously and slowly slipped his hands behind the roc's head as Murray and Muhai had done upon greeting.

The Tanri boy jerked the roc to the side and threw a low foot, trying to kick out one of the creature's lanky legs. The roc responded by driving forward with ferocity, knowing this game they played. The bird tossed the boy to the ground. He stood and bowed his head to the avian opponent before taking a seat back at the sidelines.

Another Tanri, larger than the first with red-flushed cheeks and feline eyes, started the ritual again, wrapping his hands behind the roc's head. This boy's strategy was different, though; he pulled the roc toward him and tried to unbalance it. Murray recognized de-ashi harai, one of his favorite foot sweeps.

But the bird's balance was spectacular; it righted itself and twisted its long neck to the side, forcing the boy forward before jerking the other direction and easily tossing its opponent into the grass.

The Whelps stared wide-eyed at the bird wrestling, something they'd never seen before.

"The Tanri learn much of their wrestling working with the birds," Murray explained.

"Doesn't it hurt the rocs?" Brynn asked, the girl's expression sour as another Tanri grasped the roc's feathered neck.

Muhai laughed from beside them. "You city kin! Always ask same question. Bird hurt? When we fight, Grievar hurt so often, but you worried about bird. But no, bird is honored, given good home, food, mate. Most often, boys get bashed up but bird hearty. When they fight each other, it much worse. This fun for them!"

Murray watched as another Tanri boy was tossed into the dirt by the rearing roc.

"I want at it!" Dozer yelled, standing up.

Muhai smiled and extended his hand for Dozer to step into the circle. Dozer did as he had seen, placing his hands behind the bird's head in a clinch and setting his stance.

Murray could see Dozer's arms straining already. That wouldn't do; he was too taut. The bird, however, was fluid like a whip. It curled its neck inward and retreated on its hindquarters abruptly. Dozer attempted to hold on, even impose his will and push the bird the other way, but he flailed to the ground.

"Bird's darkin' strong!" Dozer huffed from the grass. "Don't even think Coach would be able to hold on."

"I'd tend to agree with you, kid, given the luck I've had with my own bird," Murray said.

"Watch," Muhai said, as he motioned for another Tanri to step forward, this time a smaller, squat girl who had the chief's bulbous nose.

The girl assumed the starting position with the roc. Instead of tightening up and grasping hard at the back of the bird's head, the girl gently brushed against the nape of its neck with both hands.

She pulled forward and the roc retreated. The girl moved with it, taking two steps until the bird stopped and started to move in the opposite direction. The girl stepped back twice, in time with the bird. The two shuffled to the side, almost in synchronization.

"She good at bird dance," Muhai said, his chest puffed out proudly.

"That your girl there?" Murray asked.

Muhai nodded as his daughter and the roc continued to move in unison, the girl guiding the bird gently.

"What's going on here?" Dozer guffawed.

"She's timing her sweep," Murray said, keeping his eyes trained on the girl's feet. "Instead of trying to force the roc in a direction, she's lulling it into a pattern."

As if on cue, the girl shuffled to the side and changed cadence, rapidly sweeping her outside leg low into the bird's weight-bearing talon. The roc toppled to the ground, squawking from the grass.

"Isn't that cheating, the way she calmed it?" Dozer protested.

Muhai turned to Dozer, a big smile spread across the man's face. "Like any fight. Need to make pattern, then break pattern."

Murray motioned at the watching Whelps. "When you go up against the Tanri, you'll need to keep that in mind."

An abrupt blaring sound broke up the bird wrestling. Muhai held a large ram's horn to his lips and blasted it again in several quick, short bursts.

The signal prompted the Tanri to shout as they herded their rocs into formation. The birds settled on their haunches in multiple circles, lowering their heads to the grass floor while watching with upturned eyes.

Muhai gestured toward the makeshift rings. "Your challenge."

Murray nodded, and Dozer, Brynn, and Knees stepped forward. Muhai handed each a leather vest to wear.

Muhai brought a group of the Tanri kids into a huddle, each pressing their heads into the center.

Murray shrugged and did the same, gathering the Whelps around him with linked arms. "This will be a bit different than what you're used to. No strikes and only goal is to get your opponent off his feet, like Dozer tried with the bird."

"So, it be like wrestling class, then?" Knees asked from the huddle.

"Well, not quite," Murray said. "You can't shoot low for the legs, and you need to use that leather vest as a grip. Goal is to use your trips and throws to get them on their ass."

"Seems easy enough." Dozer found his confidence again. "Can't be as hard as fighting a roc!"

The Whelps broke apart, Dozer clapping his hands in excitement as he strode into a circle across from Muhai's daughter. Knees and Brynn did the same, stepping over the outstretched bird necks to stand across from their opponents.

Dozer nodded and smiled at the stout Tanri girl with red cheeks, who smiled back. Muhai's daughter was happy to show Dozer the proper way to begin, one hand on the leather collar, the other in a clinch behind the head.

Murray stood beside Muhai and watched. He remembered doing the same two decades before, on his own Pilgrimage. He'd been brash like Dozer.

Muhai blasted the horn, and the action began in the high grass, combatants shifting their weight, gripping and grasping leather vests in attempts to unbalance their partners.

"How has nothing changed?" Murray whispered from beside Muhai. He wasn't quite sure if he was asking himself or the Tanri chieftain.

"Everything change," Muhai said as he watched his daughter grapple with Dozer, unbalancing the boy with a well-timed inside sweep.

"This is as I remember, though," Murray said. "The endless sky overhead, the games in the grass, your people smiling, fighting for the true spirit of it. Like Grievar should be."

Knees was nearly able to throw his opponent with a quick hip toss, but the Tanri reacted with a strong base and an outside trip, which brought the lanky Venturian onto his back.

"Here, we fight to keep the same," Muhai said. "But is not. Empire been coming, taking our birds. Says they need them against rebels in forests and mountains where mechs can't reach."

"The empire came to the tribes?" Murray asked.

Muhai nodded. "They got weapons. We can't do anything but say yes. And they try to bring us in, too, get our boys to fight for them against—"

"The Flux," Murray finished Muhai's sentence. "They're trying to conscript you to make sure the Flux doesn't enlist your people."

"Don't want any of it!" Muhai's voice rose. "Not what the Tanri-kin are meant for. We meant for riding, fighting here under blue sky. The empire, the Flux, we don't care about them."

"I got you now!" Murray heard Dozer yell from his grass circle. Dozer had driven Muhai's daughter to the edge and was on the verge of picking the smaller girl up by her leather vest. At the last moment, the girl changed her direction and lifted a leg high between Dozer's knees, taking the big Grievar fully off his feet and throwing him on top of two surprised rocs.

Dozer looked up incredulously from a ruffle of feathers and squawks.

"Thought I had her."

*   *   *

Several giant bonfires sent crackling embers up toward the night sky.

Murray couldn't remember the last time he'd seen so many stars. His view from the barracks in Ezo was polluted by spectral light and cloud cover.

The Whelps sat beside the Tanri tribe in the same grass field they had competed in, the slumbering forms of their rocs surrounding them.

Dozer downed another skin of bird's milk, the stuff dripping down the side of his face as some Tanri kids watched him with wide eyes. "I'm starting to like this stuff!"

"Your boy fit right in here, mighty," Muhai said from beside Murray. "You like to leave him? We take care of him."

Murray nodded. "Might just do that."

He listened to Knees trying to converse with Muhai's daughter, who sat beside him on a log. The girl had a good grasp of Tikretian, which was surprising, given how far out the Tanri roamed from the empire's major cities.

"You do well early, good grip," the girl said as an offering, referring to her match with Knees where she'd tossed him in about twenty seconds.

"Not near as good as I needed," Knees said. "Thought I knew proper leg sweeps until I went up against you."

"More practice with birds, next time." Muhai's daughter smiled.

"Right, maybe I'll try that," Knees said. "Why aren't any of you Tanri taking the Grievar Road, doing the Pilgrimage this year? Think you'd do great."

"Not our place," the girl said. "Place is where birds go. We follow them, fight where they take us."

Knees took a swig from his waterskin. "Sounds nice. Where we are at the Lyceum, we need to worry about classes and homework, teams and scores."

Muhai's daughter nodded, though she did not seem to quite understand.

"There is one Tanri, though, on your Pilgrimage," the girl said as she held her hands up to the fire. "He appeared from the night, riding on bird even bigger than my father's with feathers burning like this fire."

Brynn turned from her quiet vigil in front of the fire to chime in. "We've heard about him. They call him the Firebird. He wears a Tanri mask when he fights, and they say he's undefeated on Pilgrimage so far. Probably will win the whole thing."

"Unless I take it all!" Dozer stood up and shamelessly flexed for the group.

"Unlikely, given your performance today," Knees said to his friend. "And don't forget Kōri Shimo also be winning every match he's had."

Dozer sat down, clearly deflated at the mention of his classmate. "Just our luck Shimo's on Pilgrimage with us this year. The one freak from the entire place that gives me the shivers..."

"I think you can best Firebird, or this Shimo you speak of," Muhai's daughter whispered from beside Knees. "You must trust your throw."

A smile curved up on Knees's face, something Murray didn't see too often. "I'll try."

"Your daughter speaks good Tikretian." Murray turned back to Muhai.

"Yes, yes," Muhai said. "At first, I against it, but as I say, even here things must change. Need people to talk with hawkers for trade and deal with empire."

The two old friends were silent as some of the Tanri kids began to dance in front of the fire. Muhai broke the silence.

"You too, mighty," Muhai said. "You welcome to stay with us. You said you hate them soap-eaters, politiks. So, stay out of the dealings."

"Much as I'd love to, can't do that." Murray sighed, watching Dozer start to make a fool of himself and dance in the firelight beside the Tanri.

"You got that look," Muhai said. "You chasing something else here. Not only Pilgrimage."

Murray nodded. "Someone. Someone I lost. A debt that needs be paid."

"Knowing you," Muhai said, "you be right up knocking on emperor's door to keep your promise."

"Not the empire I'm seeking this time, Muhai," Murray said. "It's the other side. The Slayer."

"What you want with a demon?" Muhai whispered. "We hear stories from the northern tribes about this Slayer. The demon, he never sleeps, never eats, never pisses. He never stops. He goes to the tribes, the villages, tells the best fighters to join him. If they don't, he kills them, bleeds them right there in front of their chicks. If they join, they disappear. No one knows where to."

"I got some idea where," Murray said. "Least, I'm looking."

"Mighty, you a warrior," Muhai said. "The fight runs deep in your blood. But you don't want nothing to do with this Slayer."

"Told you, Muhai, he's got someone I lost. Someone I should never have taken my eye off."

"Must be important," Muhai said.

"Suppose so," Murray murmured as he stared into the fire.

Dozer had stripped down to nothing but his underwear as he

huddled with a group of Tanri, their arms encircled and their heads pressed in together as they danced around the fire.

"Sure you don't want to leave the big one?" Muhai asked.

"I'd love to, but we'll need as much help as we can get to get where we're going," Murray said.

A thunderclap above turned all heads in the camp toward the sky. Three bright trails plummeted past like meteorites, blazing to the horizon.

The Tanri were silent; the laughter quieted.

"What was that?" Dozer stared out to where the flashes had disappeared.

"Flyers," Murray said. "Likely empire mechs out looking for Flux rebels."

"We seen those thunderbirds fly past many times," Muhai said as he moved to calm some of the rocs that had been startled. "Bad luck."

Murray sat back down and stared into the fire.

He needed to find Silas before the empire did.

*   *   *

The Whelps followed the Grievar Road east a full day after leaving the Tanri. Murray planned to keep to the road as long as it clung to the Beodar River before cutting north through the Kavel Mountains pass. Once their birds trekked over the craggy terrain, they would land in the Venturian desert.

Dark clouds hovered over the tallest of the peaks in the distance. The storms could wander south and bring weeklong rains with them. The crew already had to take cover at the start of their journey because of landslides along the road. Murray hoped they could keep a steady pace all the way to the mountain pass without more interference.

"First proper city challenge we got, I'm ready," Dozer said with a muffled voice from atop his roc. The big kid still proudly wore the bird mask Muhai had given him as they'd said their farewells, though it was too small and squished his face inward.

"Please don't tell me you'll be wearing that all the way to Venturi," Knees said from the front of the roc.

"You're just jealous the Tanri didn't think enough of you to give a mask over," Dozer said.

Murray smiled as he remembered the farewell, the Tanri and Whelps with arms encircled, pressing their foreheads in together like a flock of rocs greeting each other on the plains.

"I think it's quite an improvement for you, Dozer," Brynn said as she pulled up beside the two boys.

"Hey, what's that supposed to mean?" Dozer said. "Don't tell me you're still holding a grudge because that girl back in Mirstok fancied me better than you."

"Did you forget she robbed you blind?" Brynn laughed. "And I told you, she wasn't my type. Too skinny."

"Who's your type, then?" Dozer asked. "Maybe more like Muhai's girl, one that can throw Knees five times without breaking a sweat?"

"Not so much," Brynn said. "And I think Muhai's girl was taking a liking to Knees more than either of us."

"Hear that?" Dozer slapped Knees on the shoulder. "I noticed you two talking last night fireside."

Knees didn't notice the banter between his friends; he stared off toward the Kavel Mountains rising from the highland plains like a wall of granite.

Murray knew the kid was likely thinking about what lay beyond those mountains: the sprawl of the Venturian desert where he was born and where the next challenge lay ahead.

Murray pulled at Bird's reins and muttered one of the Tanri phrases Muhai had taught him. To his surprise, the roc followed his lead this time, kicking it up a gear into a gallop along the Grievar Road.

"Hey!" Knees's sharp voice caught Murray's attention.

The Venturian pointed far east along the road to the base of the forest several miles away. Murray squinted his eye, his vision not what it had been a decade before, but he could still see the large forms clearly.

Mechs.

The Enforcers were unmistakable, glaringly sharp steel suits of armor set against the high muted yellow-green grass and brown dirt.

"How many?" Murray asked Knees. The boy had remarkably sharp eyes.

"Three," Knees replied.

Murray pulled on Bird's reins, and he ground to a halt along the road. He held his hand up to stop the others.

Dozer spoke in a whisper as he lifted the mask off his face. "What should we do? They're blocking the road."

The group had encountered mechs early on in their journey, two empire Sentinels set to weed out rebels at the gates of the western province of Glynthik. Murray had shown the Daimyo their safe-passage tattoos, and luckily, they'd taken more interest in some Desovian hawkers.

This was different, though. Why would Enforcers be posted at the crossroads to Venturi?

"Let's get off the road," Murray said. He directed their birds over into the high grass and behind a rocky elemental outcropping, one of the many depleted rubellium reserves that jutted from the highland earth.

Murray needed to get more information. He had to know whether avoiding these mechs was worth the risk of cutting into the Kavels early and bypassing the clear path through the mountain. The terrain would be risky, even on rocs.

He had to get a closer look, but he couldn't bring all the Whelps with him. Especially with the heavy-footed Dozer, they'd be given away before they made it within earshot.

"Dozer, I'm leaving you in charge of watching the birds," Murray said. "You stay with Brynn. I'll take Knees with me on foot to get a closer look."

"What?" Dozer protested. "But I want to see what's—"

"We need our strongest fighter here in case more mechs cut us off from behind," Murray said. After so much time with the boy, Murray certainly knew how to play to his vanity.

"Right, right." Dozer puffed his chest out. "Don't worry, Coach; nothing will happen while I'm here."

Murray nodded and motioned for Knees to follow. They stayed low in the high grass as they jogged toward the Enforcers.

"These be the same sorts that blew a hole through Joba," Knees said softly.

Murray knew well what Knees referred to, what had happened to the largest member of the Whelps last year. While Murray had been drunk in the Deep, Joba Maglin had been disemboweled by an Enforcer's cannon. The silent giant had sacrificed himself to save Cego; he'd staved off the kid's execution by the Goliath.

Murray knew what it was to confront the darkness. He motioned for Knees to follow closely.

The two stayed tight to the shadows of a string of elemental deposits, slowly creeping closer to the Enforcers. As they approached, Murray could now make out smaller forms set in a line beside the three steel beasts.

Five men were chained together, on their knees in front of the Enforcers. Several bodies lay strewn on the dirt, including two avian forms in an exploded pile of feathers.

One of the mechs was pacing back and forth in front of the men; Murray could now make out the grating mechanical voice of the beast over the highland wind.

"You won't have another chance to respond, Flux scum. I'll ask you again. Where is your base of operation?"

Murray held a hand up for Knees to stop so they could get down on their stomachs. Enforcers were known to have a variety of heightened senses; they couldn't risk getting any closer. From the vantage in the grass, Murray could see that the men on their knees wore black leathers and had the tops of their heads shaven. Flux rebels; these were Silas's men.

One of the men, a lanky, mustached Grievar with his hands manacled behind his back, spat into the dirt. He looked directly into the encasing that housed the Enforcer's Daimyo pilot.

"Dark you and your metal arse. Dark your little beady eyes behind that glass. And dark your emperor, who sent you down to do his dirty work."

"So be it."

Even from a distance, Murray could hear the hum of the pulse cannon charging at the Enforcer's arm. Murray heard a strange sound from beside him and saw Knees was shaking. Though the Venturian was as tough as they come, Murray knew the fear that coursed through the boy now.

He placed a hand against Knees's arm. He met his eyes.

Nothing will happen to you; I'll keep you safe, Murray wanted to say.

"You have one final chance to reconsider." The Enforcer's cannon was nearly fully charged, emanating an azure light from its barrel.

The mustached rebel abruptly stood and charged, screaming.

"Free to fight!"

The other four rebels also stood and echoed the call. "Fight to be free!"

The Enforcer released its cannon charge and a brilliant pulse burned across the road, engulfing the mustached Grievar. Murray held a hand over his eye and squinted to keep looking through the brightness.

When he lowered his hand, he saw carnage. All five rebels were floored, their bodies scattered about like cuts of meat at a butcher shop. He couldn't tell whose parts belonged to whom.

"Darkin' spirits above," Knees breathed. The kid had forced himself to watch the entire thing. A tear streaked from his eye, and Murray saw his arms tense. Knees was ready to move, ready to spring into action.

Murray grabbed the kid's arm tightly.

"No," he whispered. "I know you want revenge. I know you want to teach them a lesson after Joba. Now is not the time. Your life will go to waste. Sometimes, we need to pick our fights. Sometimes, the fight isn't the one in front of us."

Knees trembled and let out a silent scream.

They crawled on their bellies through the high grass to get some distance before jogging back to the outcropping where the others were waiting.

"What happened?" Dozer asked, looking worriedly at Knees, whose face was now pale.

"We can't go that way; it's too dangerous," Murray said, hitting Dozer with a hard glare to let the boy know he'd best drop it.

Murray unfurled his map and pointed to a closer pass through the mountain range. The terrain would be risky, but it was the only way through now.

"We'll head due north and cut through the Kavels here," Murray said. He looked at Knees as the kid climbed onto his roc's back.

"From there, we head to Venturi."

CHAPTER 3

Compromised Position

Neophytes will say that strength is no advantage, that technique can conquer all. This is not so. Brute strength over an opponent provides ample advantage; however, it takes energy to feed such strength. The more strength a combatant possesses, the harder it will be to maintain for the duration of a bout. A well-practiced Grievar knows this truth.

Passage Three, Fifty-Eighth Precept of
the Combat Codes

The vast Venturian desert swallowed them after they came down the mountain pass.

Murray found a path of hard-packed sand for the rocs to follow in the valley between two dunes. A pack of scrawny sand foxes trailed them for miles, hoping for some discarded scraps off the backs of their birds.

Venturi abruptly appeared on the horizon like a mirage in the rising morning heat, the mech-repair shops, bounty brokers, and red-roofed tanneries sitting on the outskirts of the desert town.

The Whelps came in bleary-eyed, dizzy from riding through the night, looking over their shoulders to see if the Enforcers had caught their trail. Murray had told the crew it was unlikely the armored beasts would follow; they'd want to return to Karstock to report their recent victory.

But Murray could still smell the burning flesh, see the mess of limbs and bones the pulse cannon had made of the rebels. He could still see Knees's silent scream, the sheer agony the kid held in his eyes as he relived Joba's death all over again.

Murray glanced over at Knees as he bounced up and down on his roc. Dozer rode behind him, his arms draped around his friend with his head resting on Knees's shoulder.

Knees acted strong for his friends, but Murray could see the weight the kid carried. Seeing such things lived with you, like a bad bone break that might mend with time but always left you moving different.

The kid stared ahead and yawned as the pale dawn crept across the desert.

Dozer woke with a start from behind Knees. "I wasn't asleep."

Knees chuckled, wiping at his cloak. "Right, then this must not be Dozer drool all over my shoulder."

Dozer scratched his head sheepishly. "Was tired, that's all. Needed some rest for the upcoming fights."

Murray hadn't even thought about the crew's next challenge in Venturi. Pilgrims gathered the second month of every summer in the desert region to participate in the anticipated bouts. The Venturi challenges were a proving ground for all the Pilgrims that had made it so far, and often decided who would go on to win the entire three-month-long contest.

"Wish I could've been the one to get some sleep, but someone had to steer the bird," Knees muttered.

The group trotted past a pair of soot-faced kids in the dirt outside a repair shop, munching on their breakfast and watching the road disinterestedly. They were used to seeing foreigners come in on Pilgrimage every year.

"This is home, right, Knees?" Brynn asked from atop her black bird.

"Haven't seen Venturi since the slavers took me Deep," Knees said. "Since my uncle sold me off. Surprised to still see the place here in one piece."

"You think you're gonna see your family here?" Dozer asked.

"Don't know, don't care," Knees said.

"Right, but don't you have a sister? I mean, if I knew I had family still alive, I'd be—"

"Dozer," Murray cut the boy off. "Let it be."

Dozer quieted as the Whelps trotted down Venturi's main thoroughfare. Though it was still dawn, other Pilgrims had already started to trickle into the town.

Murray watched a group of lanky Desovians sparring in front of a red-shingled hostel, their coach sneering as the Whelps passed by. Two thick-shouldered Myrkonians wrestled in a small grove of kaöt trees. Murray even caught sight of the indigo second skins of another Lyceum group of Level Threes.

Dozer changed the subject as they rode past potential opponents. "Think Firebird will be here?"

Brynn piped up from her roc. "I'd like to see him in action. Heard no one's even come close to taking any points on him so far."

"Would rather be taking our wins here and moving on," Knees countered. "If Firebird's on a roll, best not to take him when he's got momentum. Better be learning more about his style before facing off."

"Nah," Dozer said. "I say bring Firebird. He can't be any better than what we've already faced. Plus, I've some new sweeps from the Tanri I'm itching to try out."

"Let's get to Hanrin's for some food and rest," Murray said.

They steered their rocs past a line of adobe homes with cacti gardens out front and a trio of squares full of dried-up fountains and crumbled statues.

"What in the dark is that?" Dozer asked as he peered down a cross street. Several blocks ahead, a building rose higher than the rest, a cast-copper cylinder clearing the tops of the trees. Both crimson spectrals and desert birds circled and nested on the frayed wires set on top of the structure.

"The Fire Can," Knees said. "Been there since I was a little kik. That's where we be fighting tomorrow."

"That's no proper arena," Dozer said as they steered their rocs down a smaller thoroughfare, the red sun glinting against broken windows.

"No proper fights in there either," Knees said. "Those that don't get put down by their opponent go down by the heat or the rage."

"The rage—" Dozer started, but Murray cut him off, a trend throughout the journey.

"We'll talk more about fight strategy tonight and morning before," Murray said as the rocs began to climb the only hill in town, a gradient that soon took them above the slums they'd passed through.

"Here we are, the Barrack Quarters," Murray said as they rode beside a faded limestone building with carved-wood latticework windows. The Whelps peered into one open door to see a steamy room full of fighters trading blows in a polished ring, even more striking heavy bags and jumping rope.

"Nice training spot," Brynn remarked as they moved farther in.

They stopped in front of a long building with graffiti plastered across the faded façade. The once-ornate window up front was blasted out and gave a view of a little courtyard within.

Murray spoke a sharp Tanri command, and to his surprise, Bird lowered his head to obey.

"Good Bird." Murray ruffled the grey roc's feathers as he slid to the ground. He smiled at Brynn, who nodded in approval.

Murray rapped his fist on the door lightly, not wanting to punch through the flimsy wood.

"Ah, my brother!" a voice came from the courtyard, and the door creaked open.

A man stepped outside in front of the Whelps, greeting Murray with a firm embrace. Murray hadn't seen Hanrin Tuvlov since their service together. In fact, he hadn't seen the man since he'd lost his legs.

Murray immediately realized he should have warned the crew about the steel prosthetics when he looked at Dozer's wide eyes.

"Hey! You didn't tell us Hanrin had mech legs!" The big kid pointed at the steel frames shamelessly.

"Dozer, have some darkin' respect, you dank—"

"No, no problem at all, Murray," Hanrin said, smiling through his blackened teeth at Dozer. "Only natural the kiks would be curious about Grievar-kin having a pair of these."

"Sorry." Dozer looked down. "Thought it was against Codes to have tech like that."

"Only code out in the desert is to stay alive," Hanrin said. He sprang agilely back and forth on the hydraulic legs. "And these gears do the trick."

Murray could see the crew was weary from the long journey. "Hanrin, can we get out of the heat?"

"Yes, bring the birds in here for a drink." The man waved the crew through the run-down stucco courtyard with a cracked fountain sputtering at its center and into the main structure.

The entire barracks consisted of one large room. Worn heavy bags hung from chains set above the ripped-up tile flooring. Several sections of frayed tatami were set piecemeal across the dusty ground. Two fans spun lethargically above the room's centerpiece: a large red-wired cage.

"It's not much but should do the trick for you Pilgrims," Hanrin said. "Got a good rubellium exterior to that cage too. You'll need some acclimation for the Can."

"Thank you, Hanrin," Murray said as he took a deep whiff of the musty training room. "Place like this is a sight for sore eyes after being on the road so many days."

"After what you did for me those years ago, I owe you my debt and more," Hanrin said, putting a hand on Murray's shoulder and meeting his eye.

"Was nothing more than any fellow Knight would do." Murray shook off the praise.

"Nothing more?" Hanrin said. "You carried my busted ass near twenty miles to get me back to the ward in Stanthas. If not for you, I'd have lost far more than my legs."

Murray jabbed at one of the heavy bags to set it swinging. "Yeah. You got darkin' stomped that day, huh?"

Hanrin laughed as he hopped over to one of the bags. "Wasn't my finest, that's for sure."

The man planted one of his prosthetic feet and whipped his other into a wicked round kick, sending the nearby bag swinging toward the ceiling.

He turned back to Murray and winked. "Still got some juice in me, though."

"Thought as much," Murray said.

"Nice place." Brynn entered the barracks after settling the birds in the courtyard. "Where do we sleep?"

"On the mats," Murray said as he turned to the waiting crew.

*   *   *

Murray woke with a start, sweat pouring off his forehead.

He'd dreamed of the execution in the highlands, except in the rebel crew's place, it was Cego standing in the cannon's blast. The kid had cried out for him.

He took stock of the still-dark barracks, the hanging heavy bags catching moonlight and the cage pulsing crimson. The fans above creaked alongside the noisy desert locusts outside.

Dozer was sprawled out on the mats with a tattered blanket pulled over him, using his cloak as a pillow and snoring as usual.

Brynn slept the traditional Jadean way, no blanket or pillow, lying flat and calm like a corpse. Murray had fallen asleep upright, wedged into the corner of the gym, as if he were waiting for an Enforcer to smash through the wall at any moment.

He slowly stood and trod toward the cage set at room's center.

He could feel it even from several feet away. The cage was far stronger than Violet, Murray's own Circle back in Ezo. He knew Hanrin's cage was built of the rubellium harvested from the nearby Kivimi mine, known to possess the purest composition of the element in the empire.

The second Murray stepped into the cage, his heart beat faster, adrenaline pumping through him. Several glinting red spectrals flitted above his head.

Murray remembered the time Hanrin had caught him with a sneaky low kick to the groin back when they trained together. Murray's temples pulsed as his anger flared. He knew the element was manipulating him. He'd fought in hundreds of rubellium Circles before, but this stuff was stronger than most.

You are not the rage.

He breathed deeply, focused on the anger. It was there, that was for sure, but what was it? Was it any different from a pang of hunger or that urge he still had for a stiff drink?

You are not the rage.

The fire began to subside, and not until then did Murray step out of the Circle. The Whelps were to be fighting in less than two days within Venturi's famed Fire Can, full of pure rubellium rings that were even stronger than Hanrin's. Murray had heard stories of the anger consuming fighters within the Can, not only making them brash in combat but urging them to lash out at the crowd and even their own friends.

Murray was deciding how he'd best get the Whelps acclimated using Hanrin's cage when he noticed Knees was missing. He moved to the gym's door and stepped outside. Knees stood straight-backed by an empty fountain, a frozen shadow in the moonlight.

"You okay?" Murray tried not to startle the kid, though he knew Knees probably had heard him already.

Knees was silent a moment, staring out at the still town below. "I remember coming up here."

"Barrack Quarters?" Murray asked.

"Me and my sis, we used to make believe we'd gotten invited on Pilgrimage," Knees said. "Pretended we be purelights, practicing here in these fancy barracks."

An old shame settled in the pit of Murray's stomach. He had been one of those purelight kids. He'd grown up destined to become a Grievar Knight, a champion. He'd come to Venturi a lifetime before, a cocky student, looking down at the slums with pity.

"'Course, we both knew they'd never be letting lacklights like us fight here," Knees said. "We knew my uncle was going to sell both of us when the next slaver came round."

"You're here now," Murray said. "You proved them wrong. You're on your Pilgrimage, and you're going to give them hell."

"That be the strange thing," Knees said. "I been thinking about heading home this entire journey. Thinking I'd be feeling that pride, coming back when no one said we be able to make it so far. But I haven't been feeling pride. I only be feeling..."

Murray finished the boy's words. "Fear."

Knees nodded.

Murray knew what it was like, coming back to a place from the past. He still remembered going Deep after so long, the clamor of Markspar Row hitting him like a brother's familiar fist, the expectations of the past weighing heavy on his shoulders.

"Your sister," Murray said. "You fear she's dead?"

"I'm more worried she's somewhere down there." Knees looked out at the slums. "That she's been having to live for all this time.

Getting pitied and looked down on, beaten every day and worse. My uncle was no good. This scar, the one I've lived my life with, wasn't from the slave Circles."

Murray clenched his fists, though he stood in no rubellium this time.

"We've got to move forward," Murray said. "Some days are good, some bad. Doesn't matter; we keep moving forward. Sometimes, though, we need to take one step backward to fix what's wrong."

"That's why you're out here with us, isn't it?" Knees looked to Murray.

"I'm here to guide you kids on Pilgrimage," Murray replied.

"You be a shit liar, Coach," Knees said. "Where'd you really go in Wazari Market that day?"

Murray looked into the Venturian's eyes and he knew he'd need to be out with it. He'd kept the secret because he wanted the Whelps to focus on their training, but eventually they would need to know.

"I went into Wazari looking for information on Cego's whereabouts," Murray said.

"I knew it." Knees smiled. "I knew you couldn't let it go, not knowing where he was."

"Would you be able to?" Murray asked.

"No," Knees said. "And I wasn't planning on it. But I was hoping I wouldn't be fronting the way, searching for my friend across this entire forsaken empire."

"You won't have to," Murray said. "I've got a good lead, but you'll need to keep the secret a bit longer. I want the rest of the crew focusing on their fights. We're here for Pilgrimage; don't forget it. When the time is right to go after Cego, you'll know."

Knees nodded and was silent for several seconds. "Coach, I need be stepping back for a moment now before I can move forward again."

Murray met Knees's eyes. He knew the kid was heading back

down to the slums, to his old home. He needed to take care of unfinished business.

"You need me to come?"

"Thanks, Coach, but I got this one on my own."

Murray wasn't sure why he did it, but he pulled Knees in close and pressed their foreheads together, like the Tanri did.

He felt the kid's pain, witnessing the execution on the road, reliving his friend's death. He felt his fear, having to go down there alone and see if his sister was alive. He felt Knees's brittle anger waiting to be released on those who had caused him such pain.

Murray held Knees, probably too long for comfort, but he didn't want to let him go. He didn't want to lose another.

But Murray knew better than to get in the way of someone trying to figure out their darked-up past.

"I'll be close if you need me," Murray whispered.

He released Knees and turned back to the barracks.

*　*　*

Knees returned to Hanrin's barracks midday, as the Whelps were making their final preparations for the Fire Can.

Dozer stopped hitting the heavy bag, panting and staring at Knees. "You get hit by a mech?"

Knees had a large lump under one eye and a gash on top of his lip. He flashed a curved smile, breaking open the gash and leaking fresh blood onto the mats. "Just be taking care of some business."

Dozer nodded in understanding, for once not filled with the need for any brash comment.

Brynn approached Knees with a frown on her face, though. "What's wrong with you? Going out and fighting before our challenge?"

"As I said, taking care of business." Knees avoided the Jadean's stare as he started to wrap his hands for practice. "Let's be focusing on getting ready."

Brynn did not let up. "Maybe if you weren't disappearing in the middle of the night, getting yourself banged up, we'd be more than ready."

Murray watched as Knees's face transformed, coiled in anger. "You be the weakest link here, Brynn, so why don't you pay some attention to yourself instead of me."

Brynn gave Knees a hard glare and held up the ice pack she had retrieved for him to hold to his face.

"Forget it," she said as she whirled away.

Hanrin defused the tension as he stepped into the barracks with a sheet of paper in hand, Venturian characters scrawled across the parchment. He handed it to Murray. "Your crew got their placements."

Murray nodded and looked at the indecipherable words. "Knees, you still remember how to read Venturian?"

Knees snatched the parchment and furrowed his brow. Better for the kid to have some distraction from what had happened last night.

"Well, what are they?" Dozer asked impatiently.

"Brynn, you're matched with Avir Klober," Knees said. "Empire stock coming directly from Karstock's fight school."

"Good," Brynn said, not meeting Knees's eyes. "Karstock students always play the same games, ones I can play better."

"Dozer." Knees stopped in front of his friend. "You got Kōri Shimo; he's here."

"Deepshit," Dozer yelled. "Of anyone, in the entire bloody empire, I got to get the freak from our own Lyceum!"

Knees took a deep breath and put his hand to his friend's shoulder. "You'll do fine; you know how he fights."

"Right, like a darkin' zombie," Dozer growled, cracking his knuckles. "Well, get on with it. Who you got?"

Knees stared back at the parchment. "I got the Firebird."

Dozer guffawed and slapped Knees on the back. "Well, in that case, guess Kōri Shimo isn't so bad."

"Enough with that," Murray interrupted. "Your opponent tomorrow will be less important than how you handle the rubellium. We need to get you Whelps acclimated. You've practiced in the red stuff at the Lyceum before. But you've seen nothing like the Fire Can."

"Is it true... this rubellium can make you see people? Faces that aren't there?" Brynn asked.

"Yeah, it'll make you see things. That and more," Murray said cautiously. "Pure rubellium is simply dangerous, and if I had my way, you'd be acclimating to it much longer, over a span of many weeks. But we'll take what we can get, and Hanrin's cage here is good enough to dip your toes in."

The crew set to work. They'd have two partners at a time taking turns in Hanrin's cage. Murray was careful to not overexpose the Whelps; too much time in the rubellium would wear their minds down. But they needed to know the intensity of their anger and how to fight it.

Knees stepped into the cage first, his eyes already fiery prior to crossing into its red glow. His expression turned from annoyance to outright anger as he waited. His teeth ground together as he raised his hands.

"Well, who be coming in here to darkin' practice with me?!"

Dozer stepped up to the task warily.

"Remember," Murray said. "You are not the rage."

CHAPTER 4

Fire and Ice

A Grievar should always keep their gaze wide. Undue focus on any single detail will prevent one from seeing the full range of opportunity.

Passage Two, One Hundred Eleventh Precept
of the Combat Codes

"Can't get any hotter than this," Dozer said.

The big kid was shirtless again, with his sweat-soaked uniform wrapped around his head as the crew walked the sandstone Venturian street.

"This be nothing," Knees said from beside him. "Just wait until we're in the Can."

They passed tan buildings with blasted-out windows and lime-green vines crawling along the façades. Murray eyed the crowd set alongside the thoroughfare, hawkers peddling desert fruits, water-diggers wrapped in linens to shield from the high sun, and toothless kids begging for bits.

Murray wiped a sleeve across his brow, wishing he had some of Dozer's brashness and could remove his clothing on a whim.

Other Pilgrims packed the thoroughfare alongside them, their closeness only exacerbating the sweltering desert heat.

Murray knew Knees was right, though; it would only get worse when they entered the Can.

A bearded Myrkonian, sweating even worse than Murray, shouldered Dozer to move ahead of him in the informal procession.

"Hey!" Dozer barked, about to grab the Northman from behind until Murray held him back.

"Focus on your own game," Murray said, hoping Dozer would be able to contain himself in the Fire Can.

"Hope I see that ice-skidder inside," Dozer growled.

The fight always begins before the fight.

Something Farmer used to say. Murray had never fully understood it until he started coaching. He saw how Grievar sized each other up, played mental games to gain an edge before stepping in the Circle. Such games were especially apparent here, when an opponent knew that any imbalance carried into a fight could be a potential path to victory.

Murray looked ahead to the Can looming from the desert floor like some tin cactus. Long-necked carrion birds circled above, screeching as they passed through the mists that jetted from the steam valves set on the roof. The entire building throbbed as more people squeezed in, as if it might burst at any moment.

The Pilgrims came to a halt about twenty meters outside the Can, where a line had formed. As they approached the tiny entryway, Murray took another deep breath, knowing he'd need to savor the outside air.

"What's that smell?" Dozer scrunched his face. Though Dozer wasn't known for his hygiene, even he could detect the wafting odor of hot sweat, piss, and shit pushed out the few ventilation shafts set at the building's side.

The crew entered the Can and were overwhelmed by both the unbearable menagerie of odors and the ear-splitting clamor. Each sound was intensified within the copper building, from the tread of boots on the spiral metal stairs running the height of the structure, to the amplified screams of onlookers, to the thud of ongoing violence on each level.

Murray could already feel the rubellium pulsing through the throngs pressed up against the cages, grasping and screaming vitriol as they soaked in the rage.

Frayed boards blared from the walls, and acrid burner smoke mixed with the scent of sweat and blood. Murray watched Brynn gag, holding a hand to her mouth as they trudged forward in line.

Bars were set along the far walls and drinks poured freely. Murray felt the familiar tug of want and produced a vial of beelbub ichor from his vest pocket. He downed it, savoring the punishing burn.

A strange creature stood at the top of the first-level stair, looking half rusted mech and half man, a buzzing red light on top of his dented helmet.

"Pilgrim or spectator?" the man said through an implanted audio box. "Step up for a scan."

Knees stepped forward and the red light flashed in his eyes. "Next," the man monotoned, to have Dozer and the rest of the crew do the same.

Murray marveled at how scans had become such a normal part of the fight trade. Grievar voluntarily letting the light pull their history, fight record, who knows what else, all so that the Daimyo could know where they fit in this world.

Processing us like every other product they hawk.

Dozer had drifted along to a free spot at the edge of one of the cages. He watched an empire cadet up against a tall Desovian warrior, trading blows at a frenetic pace.

"Toss him on his ass!" Dozer yelled, joining in the palpable fervor alongside the cage.

"Come on; we got to go up two more floors." Murray guided his crew, spiraling past ongoing fights in all directions. Finally, they carved out a small space in the crowd and huddled together.

"I can't coach you all, and you'll be divided across different cages." Sweat sheened Murray's face in the stifling air. "Dozer, you do better without much coaching. Even against Shimo, you know what you need to do. Overwhelm him. Don't let this become a battle of strategy or speed. You need to blitz that darkin' zombie."

Dozer nodded. "Got it, Coach."

"I'll be near, though," Murray added. He didn't want the kid to think he'd be on his own.

"Knees, I'll coach you against Firebird; ten minutes until go time," Murray said. "Brynn, you'll stick with me while you warm up for your match."

"Yes, Ku," Knees and Brynn said in unison, though their eyes were on the action elsewhere.

"All right, now, come on in," Murray said. He gathered the Whelps together, their four sweaty brows pressed close at the center of their ring of arms.

Murray knew these kids were brave, that they'd fight to the end for what they believed in. But he could still smell the fear on them, feel it in their tensed shoulders.

"It's places like this, in the heat and stink and chaos, when we realize what we fight for," Murray growled. "We might not be in those cages together, but we've worked hard over the last months. We've walked the long road in darkness and fear, and we've bled and broken ourselves more times than anyone else in this tin shitcan. We've earned our place here, together. Now I want you each to go and take it!"

Murray bellowed and his crew responded, their voices melding into the thrum of violence.

*   *   *

Knees pushed through the throng of sweaty spectators to the cage door, stepping in as his name reverberated on the overhead audio box. He could feel the crimson spectrals circling and fomenting a seething rage deep in his gut.

Knees suddenly hated the folk that surrounded him.

The buttoned-up empire kids, purelights from the surrounding schools ready to claim their place on Pilgrimage, Knees wanted to watch them bleed. The mercs and hawkers and Grunts, a seething mass of leeches getting roiled up and ready for blood to spill that was not theirs.

Most of all, though, Knees hated his own people, the many hometown Venturians that surrounded the cage, faces pressed against the wire frame. Some of those faces were familiar, though he knew they shouldn't be.

Knees had gone to the slums a night ago, visited his old home.

Knees had dreamed that he'd find his uncle, meet the man so that he could exact his vengeance and make him pay for all he'd done. He'd found him, but his uncle had been a husk of what he'd been, a shriveled old man who could barely feed himself, barely shit in the pot.

Knees had left the house, left his uncle alone to die.

He didn't even remember how he'd gotten in the fight with the street thugs on the way back to the barracks. All Knees could remember was the empty home with the empty man inside it.

But now, in the Fire Can, Knees finally saw his family.

His little sis pressed up against the cage, looking exactly as Knees remembered her from years ago, with that sly grin and auburn mane of hair. Seeing his sister's face in the crowd didn't bring Knees any comfort, though. Even though she knew Knees would feel the emptiness, the sorrow upon seeing her, she still dared to show her face.

And his da was there too, looking at Knees with those wide, fearful eyes. Always scared and never standing up for them when they needed him most. He'd let that monster do his worst to them.

A spear of pressure pressed against the base of Knees's skull as he clenched his teeth.

He saw his uncle again, the man staring back at Knees with his broken-toothed face and manic eyes. There was the man that had sold him as a slave to the Deep, the man that had taken his little sis from this world. The man that had tormented his mind every night. Knees screamed. He bit his tongue and tasted the blood. He raised his hands to the air as the rage engulfed him like a demonic presence.

Another Grievar stepped into the cage, and Knees's fire became focused. His diffuse anger, swirling at the multitude of faces around him, homed in on the opponent across from him.

Firebird.

Firebird wasn't formidable-looking, not broad-shouldered or rippled with muscle like some of the other fighters within the Can. In fact, Firebird was wiry. Knees had expected otherwise after hearing so many stories over the past few months.

His opponent wore the traditional Tanri mask: ruffled crimson feathers pointing skyward and a black hooked beak curving toward the floor. Two yellow eyes peered out from the mask, meeting Knees's hateful gaze.

The two combatants stood frozen, waiting for the sounding bell that would send all the fighters up and down the Can's seven floors into action. Dozer was somewhere above, likely flexing to intimidate the stoic Kōri Shimo. And below, Brynn would be readying herself against some polished empire brat.

Knees's anger coiled, ready to lash out like a whip. He'd charge straight ahead and take Firebird's head off in a blitz. Not many could match Knees's speed and precision.

Knees took his eyes off his opponent for a split second, glancing cage-side, where he expected to see the rubellium-conjured mirages of his family again, taunting him. Instead, he saw Murray, right up against the chains, meeting his eyes with a measured gaze.

Coach mouthed the familiar words: *You are not the rage.*

Knees attempted to steady himself. The rage was within him, a festering bubble ready to burst. But it was like all else within him: a perception. It was not him.

Knees breathed deeply, realizing he'd been lost. He tried to recoup a real strategy, but the bell screeched and his opponent came at him.

Firebird moved forward deliberately, like a raptor edging toward Knees with that hooked beak ready to lash out. Knees had expected an all-out onslaught after the stories he'd heard of the fighter, not having a single strike scored on him through the entirety of Pilgrimage, finishing each opponent in a decisive fashion.

He noticed Firebird's left leg forward, right leg light. Prepping the high kick.

Knees circled to his left, baiting the kick. He had a loaded cross in response to a parried right high kick. But the kick did not come.

The rage bubbled up within Knees again, urging him forward. Who was this Tanri with the arrogant, curved beak? Did he think he was better than Knees? All these tribesfolk, people with no homes, no real allegiances or loyalty. What use were they to anyone?

Knees barely restrained himself from throwing his cross, despite not having any opening. Only catching Murray's steady stare held back the misplaced strike.

Firebird again shuffled forward, hands up, those yellow eyes peering out at him. Knees met those bird eyes and they seemed familiar, another face from his past. Another mirage to enrage him.

Knees couldn't hold his strike back this time. The redlight coursed through his body, pulling him forward like a marionette. He threw a leading front kick followed by a barrage of winging punches.

Firebird moved as if unrestrained by a viscosity that slowed

Knees. The fighter dodged the strikes with ease, weaving his head, turning his body at just the right angles without having to use his raised hands to parry.

But the Tanri did not counter. He stared back at Knees with those familiar yellow eyes, taunting him.

Knees knew he needed to be more calculated. He could see Firebird's technical skill now, the way the fighter left no movement unaccounted for. The Tanri was waiting for the right opening. A split second was all he would need to land a finishing strike on Knees.

A roar, like some unrestrained beast, dropped from the cage above. Dozer.

The rubellium was doing its work, and Knees guessed it wasn't giving Dozer any advantage against the stoic Kōri Shimo.

Knees met Firebird's eyes again.

They were the eyes of Weep, the slave Circle boy who had been too weak to defend himself against the jackal. They were the eyes of Joba, who had selfishly sacrificed himself, who'd left his crew behind. They were the eyes of Cego, who had abandoned his team, gotten himself arrested and taken to Arklight.

Firebird launched forward in a blur, the right high kick that had been cocked anchored to the ground, and instead, the left foot rose swiftly to catch Knees directly at the crown of his skull.

He dropped like an anchor, the Can spinning around him before his head bounced against the plate-metal floor.

Knees breathed, waited for the bell, but it did not come. The rage still pulsed within him, though he was barely conscious. Knees's anger kept his biometrics elevated, kept the fight going.

This was why Murray had said high levels of rubellium could be so dangerous. Knees's rage wouldn't let him be finished, not until he was dead, not until his brain function shut off like a switch.

He listened to the screeching crowd calling for the crushing blow, an end to his torment, the only way to extinguish the fire within him.

But through the chaos and the thudding pulse of blood in his skull, Knees heard something else. A whisper in his ear.

"Stay down."

*   *   *

"What'd Firebird say to you?" Dozer asked from beside Knees.

Murray looked down at the Venturian kid shivering on the dirty tin floor of the Can.

"I caught the end of your fight…" Dozer trailed off. "Shimo got me pretty quick with the strangle, so I had the time. The freak, took my back like a cat on a Deep rat."

"Really cold." Knees's teeth chattered as he shivered against the wall, though the room was still nauseatingly hot as the challenges were ongoing.

"Rage will do that," Murray said as he threw his heavy cloak over Knees. "Runs red hot while you're in the rubellium, but when you're back out, it's like your body has nothing left."

"You need some of this ice?" Brynn asked. The Jadean girl was wielding two ice packs, one to Dozer's forehead and the other to her own knee. "Funny how I was the only one of us who got past round one."

"Ha-ha." Knees shook his head. Murray admired the girl's tenacity to hold a grudge after her and Knees's exchange back at the barracks.

"So, what *did* Firebird say to you?" Brynn asked. "I'd already finished my empire cadet, so I got to catch the end of your match too."

"Stay down," Knees whispered. "He said, *stay down*."

"Huh, that's strange," Dozer said as he stood up to get a look at the fight in the cage across from them. "Why would he not put you out?"

"Not sure." Knees's teeth chattered again.

Murray had seen the end and also thought it strange that Knees's opponent had let the light fade instead of putting a quick end to the bout. Perhaps Firebird thought Knees unworthy of any more effort.

"Darkin' Shimo…" Dozer muttered, still upset over his loss. "Don't know how he got me so fast."

"We're lucky the way he finished both of us," Brynn said. "Bet his round-three opponent wished he'd been strangled unconscious."

"Shimo got you too, Brynn?" Knees asked as he wrapped Murray's cloak tighter to himself.

"Yeah, I had him second round after Dozer," Brynn said. "Same thing, quick back take to a strangle."

"How long was I out?" Knees asked.

"About an hour," Murray said. "As I said, though you didn't throw more than a few strikes in there, rubellium takes its toll."

"Sorry." Knees looked down at the floor.

Murray knew what the kid was feeling right now. Shame. The emotion always came on strong after the anger.

"I let the rage win in there," Knees said, looking up at Murray.

"No," Murray said. "You didn't. You fought the demons and you won. You didn't overcommit; you waited long enough for an opening. I'm proud of you. Firebird was better today and caught you with the switch kick."

Knees looked like he was about to disagree, but the central audio box rang out from above them with the announcer's gravelly voice.

"We've narrowed down today's matches to our two final fighters!"

Murray knew who they would be.

"Kōri Shimo and Firebird!"

"We've got to stay and watch this one," Dozer said as he pushed his way through the growing throng of spectators to the edge of the cage. The rest of the crew followed the path the big kid cleared, with Murray at the rear.

The room became even hotter, more stifling, as the lower floors crowded up to watch the final match.

A group of spectators screeched on one side of the cage, the Firebird stoic among them, readying himself for entry.

Shimo stood alone on the other end, staring off into some

unseen world. He was uncoached and with no supporters. If the strange kid had come with a team on Pilgrimage, he must have left them behind long since.

"Who you got now?" Dozer asked.

"Firebird," Knees said. "It was like he didn't even feel the rubellium. He waited for me to make a mistake and then I was out."

"Same with Shimo, though," Dozer said. "I mean, I always knew the kid was a freak, but I at least expected the rubellium to have some play. But the redlight went through him like two-day-old porridge from the dining hall. Meanwhile, I was seeing visions of Shiar all over again, wanting to put his jackal head through the floor from the bell."

The finalists stepped into the cage, both cast in the rubellium's crimson glow as they stared each other down. Firebird was undaunted by Shimo's blood-spattered second skin, the Tanri staring out from behind his hooked bird mask.

The sounding bell rang, and the two combatants stood completely stationary. The crowd quieted, surprised at the lack of aggression after seeing multiple rage-fueled bouts. Neither Firebird nor Shimo appeared to be affected by the pure rubellium Circle they stood within.

It was as if the two fighters were in a standoff to see who would flinch first, as if a single movement would dictate the rest of the fight.

The quiet was soon interrupted by an impatient Myrkonian screaming, "Get after it!" which prompted the rest of the crowd to begin their raucous bellows again.

Finally, it was Firebird who made the first move: a single step toward the center of the ring. Shimo replied with an equivalent stride forward. The two stopped again, staring at each other.

"What the dark is wrong with you two?" another impatient spectator screamed. "Let's see some blood!"

Unmoved by the crowd or the light, Firebird took another step, this time diagonally to cut off an angle of attack. Shimo paused and crouched low, turning toward the Tanri fighter but not advancing this time.

Firebird mirrored the crouch and edged toward Shimo until he was within a front kick's reach.

The two remained coiled like springs, waiting for a reaction.

It was Firebird again who made the first move, diving forward into a low single-leg and latching on to Shimo's knee. Kōri calmly hopped around the ring to defend the takedown. Murray noticed Shimo didn't even attempt to waste energy to drop an elbow against Firebird's exposed head.

Shimo freed his elevated leg to the outside and wrapped a hand around Firebird's back, quickly shifting his hips and tossing the Tanri fighter to the ground.

Darkin' smooth tai otoshi.

Firebird reacted instantaneously, entangling his legs around Shimo's from the bottom to bring him to the floor as well.

"That was nice," Dozer exclaimed. "Feel like I've seen that one somewhere before."

Firebird twisted his body around Shimo's leg and wrapped up a heel in the crook of his elbow. The Tanri started to apply breaking pressure.

Still, Shimo was unfazed, turning with the heel hook and pointing his toe to alleviate the pressure on his knee. He ripped his leg free and pressured back into Firebird's guard.

"Um…why aren't they hitting each other?" Dozer asked.

It was a good question that Murray had considered already. The two combatants had opportunities to throw strikes, but it was almost as if they'd made a pact to not do so.

Firebird threw his legs high to attempt a triangle choke, but Shimo sensed the trap and defended.

"They're not wasting anything with strikes," Murray replied. He'd seen it before. Grapplers so confident in their skills that they'd rather not waste energy throwing punches, always snaking one step forward for a finish. Cego had that ability. So had Farmer.

"Guess I don't feel so bad anymore that Shimo put me out," Dozer said sheepishly.

Firebird rapidly sat up and wrapped an arm around Shimo's neck before dropping back for a guillotine choke, but Shimo threw his legs over and passed into side control, rendering the choke ineffective.

Shimo was getting the edge in the exchange. He had passed Firebird's guard again and moved into a solid side control on top. He slid his knee over into mount and pressed his weight down on the Tanri's chest.

Firebird attempted to buck his hips to escape, but Shimo's mount from top was too strong. He pressured downward, pushing his shoulder into Firebird's chin, slowly ratcheting an arm up to set up a strangle.

"Think Shimo's got him," Dozer commented, wide-eyed at the prospect of either combatant being finished.

Firebird's tucked chin was the only thing preventing the finish. Shimo wedged his hand under the Tanri's hooked beak and drove his shoulder forward, popping the feathered mask off.

The entire crowd gasped, but not for the same reason the Whelps did. The crowd's surprise was in finding out the Firebird was female. A girl with high cheekbones, piercing yellow eyes, and an auburn braid of hair.

But the crew gasped because they knew this female warrior, this unmasked Firebird.

"Sol?" Dozer yelled in confusion as Shimo tightened the choke and their friend in the cage went out.

CHAPTER 5

Survival

A Grievar shall sacrifice all semblance of a civilized soul to walk the martial path. However, sacrifice is not some lofty ideal; it is an everyday circumstance. The sacrifice of comfort and well-being to temper the iron of one's body and mind. The sacrifice of family and friendship to devote every waking hour toward perfection. In training, the sacrifice of tried-and-true technique to practice unfamiliar movements. In the heat of combat, the sacrifice of stable defensive positions to attack and exploit vulnerabilities.

Passage Two, Thirty-Fifth Precept of
the Combat Codes

Sol's massive red roc streaked across the desert as if the sand were on fire.

Brynn followed not too far behind on her lithe black bird, with Knees and Dozer behind her atop their plump brown mounts. Murray's bird had taken a wrong turn into the underbrush surrounding the nearby oasis.

Sol looked over her shoulder and saw the curly-haired Jadean gaining on her, kicking up sand as they both neared the finish. The grizzled man with steel legs, Hanrin, stood by a series of rocks to designate where the race would end.

"Let's go, Akari!" Brynn yelled as she spurred her bird on. She nearly caught Sol, but Firenze leapt to the air, flapping his wings as if the little things would take his massive frame over the final hurdle.

"Firebird takes it!" Hanrin yelled as he waved his hands enthusiastically.

Brynn pulled up behind Sol and nodded begrudgingly. "Good run, Solara Halberd."

"Your bird is fast." Sol tried to offer a compliment, though she knew the Jadean girl would likely ignore it.

"Not as fast as yours," Brynn said as Dozer and Knees crossed the rock line.

"Sol won?" Dozer asked as his bird wheeled around. "Wish I hadn't bet my night's rations on Brynn now."

"She does have the advantage of riding a racing roc, probably only a few of his breed off the Isles." Brynn frowned at Firenze.

"It's true, then?" Dozer asked, out of breath though it'd been his roc doing the racing. "You stole that bird from a Daimyo lord on the Emerald?"

Sol nodded, accustomed to Dozer's numerous questions about her travels. She stroked the ruffle of crimson feathers on the bird's forehead. "Yes, Firenze was Lord Cantino's prime roc."

"Some of us need to ride what's available, can't take pick of prime rocs." Brynn turned her bird away and guided it toward the oasis set at the bottom of a sloping dune.

"What's with her?" Sol asked.

"She be a tad bit competitive, like yourself," Knees said. "Don't worry; she'll warm up to you once she gets to know you."

Sol understood the Jadean girl's reluctance to show her warmth since they'd first met back in Venturi. Sol was the newcomer here,

even though she'd been with the Whelps since they were Level
Ones at the Lyceum. But Sol had left them, spent a year on a jour-
ney to the Isles and then more time away at her family's estate. To
Brynn, Sol was an outsider.

"That, or maybe she's taking a liking to you," Dozer added as he
winked at Sol.

"What do you mean?" Sol asked as her cheeks flushed.

"Don't think Sol be her type either," Knees offered.

"So, who's her type?" Dozer asked from behind the Venturian.

"Guess we'll know when we see it," Knees replied as a squawk
emerged from the underbrush beside them. Murray burst out atop
his grey bird, branches and leaves attached to both of them.

"Least you didn't toss me this time, Bird," Murray muttered as
he patted his roc's head. Sol found it strange to see the normally
gruff Grievar showing affection to his grey mount. She noticed
that the two were well paired, though, both with unruly grey tufts
of hair and feathers sprouting from their heads.

"Let's get these birds drink and feed before we move again,"
Murray said as he guided his roc down after Brynn. Hanrin followed on foot, sliding down the sand dune with surprising agility
on the uneven terrain. Sol had learned the disabled man needed
neither pity nor help on their trek so far; Hanrin had jogged the
entire journey across the desert alongside the crew mounted on rocs.

"Could use something to eat myself." Dozer rubbed his stomach.

"You ate half our day's rations this morning, you block," Knees
said.

"Can't help I'm still growing," Dozer said as they pulled up
beside Brynn and dismounted in front of the shimmering body of
water. The oasis was one of the few they'd encountered in the vast
desert heading out of Venturi.

Sol still couldn't believe she was back with the Whelps. After
having spent so long on her own, it was strange seeing the familiar
camaraderie between her friends.

"Knees." Dozer turned to the Venturian. "Now that you've had some time to let it sink in that it was actually Sol who knocked you senseless in the Can, how do you feel?"

Knees held a hand to the welt still bulging from his forehead and smirked at Sol. "Besides this lump, glad it was her."

"You could have taken the whole challenge, Sol!" Dozer splashed water onto his sweaty face. "Too bad Shimo went through all of us like that."

Sol had replayed her fight with Shimo over and over in her head throughout the trek across the desert. She hadn't lost like that since she'd faced Wraith, the mysterious rebel she'd met on the Isles. It was as if Shimo had always been a step ahead of her, as if he knew what she was going to do before it happened. It bothered her immensely that a fighter could dismantle her in such a way.

Sol smiled though and punched Knees in the shoulder. "Only reason I got through Knees was we've trained a thousand times together, so I knew his defenses pretty good."

Brynn made a dismissive sound from by the water. Sol thought the Jadean would say something, but she remained quiet and tended to the rocs as they dipped their long necks down into the oasis for drinks.

The companions sat quietly by the oasis, filling their skins and enjoying the scant shade of a kaöt tree. The silence was nice, though it wasn't long before Dozer started his interrogation again.

"So, how'd you do it?" the big kid asked.

"Um...how'd I do what?" Sol said.

"How'd you off the lord?" Dozer attempted to keep his voice low, though it was hardly a whisper. "You punch the little blueblood in the throat or something?"

"Dozer," Murray growled from beside him. "I've told you, what Solara's been up to is none of your—"

"It's okay, Murray-Ku," Sol responded. "I'm back with the team now. I don't want to keep any secrets from them."

"Seems like that will be difficult, considering how many secrets you've got," Brynn muttered.

Though Sol was trying to be patient, she knew some wounds needed to be nipped before they could fester.

"Have you got something to say to me?" She stood from her crouch and turned to Brynn.

"Ooh...this should be good," Dozer said as Brynn met Sol's stare.

"We're supposed to believe that you're with us now, a part of the team?" Brynn spat on the sand. "After you've been off traveling the world in disguise for a year, wearing that bird mask, consorting with the rebels—"

"I'm not with the Flux," Sol said flatly. "I was unwittingly brought in on one of their plans while I was on the Emerald."

"Convenient," Brynn said. "On the Jade we have a saying: If you're in the water and see red and gold slither by you, you must believe it's a venomous sea snake. Because even if it's a blind worm, better be cautious and wrong than stupid and dead."

"So, that's what you think?" Sol asked, holding her hands up in frustration. "You think I've had some plot all along to join up with the Flux on the Isles, then track you all down on Pilgrimage so I can, what—betray you for the Slayer and his rebels?"

Brynn stood with her arms crossed, her mouth flat. "You seem like you've got one too many secrets."

"Solara is to be trusted," Murray interjected, watching the exchange wearily. "She's been with us for a while, just as you have, Brynn. And we all have our secrets to keep."

Brynn wasn't convinced, though she backed off at Murray's glare and crouched to the water.

"Maybe now's a good time to tell them, Coach," Knees said from beside Murray. "While we're on the talk of keeping secrets."

"Not now, Knees." Murray shook his head and did not meet the Venturian's gaze.

"Tell us what?" Dozer looked up.

"Coach," Knees said. "You be owing it to them."

"You're darkin' right as usual, Knees." Murray breathed out heavily. He turned to the crew, who were looking up at him expectantly.

"I'm not only here to guide you kids on Pilgrimage," Murray said. "I'm here to find Cego."

"I knew it!" Dozer hooted and splashed a hand into the water in front of him. "Knew you wouldn't let our boy down!"

Relief flooded Sol. She'd not spoken of her motive for coming out to Kiroth and joining Pilgrimage either. After she'd buried her father, word had come to her estate of what had happened at the Lyceum. She'd learned that Cego had been taken to Arklight Prison before he was broken out by his brother Silas.

Sol had decided she wouldn't return to the Lyceum. She'd head north and find Cego as well.

"Now," Murray said. "I don't expect any of you to take on the burden with me, but when the time's right, I plan on finding Cego out here and bringing him home."

"And you be expecting us to keep on Pilgrimage?" Knees asked. "Fighting for scores and studies across Kiroth while you're rescuing our friend? Forget that."

"Right, forget that!" Dozer echoed his friend. "No way I'm leaving Cego if we know he's out there."

Murray sighed, as if he'd been expecting such a response from the loyal crew.

"I've got some information on where he might be," Murray said. "The Flux activity is concentrated around the capital, Karstock. It's rumored Silas is hiding in plain sight there, and Cego's most often by his side."

"I know," Sol said. "That's why I came out here too."

"See!" Brynn shook her head. "More secrets!"

"These be good secrets, though." Knees put his hand on Brynn's shoulder to calm her. "She's here to help her friend. Just like all the rest of us, right?"

The Jadean girl took a deep breath. "Yes, spirits said, we best get that boy back to us."

"It will be dangerous," Murray said. "We'll have to get through the Flux, through Silas to get to Cego. I took on this path, but none of you have to—"

"This be our path, too, Coach, and you know it," Knees said.

"Cego would put his life on the line for us," Dozer added. "We can't let him go."

"So, we're all in, then." Murray nodded in approval. "Tomorrow we head north through the desert to Karstock."

*   *   *

Murray shook his head as Bird sniffed at the bucket before rearing up and snorting.

"You're too good for darkin' sand rats now?"

He held the bucket of dead rodents up.

"Yum, mousey," Murray cooed in vain, as Bird pushed the bucket away with his beak and scratched at the sand with his talons.

"Firenze only likes his food live," Sol said as she emerged from the darkness. The girl was carrying two long-tailed weasels over her shoulder, both bloodied but still writhing. She held one up to the nostrils of her massive roc. The crimson bird lowered its head and opened its beak toward the stars. Sol tossed the squealing weasel into the air and Firenze snapped it up in one great bite.

"How'd you snag two live ones?" Murray chuckled.

"Been spending a lot of time camping these past few months," Sol replied. "I moved with the Tanri every so often and learned much from them, but mostly, I needed to fend for myself."

"Lot to learn from the Tanri," Murray said.

Sol handed Murray the other weasel. "Give it a try."

Murray held the morsel up to his roc's beak. Bird stared at him skeptically before ripping the weasel from his hands. He tore the thing apart, leaving the sand bloodstained beneath him.

"Darkin' picky," Murray growled.

"Well, have you considered giving him a proper name?" Sol said. "Maybe *Bird* isn't cutting it."

"Brynn says the same thing," Murray said. "Bird's his proper name." The two walked back from where the rocs were tethered several meters from camp. The orange glow of the fire cut through the darkness.

"—but doesn't that scare the Deep out of you?" Dozer's voice was always the loudest, even out there in the vast desert.

"Yes, it be bothering me since I saw it," Knees replied.

Murray held back and let Sol step forward into the clearing. The Whelps sat around the campfire on a bed of wide tafola leaves. Hanrin was snoring, looking comfortable on the sand with his prosthetics propped up on a rock.

"What's been bothering you?" Sol interjected, as if she'd not been gone for over a year.

"Oh...erm..." Knees trailed off.

"Cego," Brynn said flatly.

"But we have a plan now," Sol said, sitting beside Dozer and popping a morsel of fennel corn into her mouth. "We talked it over all evening. We'll find him; we'll get him back."

"You didn't see it, Sol," Dozer said. "You didn't see him in Central Square against the Goliath last year. You didn't see what happened to Joba."

Sol watched the fire, frowning. "I'm sorry I wasn't there. I could have done something, maybe prevented Joba from..."

Murray sighed, watching from the darkness beyond the illumination. He could have been there too. He could have done something. Instead, he'd been drunk and pissing himself on the Deep streets.

"You couldn't have done shit, Sol." Knees stood up, anger rising in his voice. "The Goliath, you've heard about the thing, but you didn't see it. It was a monster."

Sol didn't reply.

"I'm sorry still that I wasn't there for you all." Her voice cracked.

"It's okay," Brynn said. "We didn't need you there. As Knees said, nothing you could have done."

Sol met Brynn's eyes and shook her head.

"But the Goliath wasn't the scary part of it all," Dozer said. "Cego was."

Knees nodded in agreement. "That be the truth. The way Cego transformed after the Enforcer blasted Joba. He became something else, tore into Goliath like a piece of meat. It was like that time in the finals matches years ago, against Shiar. But worse."

"How could he have done it?" Dozer said as he tossed a stick into the fire, sending embers crackling toward the stars. "I still think it's impossible how it went down. I mean, we all knew Cego was the best of our crew, maybe even the best in class, but…the Goliath?"

Murray stepped forward into the light. "Not impossible."

The red embers reflected in Knees's eyes.

"There's something you all need to know before we go further down this path together," Murray started. It had been long enough. These kids sitting around the fire were Cego's best friends. They were his family.

"Cego's not from the Deep," Murray said.

"We knew that one," Dozer replied. "Think we couldn't hear him screaming in his sleep all the time? About the island."

"Yes, he sometimes used to talk about the island," Sol agreed. "Growing up with his brothers there. The old master who taught him to fight."

Murray nodded. "That's true, sort of. But the island, it's not what you think it was."

Knees's eyes were closed, his body slightly trembling.

"The Citadel and a few other nations have been running a training program for over a decade now." Murray breathed measuredly. "The program is like the Sim, where you kids took your Trials, a virtual environment where you can train or be tested."

"I knew it," Knees whispered, his eyes still closed.

"Knew what?" Dozer asked impatiently. "What was with the island?"

Murray let it out. "The new training program was called the Cradle. They put Grievar babies in the simulation from the start. The kids lived their whole lives suspended in some vat, though their minds were someplace else, on the island."

"You mean to say Cego was in the Cradle? Living in some tube until he ended up in the Deep?" Sol raised her voice as another ember popped in the fire.

"Yes," Murray said.

"Why didn't you do anything?!" Knees's eyes flared open. "You were there, working with the Citadel! This whole time, how could you let this happen?"

Murray bowed his head. "I...I didn't know until I saw him. I found out after it was too late."

Knees whirled away from the campfire and stalked into the darkness.

Sol stood and put a hand on Murray's shoulder. "We know you've done all you can to help Cego. To help all of us."

Murray shook his head and ground his teeth together. He'd spent months drunk in the Underground, feeling sorry for himself, while Cego was a prisoner at Arklight Prison.

"So, that's how Cego went wild and killed the Goliath?" Dozer asked. "Because he's born of the Cradle?"

Sol nodded. "Can you imagine? Training in the Sim is like training outside of time. You feel like you've fought hours on end, but you've only been in there a minute. Now, if Cego spent his entire childhood growing up and training in the Cradle, it's like he's been fighting for hundreds of years!"

"So, why in the dark hasn't Cego been kicking our asses all over the place the entire time?" Dozer asked. "I mean, we've seen him beaten. Couldn't he have run the Lyceum, even taken out the Level Sixers on top?"

"Cego doesn't know," Murray explained. "He doesn't fully

understand the power within him. He's still learning how to access it. We saw it in the finals that year and against the Goliath, but it was as if something triggered him."

"But he's with the Slayer now…" Sol trailed off. "And Silas, he took my father out like it was nothing. He must have full access to his abilities—"

"Which means Cego probably does now too," Murray finished Sol's sentence. "I hope he's not lost. I hope it's not too late."

*   *   *

The Venturian desert sprawled out before them, a sea of never-ending sand. Though it was technically a part of Kiroth, the region had its own distinct geography and culture that set it apart from the rest of the empire.

Murray held his flask to Bird's upheld beak, and the roc greedily let the liquid trickle down his gullet.

"Not complaining any longer now, are we, Bird?" Murray said, feeling satisfied. He absentmindedly stroked the dirty grey feathers alongside the creature's head.

"Getting a bit attached, Ku?" Brynn smiled from beside him as she hydrated Akari.

"Just happy he's staying alive," Murray said. "Going on foot through this darkin' desert would be a death sentence, unless you got steel legs like Hanrin."

Hanrin had kept up with the crew the entire journey, his legs outlasting even the rocs, who needed to stop and replenish their sustenance in the heat. The man stood atop a sand dune, the red sun hanging behind him. "Come on, bird riders, not far to go!"

Brynn laughed as the crew remounted and moved on. Great red Firenze led the way, scouting ahead like a signal flare against the sand, with Sol astride his back.

"So, you and Sol trading techniques yet?" Murray asked Brynn. He prodded Bird ahead as the roc stopped to sniff at a desert rodent that squirmed beneath the sand.

"Why, you think I need be taking techniques from her, Ku?" Brynn asked defensively.

"Nah, I just know that Sol's been off on the Isles, training with the Emeraldis. And I know how you Jadeans and the Emerald-folk get along…"

Brynn shook her head. "I see what you're saying, Ku. Yeah, my parents had no love for Emeraldis, said they brought bad spirits with them. But I never had a problem."

"So, why the hard looks at the girl?" Murray asked.

Brynn sighed. "Ku, you see through it all, don't you? You trust her after this?"

Murray watched the Jadean girl carefully.

"Yes, I trust her," Murray said. "But I don't think that's what your problem is. You're worried about Sol coming back to the crew and where you fit in now."

"No, it's not—"

"Don't worry," Murray said. "You've got value that Sol doesn't have. She may be too smart for her own good and technical as a professor, but she doesn't know how to help sometimes. You can read folk; you know what they need, how to make them move. You have faith in them. And the crew knows that. I know that."

Brynn let a broad smile cross her face. "Thanks, Ku."

"Approaching homestead!" Hanrin yelled from ahead. They crested a high dune to see Firenze had stopped fifty meters down. Farther past lay rows of crops lining the desert valley floor. Harvesters in wide-brimmed hats dotted the crops, plucking at large husks and tossing them into cylindrical backpacks.

Most notable was a massive steel mech with a wide, curved maw that crawled up and down the rows, the harvesters depositing what they carried into its gaping mouth.

"What's that mech doing here?" Dozer asked. "And what're they growing?"

"Urgh," Knees groaned from in front of Dozer. "Stop squeezing me so hard, you brute. You probably can't eat the stuff, whatever it is."

"Those are my caucas!" Hanrin yelled proudly, extending his hands toward the crops.

The crew followed Hanrin down to the valley floor, directly onto a small path that cut through the crops. The whir of the mech drowned out all else as it made another pass.

"Hey there, Kai!" Hanrin greeted one of the many harvesters working the crop. An old, sun-weathered Grunt plucked a plump green plant from the stalk in front of him and held it up.

"Got a good batch right here, Hanrin." The man had several teeth missing from his grin. He tossed the hefty plant to Hanrin, who deftly plucked it from the air.

Hanrin dug his thumbs into the base of the plant and held it above his open mouth to let a stream of juice flow from the puncture. He wiped his mouth and smiled at the crew. "Caucas juice. Good stuff there. 'Course, the meat of the plant is what we bundle and ship off."

Dozer looked at the plant with thirst, and Hanrin caught the boy's eyes. "Ah, don't worry; we got some fresh juice at the homestead ready for you. Come on, now."

Hanrin nodded to Kai. "Keep up the good path, fella."

He led the crew down a row of the crops toward a flat house with a long wooden terrace surrounding it.

"Papa!" A little boy burst from one of the screened doors.

Hanrin leapt forward and wrapped up the boy in his arms. "You won't believe who I got with me for you to meet."

The little boy's tousled hair fell across his wide eyes as he watched the approaching riders.

"That's a big flackin' bird!" the boy yelled as he caught sight of Firenze.

"Effi! Watch your language in front of our guests." A muscled woman stepped out onto the terrace, a baby on one shoulder and a large steel sledgehammer slung over the other.

"But look at the size of it, Mama!" the boy yelled, running to Sol's side fearlessly and jumping with his hands in the air. "Can't even reach the top of the saddle!"

Sol slid off and smiled at the little boy, extending her hand. "Hi there, I'm Solara."

The boy took it. "I'm Effi and you've got a big roc."

Murray attempted to do the same, except Bird bucked him off, sending him tumbling into the sand at the foot of the home.

Effi laughed and the baby clapped its hands as Murray spat sand from his mouth and dusted himself off. "Darkin' Bird."

"This is the one I wanted you to meet, Effi," Hanrin said proudly. "May I present the Mighty Murray Pearson."

Effi stepped close to Murray, sizing him up with a suspicious look. "No way this is Mighty Murray, Papa. He's too old and too... oafy-looking."

"Hey now, didn't your ma there tell you to mind your language?" Murray growled at the boy, who responded by sticking his tongue out. Murray took a lazy swat at the kid.

"And he's slow, Papa!" The boy ducked the playful slap and ran back to the porch to hold on to the hem of his mother's pants.

"Now, you give Murray a break, Effi." Hanrin smirked and jumped onto the porch. "Not all of us can stay quite as strong and fast as your papa over the years."

Murray cracked his neck to the side. "Been a tough few months."

Murray's old friend held the screen door open and waved the crew in.

"Well, take the load off for a while," Hanrin said. "Welcome home."

*   *   *

"Now, this is what I'm talking about." Dozer could barely speak as he stuffed a roll into his mouth.

"Glad you've taken a liking to my cooking," Hanrin said as he stood in front of the iron sizzler set at the edge of the kitchen.

He flipped a strip of greasy meat that crackled as it met the hot surface.

"You do all the cooking here?" Dozer asked as he ripped into a large, stringy fruit. "I mean, doesn't Mira cook at all?"

"Don't be an ass, now, kid," Murray said, sitting beside Dozer at the long table. He looked over to Hanrin's wife, Mira, who was nursing the baby at the far end.

"Not a worry." Mira smiled. "Boy's only curious about the way we do things here. Hanrin is best cook in the house; that's for sure. Don't think I could sizzle a rat for a hungry desert snake. But I did pick that paya fruit you're munching from the tree outside."

"Don't let that humility fool you," Hanrin said as he tossed the steaming strips of meat onto a wooden board and placed it in front of the crew. "Mira here is best mech-mender south of Karstock."

Murray watched Sol raise her eyebrows. "You know how to fix those things?"

Mira nodded as she cradled the baby in her arms. "I sure hope so. Been doing so since I was littler a lass than you."

"But isn't that against the Codes?" Dozer asked. "Working with tech like that?"

Mira chuckled as she shared a look with her husband. "Well, first, not sure how many Grievar listen to those Codes any longer. And second, I'm no Grievar that needs to be listening at all."

Dozer's eyes widened. "You mean you're—"

"—a Grunt, yeah," Mira finished his words.

"Maybe you should start minding yourself again, Dozer," Sol chimed in from her seat as she chewed at one of the meat strips.

"It's all good," Mira said. She lifted her free arm and proudly flexed her bicep. "That's from my craft. Working the caucas fields with the rest of our harvesters and fixing up our mech. Not to mention keeping my husband on his feet."

Dozer nodded and got back to shoveling food into his mouth.

Hanrin removed his greasy apron and sat down beside the crew, placing a tray with several small glasses of clear liquid at the center of the table. "Caucas liquor. Stuff's strong, so watch yourself."

"The food was delicious," Brynn said as she wiped her mouth and took one of the glasses. "May the spirits bless you for this offering."

"What's a spirit?" little Effi asked, who'd been trying hard not to wiggle out of his seat the entire meal.

"I'll explain it some other time, Effi," Mira said. "If you're done eating, why don't you go hit that dummy out back before night's out."

"The dummy again? That's no fun; can't Papa hold some pads for me now that he's—"

"Don't you see your pa is busy right now, Effi?" Mira scowled.

"Would I be good enough to hold some pads for you?" Knees offered, wiping some brown gravy off his face to stand.

"Yeah, yeah!" Effi yipped enthusiastically as he grabbed Knees by the hand and led him out of the kitchen.

Hanrin chuckled as he passed the drinks out to the crew. "Effi was excited to meet you, Murray. Used to tell him stories of your fights to put him to sleep every night."

Murray brushed off the compliment and turned down the drink. "That was a long time ago; lot's changed since then."

"So I can see," Hanrin said as he lifted his own drink to his mouth. "Here's to changes."

Murray nodded. "Changes."

Dozer, having put down the entire glass, met the call loudly. "To changes!"

"Not all changes are good lately, though," Hanrin said, taking another sip of the clear liquor.

"Not all," Murray said. "They been by here yet?"

Hanrin clenched his jaw. "A lieutenant and some muscle. Came by a month back, asking about our operation, how long our harvesters had been working these crops. Said we better be ready if they need our help."

"Those shits," Mira said as she downed her drink. "Daring to come to our home, our own operation we've been running for a decade, and they try to take our men away for their rebellion."

"The Flux came here?" Sol asked. She sipped at the liquor. Murray was impressed the girl didn't break into coughing.

"They've been sending men out to all the harvesters," Hanrin said. "Looking to recruit the Grunts to their cause. I hear on the western range, they stopped an entire mining operation; every single last Grunt dropped their pick to take up the Flux banner."

"But why?" Sol asked. "The Flux already has taken in thousands of Grievar. Why do they need the Grunts too?"

"Numbers," Murray said. "To actually do what they want—overthrow the empire—they need the numbers. Even if the Flux has a bunch of fighting men, even if they can stand up to the mechs and the firepower, they still don't have enough folk to take every major city in the empire."

"And if they can pull the Grunts from their work, industry stops," Hanrin added. "Those elemental reserves that fuel tech, the ships at the dockyard that carry trade, the harvesters in the fields that feed mouths, it all stops if the Grunts stop."

"Why didn't the Grunts stop working a long time ago, then?" Dozer asked, his cheeks flushed from the drink. "If they got all that power over the Daimyo?"

"Why didn't you stop fighting long ago?" Mira returned. "That's what the Daimyo want, for you to fight for them."

"I don't fight for them." Dozer shook his head. "I fight for myself."

"And so do I," Mira said. "I work the mechs for myself. Harvest for my family. Which is why I don't appreciate those so-called rebels coming to my doorstep, trying to take my work from me."

"Empire's no better, though," Hanrin said. "Even before the rebellion, they've been coming by yearly, checking licenses on our mechs and of course taking a cut. It's only got worse since the Slayer's come to town."

"Way it's always been." Mira knocked her glass back and looked down at the baby. "Those that want power tread on the rest of us."

Sol stood up, her glass of liquor empty and her face flushed red. "Think I might need some air."

"Told you kids to watch yourself." Hanrin winked. "That stuff will make your head feel like a thousand pounds come morning."

Murray sat back in his chair and sighed, his belly full with good food for the first time in weeks.

"I've heard rumors about Coach." Hanrin lowered his voice as he turned to Murray. "That he was embroiled in some Daimyo machinations after he left. And that he's really gone for good now."

Murray suddenly felt an urge to grab one of the remaining drinks on the table. He clenched his teeth. "Yes, darkin' bad stuff, all of it."

"How can that be?" Hanrin asked. "The Coach…the Farmer I knew wouldn't have nothing to do with no Daimyo tech. No tools, no tech. The Code he abided by most of all. Could he really have strayed so far?"

"Codes aren't what they seem anymore, Hanrin," Murray said. "And…Coach had his reasons. I think."

"How do you know? Have you heard from—"

"I saw him." Murray knew he could trust his old comrade. He needed to tell someone. "Down Deep, last year. I saw Coach… Real enough to touch, same man who taught us, who we knew so well, right there in front of my nose. Though not so sure anyone else did. But I darkin' swear the man helped me. Saved my life right from beneath the foot of a thousand-pound Sentinel. He was there, I darkin' swear it."

"I believe you." Hanrin picked up the remaining drink and slung it back, as if Murray's old friend knew it would take a load off. "How many times did that man save me during our training years? If anyone could come back from the dead to save one of our asses, it'd be that man. It'd be Coach."

Murray's face felt flush suddenly, though he hadn't done any of the drinking tonight. "Need some air."

*   *   *

Murray stepped out to the veranda to find Sol with her legs dangling from it, eyes distant at the moonlit rows of crop.

"You all right?" Murray asked.

Sol nodded. "Yeah, just needed some quiet."

Murray still saw her father when he looked at her. Those feline yellow eyes, the same sharp nose he remembered on Artemis Halberd.

"Hanrin hit me with some of that caucas liquor two decades ago when we first met on Pilgrimage," Murray said. "Strong stuff."

"Not bad," Sol said. "Had some drink on the Isles that made caucas taste like sweet juice."

Murray sat down beside Sol and stared out at the fields. The stars crowned the night, casting white light off the steel bulk of the slumbering harvest mech. He could make out the swaying forms of their rocs, the birds reined in under a tent beside the fields.

"What happened to Hanrin's legs?" Sol asked bluntly.

"He was fighting fit when we were kids," Murray said. "Top of class at the Lyceum with me. First year as a Knight, he went up against the best kicker Kiroth had to offer, one who'd been sharpening his shins for years. Hanrin won the fight, but his legs were such a mess, clerics had to take them off."

"Looks like he's doing okay now," Sol said quietly.

"It's a good life here," Murray agreed. "Wake early with the sun, work the fields. Settle home to a family and hot meal. I know it's no Grievar path, but I could see myself here."

Sol chuckled. "Not sure you know yourself well enough, Murray-Ku. I'd venture you'd be out the door in a day looking for a fight."

"You might be right." Murray rubbed at the skin beneath his missing eye. "And you—think you'd be happy settling in a place like this?"

"I suppose," Sol said. "But I sort of enjoy moving about, meeting new folk, hearing their stories. Setting off on new adventures."

"Right," Murray said. "From what I hear, was quite an adventure you had on the Isles."

"It was," Sol said distantly.

"Did you find what you were looking for?"

"I brought my father home," Sol said. "If that's what you're asking."

"Yeah, you did," Murray said. "The man deserved a proper burial. But did you find all you were looking for out there?"

Sol was quiet for several moments; Murray watched a streak of white flash across the sky and heard Dozer hooting from within the house, retelling one of his fight stories.

"My . . . my mother, she was . . ." Sol had trouble finding the words.

"She was a courtesan," Sol let out. "She and my father kept it secret, for a while. But eventually, they couldn't any longer. It was too hard. And so, she left. I never knew her."

Murray nodded. He'd heard rumors of how Artemis Halberd's wife had died at childbirth.

"Many kids born of such meetings," Murray said.

Sol turned toward him. "You're the first person I've told that to. That my mother was a Daimyo. That their blood runs through me."

"So what?" Murray said.

"The Codes forbid it." Sol's voice broke. "My blood is not pure as everyone believes. I'm a half-blood."

"Codes are deepshit," Murray replied. "Silas is right on that end. The Daimyo wrote those words to control us."

"It's hard to keep track of who's right lately," Sol said. "And I'm not sure where I fit in anymore."

"I sure as Deep don't know who or what is right anymore either," Murray said. "But I do know that Grievar, Daimyo, it doesn't much matter. There's bad ones all around and a little good to go with it. You're that little good, Sol. You're still that Level One girl I saw making so many prissy purelight kids pay the price in the Circle. You're the one who went after your father's body, even though it was a deepshit crazy plan. And you're here now, Sol. With the rest of us, come to bring Cego back home."

A tear crept from Sol's eyes as she squeezed them shut. She sniffed and turned back to Murray.

"You're a good man, Murray Pearson," she said. "It's a shame you never had kids. Because you'd have made a good father too."

"Well, now, wouldn't go that darkin' far," Murray said as he felt a lump catch in his throat.

"Hey, Sol, you coming back in for round two or what?" Dozer popped his head out the screen door, dangling the bottle of drink in his hand.

Murray chuckled. "He's a big kid, but he's going to feel that in the morning."

"We're off in the morning?" Sol asked.

Murray nodded. "Once we're out of the desert, three days on the Grievar Road to make it to Karstock."

"You think the plan will work?" Sol questioned.

"Probably not," Murray said. "But it's all we got."

CHAPTER 6

The Purification

There are many outlandish and unorthodox techniques that might work against an unprepared opponent. Such techniques should be studied carefully. However, the mainstay of a Grievar's martial training should be devoted to proven movements that have stood the test of time.

Passage Three, Seventy-Third Precept of
the Combat Codes

Though Murray had to admit he'd taken a liking to Bird, he was glad to be moving on foot.

The crew had left the rocs behind with a Tanri trainer Hanrin had set them up with outside Karstock. Riding in on the birds, especially with massive Firenze in the lead, would attract far too much attention.

Murray cracked his neck side to side as the crew walked the dusty mech road along the outskirts of Karstock, Kiroth's capital city. They'd purposefully circumvented the High Street that met the city's main gates and bisected the empire's seat. The crew instead followed in the fumes of the numerous transport mechs heading to the eastern docks.

From the road, Murray could make out the towering buildings of the empire's capital, like knobbed fingers protruding from the highlands with the Andal Mountain Range shading the horizon beyond.

West of downtown, Flyers swooped in and out of Karstock Airbase, a massive underground hangar that looked like the maw of some giant beast gaping from the earth. Some of the Flyers streaked in formation over the Andals, likely heading to the Northlands to try to regain control over the Myrkonian Ice Tribes, who had been in rebellion there for over a year now.

It was strange, Murray thought, that he was also there to find Flux rebels. And where they found rebels, he hoped they'd find Cego.

"People live in those darkin' things?!" Dozer exclaimed over the whir of a heavy transport up ahead. "Nearly up in the clouds?"

The crew watched the city skyline in awe. Most had never even visited Ezo's Tendrum, seen their own nation's skyscrapers, which grew from the streets of Daimyo-only districts.

Murray nodded.

"Aren't they afraid they'll fall over with some big gust of wind?" the big Grievar asked.

"They build those to resist quakes and storms," Sol responded, fitting snugly back into her role as the group's resident expert. "But, yeah, I agree with you. Not a good idea to be up so high."

The sparse farm homes they passed alongside the mech road started to appear in denser clumps and soon became small factories, smiths, anchor yards, and pubs. Murray could now smell the sea on the air. Featherwing gulls circled overhead, searching for scraps.

"You sure these friends of yours with the Flux, they'll see us?" Murray turned to Sol.

"No," Sol replied. "I'm not sure. But I think they trust me after what we went through on the Isles. So, we'll at least get some information and closer to where Cego might be. And I know they've got a direct line to Silas."

"Hate doing things like this lately," Murray muttered as they approached the dockyards ahead. He could see the masts of tall ships bobbing above the flat-roofed buildings.

"Doing things like what?" asked Sol.

"Slinking around corners like hawkers," Murray said. "Laying down lies instead of standing up and fighting."

"Murray-Ku," Sol said. "You were the one who told me there's no way we'd be able to fight our way in. We'd be sealing our own death and leaving Cego with no chance for escape."

"I know it," Murray said. "The fight's not always the one in front of us. But doesn't mean I like the way we need to go about it."

Murray's boot crunched some old fish bones as the crew stepped onto the docks. Giant warehouses, holding the machinery for both old galleons and modern Dyvers, sat beside a variety of pubs to feed and liquor the sailors.

"Hey there, lass!" One such sailor, a Grunt with barely any teeth to call his own, stumbled into the street in front of Sol, tugging on a burner. "Has anyone told you Gastu here prefers the Grievar gals? You can hit me anywhere you like!"

Murray was about to intercede, but Sol met the drunken man with such a fiery look, violence behind her eyes, that he backed away.

"Maybe next time." The man flipped the burner to the curb and stumbled indoors.

"Nice work," Brynn said. "Though I'd have put him down for that much."

"Sometimes, the fight's not the one in front of us." Sol looked to Murray and nodded.

The crew followed Sol to one of the wider docks. Multi-sailed barks brimmed on one side and Dyvers with humming elemental engines on the other. Grunts covered all the boats like barnacles, hammering and patching them for the next route. Transport mechs rumbled past the crew to unload their wares into waiting hulls.

Karstock's docks were one of the world's foremost trade ports, set on the Adrian Sea to send out rations, elemental alloys, and slaves to every corner of the planet. Murray wasn't surprised the Flux had set their base of operations there, given the access it would provide them. What he didn't understand was how the rebels could hide in such plain sight, right beneath the nose of the empire.

"Dock nine," Sol said, looking up at some scrawled letters hanging from a wooden torii gate. A sleek obsidian Dyver was held partially out of the water by a lift at the end of the dock. The top section of the boat was still dripping wet and had hot fumes coming off its exterior, likely just returned from a trade run.

A cloaked man stood at the ladder entry to the Dyver, his hands folded in front of him. He didn't waver as Sol approached.

"Hello, Wraith," Sol said.

"Solara Halberd," the man responded without surprise, lifting his hood to look out at the crew behind her.

"Wraith, I'd like you to meet Murray Pearson," Sol said.

Murray stepped forward and nodded at the man called Wraith, his bald head as white as a cleaned bone with scars crisscrossing his face.

"Of course I know of Murray Pearson," Wraith said, his wolfish eyes twinkling. "I've always wanted to see if I might be able to withstand an onslaught of ground-and-pound from the best in the trade."

Always with the challenges. Murray sighed. "You'd best be hoping you don't need to see that."

"We're not here for sparring, Wraith," Sol said, stepping between the two men.

"I wouldn't mind seeing that either," Dozer said as he made himself apparent.

The big kid grasped Wraith's hand in greeting even though the pale man didn't offer it. "I'm Dozer. And this here's my crew, Knees and Brynn."

"Your crew?" Brynn stepped forward and smacked Dozer on the back of the head.

"Well…we're all working together," Dozer muttered. "But either way, we want in."

"What is it that you want in with?" Wraith said as he scanned the group with distrust. "You don't look suited for dock work. In fact, based on those safe-passage fluxes I see, you've been on Pilgrimage. What would Pilgrims playing school games want with dock work?"

"We're not playing any darkin' game," Murray interjected. "Sol, let's get out of here; we can find—"

"Wait, no," Sol said pleadingly. "You two would get along if you only gave it a chance. And yes, we've been on Pilgrimage, but we're here for more."

"What did I hear, now?" a voice swung from above, along with a sleek, muscled form that tumbled from the Dyver and landed on the dock. "Sayana, returned in the flesh!"

A smile broke across Sol's face as she embraced the girl with the shaved head. "N'auri. *Kinvasa tuvisi.*"

"*Kinvasa tuvisi,*" N'auri said as she looked Sol up and down. "I was hoping to see you sometime soon."

"N'auri, we should get back to work," Wraith said sternly, as he turned back toward the Dyver.

"What, Wraith, you don't trust our old friend Solara here?" N'auri said. "You the one said we need more dockhands for next big trade run."

"N'auri." Wraith spun back. "Solara is a friend. But we don't need her or any of these others, despite the famous names some of them carry."

Wraith stared Murray down again, rapidly blinking several times.

"This old Knight?" N'auri stepped toward Murray and gave him a sniff. "Sure, he looks a bit broken, but bet he can still help."

The Emeraldi girl continued past Murray and stood in front of Dozer. "This one seems thick but looks like he can carry a load on that back."

"Hey!" Dozer started to protest, but Sol elbowed him.

N'auri stopped in front of Brynn and smiled, getting awkwardly close. "And you got one from the Jade! Bet you can hold your own, eh?"

"You bet right," Brynn growled, meeting N'auri's feral stare. "Why don't we find out?"

Wraith stepped back toward the crew. "It's good to reunite, Solara, but we don't need more hands right now."

"We're here to see Cego," Sol said abruptly.

N'auri hissed in her direction. "Don't say that name out loud here."

"Well, if Wraith doesn't want to hear us out, we'll likely be walking these docks, calling out our old friend's name," Sol said. "You want that now?"

Wraith's eyes blazed. "I like you, Solara Halberd. But that won't stop me from putting you down if need be."

Murray started to move for the man. He'd stood face-to-face with too many killers to let this one threaten his crew.

N'auri intercepted him, standing in front of Wraith with her hands out. "Wraith, let us hear them out; least we can do to prevent losing our position here on the docks, right?"

Wraith didn't say anything for several moments. Finally, the pale man nodded and gestured toward the Dyver beside them.

"We speak inside."

* * *

Sol descended the ladder into the top of the Dyver, feeling as if she were crawling into the blowhole of some sea beast.

"Isn't this against the Codes or something?" Dozer asked from above as a flashing crimson light illuminated the entry chute.

N'auri laughed from below. "Codes! Such funny friends you've brought with you, Solara."

Sol leapt down the last several rungs, landing with an echoed clang against the metal floor of the craft's hold. A glowing cylindrical steel core occupied the center of the room, with another ladder set beside it that led even farther down. Several control panels blinked on one side of the room, and a massive windshield wrapped around the other with the inky black sea pressed up against it.

The rest of the crew filled the hold, Murray's bulky form coming down the ladder last.

Dozer pressed his face up against the glass window, watching a large, silvery fish shoot by. "Did you see that?"

"Dozer." Brynn glared at him.

"This is a surveillance-safe space," Wraith said, standing beside the craft's core. "So, let's cut to the kill in case anyone spotted you coming down here."

"You know what we're here for, Solara," N'auri said. "And it's not loading up no galleons with caucas fruit."

"I do," Sol said. "As do the rest of my friends."

"You've betrayed our trust, Solara," Wraith said. Murray stepped forward aggressively, and Sol knew she had to speak quick.

"I didn't," Sol said. "You told me that if I ever wanted to join up, you'd have me. You told me to come to Karstock. Well, now's that time."

"We did not tell you to bring strangers along, though," Wraith said.

"These are my friends," Sol said. "And they want to join the cause as well. We've come a long way."

Wraith eyed Murray. "Why would a Citadel professor, under the thumb of our enemy, come and join us?"

"Same darkin' reason you're here," Murray growled. "I'm done with it all. The bluebloods controlling us. Fighting for them. I'm ready for my freedom."

"Maybe so," Wraith said, his eyes flicking back and forth between Murray and Sol as if trying to decipher some unspoken language. "But what of Cego?"

Brynn stepped forward. "Cego is our friend. We schooled with him, as I'm sure you know. He was Ku's student. We heard the Slayer had broken him out of Arklight, that he'd joined up with the cause. And we came to do the same."

"You know who Cego really is, Jadean?" N'auri asked, displaying her sharp teeth to Brynn.

"We know he's our darkin' friend," Dozer said to N'auri. "Do you know *where* he is?"

Wraith stepped in front of N'auri protectively, his cold eyes meeting Dozer's. "Back off, now."

Sol could feel the situation getting away from them. They'd come to the docks to find out where Cego was, not end up in a bloodbath beneath the waters.

The fight is not always the one in front of you.

"We know Cego is the Slayer's brother," Sol said. "As Dozer mentioned, he's our friend. And if Cego follows the Slayer, so will we."

"And we be wanting the chance to put some soap-eaters in the ground," Knees added. "They sold me to slave Circles when I was a little kik. I'm here to repay that debt."

Wraith's eyes flitted across the crew and met Murray's again. "The one you knew as Cego...he isn't here any longer."

Murray's fists balled up, and Sol was worried about that bloodbath once again. "Where the dark is he, then?"

"What Wraith means is your friend is far different than you knew him," N'auri explained. "They don't call him Cego, for one."

"What do they call him, then?" Dozer asked, his eyes wide now.

"The Strangler," Wraith said, almost begrudgingly. "He's second only to the Slayer himself in disposing of Daimyo targets."

The crew was silent for too long.

"Times like these change us all," Murray said, breaking the

silence. "Doesn't make a difference far as what we want: to join up with the Flux. And I plan on making a run on the kid's kill count soon as you tell us how we darkin' get started."

A faint smirk finally broke across Wraith's face. They'd gotten through. Now they needed to make their move while defenses were down.

"I knew you two would get along," Sol said.

Wraith looked out into the inky water. "I run the operation here in the dockyard. We're about twenty strong, working for the Daimyo during the day and running ops at night. Slayer and Strangler are in and out, going after high-value targets across the empire and recruiting new conscripts."

"Makes sense," Murray said. "I've done the same, working for the bluebloods. I know how they think, that we're fulfilling our paths by serving them. They can't see past their own darkin' arrogance."

"So, is it true what I've heard from our sources in the Deep?" Wraith asked. "That you destroyed one of the trade lords?"

Murray nodded, meeting Sol's eyes. "Yes."

"You've done the Flux a service, then," Wraith said. "The Slayer will be pleased to hear it. Our goal is to hit the Daimyo vital points: mining operations, stim, and mech production."

"We took out the biggest rubellium reserve west of the capital only last week," N'auri said. "It was glory, to see those slave mines go up in flames."

"Spirits be asked, I'd like to see something like that." Brynn smiled.

"And you will, Jadean," N'auri said. "First steps, though. Wraith, what you say? Should we put these ones in the purifier?"

"The purifier?" Dozer asked. "What's that, some initiation to join up with the gang?"

N'auri pulled her worker's leathers over the top of her head, displaying her taut, ebony-muscled frame. "What you notice here, big boy?"

"Uh…" Dozer stared at the near-naked Besaydian.

"No fluxes," Sol said. "You've gone and removed all your flux tattoos."

"They are a symbol of Daimyo control," Wraith said, blinking rapidly. "They brand their slaves with them. Their schools promote fluxes to show off the deeds of Grievar brood. And their champions proudly wear the fluxes they win, though the designs only flaunt their forced service to the Daimyo."

"You mean… you've got a way to take the tattoos off of us?" Dozer stuttered.

"Yes," Wraith said. "No rebels will have a painted body. The words of the Slayer himself. We have purification machinery in this Dyver that will take them off cleanly."

"It won't be without pain, though." N'auri bared her sharp teeth again.

Sol shuddered. She'd never cared too much for the tattoos she'd earned at the Lyceum, the little Whelp design that still hatched along her neck. But she knew Dozer prided himself on the fluxes he'd earned; each was a symbol of what the big kid had fought so hard for all the way out of the slave Circles.

And Murray. Sol eyed the ex-Knight, not sure how he'd react. The man had won champion fluxes from Circles across the world, defending the nation of Ezo. Those fluxes etched across Murray's body displayed his legendary path, all the man had fought for and believed in.

Most Knights would die before having their fluxes removed.

"Let's get it done," Murray said as he pulled his vest off.

* * *

The Whelps stood in the back compartment of the Dyver, which looked like a storage room. Knees noticed this craft commandeered by the rebels appeared to have a specific purpose, though.

Six steel capsules stood upright in the room, a small glass window embedded in each.

"Once, these were cryo-coffins." Wraith invited the crew into the neon-lit room. "Containers the Daimyo use to bury their kind."

"Why in the dark would any person want to go under in a steel box?" Murray asked.

"To be kept alive," Wraith said. "Even after prolonging their lives beyond the natural order of things, even when death finally calls to them, the Daimyo still seek to further the coil, freeze themselves in the hopes that someday they will be revived with ever more advanced tech."

"Still don't darkin' understand why you got to take our fluxes," Dozer growled.

Knees eyed his big friend and knew how he felt. The two had talked of getting flux tattoos from the Lyceum ever since they'd been fighting for Tasker Ozark in the slave Circles together.

"If you are ready to give yourself to the cause, all the previous vestiges of your Daimyo-controlled lives must be erased," Wraith said.

"But I earned these…" Dozer argued, pointing to the glowing lizard on his bicep. "Fought in the Circle to get them. Bled for 'em. No Daimyo gifted these to me."

"Didn't they?" N'auri interrupted. "You thinking too small, big guy. You got the fluxes at your Citadel. Who the Citadel training students for? Who those Knights fighting for in the end? For themselves? No, for them bluebloods."

"But—"

Murray placed a hand on Dozer's shoulder, grasping it hard and meeting the boy's eyes. Murray ripped the shirt off his back, revealing dozens of fluxes he'd earned as a student, a Knight, and a champion. Dozer watched the patterns in awe.

"I also earned mine," Murray said. "But some things must change, and these designs don't define you."

Murray turned to Wraith. "Let's get this over with."

N'auri moved alongside the steel capsules, waving her hand

over a lightpad on each. The curved doors to the compartments slid open, cold smoke drifting from the innards.

"You be sure these things aren't still coffins?" Knees asked warily as he stripped off his shirt and approached one.

"Yes, they've been repurposed," Wraith replied. "They'll cleanse the Daimyo filth from your backs, make you whole again."

Murray stepped into a capsule, his large frame filling the entire thing. The door slid shut and a mist swirled around his face in the small window.

Knees watched Sol pull down the nape of her shirt and look at the little Whelp flux peering back at her, admonishing her with its wide eyes before it slithered back across her shoulder. The girl took stock of the fiery roc flux she'd had done at Cantino's compound, the proud bird stalking across her opposite shoulder. Knees knew the take, he knew what Sol had gone through in her adventure across the world to recover her father's body.

Sol shook her head, sighed, and walked into her capsule.

"For Cego," Knees whispered to Dozer before stepping inside his own capsule, feeling the cold mist surround him as the door slid shut. He removed his clothes and stared out the window, watching first Brynn and then Dozer as the last to reluctantly step in.

Knees shivered, thinking about being stuck in this box. He thought about Cego, how his friend had grown up in such a capsule, spending his entire childhood in the Cradle. He thought about his own experience in the Sim during the Trials, the darkness that had crept into him and been so hard to shake, that still lived somewhere within him.

He watched N'auri pull a handle on the wall panel, and the darkness within his capsule was replaced with brilliant light. Knees clamped his eyes shut, but the light pierced his lids.

His body began to burn, as if someone had set fire to it.

Knees screamed, pounded his hand against the glass in a desperate attempt at survival. These rebels had tricked them. They were incinerating them. The fire burned hotter and the pain became more excruciating.

Abruptly, the light dissipated and an ice-cold, soothing mist enveloped Knees's body. He crumpled to the floor in relief, slowly opening his eyes as the bright flares receded from the darkness of his lids. He looked down at his body. His flux tattoos were gone, only naked skin where the designs had been etched. The little whelp with the curious eyes had vanished.

Knees slowly stood and dressed. He pushed the inside of the capsule and the door released, letting in the warmth from the Dyver.

Sol and Brynn were outside with Murray, looking solemn. They were doing the right thing. This was for Cego.

Dozer's compartment was still closed. Knees could see his big friend standing in the window. "Dozer okay?"

Murray nodded. "Give him a minute."

"Welcome to the Flux!" N'auri smiled with her sharp teeth. "How do you feel?"

Murray looked down at his naked arms, absent the many trophies he'd won through his career. "I feel ready."

"Better now that I'm out of that thing," Brynn said as she pulled the shirt back over her head.

Dozer's capsule door swung open and the big Grievar walked out, slowly. He'd only put his trousers on and was looking down at his bare body as if it weren't his own. Knees could tell his friend was trying to hold it together, but a deep sob racked the big kid's body and he fell to his knees.

He knelt beside Dozer. "It'll be all right. More, bigger prizes to earn ahead, my friend."

Dozer looked at him through misty eyes. "I don't feel myself anymore."

Knees nodded; neither did he.

Sol offered Dozer her hand, hefting the big boy back to his feet.

"We've done this now for the cause; we've removed what we were," Sol said softly to Wraith. "So, now what will you have us do?"

Wraith's eyes fluttered. "That you have. I'm glad to have so many proven Grievar added to our ranks. I know the Slayer will be pleased as well."

"We're not here to please the Slayer." Murray pulled his studded vest back on and cracked his neck. "We're here to bring down the Daimyo."

"And you will, in due time," Wraith said. "But you must realize, as new initiates to the Flux, you still must be tested and trained to ensure you are ready for the mission when it comes to you."

"Once you step in shit, you gotta keep walking across the field," Murray muttered.

"What was that?" Wraith asked.

"Something an old man used to say to me," Murray replied. "So, take us to this new test of yours, this training."

"Guard duty on the docks to start for you." N'auri chuckled as she opened one of the storage closets, pulled down a stack of black uniforms, and handed them out to the crew. "Start where we all did, watching shipments come in and out, make sure they're protected. Like the Daimyo watch their goods, we need to keep an eye on our own retrievals."

"You mean to say"—Murray shook his head—"now that you've had us burn up our fluxes in one of those death traps, you'll have us sitting on our asses, watching hawkers deal out goods?"

Wraith nodded. "Call it what you want; it's important work that needs to be done. The Flux has forces amassing across the empire, and they need these shipments to sustain their momentum."

"What about raids? Going after the good stuff?" Dozer stood up. "Getting to work with the Strangler and the Slayer."

Knees glared at his friend. They couldn't appear too eager.

"I understand you want to be reunited with your old friend, the one who used to be called Cego," Wraith said. "As I told you, he's often on the move to track and destroy high-value targets. So, do not expect to see him until he needs you, until you can be fully trusted to take on the task."

Dozer looked like he was about to protest but luckily shut his mouth.

"Let's be doing this," Knees said, pulling his black uniform over his head. "Guard duty it is."

CHAPTER 7

The Slayer

The world does not care of dreams or hopes. Such are concepts that live solely within the mind, and though they may propel a Grievar to strive for greatness, they may also weigh one down. A Grievar should have sight of the horizon, but not at the expense of the next step forward.

Passage Four, Sixty-Third Precept of
the Combat Codes

Murray shifted his weight back and forth, standing among the crates in the dimly lit warehouse.

Across the dusty floor, N'auri sat with her legs swinging off one of the nailed-and-bolted boxes, casually chatting with Brynn and Sol.

"That fishmonger on the Emerald still there, the one with the spiced sarpin?" Brynn asked.

"Yup, as good as you remember it too," N'auri said. "Solara here didn't get a taste of that, though. Too busy helping us take out Daimyo lords."

Sol shook her head sheepishly. "Still haven't forgiven you for tricking me like that."

"And I still haven't forgiven you for thinking we were stupid enough to think your name's Sayana." N'auri laughed.

Murray couldn't believe these kids who called themselves rebels had taken down a figure as powerful as Lord Cantino. Though Wraith was the one who had led that operation, N'auri appeared more cheery islander than cold-blooded assassin. Nothing was as it seemed in this new world.

Nearby, Dozer and Knees passed the time working on striking drills, the big kid's hands moving as mitts as Knees teed off on them.

"Two, four, three!" Dozer bellowed, and Knees threw a cross, uppercut, body shot combo.

"Jabs!" Dozer yelled as Knees followed up with three quick jabs.

Dozer threw a roundhouse, which Knees ducked under, and a push kick that knocked the Venturian backward.

"Don't forget that kick coming down the center," Dozer instructed sagely as he glanced out of the corner of his eye at N'auri sitting up on the boxes.

"You told me we're only working hands today, you block." Knees dusted himself off. "Showing off to the Emeraldi again?"

"No," Dozer said. He raised his voice. "Just want to make sure my crew is prepped for anything we encounter."

Knees rolled his eyes and took advantage of Dozer's distraction by dragging the boy's arm across his body and leaping onto his back.

"Hey!" Dozer protected his neck as Knees fought for the strangle, a ritual the two often played at.

Murray watched as Knees sank the strangle, then whispered something in Dozer's ear before popping off the big kid's back.

"What do you mean, she's more Brynn's type than mine?" Dozer shoved Knees, who had a smirk across his face.

Murray shook his head, though he was glad Dozer had regained some of his personality after getting de-fluxed. For two weeks, the big kid had moped around, not even eating his fair share of rations.

Murray paced to the far end of the warehouse and stood beside a heavy steel door, the one place his crew hadn't been allowed to enter after the month they'd worked for the Flux.

"Your games won't last." Murray heard Wraith's muffled voice from within.

"A Grievar shall not accumulate land, wealth, servants, beyond what is necessary for survival," came another voice from behind the door.

Murray heard a thud, the familiar sound of a fist striking flesh, and then Wraith's voice again.

"Enough with the Codes; tell us how we can activate it."

"A wave rolling to shore and receding to sea knows neither purpose nor—"

The steel door opened and Wraith's pale face appeared.

"Something you need, Murray Pearson?"

"Seeing as we're a part of this operation now, thought you'd tell us about the prisoner you've been interrogating in there for the past week." Murray met the lieutenant's eyes.

Murray had seen the bedraggled Grievar carried in by Wraith's men, thrown into the prison. Whoever he was, Murray was impressed with his grit. The man hadn't broken yet. Though Wraith had punished him every day, the man only repeated random scripts from the Codes, as if to antagonize the Flux lieutenant.

"Not something you need to know," Wraith replied, shutting the door behind him.

"He's a Grievar," Murray said. "Man you're beating in there is our kin. Thought we're fighting the bluebloods?"

"We are," Wraith replied as he led Murray away from the door. "Though sometimes our own kind are confused about which side they are on. We need to remind them."

Murray clenched his fists. The lieutenant's words were the same as the Daimyo's. Justifying dishonor and servitude with the notion of keeping order and closing ranks.

"You seem...impatient." Wraith noticed Murray's scowl.

"Ready to get on with this," Murray replied, relaxing his hands. He needed to stay the path. "Where are they?"

"They will come when they are ready," Wraith said. "We must not rush into anything. One misstep and the empire catches on. Last week, our hideout in the Andal foothills was hit hard by Enforcers. No survivors."

Murray nodded grimly. It was dangerous business, not complying with the empire. Going head-to-head with the Daimyo was a near death sentence.

"We've been waiting," Murray said. "Standing guard at the docks and the depots, every day for a month now. My crew is ready for the next step."

"I know why you're nervous, of course," Wraith said. "All the anxious energy within your crew. It is your past with the Strangler."

Murray still couldn't get used to these rebels calling Cego by that name.

"Yeah," Murray admitted. "I am nervous to see him again. A lot has changed since we last crossed paths."

"I know about your past," Wraith said. "All Solara has told us. And the Flux does our due diligence with all initiates. You were the one who saved him, took him from the slave Circles and brought him to the Citadel."

"Seems like a lifetime ago now," Murray said.

"It was," Wraith said. "The world has changed since. And the one you called Cego, he's changed since the Slayer took him from the Daimyo prison. After the things they did to him, he's not the kid you knew anymore, Murray Pearson. You need to remember that."

Wraith turned and walked back into the interrogation room.

Every day after standing their rounds on the docks, the crew returned to the warehouse to report to Wraith. Most often, it was business as usual: A shipment came in by Dyver, was loaded onto transport, and they made sure it got back to the warehouse safely.

Murray didn't ask questions about the contents of the shipments, many of the crates now housed in the corners of the expansive warehouse. He didn't ask why the Flux needed an entire team to ensure the safety of these goods.

One thing Murray did know was these boxes weren't all full of rations to support the growing rebel armies, as Wraith had told them.

The chatter within the warehouse stopped as the chain winch attached to the large steel gate began to turn. Transport mechs usually entered by the main portal a few times per day but never this late at night.

The heavy metal sheet slid up to reveal at least a dozen men standing at the entryway, the dockyards moonlit behind them.

Several in matching studded black leather marched in with authority. Murray could smell empire Knighthood on the lot, the way they carried themselves, their mangled ears and the scars crisscrossing their faces. Even though the Knights no longer bore any recognizable tattoos from their service, Murray knew he'd tangled with their sort in the Circles before.

The men made a quick sweep of the warehouse, eyeing the crew with suspicion without saying a word.

"Clear!" one of them yelled, a giant of a man with a missing ear.

"Hello, Wraith." The large Knight slapped the Flux lieutenant on the back. "Still got no sense of humor?"

"Ulrich." Wraith nodded.

Several more figures emerged to the dim warehouse light.

Wraith stepped forward and bowed his head. "Slayer."

A chill wind crossed the space as a tall, cloaked figure stepped forward. He threw his cowl back, revealing the face Murray had seen on so many feeds across the empire: the leader of the Flux rebellion, Silas the Slayer.

"You've heard of our loss on the ridge." Silas turned to Wraith.

"Yes." Wraith's voice wavered. For the first time, Murray saw the pale lieutenant's stoic demeanor broken.

"We'll need to recoup our foothold there, soon," Silas said. "Are you up to the task?"

"Yes, Slayer," Wraith said.

"Good." Silas turned and met Murray's eyes.

Murray had stared down many killers in his life. He'd fought every sort of Grievar, those from the northern ice all the way down to the southern isles. He'd faced death enough times to consider the reaper a friend. And yet, Murray feared the man standing before him.

"It's about time you darkin' gave my crew something better to do than watching water fruit shipments on the docks," Murray said.

Murray also knew that if he felt the fear, he'd rather dig his own grave than show it to this lot.

"Just as I'd heard about you, Murray Pearson," Silas said, his eyes flashing. "Always telling things as they are."

"No other way to do it," Murray replied.

Silas waved to the rest of the crew, still on the outskirts of the warehouse. "Let's all come in and acquaint ourselves before we start briefing on the operation ahead. In fact, I know there are some reunions to be had here."

Another hooded figure stepped forward from amid the battalion of Knights. Murray could see golden eyes shining out from beneath the cowl of a cloak.

"Cego!" Dozer yelled, rushing forward. The tall Knight named Ulrich stepped in front of Dozer, shoving him backward a step.

"Hey!" Dozer growled. "What gives—"

"It's okay," Cego said quietly. "I know him."

The kid pulled his cowl back. His head was shaved, as it had been when Murray had first found him fighting for his life in the Deep.

Ulrich stepped aside, and Dozer shuffled toward Cego again, this time more cautiously.

"Is it really you?" Dozer asked.

"Yes, it's me," Cego replied.

Dozer couldn't hold back any longer, like a wolf that had been apart from his pack for too long; he pulled Cego into his trademark double-unders, lifting the kid off the ground.

Cego didn't return the hug, though he let Dozer wrap him up. He was looking past Dozer, his golden eyes meeting Murray's.

"Hello, Murray," Cego said. It'd been almost two years since he'd seen the kid. Cego had grown into a man, nearly as tall as Silas now, his black leather corded with the muscles beneath.

"It's been a while, kid," Murray said.

Sol had started to cross the floor toward Cego when she stopped in front of Silas. The girl met the Slayer's eyes.

"Solara Halberd," Silas said. "Wraith has told me you were an asset on the Isles. I thank you for your service."

"I was on the Isles to recover my father's body," Sol said unflinchingly.

"This I know," Silas responded. "Your father fought well against me. He died an honorable death. I never wished his body to be sold to the Daimyo. In fact, I requested he be sent back home for proper burial."

Murray saw Sol's jaw clench, and he prepared for things to go sideways.

"I thank you for that," Sol responded calmly. "And I'm ready to take down all who would tarnish my father's memory."

The girl moved on to stand in front of Cego.

"Are you okay?" Sol wasn't one to pull punches.

"Yes," Cego said listlessly.

"I heard what they did to you," Sol said. "I'm sorry I wasn't there to help."

"There's nothing you could have done," Cego said. "And what they did to me has made me stronger."

Sol nodded and appeared ready to turn away before she added, "We've missed you, Cego."

Cego was quiet for a moment, as if processing the strange words Sol had uttered.

"It's good you are here," Cego said. "We need strong fighters for what lies ahead."

Sol looked hurt, though she recovered quickly. They needed to hold their cover.

"Last time I laid eyes on you, you'd put your hand through the Goliath's skull," Brynn said as she approached the kid. "Spirits be praised, you're alive and well."

"Good to see you again, brother." Knees punched Cego in the shoulder. "We be ready to finally put down some soap-eaters with the famous Strangler."

"I didn't ask for the name," Cego said blankly.

"It's well deserved," Silas said. "And now that you're all reunited, we need to bring our new recruits up-to-date with the task at hand. Lieutenant?"

Wraith stepped forward and raised his voice uncharacteristically. "How does one defeat a larger, stronger opponent?"

The Flux Knights barked in unison, "Wear them down! Move fast! Strike to bleed!"

"Correct," Silas said as Wraith stepped back.

The Slayer eyed the new recruits. "These are the tenets of the Flux. This is the strategy we've employed to wage war against the empire. This has been our path against the vast Daimyo machine, those who have made slaves of our kin for millennia."

Murray looked to Cego again. The kid stood straight-backed as his brother paced in front of the rebels. He stared into the shadows of the warehouse. Perhaps he'd heard the speech one too many times.

"As most of you know, we've been making steady progress wearing down the empire's main supply lines. We've not overcommitted our attacks or centralized our forces. We've made this a war of attrition," Silas said.

"And we've used our speed to remain largely undetectable," Silas continued. "We attack, do damage, and move out, giving our opponent little ability to counter."

Silas stopped pacing and cocked his head, as if listening to some unseen voice. The Slayer stood like that for several moments. Murray looked to the Knights, and clearly, they were used to the strange behavior, not batting an eye.

Murray couldn't help but stare at Cego again. The kid was there, in the flesh. Certainly broken, and changed, but alive. He wanted to go to him, wrap the kid in his arms. Murray wanted to tell him he was sorry he'd not been there when he needed him most. Murray wanted to tell Cego he'd brought Sam back to the Citadel.

"We've bled the empire," Silas said abruptly, breaking his silence. "We've struck fear into the hearts of their nobles, brought the violence to their homes, their wards, their parlors, their eateries. We've littered blueblooded bodies in our wake so that they feel safe no longer."

Murray disliked the soap-eaters, but he could feel Silas's hatred for the Daimyo, a palpable energy coming off the Slayer.

"Our forces to the west have struck their key mining operations, cutting off supply of precious elements to hinder production of mech weaponry," Silas said as he continued to pace. "We destroyed one of their largest factories on the Desovian border, a place where their steel beasts were being churned out."

Murray felt exposed in this place, in front of these rebels. How could these kids under his care hope to blend in? How could they follow this zealot on his blood-soaked path?

He saw the emptiness in Cego. Maybe he'd already lost that one, but now Murray had led the rest of the crew right into the wolf's lair. The bile rose in his throat.

"We've done so far what no rebel force has ever achieved against the empire," Silas said with pride. "The enemy is bleeding, breathing hard, on their heels. We need to keep pushing forward, striking at our opponent where their defenses are down, ensuring that not only their bodies are broken but so are their wills."

Murray wasn't sure if his eyes were deceiving him, but he could swear a fine mist was rising from Silas's shoulders toward the warehouse ceiling. And then he caught a flash of movement at Silas's arm—a glowing flux tattoo in the form of a wolf prowled down to the Grievar's wrist.

Murray caught Dozer glaring at the elaborate canine design. He knew what the big kid was thinking; the Whelps had been forced to rid themselves of their fluxes, while the leader of this entire movement somehow had kept his own intact.

"Shirōkami." Silas's glowing eyes met Dozer's. "This is not a mark of the Daimyo, like your flux tattoos were reminders of. This isn't something they've forced upon us. This is a mark from within, given to me by the blacklight."

Dozer looked like he was about to argue, but Murray grabbed the boy's shoulder and squeezed it.

"Though we've had much success, we've also had to sacrifice," Silas continued. "We've seen our enemy's strength, their ability to destroy us with their mechs. Our opponent is not near finished. We cannot underestimate their strength; at any moment, they can strike back with a finishing blow.

"There will be a time when we amass our forces. There will be a time when Grievar-kin ride out into the open field of battle. There will be a time when we show them our full might so that they can quiver in their estates, watching on their feeds. But that time has not yet come.

"The fight is not always the one in front of us," Silas said.

The words rang out in Murray's head. *Those were Farmer's words.*

"First, we must strike at another breaking point, one deep in the heart of enemy territory," Silas said. "Here in Karstock, where we've operated in plain sight, purposefully avoiding conflict. But the time has come to trade our spot in the shadows for a vital target in the open. Karstock Labs."

Of course, Murray had heard of the famed facility where the empire's top makers worked. Karstock Labs was planted right in the center of the capital.

"We're here to help with the cause, not become corpses for you." Murray couldn't hold back anymore. "How could attacking Karstock Labs be anything but a death sentence to all involved?"

Wraith snarled. "You dare doubt the Slayer when you've only—"

"Murray Pearson is right to be concerned," Silas said. "He is a veteran fighter, one that's seen more Circles than most in this room. Yet he hasn't seen what we can do…"

"We're not here to sacrifice ourselves," Murray said. "I want to be alive to see the look on their blueblooded faces when we knock at their doors."

"You will not be a sacrifice," Silas said as he pulled the hood back over his head and began to walk away. "Lieutenant, outline the plan to the recruits."

"You aren't fighting with us?" Murray shouted after Silas as he passed beneath the warehouse gate. "On this mission you've said is so important?"

"You're in able hands, Murray Pearson." Silas turned back. "And there's a certain marshal who ordered the execution of several of our rebels recently. I owe him a visit."

The Slayer vanished to the shadows of the dockyard.

Wraith stepped forward to take his place.

"Karstock Labs is the largest producer of neurostimulants in the world. They flood the market with these enhancements, pawning them to both the highest empire supply lines and to the lowest black-market dregs," Wraith said. "Our primary objective is to destroy the lab's production capacity."

Murray didn't hear the same hatred Silas had for the Daimyo in Wraith's voice. The lieutenant had a different flavor of cold calculus behind his words.

"Our second objective is to capture a high-value target," Wraith said. "Master Maker Stalyr Varakas, leading the research and development of new neurostimulants for the past three years and responsible for many of the new strains on the market today.

"In the past, we've simply assassinated similar targets," Wraith continued, nodding to Cego. "But we believe Varakas to be in possession of integral information that will help with our next phase of attack against the empire. So, we must capture him alive and return him here for interrogation."

Wraith passed a handful of what appeared to be small black seeds to N'auri. The Emeraldi girl distributed them among the crew.

"You're going to be telling us how to throw punches through this thing?" Murray asked as he fit the small rubber piece into his swollen ear.

"These receivers will allow us to be in communication throughout the operation," Wraith said. "I won't always be in sight, but you'll be able to hear me and know that we'll be watching."

Was that a threat?

"We have an inside operative at Karstock Labs," Wraith said. "Using her intelligence, we've determined the precise time to strike. The highest-level security protocols will be disabled at this moment, but we'll still need to get by a large and highly trained security force."

"There be Enforcers waiting for us?" Knees asked, though Murray knew the question was on everyone's mind.

"Yes," Wraith answered. "There are several mechs guarding Karstock Labs, though we hope to bypass them. In the case we do encounter one, we'll take care of it."

"Take care of?" Dozer asked. "You mean, like fight one of those things? I've seen what they can do to a body—"

"You will not need to worry about the mechs," Cego said quietly. "I'll handle it."

The words of his friend silenced Dozer, and Wraith continued.

"Murray, we will use you as a distraction," Wraith said. "You and Dozer will walk in the front doors of the facility."

"And how do we suppose that will happen?" Murray said.

"It so happens that the empire official who runs the lab is a fan of yours," Wraith said, a faint smile almost blossoming on his ghostly face. "We've set up a personal audience for him."

It all makes sense now.

"You never cared about our training, what we added to the team," Murray growled. "You've been wanting to use me as a distraction for this op the entire time."

"Yes," Wraith said flatly. "But we needed to see your loyalty first. And as you know, throwing a feint is most often the best way to bring an opponent's hands high to land a proper body blow."

Wraith demonstrated the technique, moving with precise speed, the steel bracers on the wrists of his leather uniform reflecting in the low light as he threw his punches.

Murray couldn't argue with the man's logic. And it would be otherwise impossible to gain entrance to a place like Karstock Labs without setting off alarms.

"So, you want me and Dozer here to dance for some politik while you do the dirty work?"

"Don't worry," Wraith said. "There will be plenty of dirty work for you as well. Once you are isolated with the official, you will take him hostage. You will sound the breach alarm and draw security forces to your location."

Murray shook his head. Despite the lieutenant's calm demeanor, it still sounded like he was sending his crew on a suicide mission.

"We will be ready to bail you and Dozer out." Wraith watched Murray frown. "But first, I will lead the bulk of our force to infiltrate the lab's core production facility. We will enter via the sewage system below the labs, which we've gained access to via our network of Grunt operatives."

"Great, we be walking through the shit now," Knees muttered.

Wraith ignored the Venturian and turned to Cego.

"The Strangler knows his objective. Capture Master Maker Varakas alive and destroy all else in the way. You'll climb the disabled lift shaft for roof access and come back down into Varakas's research lab through the ventilation."

Cego nodded.

"Solara," Wraith said. "You'll be accompanying the Strangler."

Cego shook his head. "I don't need anybody with me; she'll only hold me back."

Sol stepped forward. "What did you say?"

Cego ignored his old friend and spoke directly to Wraith. "You know I can handle it on my own."

"The Slayer has given me these instructions," Wraith said. "He wants other Flux operatives to be trained in your particular... skill set."

"Now is not the time for me to be brood-sitting," Cego said.

Murray watched Sol's brow furrow.

"I've worked with Solara before, and you know her as well," Wraith said. "She's quick enough to keep up, good enough in a pinch to help out. Especially because you'll need to go through Varakas's personal guard to get to him. Take her; you've got no choice."

Cego paced away, unresponsive.

"We'll run training exercises for the next week instead of having you on guard duty at the docks," Wraith said.

"Finally!" Dozer stepped forward. "I've been waiting for some real action."

Murray couldn't quite tell whether the big kid was still playing his part or if he was genuine in his excitement. He feared the Slayer's words had seeped into these kids' minds, pulled them toward this hopeless cause. The cause that Cego seemed to be lost within.

Murray looked to the shadows where Cego had retreated. He didn't recognize him anymore. The kid he'd pulled from the slave

Circles. The boy who had always stood up for the weak, who had possessed an innate sense of honor that transcended these games for power. Now Murray only saw the Strangler in the shadows, born of the blacklight and shaped by Silas over the past year.

Wraith turned to the dozen Knights who had stood at attention, unmoving like mechs throughout the operational details.

"Free to fight," Wraith whispered.

"Fight to be free!" the Knights called out.

Murray heard the voices of his own crew joining the chorus.

CHAPTER 8

The Strangler

The lord must fully realize the attributes of all those in his service. From the gardeners on his grounds to the harvesters in his fields to the warriors in his court, a lord must strive to know every individual's strength and weakness. As with an assorted garden, each plant must be tended in a precise and unique manner to bear fruit.

Passage Five, The Lost Precepts

Murray and Dozer waited in the west-end industrial reaches of Karstock, made up of flat buildings that smelled of motor oil and fumes. Only a short sprint away, downtown's forest of sky-scrapers sprang up from the cement streets and reached to the clouds.

It was rare for Daimyo citizens to traverse the lower levels of Karstock, where Murray and Dozer currently squatted in front of a shuttered repair station. Most bluebloods traveled in the aerial pods above, the nighttime traffic an unending stream of spectral light, luminous wisps following in the wake of the mechs that flowed in and out of the city.

"So boring," Dozer yawned, staring up at the traffic.

"Not boring for them," Murray said.

"How come we don't get to be a part of the infiltration team down below?" Dozer asked.

"That's the plan," Murray said, eyeing the entrance to Karstock Labs two blocks down. "They need us for a distraction."

Other than the tall, barbed fence surrounding it, the building was nondescript. Murray peered up toward the roof of the lab, where an iron smokestack pumped out black fumes. Cego and Sol were likely already scaling the lift shaft toward the roof.

A small guardhouse sat along the fence, where Murray and Dozer had been watching a pot-bellied merc recline in front of a feed.

"How much longer?" Dozer asked, as he reached into his pocket and produced a strip of jerky.

"Where'd you get that?" Murray whispered.

"Took it out of the stash at headquarters," Dozer said. "You want one?"

Murray shrugged, marveling at the kid's ingenuity in finding food wherever he went. "Sure."

From their vantage, Murray could make out the fuzzy picture coming into the guard's screen. Murray knew the fight the man was watching: Artemis Halberd vs. Yongl Floree. He was likely playing a top-ten Halberd feed.

"You think Cego's so different now?" Dozer whispered as the two squinted their eyes to watch the fight. "I mean…didn't seem like he even cared that we'd come to get him."

"Well, he thinks we're here to join up, so he doesn't know we came for him," Murray said.

"'Course he does," Dozer said. "But I mean, if I'd been put on trial, fought the Goliath and beat him, then sent to prison before getting jacked out by my famous brother, guess I'd not care that my friends showed up either."

Murray looked at the big kid. Though he sometimes acted like he wasn't the smartest, Murray knew he understood more than he let on.

"Cego's gone through a lot." Murray ripped at the jerky. "At Arklight, they did things to him. Things no kid, no person, should have done to them. Stuff like that messes with your brain, can make you change—"

Murray held his hand to his ear and Dozer's head perked up.

Wraith's steady voice came over the com.

"Squad Two, move in for interference."

"We're on." Murray downed the jerky and stood, putting his hand on Dozer's shoulder. "You ready?"

"Yeah, I'm good," Dozer said. "Let's do this."

The two walked around the corner and across the street. Murray rapped on the glass of the guard enclosure.

The man frowned, threw his feet off the table, and switched the feed off. "What do you want?"

"Got an audience with the folks who run this place," Murray said.

The guard quickly straightened himself up and peered closer at Murray before breaking into a wide grin. "Well, if it isn't... Mighty Murray himself!"

Murray nodded, wanting to be on with it.

"I remember watching you fight when I was a little kik," the guard said. "Can see it as clear as yesterday when you put Maverick down with that cross. Thing of beauty it was, even though he was empire team. Think I watched every one of your matches on SystemView after that. Even the last one... But hey, we've all got bad days, right?"

"Right," Murray said. "We're in a rush, if you don't mind."

"Got it." The guard touched his hand to a receiver on the desk in front of him. "We got Murray Pearson at front gate."

The guard stopped and eyed Dozer. "Who's he?"

"My squire," Murray said. "Even though I'm retired, still can use a bit of help getting around these days."

"I know how it is," the guard said. "Busted my hip training five years ago. Haven't been the same since."

The man stepped out of the guard booth. "Hate to do this to you, Murray, but I've got to make sure you two aren't carrying."

"I understand," Murray said, as the man ran a steel rod with a blue spectral buzzing around it across Murray's body and then Dozer's.

The guard returned to his booth and pressed the receiver again. "Pearson and his squire, cleared and coming up."

A red light flashed on the gate in front of them before it slid open. Two more armed men in uniform emerged to escort them.

"Was an honor to meet you," the guard said. "My brother won't believe it. Best of luck in there."

Murray and Dozer started to walk toward the facility entrance.

"Wait!"

Murray's heart jumped as he slowly turned back toward the guard.

"We fight so the rest shall not have to," the man said.

Murray breathed a sigh of relief. He hadn't spoken the Codes for some time now.

"We fight so the rest shall not have to," Murray replied.

*   *   *

Sol watched Cego scale the thick chain above her. Sweat trickled off her brow, and her shoulders started to tighten, trying to keep up with him.

"I hope the lift really is disabled, as Wraith told us," Sol said, fruitlessly trying to get something out of Cego.

Her friend was quiet, as he'd been for the entire week preceding the mission.

At first, Sol had been upset that Cego hadn't wanted her by his side. But she remembered what he'd been through. All Sol needed to do was think about Cego's time at Arklight, and any grudge she had was replaced by the gnawing worry that her friend was gone, replaced by this stranger mechanically climbing above her.

They slowly made their way up the shaft in the darkness. Cego moved methodically, his hands and feet in sync as they gripped the chain.

Sol looked down the way they'd come. A fall from this height onto the hard steel ceiling of the disabled lift compartment would mean certain death, even with a rolling breakfall. She wondered if Cego would even care if she fell. He hadn't turned back even once so far.

Wraith's voice abruptly broke the silence, coming in through Sol's com. "Status update, Squad Three."

Cego responded as he reached for his next handhold. "We're halfway up the shaft."

"Good," Wraith said. "Update again when you've reached the roof."

Wraith and his team of Knights, along with N'auri, Brynn, and Knees, were now waiting in the sewage tunnels beneath the building. Cego and Sol had started alongside them but had parted ways to gain access to the bottom of the lift shaft.

"It's strange how we've been connected, you and I, even though we've been apart," Sol said, settling for talking to herself to keep her mind off the strain of the climb.

"I first met N'auri and Wraith during my travels on the Isles," Sol continued. "And you've been working alongside them out here for the past year. Don't you find that strange?"

Sol paused for Cego to respond but only heard the faint chatter of the bats nesting in the shaft.

"I haven't been back to the Lyceum either," Sol said. "After I returned from the Isles and buried my father, I stayed on my family's plot to look after things. I was planning on returning for the next semester, but when I got word about you...I knew I had to head north."

She kept talking as they climbed, hoping something might break through to Cego.

"I tried to find work in Karstock; looked to make a name for myself in the local Circles, gain some trust to see if anyone would mention you or your brother. Of course, no one would trust some Ezonian girl. I'm not sure what I expected, but I only found hostility and tight lips."

Sol could feel her arms straining as she continued to climb. "Eventually I left Karstock, took to the road again on Firenze, and I found the Tanri. The bird people I'd heard so many stories of from my father. Cego, they took me in right away. Though we could barely communicate, somehow, they knew who I was: the daughter of Artemis Halberd. They let me live with them, fight and earn my place in their tribe. They let me wear their mask. They let me become the Firebird."

Sol could make out a glimmer of moonlight creeping through the seams of the shaft's ceiling. They were nearing the top.

"Cego," Sol said. "All I knew is that if I kept fighting, if I didn't give up, I'd find you again. And I did. That's why we're all out here. We're here to help you."

Sol wanted to tell Cego they were here to bring him home, that they were here to get him away from his maniacal brother. But she wasn't sure how this stranger climbing above her would react; at this point, it wouldn't surprise her if he accused her of being a traitor to the Flux.

As Sol reached to brush the matted hair from her face, a sudden blur of movement rushed by her shoulder. A large bat shot up the shaft with a screech. Sol's hand missed its mark on the chain and she dropped backward, the darkness rushing up from below.

She crossed her ankles around the chain at the last moment, squeezing tight as her upper body was flung upside down. She hung there, suspended in the darkness, breathing hard, before she used her core to pull herself back to the chain and find her handhold again.

Cego had finally stopped. He was looking down at her.

Perhaps if she'd fallen to her death, he would have made some sound, some utterance to acknowledge Sol had accompanied him on a mission to kidnap the empire's famed master maker.

But he stayed silent.

"Good thing I've got a good closed guard." Sol laughed nervously.

Cego nodded and reached again for his next grip.

"You used to tell me about climbing on the island," Sol said as she wiped her brow and worked to catch up. "You told me how your teacher would have you scale the cliffs with your brothers. Wonder if that's why you're so comfortable on this chain."

Cego didn't respond; he kept moving upward, closing in on the shaft's ceiling.

"Murray told us," Sol said. "He let us know about the Cradle. How the island you grew up on was a simulation."

Cego stopped again.

"All you've gone through," Sol said. "During the Trials and at the Lyceum, the nightmares. It makes sense now. I wish you'd told me. Maybe I could have helped."

Cego stared down into the darkness, as if he were occupying another world. Finally, his golden eyes locked on to Sol's. She realized it was the first time Cego had actually seen her since they'd arrived at the dockyards.

"It was my home," he said.

"I know," Sol replied.

Cego turned and rapidly ascended the last few meters of the climb.

He pressed his hand against the metal grate on top and punched it hard, popping it out. Moonlight streamed down into the shaft, bathing Sol's face.

Cego turned back to look at Sol once more and lifted himself to the roof.

*   *   *

Knees stood ankle-deep in shit.

He'd gotten used to the smell after waiting over an hour in the sewage tunnel beneath Karstock Labs. But Knees had not gotten used to the three-foot-long rats that would occasionally scamper along the ledge of the tunnel walls, their red eyes peering at him through the darkness.

"Darkin' swear they're bigger than my hunting hounds," Ulrich muttered as he paced back and forth in the muck. Of the dozen Knights on Flux Squad One, Knees didn't dislike Ulrich quite as much as the others. The giant man at least had a sense of humor.

"It's because of what they're cooking up above," a balding Knight said. "Stims seeping down into the sewage. Rats are eating it and getting bigger, stronger."

"Until they waste away," another Knight with a cloth tied over his face said in a muffled voice. He pointed to a rodent body floating belly-up atop the brown water, its mouth hanging open.

"Least the live ones are good for kicking," Ulrich said as he sprang forward through the muck to launch a kick at a rat baring its teeth at him. He missed widely and showered another merc with brown water.

"Darkin' idiot." The Knight wiped a streaked arm across his face and stepped toward Ulrich threateningly.

"Stop," Wraith said from the shadows, and the Knight froze. "I'll not have this entire mission compromised because my team can't sit still for a moment."

"Sorry, Lieutenant," the Knight said. "Just that we're ready for action. Been near an entire shift we've been waiting down here."

"I've told you, we're waiting on word from Pearson," Wraith said. "If we move ahead beneath the main facility and security has not yet been diverted, we'll be up against odds we can't handle."

"Bet we can take anything these soap-eaters throw at us," Ulrich boasted.

"Perhaps you wouldn't mind telling the Slayer himself why

you botched the mission because of your arrogance," Wraith responded.

"Uh…no," Ulrich said. "I'll be fine waiting."

"Take note of the new recruits, who've stood patiently without a word of complaint, unlike my elite team of trained rebels." Wraith nodded to Knees and Brynn.

"Give the men a break, Wraith," N'auri said from her perch on the thin ledge with her back to the tunnel wall. "These two have the pleasure of listening to my stories. We could wait all day."

The islander was comfortable with the rats. Knees saw one of the things brush behind her, rub right against her leg, and she didn't even flinch.

"We've got bugs as big as those in the bush back home!" The Emeraldi laughed as she caught Knees's eyes. "Same on the Jade, right, Brynn?"

Brynn shook her head. "My family wasn't near the jungles, so not sure."

"Ah, the sorts up in the hills, then?" N'auri raised an eyebrow. "Sittin' back and getting fresh deliveries from the fishmongers, I bet."

"Doesn't mean we didn't work hard," Brynn said defensively. "We trained from sunup all the way until we couldn't sweat anymore in the high heat."

"Didn't mean no disrespect, Jadean." N'auri held her hands up and flashed her sharp smile. "Just saying it's probably why you're standing in the shit over there to keep away from the little mice. You know, you could come and stay nice and dry over here with me."

Knees could almost swear he saw Brynn blush as she waved dismissively at N'auri.

Wraith held his fist in the air and the group froze in the darkness.

"I've gotten word from Pearson," Wraith said. "They've successfully captured the target. Security forces are being diverted as we speak."

"Can't believe the old man did it," Ulrich said. "Didn't think he'd be able to pull it off."

"Let's hope he can hold position until we've infiltrated the production facility," Wraith said as he blinked rapidly. "You've got your wish, Flux Squad One. It's time to move."

Knees breathed a sigh of relief, knowing that Murray and Dozer had completed the first part of their mission without a problem. He wondered if Cego and Sol had made it atop the roof yet.

Wraith marched down the tunnel and waved the rebels on behind him.

Brynn offered a hand to N'auri and bowed her head slightly. "Shall I escort you from your perch, my lady, into the shit?"

N'auri smiled as she took Brynn's hand and leapt from her perch into the sewage. "Maybe I'd get used to living up in the hills too if that's how they talk to me."

The companions followed Wraith down the tunnel until they stopped beside a ladder that led above. Knees heard the grating of machinery shaking the pipes running along the sewer ceiling.

"We're here," Wraith said. "Ulrich, you lead the way up with two men, ensure the room's clear, we'll—"

The lieutenant froze, staring straight ahead into the darkness.

A crimson glow had flared to life several meters down, illuminating a tiny man, a Daimyo. Knees couldn't tell if his eyes were playing tricks on him in the darkness, but the little blueblood appeared to be floating in midair, his black eyes peering back at the group.

The man floated toward them, and the massive black mech he sat within came into view.

"Sentinel!" Wraith screamed.

*　　*　　*

Sol heard the muffled shouts in her earpiece. She listened to Wraith's scream right before her com filled with static.

Cego had frozen in place atop the roof, listening as well, his black cloak catching the steady wind.

"We've got to help them!" Sol yelled. "This wasn't supposed to happen; they were ambushed!"

"We can't do anything for them now," Cego said as he lifted a black mask over his face and swiftly walked toward the other side of the roof. The lights of the surrounding skyscrapers sparkled across the cityscape.

Sol ran to Cego, put a hand on his shoulder to turn him around, and suddenly she was flat on her back. Cego stood above Sol with her arm torqued, his golden eyes staring down at her through the slit in his mask.

Sol rolled over her shoulder to relieve the pressure and sprang back to her feet. Her hands were up, fists curled tight.

"Who are you?" Sol snarled. "It's Knees down there in the sewers; it's Brynn and N'auri! Your friends!"

Cego stared blankly back at her before whispering, "I don't know who I am anymore."

Sol let her hands fall back to her sides, her heart jumping in her chest.

"We need to help them, Cego." She turned back the way they'd come, ready to scale the long chain down the lift.

"We can't," Cego said. "If they've been ambushed, we won't be able to get to them in time. We need to trust them and stay on task. Wraith and N'auri are down there with the Knights. Knees and Brynn can handle themselves. If we don't do this, it will all be for nothing."

Sol kept walking. Who was this stranger to tell her to not help her friends? Who was this assassin they called the Strangler? Certainly not the boy she had once known who would do anything for his friends. This was not her old training partner with the kind, curious eyes.

She turned back as she reached the open entry of the lift. Cego was walking in the opposite direction, toward the smokestack pumping black fumes to the sky. She knew he would continue on the mission without her. He'd enter the research lab and take on anything that got in his way to get to the master maker. Even if it meant his death.

She'd told Cego she'd have his back. She hadn't been there for him before when he needed her most, when he'd gone to trial and been sentenced to execution. When Cego had been sent to Arklight, Sol had been absent on her own journey, for her own reasons.

She couldn't leave him again.

Sol pulled her mask over her face and walked back across the roof toward Cego.

*   *   *

Knees watched in horror as the brown sewage turned red with the blood of rebels.

The Sentinel's armor seemed impenetrable, the entire crew attacking it all at once and not even making a dent. The beast was far stronger than any Knight and moved with a blazing speed that contradicted its sheer mass.

Two Knights floated face down in the water. Knees had watched the Sentinel shatter one with a punch to the chest and toss another like a rag doll against the tunnel wall.

Wraith was holding off more bloodshed by goading the Sentinel toward him, always standing in front of it to attract its lethal strikes. The mech launched itself at him and threw a cross, the pale man barely weaving his head from the punch. An inch of a difference and Wraith's skull would be pulp.

The mech charged again and Wraith dove out of the way into a splashing front roll.

"Come on, you tin shit!" Ulrich screamed as he threw his hardest kick into the Sentinel's exposed back. The mech slid forward a few inches in the muck before swiveling around and barreling toward the tall Knight.

The Sentinel threw a roundhouse that Ulrich ducked but followed with a cross that caught the Knight on the shoulder. Knees flinched as he watched Ulrich's arm crack.

Another Knight took Ulrich's place, throwing a kick down the middle aimed at the pilot's compartment, only serving to shatter his own foot. The Sentinel countered with its own kick, hurling the Knight's limp body into the darkness.

Another rebel leapt onto the beast's shoulders, raining down elbows atop its blocky head. The Sentinel reached back and grabbed the man, plucking him by the head like a water fruit off the vine. Knees could see the pilot within the mech encasing, the Daimyo's black eyes pulsing.

The mech wrenched the man back and forth before smashing his head against the tunnel wall. Knees watched, horrified, as the beast whirled around and tossed the limp, nearly headless body into the sewage.

Knees had sought an opening to help, but awe and fear of the Sentinel's destructive power had left him frozen. He saw not only the Sentinel standing before him in the tunnel but the mech that had ripped a hole through Joba. Knees saw the execution on the plains, the burning stench of flesh still putrid in his mind.

Wraith danced in front of the Sentinel again, barely dodging another punch that ripped concrete off the tunnel wall. The pale Grievar was bleeding from his face and tiring as he attempted to draw the beast from the remaining rebels.

A wild scream erupted from behind the mech and N'auri landed on its shoulders, looking like a feral street cat attacking a gar bear. She pounded at the thing's head, attempting to give Wraith a moment to breathe, though the Sentinel didn't even appear to notice the Emeraldi riding atop it.

"Wraith!" N'auri screamed. "It's time; we need to use it!"

"No," Wraith breathed heavily as he barely evaded another strike.

Knees caught a blur of movement out of the corner of his eye. Brynn was running directly at the beast, her eyes on N'auri atop its shoulders. The Jadean looked even smaller than normal as she neared the metal creature.

"Brynn!" Knees screamed as his fear finally broke, like a fever run too hot. He didn't care about these rebels. But Brynn was his friend. He wouldn't let her go in alone. He sprinted to join her.

The Sentinel flicked out its arm with blazing speed, and Brynn barely managed to drop backward to avoid getting crushed. The Jadean fell on her back into the sewage, staring up at the metallic beast.

N'auri screeched, pounding at the mech's head, her fists a bloody mess. The Sentinel raised its giant leg to stomp Brynn into oblivion.

The mech jerked and stopped.

Brynn scrambled out from beneath it and backed up toward Knees.

The beast turned, attempting to grasp at something, and Knees saw Wraith with his hand plunged through the Sentinel's lower back. The rebel lieutenant ripped his hand free, releasing wires and a plume of smoke from the casing.

In the place of Wraith's hands were two steel spikes, each crackling with blue energy. The Sentinel swung at Wraith, and he ducked the blow before plunging one of his hand spikes into the beast's leg.

Ulrich had staggered back into the fray, despite one of his arms hanging limply at his side.

"We're doing that now, eh?" the big Knight said.

Knees watched as Ulrich flicked his wrist. Blue flared around the man's bracer and a metallic casing engulfed his hand. The tall Knight charged the Sentinel, who was wildly swinging to detach Wraith from its leg.

Ulrich aimed for the pilot's compartment, but the mech pivoted at the last moment to protect its innards, causing the fan of energy blazing around Ulrich's fist to rip across its arm instead.

"Eye for an eye, tin shit," Ulrich growled as the mech's arm dropped to the ground, leaving a mess of writhing wires open at its shoulder.

"Spirits be asked, how are they doing this?" Brynn whispered as a flare of light burst from the top of the Sentinel's shoulders. N'auri plunged both of her now-crackling hands into the beast's head, ripping them free and blasting them back in again.

The mech whirled frantically in a lethal spin of steel arms.

Another Knight with two spikes where his hands should be was caught by the mech's flailing and dropped lifelessly into the sewage.

N'auri continued plunging her hands into the Sentinel's head, while Ulrich danced in and out of range, attempting to land another shot.

Knees watched as an explosion of blue blood splattered the pilot's compartment inside the mech. The little Daimyo pilot within slumped over, his black eyes rolling back into his head.

The giant steel Sentinel wavered as if it were drunk. N'auri leapt off the beast's shoulders, and it toppled into the muck face-first. Wraith was atop the Sentinel, his arm fully punched through its back into the inner sanctum.

The pale man breathed heavily and ripped his bloody arm free.

*   *   *

Sol dropped down from the duct behind Cego into the darkness of the laboratory.

She crouched on the floor, trying to get a bearing on her surroundings. The room smelled of sterile cleaning astringents. A centrifuge droned in a corner and panels blinked against the walls, but what drew Sol's attention was a glowing glass casing, rising from floor to ceiling.

A grey, gangly humanoid form was suspended within the translucent tube.

"Who's there?" she heard a man yell, fear tingeing his voice. She saw a little form scamper across the room and stop in front of the glowing tube.

Cego was gone from beside her, melded into the shadows of the lab.

Another voice burst into the room along with flashes of bright light, "What the dark's going on in here?"

A full squad of armed guards entered, casting their spotlights across the room.

"Make sure the maker doesn't escape," Sol heard Cego's voice emerge from the darkness.

"Someone came from the ducts as the lights went out," the little Daimyo maker screamed. "You must protect my work!"

One guard turned his spotlight on Sol, who was crouched down near a granite counter.

"Breach, get him!"

Two men rushed Sol. She ducked behind the counter and tried to creep away from the light, but a beam tracked her, cutting the shadows in the room.

One of the shadows broke from the darkness like a spear, piercing a guard and throwing him to the floor. Sol heard a sharp grunt, then a gurgle. The remaining guards stopped in their tracks.

"There's more of them..." one whispered. They lifted their charged weapons and cautiously approached Sol's position again.

"Doesn't matter how many of 'em there are," another said. "We've got our orders: Protect the maker at all costs."

Several guards crossed the lab and planted themselves in formation in front of the master maker. The little Daimyo stood protectively in front of the strange specimen within the tube. Sol couldn't help but glance back at the creature. Empty eyes stared out from a bone-white skull lacking a nose or mouth. Gnarled muscles hung listlessly from its torso like slabs of butcher's meat on display.

A shadow emerged in front of the tube, standing to face the entire squad. Cego. A guard took a swing with his blazing baton, but Cego ducked low and lanced the man with a high side kick.

Sol turned her attention back to the men closing in on her. She wasn't accustomed to fighting multiple opponents. Nearly all the drills she'd practiced were focused in the Circle, where she'd face only one attacker at a time. However, when she was younger, her father had made sure to prepare her for anything.

Fighting two, three men at once, you're likely to lose, no matter how good you are, Sol, Artemis Halberd had said. *Only chance you've got is to cut the angles; don't let them come at you at the same time.*

Sol backed herself between two granite slabs, each stacked with glass beakers and steel canisters. She pulled the mask from her face and stood to let the guard's light beam catch her.

"Ah, so—what we got here?"

A guard with a knot on his forehead advanced as Sol backed up. "A girly!"

The other guard grinned, looking over his friend's shoulder at Sol. "You get lost or something, beautiful? Maybe once we put your friend's head through the floor, we can have some fun."

Sol began to raise her hands to the air and flashed a smile at the guard. He started to lower his weapon, and Sol kicked him in the face, hard. She threw her full weight into the strike, breaking the man's nose and, more importantly, making him drop his weapon.

Sol shoved the screaming man backward into his friend before throwing a cross to his chin. The man dropped like a sack of vat flour, while the second attempted to scramble past him to get to Sol.

The guard's fallen spotlight twirled on the floor and cast its beam back at the melee across the room. Three guards were swinging simultaneously at Cego, who was moving like a demon, dancing between their strikes and countering with lethal accuracy.

One guard tried to club him with his crackling rod, but Cego wrapped up his arm and broke his shoulder in a fluid movement. He held the screaming man at bay and kicked another in the chest. The third guard came from behind and ripped his long staff across Cego's back, tearing the leather from it and searing his flesh beneath.

No matter how much Cego had changed, Sol still wanted to help him. But her own opponent was stalking her. The guard swung his steel menacingly as she backed up again.

"Know your stuff, do you, girl?"

"Why don't you fight me like a real Grievar?" Sol growled. "Need a weapon to take on a girl?"

The man laughed. "No, but I'd like to see how you smell when I fry you."

He charged.

Sol anticipated the movement and grabbed the man's weapon-wielding hand with both her arms. She sank her hips and tossed him over her shoulder.

Seoi nage. Worked even better on the big ones.

He landed on the lab counter, smashing vials and glass. Sol ripped at his weapon and pried the rod away. She held it for a moment, her eyes transfixed on the pulsing electric charge. Sol considered using it, putting her opponent down in one lethal strike.

She tossed the rod aside and backed up as the man slid off the table into a crouch. "Guess I'll be the one choosing to fight you like a Grievar," she taunted.

A loud *crack* across the room drew Sol's attention. One of the guards had swung on Cego and smashed his rod into the casing behind him. A series of fissures sprang up the side of the glass.

"My work!" the little Daimyo screeched with his hands up to the machine. "Protect my work!"

The glow from within the tube leaked its light onto Cego and the guards still surrounding him. But there was another light source now. It was coming directly from Cego. A strange radiance streaked across his arm where the leather had burned away. The guards approached him in unison.

Sol's opponent capitalized on her distraction, shooting low for a takedown and blasting her to the ground. She defended from her back, placing her feet against the man's hips to keep him at a distance.

"Got you where I want now." The man pressed forward, attempting to throw a looping overhead at Sol while she was on her back. She pushed forward as hard as she could with both feet against his hips. The man stumbled and Sol used the opportunity to stand.

The guard kept the pressure on, though, diving at her. Sol sprawled her legs back and wrapped her arm deep around his neck, fishing for the guillotine. She cinched the strangle; it was tight.

The guard reacted in desperation, lifting Sol into the air and slamming her onto one of the lab tables. She winced as a shard of glass dug into her back. The man slid her across the granite surface, wildly attempting to break the choke, but Sol held on, even as more glass shards tore into her body.

Sol kept the strangle up, and finally, the body atop her went limp. She breathed heavily as she kept her arms tight to finish the job.

She stared back across the room. Cego was glowing even brighter now, with blue flames pulsing across his back, streaking his shoulders, brightest at the strange serpentine flux flowing down his arm. Doragūn. The flux was also unremoved, like the wolf on his brother Silas's arm. Sol had seen it once before, years earlier when he'd fought in the finals match. Whatever this strange force was, it appeared stronger within Cego now.

Sol let her opponent drop lifelessly to the ground and slid off the slab of granite. She reached behind her and ripped a long shard of bloody glass from her shoulder.

She strode forward to help Cego but saw nearly all his opponents were down, unmoving on the floor. A single guard still stood between Cego and the master maker.

"Get the maker," Cego said.

Sol saw the Daimyo cowering beside the giant tube. Wisps of curly white hair were damp across his veined forehead.

The remaining guard screamed as he charged Cego, wielding a fully charged long staff in both hands. Before the man could even start to bring his weapon in a downward strike, Cego punched his burning fist into his opponent's chest.

The guard looked down with a bewildered expression at Cego's arm, which had pierced his body down to the elbow. Cego ripped his bloody hand free, and the man fell to the floor.

The lab was quiet for a moment in the battle's aftermath. Sol could hear her own heart pounding, the maker whimpering, Cego breathing hard.

"Are you...all right?" Sol asked.

Nearly half of Cego's leather uniform had burned off, whether from the guard's attacks or his own internal energy, Sol wasn't sure. But she did know he was injured, a nasty gash across his back. Sol also realized it wasn't Cego that was breathing hard. She looked up toward the tube.

It was the thing within that strained to breathe.

They turned to the broken glass casing, which was leaking a thick green ichor from the cracks. Cego stared up at the creature within, and its alien eyes met his. Its skeletal chest rose and fell like a pump.

Sol tore her gaze from the strange creature and advanced on the master maker.

"Wait," the little man whimpered. "Please don't hurt it."

"It?" Sol asked. She realized the maker wasn't concerned about his own life. He was staring up at the experiment floating in the tube beside them.

"I know what you are!" The maker scooted on his knees toward Cego. "You...you're one of them. One of the Cradle brood."

"You know nothing of me," Cego said, still staring at the creature through the glass.

"Oh, but I do!" the little man said. "In fact, I was part of the team that helped develop the vats that you were born in. Of course, the Minders did the difficult work, but—"

"Shut up." Cego moved toward the man, blue energy still pulsing up and down his arm.

"Cego!" Sol said, moving to intercept him. "We need this man for the mission. Don't you remember?"

"Don't you see the miracle of this all?" The maker began to smile maniacally. "That you...the first generation of truly enhanced Grievar, are here to witness the next evolution of your kind."

The man stood and placed his hand to the vat, staring into the creature's eyes as it continued to take labored breaths.

"You mean...this thing," Sol whispered, "is supposed to be a Grievar?"

"Yes," the maker responded. "I know she doesn't look it yet, but she's still in the first stages of her development. Give her a year... and she'll look far different. She's still growing and learning."

"No!" Cego abruptly screamed, the first time Sol had heard him raise his voice. "This thing is not like us. This is an abomination."

"An abomination?" the maker asked. "No more than you, my boy. And she will grow faster, stronger, become a better vehicle of violence than you will ever be."

"No," Cego said as he turned and smashed his blazing hand through the glass of the tube. The green ichor within rushed out, and the creature gasped desperately.

"What have you done?" The maker tried to get to the vat, but Sol held him back. "She can't breathe the air yet; her lungs are not yet fully formed. We must get her into another amniotic solution!"

"No," Cego said again. He stared into the creature's black eyes as it crumpled to the floor of the vat, heaving for air. "It's not made for this world."

"Neither were you!" the maker screamed, clawing at Sol to try to free himself. "We let you live! Who are you to decide to take her life?"

"You did not let me live," Cego whispered, turning his blazing eyes on the maker. "I survived."

Sol trembled as she watched the creature curl up on the ground among the shards of glass and ichor. Its breathing became barely discernible before its chest was still.

The Daimyo stopped struggling. The little man went limp in Sol's arms and began to sob.

A voice came over the com, startling Sol.

"Squad Three...status report."

Wraith. He was breathing hard.

He's alive.

Cego turned from staring down at the dead creature in the tube back to the Daimyo in Sol's grasp. "We have the maker; we are on the way back to the lift."

"Good," Wraith said. "We're ready to get out, then. Rendezvous by the entry point at the bottom of the lift."

"Wait!" Sol yelled. "Are Knees and Brynn all right? What happened?"

"Yes, your friends are alive, though not all of the team was so lucky," Wraith said grimly. "We'll debrief when we're clear."

The Flux lieutenant's voice faded, and Cego grabbed the little maker from Sol's arms by the neck. He pulled the Daimyo onto the top of a lab table and reached toward the handhold for the ducts above.

"Do you even care?" Sol asked, staring at Cego. "That our friends are safe?"

Cego didn't answer. He pulled himself and his new hostage above.

CHAPTER 9

The Mighty

A Grievar shall not spend undue time alongside those who work the lands. It is the Grunt's path to trod on soil, grow crops, and provide nourishment for the society around them. Keeping such a peasant's company will weaken a Grievar's spirit.

Passage Three, Two Hundred Fifteenth Precept
of the Combat Codes

Murray walked the nighttime dockyard, letting his mind settle to the smell of rotting fish and the hoots of reveling Grunts from the alehouses.

He had the vial of beelbub ichor in his pocket, but finally, he didn't feel the pull. He no longer felt the gravity that dragged him toward the drink, the gut punch he'd take each day without the stuff flowing through his blood.

At first, Murray had wondered if his newfound freedom was a result of the Flux. He thought, maybe, he was a part of something again. Maybe he'd regained the common cause that he'd lost after his service with the Citadel. Maybe that was what he'd been seeking for so long. He and Dozer had completed their mission; held some little Daimyo chief hostage to provide ample distraction for the rest of the Flux team to get the job done. Murray had felt the familiar adrenaline flooding his veins during the mission, the same feeling he used to get stepping into a Circle to fight for his nation.

But breathing the humid sea air, listening to the clamor of the bars, Murray realized the Flux mission was not what had settled him. If anything, the events of the past night alongside the rebels had only served to increase Murray's uncertainty of the path forward.

The Whelps had broken away from Pilgrimage, and now Murray had gotten them mired in this rebel cause. He could see the look in Wraith's eyes, the way the Slayer spoke. These were zealots who claimed to fight for Grievar-kin, supposed liberators, but in truth, they were power-hungry like the Daimyo.

And Cego was an entirely different problem.

Murray had watched the kid come back from the mission at the lab. He'd seen the way Cego had dragged the little maker behind him, and it didn't sit right. The kid was changed after what he'd been through, and Murray was helpless to show him the right path again.

Murray found himself at the end of one of the docks, the sounds of the bars faded and replaced with the Adrian Sea lapping against the barnacled posts. The low moon cast a crimson path out to the horizon, as if it were some road that Murray might walk out on.

"Why?" Murray whispered.

Why was Murray suddenly fine with it all? Why was he settled in the chaos now when it had amplified to maximum decibels?

"Try to control it all, and all control will be lost to you."

Farmer's white beard and wrinkled forehead peered back at Murray from the undulating waters beneath the dock.

"Blast it," Murray said, rubbing his eyes and opening them wide again to see if the old man's face was still there in the waters.

Murray shook his head, slapped his skull. "Get out! How are you doing this again? Why are you here?!"

"I'm here…for you, Murray," Farmer spoke. "Because you still have a part to play."

"Is that what it is to you?" Murray growled at the water. "A game? Bythardi pieces for you to move around on a board, just like you used to do in your Citadel study? I see the Slayer, that demon inside the warehouse, I see him speaking to himself…Is that you in his head too?"

"We must all play our part in this game, else the cost of defeat is too high, unfathomable," Farmer said. "You have yet to play your truest part."

"Where are you?" Murray tried to keep his voice low to not attract attention from the warehouse. "Are you still…in there? Floating in the Cradle?"

"Focus, Murray," Farmer said, ignoring the question. The visage of the old master in the dark waters started to fade. The man repeated the same phrase he'd opened with. "Try to control it all, and all control will be lost to you."

Farmer had said those words to Murray when he was a fresh Lyceum graduate, a bright-eyed Knight ready to take on the world. Murray's fighting style had been aggressive, always moving forward, putting on the pressure, never giving his opponent a chance to breathe. That's how he'd won his way to Knighthood. *Control.*

But once Murray entered the international circuit, when he'd encountered Grievar beyond his skills that he couldn't control, he'd been lost.

Farmer's words had saved him. Those words had made Murray a better fighter, one that realized that his opponent would move in ways that he could not control. It was in these moments that Murray had realized he needed to flow. He needed to adapt to what was given to him, let go and trust his instincts.

And after all these years passed, it wasn't until now that Murray realized that Farmer's words weren't about Circle strategy. He'd been a stubborn blockhead, as usual.

"Try to control it all, and all control will be lost to you," Murray whispered into the darkness as the old man's face became waves and froth again.

Murray knew the events of this world that had been put in motion were out of his control.

Decades before, when the Daimyo and Bit-Minders had decided that they'd conspire to create a Cradle of darkness, Murray could not have stopped it. When Farmer had gone Deep to enter the Cradle, his mind set on trying to save those kids, Murray could not have stopped him. And when Cego had been put on trial, put to execution, sent to Arklight, Murray couldn't have saved him.

Murray could control some small parts of this world, though. He could stop taking the drink. He could help his friends who were in arm's reach. He could stand up for what he believed in.

Where that path took him, Murray didn't know. But he was finally darkin' all right with that.

*   *   *

"So, I want to lose top position?" N'auri asked. "You crazy Ezonian."

Sol displayed the technique to N'auri while Brynn watched. She needed something to pass the time while waiting in the warehouse, something to help forget the events of the prior night. She needed some way to block out the screams of the captured maker behind the steel door.

"Yes, you're on top," Sol said. "You advance to high mount. But let's say you can't get anything going, your opponent's defense is too strong."

N'auri appropriately kept her elbows tight to her body, and Sol attempted to separate her arms in vain.

"You make them think they have an opportunity to post off your hip here," Sol said.

N'auri placed her hand on Sol's hip, pushing.

"Throw your leg over for a mounted triangle," Sol revealed. "Then, when they reverse to top, which they certainly will, cinch the strangle."

N'auri tapped in submission and displayed that sharp-toothed smile on her bruised face. "Always the technician you are, Solara. I think I can use some of your tricks. Though I don't think it would've worked against the Sentinel we fought in the tunnels."

"Spirits be said, nothing would have worked against that thing," Brynn agreed.

"Besides what Wraith and N'auri did to it," Knees said as he trotted over, eyeing N'auri. "Maybe next time, you should let us in on that flare."

N'auri shrugged. "Wraith said to keep it secret for now."

Sol was about to inquire further about the strange weapons she'd heard the Flux had used against the Sentinel, when a voice crept in from beside her.

"Good to see my Flux recruits honing their skills."

Sol turned to see Silas the Slayer himself, his lip curved up on one side.

Wraith hurried over, his face still streaked red with open wounds. "Slayer."

"Lieutenant," Silas said. "Well done on the mission, despite the complications you encountered."

"Yes, Slayer." Wraith bowed his head.

Sol trained her eyes on Silas. Here he was again, the leader of the Flux rebellion. The man who'd sent them on that near-death mission to Karstock Labs. Sol found those glowing eyes and had to suppress the shiver that ran down her spine.

Cego stepped up beside Silas. She hadn't spoken with him since their return from the lab.

They didn't look alike, the two brothers. But why would they look the same? They didn't share the same bloodline, only the same virtual womb within the Cradle. Silas's features were sharp, jagged, as though brushing a hand against his face would draw blood. Cego's face was smoother, rounded.

"I still see the rage within you, Solara Halberd," Silas noted.

Sol did hate Silas. She'd hated him since she saw him standing over her father's lifeless body on SystemView. But she knew that hatred wouldn't save Cego from his brother's clutches.

She looked back to Cego. She knew her friend was in there somewhere; she'd seen it on last night's mission, if for only the briefest moment.

"I saw what they were doing, at the labs," Sol said, thinking of the strange creature gasping in the broken tube. "I hate them for that."

"That is good," Silas said. "I wanted you to see the lengths the Daimyo go through to warp the world to their reality. They're no longer content meddling with Grievar; they want to create abominations to fight for them. I wanted you to feel the hatred."

"You should've seen the soap-eater!" Dozer yelled, awake from his nap in the corner. "Pissed himself when Murray and I strung him up from the lift shaft on the way out."

Sol cringed, hoping the big kid's enthusiasm wouldn't blow their cover.

"Good," Silas said, nodding at Dozer and turning to the rest of the crew. "Lieutenant Wraith has spoken to me about the well-executed mission last night. You have all proven yourselves, shown that you are willing to sacrifice for the cause."

"Right, we are," Dozer said. "What've you got for us next?"

Knees elbowed Dozer in the ribs.

"But our cause has only begun," Silas continued. "There will be many more fights ahead, and far more sacrifice than what you've already given."

Sol knew the Slayer's words were true. The crew had barely survived the last mission. How many more would they last before they could pry Cego away from his brother?

Silas turned toward the steel door of the interrogation room. "Now let's go pay a visit to Master Maker Varakas."

*   *   *

Murray quietly slid open the iron gate to the rebel warehouse, hoping to let the kids get some rest after the mission. When he peered into the dimly lit space, though, the crew was awake.

Cego had returned; Murray could see the back of the kid's shaved head. Though Cego certainly had changed, he still stood with that same posture Murray remembered when he'd first seen him in the slave Circles. Straight-backed, head on a swivel.

Beside Cego stood another figure, wrapped entirely in black leather, addressing the remaining rebel Knights, with Ulrich and Wraith standing up front.

"—we have what we need, and now we must use it to our advantage." Silas turned as he heard Murray approach.

"Ah, there he is," Silas said. "The bear has returned to the den."

"My den is back in Ezo, my barracks where I like to sit by the hearth," Murray replied, stepping up to Cego's side. "And to be honest, I'd rather be there than here."

"Have some respect when you speak to the Slayer," Wraith said.

Murray met the lieutenant's eyes. "Only the second time I've met the man; why should I have respect for him?"

"Because he is the—"

"Murray Pearson is right," Silas interrupted Wraith. "He has no reason to respect me yet."

Murray let his guard relax as Wraith backed down.

"As I was saying," Silas continued. "You've done well with your team, Wraith. Karstock Labs was one of two major processing plants in Kiroth. The team in the west is hitting the Vlastor plant as we speak. With these stim supplies taken off the map, the Kirothian trade will be amputated."

"And where does that leave us?" Murray asked. "You know as well as I the black market likely provides more than half the darkin' stim trade anyway. You'll still have the junkies on the streets, fiending for the stuff, while politiks turn to dealers instead."

Silas met Murray's eyes silently before turning his back to him and slowly walking the length of the room. "Yes, I understand. We will see."

Murray cocked his head, turning to Ulrich beside him. "Who the dark is he talking to?"

Ulrich shrugged as Silas wheeled around to face Murray.

"You're right again, Murray Pearson," Silas said. "But your vision is hindered. You aren't looking far enough ahead."

Murray growled, "My vision's just fine."

"Yes, the empire's stim depots only supply to a minority of buyers, small and large. But removing their production serves a greater purpose than simply cutting down on supply. It's about control," Silas said. "When the empire is forced to turn to hawkers and dealers, sinking deep into the black market to buy stims, their position will be weakened. When trading with Ezo, they'll be forced to sell at a higher price, and meanwhile, another seller can offer to the other nations at a lower price."

"You mean to say you're going to darkin' start selling stims?" Murray asked. "That's the big plan? The Flux rebellion, the new world order—selling stims like a dealer under a bridge?"

Wraith stepped forward this time. "You've been here for a month, Murray Pearson. You claim to know more than we who have devoted our lives to the cause?"

"No, I don't." Murray turned to the pale man. "But I know about appearances too. And to me, this looks like we're sinking to their level. Doing exactly what the Daimyo have been up to all along. Controlling trade, slinking around like hawkers. And I've heard about the weapons used in the tunnels yesterday. What happened to the Codes?"

Silas laughed, his head cracked back. "The Codes. I've heard you were still a believer. Has the veil been pulled over your eyes so far?

The Codes were created by the Daimyo to control us, to manipulate our kind."

"I know," Murray said. "I've figured that out my own way. And I say dark it, I don't care why they created the Codes. Because I live by my own, those Codes I know to be right. That's what Farmer believed. He was your coach as well as mine."

"We do share a common teacher, don't we?" Silas said, gesturing to Cego beside him. "So strange that we all stand here together, Farmer's disciples, now leading Grievar-kin to a new era. But... how well do you know your old master, Murray?"

"I know him well enough," Murray said. "Enough to catch up with him in the Deep not long ago."

For once, Silas appeared caught off guard, like Murray had thrown a strike the Slayer hadn't been expecting.

Murray turned to Cego, capitalizing on the opportunity. "Kid, listen. I know it's probably not the best time, but there's something I've been meaning to tell you."

Cego stared up at him, a glimmer of curiosity flashing across his face.

"The reason I wasn't there for you this past year..." Murray said. "I went Deep, like I said I would. I found your brother Sam. Farmer...he was there, sort of. He helped me. He's still helping me. I brought Sam back home to the Citadel."

"Sam...he's back at home?" Cego whispered.

"He's waiting for you there, kid," Murray said.

"Even if you did retrieve our brother," Silas interrupted, "it doesn't matter. Cego's home is now here, with the Flux."

"You have a choice." Murray kept his eyes on Cego. "You always have a choice. But know no matter what, we're here for you, kid. I'll stay by your side with the Flux, long as it darkin' takes."

Silas was quiet a moment, before turning and slowly walking away. "Now is the time?"

Murray watched the Slayer talk to himself again as he walked toward the steel door of the interrogation room. He knew what it was like to have such an alien voice inside his head; it wasn't long ago that Farmer had seemed as real to Murray as anyone standing in this room. Murray wondered what phantom possessed the mind of the Slayer now; was it Farmer in there too, somehow influencing the rebel leader's path?

Silas returned, holding a small, writhing form with one hand. Master Maker Varakas.

The man was subdued, no longer screaming obscenities like he was earlier. But Murray could see the fear in his eyes as Silas lifted him by the throat and carried him like one of the weasels Sol had captured in the desert.

"Please..." the Daimyo whimpered, the blue veins in his forehead bulging. "I'll give you anything. My bit-purse, my properties, my slaves, they are all yours. Anything."

Silas laughed, like a wolf howling before it ripped into its prey. He tossed the man to the floor in front of the crew.

"See?" Silas looked directly at Murray. "See how their kind thinks that they can buy anything? See how they believe that what they own is who they are?"

The Slayer looked down at the trembling Daimyo. "You will all soon learn that you've lived falsehoods. All the greed, accumulation, power that you thought you had will be taken from you. And then what will you have?"

The maker made a feeble attempt to scramble to his feet, like some trapped animal, wildly looking for an escape route from the warehouse. He broke for a small gap between two of the rebel Knights and managed to make it past them. One of the Grievar started to make a move, but Silas held a hand up.

"Let's see him try to run," Silas said.

The maker made it twenty labored paces before Silas broke into a sprint, taking long, loping strides that carried him to his prey. He leapt into the air and landed in front of the man, cutting off his only exit.

Silas howled as the man cowered. He grabbed the Daimyo by the scruff of his ripped clothes and carried him back, this time tossing him at Murray's feet.

"He's yours," Silas said, staring at Murray.

Murray shook his head, looking up at Silas. "I don't need no soap-eater for entertainment."

"No, no," Silas said. "I don't mean to keep the thing as a pet. We've gotten what we need from him already. But the creature has spent his life breaking our laws, torturing and experimenting on our kind, creating abominations. So, he must pay the price. And I'd like you to carry out the justice."

"What laws do you speak of?" Murray asked.

"The new law of the land, the real order of this world," Silas said. "The law that says any who stand in the way of Grievar-kin freeing themselves from the chains of servitude will pay the ultimate price. And this maker, he is one of the worst perpetrators. A puppet of the empire, charged with building the worst of their tech and mass-producing stims that have ruined countless Grievar lives."

"If you're making the darkin' laws now, you carry out your own judgment," Murray said. "I'm here because of Cego. We believe in him, in his cause. We're here for him as long as he stays."

Murray stared at Cego, desperately trying to get through to him again. If only the kid would snap out of it, they could be out of this forsaken place. They could head home together.

For a moment, Murray saw the kid he used to know across from him. That curious boy with the golden eyes.

"My home is here, with the Flux," Cego said, and Murray knew he was gone again, in a flicker, gazing to the shadows of the warehouse.

"We've all had to make sacrifices for the cause, Murray," Silas said. "Cego earned his name, the Strangler, for good reason. The Flux is one. We all must carry out the judgment."

Murray stared down at the broken Daimyo at his feet. The man looked so small, so scared.

Murray hated them, the Daimyo, for all they'd done to his kind. He hated them for all they stood for. But he'd met good ones before too. And he didn't hate this man in front of him. He knew, no matter what, he couldn't carry out what they asked.

"No," Murray said flatly, staring Cego in the eyes, not even looking at Silas.

"No?" Silas asked incredulously. "You, who claim to be a part of the Flux, won't do the most basic component of carrying out our justice?"

"No," Murray said again, turning to Silas. He knew now what he must do. He couldn't control everything, but he could control what was in arm's reach.

"I believe in honor," Murray said. "I believe in the Codes, whoever the dark created them. I believe in justice. But not like this."

"If you cannot do this, you cannot be trusted," Silas said with menace. Four of the rebel Knights and Wraith stepped forward.

"So, what now, you're going to have your lackeys try and take an old man out?" Murray spat on the floor. "Too afraid to take the task yourself?"

Silas's lip curled upward. He held his hand up to stay his men and turned to Wraith, nodding to the maker on the floor. "Put the pitiful dog down."

Wraith moved without hesitation, his foot going head high before dropping an axe kick to the Daimyo's head, splitting it like a ripe fruit.

The warehouse was completely silent for a moment, all looking down at Wraith's grisly work on the floor. Murray thought he could hear the tide lapping against the docks not far away outside an open window.

"Now that his justice is served, I will serve you yours," Silas said, breaking the silence.

Murray nodded and turned his back on the Slayer. He met the eyes of the kids he'd brought there, the Whelps who stood frozen to the floor. He stepped toward them, beckoning them to bring their heads into a huddle.

"You can't take on the Slayer!" Dozer whispered desperately. "He's killed everyone he's fought! He darkin' put down Artemis Halberd! Sorry, Sol…"

"No, Dozer is right," Sol said with ferocity. "You don't need to do this, Murray. Tell him you still believe… Tell him you're with him."

"I can't," Murray whispered back. He felt the warmth of the kids around him, Knees clutching at his shoulder. They were good kids. "I can't do it anymore. I can't lie about who I am."

"But this all be for Cego," Knees said. "Isn't that what you said, Coach? We're putting up this front for him."

"I was wrong, Knees," Murray said. "Even trying to get Cego back, you can't darkin' turn on who you are. And this…this isn't who I am. This isn't who any of us are. And if Cego can't see through the darkness, can't see who we are, then all is lost."

Dozer's shoulders trembled. "Coach, take him down for us."

"Spirits be asked, do it for us, Ku," Brynn said.

Sol spoke through clenched teeth. "For my father, Murray-Ku, for Cego, for us."

Murray breathed deeply, pushed his head into the huddle, and broke from the crew.

The fight was finally the one in front of him.

He turned to face Silas the Slayer.

CHAPTER 10

Waking Up

The gar bear is considered the apex predator in the forest. However, when the bear encounters the kamatar lizard, it retreats, likely aware of the reptile's venomous bite. This simply illustrates the relationship between two creatures; it does not equate to the wolf or the roc or any other predator. The same is true with the Grievar. A victory over one individual, even the most fearsome opponent, does not mean a victory over that individual's conquered foes.

Passage Seven, Eighteenth Precept of
the Combat Codes

Morning rose over Karstock, a dawn that threw shards of ruby light through the lofted windows to the wooden warehouse floor.

Cego watched his brother toss his cloak to the ground and turn toward Murray. He'd seen the look in Silas's eyes many times now before he stepped into the Circle against those who would stand up to him.

After Silas had saved Cego from the jaws of Arklight, he'd taken him into hiding. His brother had been at his side for months, helping nourish Cego, reviving his broken body. It had taken those months of healing to finally stop seeing the veined faces of the clerics at Arklight, those torturers who had pierced Cego's body and mind for so long, seeking the secrets hidden within him.

It wasn't until Silas had brought Cego back to life, until he could finally open his eyes and see the sun rising without screaming in fear, that the visions of the prison had faded.

But new visions soon came to replace those of Cego's torture. The island, the Cradle of Cego's birth, came to him.

Sometimes, Cego was in this world, the one of the rebel warehouse and Murray and his old friends from the Citadel. But more often, Cego was in a different place, one more visceral and real to him, as a prisoner within the Cradle.

For the moment, Cego remained in the warehouse, watching Murray Pearson crack his neck side to side and stare Silas down.

Cego remembered Murray. He remembered how the burly Grievar had taken him from the slave Circles of the Deep. He remembered how Murray had brought him Surface-side, given him a home, trained him, and taken him to the Lyceum.

And yet, Cego couldn't find any warmth for Murray Pearson since he'd arrived in this new world. Murray and the rest of the Whelps, other faces from his past, had appeared as unwelcome intruders.

Here, Cego was not the boy his friends remembered. In this world, he was the Strangler. And the Strangler's sole purpose was to rid the planet of the festering Daimyo infection. His path beside his brother was set before him.

Cego watched Silas cock his head, listening to his voices.

Murray was looking directly at Cego, the big Grievar watching him pleadingly. Was the man scared?

"You know who you are," Murray said to him. "Somewhere inside, there's the kid I found in the Deep."

The words made Murray real again, for a moment. The way the morning light caught his worn, bearded face and reflected on the white pearl in place of his missing eye. Once, Murray had fought for Cego's freedom. And he was doing it again now.

"Cego," Murray said, ignoring the looming figure of the Slayer across from him. "Only you know why you fight. And it's not for Silas, not for this cause."

Silas stepped in front of Murray, blocking Cego's view of the Grievar. The Slayer raised one hand to the air and beckoned him forward. "Enough of this talk. Let us do what we were meant to do."

Murray was quiet, his jaw set. He stepped toward Silas.

*   *   *

"Darkin' move," Murray muttered as he circled Silas, hands up.

The Slayer was completely still, watching him with those wolf eyes. The man didn't even cut angles as Murray rounded a corner on him, as if he couldn't be bothered to turn toward his opponent.

Of course, Murray recognized the strategy. He'd seen it in Cego so many times, watched the kid stand completely inert until the last moment, the second of impact, when he'd switch on like some machine.

But this was the Slayer, the man who had brought Artemis Halberd down with ease, the man they said would bring the world to its knees.

"You got this, Coach!" he heard Dozer yell from behind him.

He couldn't let these kids down. He couldn't let Cego down. This was the fight, here in front of him now.

Murray shuffled an arm span away from Silas. He might have the reach on his opponent, but he severely lacked in speed. His shots had to count.

Murray feinted high as if he'd throw a long-distance cross but instead shot low, taking a deep-penetration step and reaching for the ankle pick.

Murray grasped at air. The Slayer's sidestep had been blindingly fast and the blow following it even faster. The knee blasted through Murray's outstretched hands and ruptured his already-broken nose.

The warehouse swarmed Murray, the walls moving inward, the surrounding faces transformed to white flashes. And there was Silas, right in front of him again.

Murray found his senses and got his hands up. But no attacks came. Silas stood motionless.

"Darkin' fight me, why don't you," Murray growled as he wiped the blood spewing from his nose.

"Isn't that what we're doing?" Silas replied, a smirk edging his lips.

Murray came in with two stiff jabs. Silas weaved his head around both as if Murray were moving underwater.

The follow-up cross fell short too; Silas bobbed backward and threw his counter. Murray sensed the movement, saw Silas's hip jerk and the foot flash toward his face. But he wasn't fast enough to avoid the heel full on the chin that threw him back to the floor.

The warehouse spun around Murray for the second time in a matter of seconds, and Silas was above him again, his mouth curved up at the corner.

Murray's head dropped to the side and he found his gaze on Cego, the boy's eyes locked on him.

There's more to be done. Don't think I'll be put down so easy.

Murray roared despite the electric pain coursing through his broken jaw. He pushed off the ground, stumbled to his feet, and launched himself at the Slayer. He threw a looping overhand right, which he knew Silas would parry, followed by a left to the body: the liver shot he'd hit so many times, a technique that had put down so many in the Circle.

Silas stepped forward into the body punch, anticipating it and dropping his hips into Murray, aiming to toss him.

Think I haven't been here a thousand times? I've been thrown by the best.

Murray countered, sprawling his weight into his toes, but Silas was already another step ahead, switching directions and dropping low for an inside trip. Murray was helpless to defend and fell to his back with Silas's weight already on top of him.

Murray attempted to get his feet in front of him, push Silas off, but the Slayer was already slicing through his guard like a knife through vat liver.

"Don't like playing off your back?" Silas laughed as he pressed a knee down into Murray's abdomen.

"I'm not playing," Murray grunted, trying to shove Silas off him as blood clouded his eye.

Murray could feel the Slayer's weight driving into him. Silas wasn't heavier or stronger than him, yet the way he moved, the way he was connected to Murray felt as if he were a wet blanket. Murray escaped his hips and Silas was already swiveling around to the opposite side, keeping his knee directly connected with Murray's stomach.

"You don't need to play," Silas said as he floated over Murray into full mount, staring down at the older Grievar from on top. "I can play on my own."

Murray covered his face, expecting incoming ground-and-pound. But it didn't come. Silas was simply sitting on him, smirking.

Murray knew this feeling of being toyed with, like a mouse batted around by a cat before its meal. He'd felt it only once before in his career, against one man. Farmer. His own coach and the man that had trained both Cego and Silas.

There's more to be done. I can't stop now.

"Go dark yourself," Murray groaned, shoving forward into Silas's chest, knowing that he was exposing his arms. The Slayer took the bait, trapping Murray's exposed arm and swinging around to break the limb.

Murray moved with Silas's momentum, switching his hips and reversing to top position, but the lock was already in. Silas extended his body, his head propped against the floor as he drove his hips forward.

Murray heard the pop of his elbow joint. A familiar sensation, one of a hundred arm breaks in his career. And so, Murray didn't even wince as his arm crumpled in the wrong direction, and instead took the opportunity to pivot around and drop a hammer fist to the back of Silas's head.

His meaty hand connected with the Slayer's skull. And satisfyingly, he heard the Slayer grunt as his body dropped to the wood.

Can't let him recover.

Murray breathed heavily as he wrenched his hand back for another blow.

But Silas was already rolled up onto his shoulder, spinning around and back to his feet. The Slayer reached behind his head and brought back blood on his fingertips.

"So, the Slayer bleeds like the rest of us," Murray growled. "Who would have known?"

"Do it, Coach!" Knees shouted as familiar adrenaline flooded Murray's body. He felt the momentum of every match of his career, from when he was a lowly Level One at the Lyceum to a champion Grievar Knight fighting for the Citadel. The weight of Murray's history drove him forward.

No more strategy, no more letting the Slayer time his shots to make Murray feel like a junkie lured to the dregs.

Murray ran at Silas.

Silas whipped out a blindingly fast side kick and Murray took it, let it rip into his midsection, snapping one of his ribs inward. He grabbed Silas's leg and pulled him forward, timing it with a heavy punch that found the Slayer's nose and sent him reeling back.

Murray advanced and met Silas's quick counter jab. He let the Slayer's fist in, didn't care as the orbital on his good eye caved. He kept moving forward until he clinched his hands behind Silas's head.

It was the same position Muhai had greeted Murray with on the highland grass, the same huddle the Whelps had taken before their fights with their heads pressed in together. Except here, Murray meant to use his head as a battering ram.

Murray snapped his forehead down, smashing it into Silas's face. The Slayer staggered and Murray stayed on him, holding the clinch, oozing his blood onto his opponent as he slammed his head forward again and felt the satisfying crunch of a nose.

Silas was falling backward and Murray followed, not willing to give his opponent a moment to recover, meaning to bludgeon the Slayer back to whatever darkness he'd emerged from.

But Silas's feet found Murray's hips as he fell, and suddenly Murray was tumbling through the air and onto his back.

Tomoe nage.

This time, though, Silas didn't hover over him, toying with Murray. The wolf came in for the kill, a foot hurtling down toward Murray's skull. Murray barely was able to lift his hands in time, deflecting the strike directly into his own throat.

Murray's windpipe crumpled beneath the heel. He rolled in time to avoid the second kick and managed to stand again. He tried to suck in air, but only a sliver came through his bloody nose. He heard himself wheeze as the world darkened.

There's more to be done. I can't stop now.

Murray charged Silas again, desperately seeking the violence that had kept him alive so many times before, reaching for it like an old friend. He threw a volley of punches, trying to make each one count.

The Slayer countered, battering him like a piece of meat, but Murray kept coming forward. He knew if he stopped now, he'd not start again.

There's more to be done. The kid needs me.

Murray charged and wrapped his arms around Silas, trying to pick the man up as if he'd draw the life force from him, squeeze out the Bit-Minder tech that had borne this creature. But the Slayer was too heavy, an otherworldly form that he couldn't lift with these broken arms.

Silas pushed him off like a misbehaving kid, spun around, and lashed a heel out to connect with Murray's chin.

Murray was falling backward.

He'd fallen many times in his life and always returned to his feet. But the gravity that pulled him down this time was stronger, as if the space between his bones and tissues had become dense like stone.

Murray was scared. Not of pain or what came beyond this, but that Silas would be there again, standing above him. Murray was afraid that this man's face would be the last he'd ever see.

But as Murray's skull bounced against the wood floor and he glimpsed the morning light of dawn through the broken warehouse window, he only saw Cego.

There's more to be done.

* * *

Sol watched as Murray-Ku was torn apart.

It had been as if some invisible force had propped the big Grievar up, constantly driving his broken body toward Silas even as he was punished for it.

She'd heard the cries of anguish from her teammates beside her, their last flickering hopes fading as Murray finally fell and did not stand again.

Sol saw the Slayer standing over Murray. A strange white mist poured off Silas's shoulders and that crooked smile creased his face. Just as when Sol had seen him standing over her father's body.

The rage coursed through Sol, a heat that had been building through the years since Artemis Halberd's death. Who was this man to take away their coach, their friend? Who was this man to take another father away from her?

It was Murray's words that stayed Sol's hand, that kept her rage simmering within.

The fight is not always the one in front of you.

But Dozer was not imbued with the same patience as Sol. The big kid sprinted at Silas, aiming to spear the man with a shoulder tackle. The Slayer saw him coming, stepped to the side, and threw a feline elbow that cut the air like a blade, landing hard to the back of Dozer's head to send him sprawling face-first to the floor beside Murray.

Dozer did not move and Sol ran to his side, turning him over, making sure he was still breathing. The big kid's chest heaved, and beside him Sol felt the stillness of Murray's body, the chill coming off it.

She forced herself to turn her head, to look up and meet Silas's eyes. She held the hurt from racing up her lungs and escaping in a scream.

"Rage," Silas said, staring at Sol. "Not something your father had enough of. But I see it in you, Solara Halberd. That rage would work for the cause."

"I'll never be a part of your cause." Sol cradled Dozer's head. He was awake now and sobbing as he stared at Murray's lifeless corpse.

"Traitors, then," Wraith said as he and the other rebels began to close in.

Knees and Brynn stepped in front of Murray's body.

"Don't think you be taking us easy," Knees growled, his fists in the air while Brynn crouched, ready to pounce.

N'auri leapt in front of the crew, her hands up and her eyes frantic.

"Don't hurt them," she yelled toward the Flux rebels.

"They're with us or they're against us, N'auri." Wraith stepped forward again, his eyes cold. "Even Sol must face the truth. Murray made his choice and he died for it."

"They can change still!" N'auri insisted. "They don't realize the cause yet. They will still see the path. They came here to help."

"We won't change," Sol said softly to her friend, the anger fading and replaced by a deep weariness. "We never were a part of this. We didn't come to help; we only came for Cego."

N'auri was silenced by Sol's admission. The Emeraldi looked up with fiery eyes. "You told me long ago, on the Emeraldi shores, that you'd only ever tell me the truth again. So, you meant to betray us? For what? So you can bring your friend back to your school in Ezo? So you can take your classes, live your life as if nothing is happening? As if we aren't slaves to the Daimyo?"

Sol met N'auri's eyes. "This new world you want to create, we don't have a place in it."

N'auri whirled and stalked away. Sol's gaze was drawn to Cego. He stood apart from the rising fury. Cego was silent, his head down, looking toward the floor where Murray lay.

Sol stepped toward him. She knew her friend was in there somewhere.

"Cego, Murray is gone," Sol said. "He died for what he believed in."

Cego closed his eyes, put his hands to his head, as if he were having some conversation within.

"Cego," Sol said. "We need to bring Murray home, give him a proper burial. Come home with us."

"Murray died in vain," Silas said, looking down at the prey he'd brought down. "He died for no cause other than the beliefs the Daimyo poisoned him with. False concepts of honor. Our home is here with the Flux, breaking the Daimyo to build a new world, one where we are free to fight."

Sol ignored Silas and took another step toward Cego, her hand extended. "Cego, come home with us. Please."

Cego turned and began to walk away from her.

"Cego!" Knees followed him, yelling at the back of his head. "Look what your brother did! He killed Murray. Coach's blood be on your hands. And now you're going to stay here as if nothing happened? Forget that!"

Knees spat on the ground and turned, letting Cego walk away.

Sol breathed deeply and turned to Silas. "Will you let us go?"

The Slayer nodded. "You are permitted to go. Bring Murray Pearson's body back for proper burial. But know this. If you are not with the Flux, you will be our enemy. And we will come for Ezo; we will come for you."

Sol nodded and helped Dozer to his feet.

"Help me," Sol said, kneeling and hefting one of Murray's lifeless arms onto her shoulder. Dozer wiped the tears from his face and followed suit, lifting the man's upper body while Knees and Brynn grabbed his legs.

Together, the crew hefted Murray onto their shoulders and began to walk toward the gate.

They stopped when they reached the docks outside, and Sol turned back toward the shadows of the warehouse.

Cego was gone.

*　　*　　*

Sol felt Firenze carrying the weight.

The great red roc's long gait was shortened and slowed by the wrapped bundle draped across his hindquarters.

The bird was too familiar with such a weight, Sol thought. It had been only a year before that he'd carried Sol's father, and now the heavy burden of Murray Pearson lay across his back.

Sol carried the weight too. It seemed like only yesterday that she'd laid her father to rest, set him beneath wet earth and dry leaves back at the homestead. And now, they needed to bury another of their own.

Sol brushed the feathers alongside the bird's head as the crew crested the sloping hill, already miles outside of Karstock and back into the heat of the Venturian desert. They had traveled the distance in silence, a reverence for the load they carried with them.

The sun rose over acres of caucas crop, casting crimson light on the hundreds of harvesters out in the fields. Hanrin's harvest mech crept across the crops like a steel behemoth. The path ahead cut the center of the fields like an outstretched arm, reaching beyond to the desert sands and the distant horizon.

The Whelps dismounted at the top of the crest, looking out at the familiar sight as they fed and watered their rocs. They watched the sun slowly lift to the sky and listened to the morning swallows begin to chatter in the sparse kaöt trees.

Several harvesters at the base of the slope turned upward, peering beneath their wide-brimmed hats at the sight atop the hill, the silhouette of four riders.

"Spirits wept, Ku would have liked it," Brynn said, breaking the long silence as she held her waterskin to her thirsty black roc. "The view from this side."

Knees shook his head. "He'd likely be telling us to stop taking our darkin' time, dallying here on this hill. Get going where we need to be going."

Bird screeched loudly, prompting the nesting swallows to swarm to the sky. The unruly grey roc had been unsettled since they'd set off from Karstock. Bird had looked for the big man, prodding the bundle on Firenze's back with his beak. He'd reluctantly taken Dozer atop his back.

Dozer sighed with his eyes closed as the sun met his freckled face. "How can we fight someone like that?"

"Murray fought him," Knees said. "Almost had him too."

"Silas is too strong," Dozer said. "Murray didn't have a chance and neither do we."

Sol held her tongue. She wanted to tell Dozer how they needed to return to the Lyceum to train. She wanted to tell him of the specific techniques they'd need to work, how if they met the Flux again, they'd be ready next time.

But such words would be empty because Sol felt hopeless. What power did they have against such fighters as Silas? Against the might of the Daimyo? What good could a bunch of kids do against such odds?

Firenze nuzzled his feathered head against Sol and shifted his weight, trying to compensate for the burden across his back. She placed a hand on Murray's body.

"Forget our chances," Sol growled.

Sol met the eyes of her companions, those she would certainly give her life for as Murray had done.

"Forget what chances we have; that's what Murray would say," Sol said. "We can't live by what could or might happen. We can't be paralyzed by fear and find ourselves standing still, because then we have zero chance, no way forward. So, forget what's to come and let's keep moving. I think that's what he'd say, at least."

"Forget the chances," Dozer echoed. "You're right, Sol; Murray would say that. You know what else he'd say?"

"What?" Sol asked.

"Dark it! Dark it all to the Deep and back!" Dozer bellowed the words to the rising sun, letting tears fall freely across his cheek as he raised his fist to the air.

Brynn joined in, howling beside Dozer, as her black roc screeched along with her.

Sol looked to Knees, shrugged, and let the raw dark escape from her own lips. A scream that she'd have liked to let loose at Silas. At Wraith and N'auri. At the Daimyo. At all those in this world who caused such pain to others.

The harvesters below stared up with wide eyes at the four riders, all screaming like wildcats to the sunrise.

A fifth rider appeared at the crest of the hill.

Dozer gaped wide-eyed at the newcomer.

"Cego?!" Dozer said in disbelief. "You came! How...how did you come?"

Sol stared at Cego as if he were a mirage cast by the desert heat.

Cego dismounted from a muddy brown roc across from the crew. He nudged its flank and it sprinted back the way it came.

Knees stepped forward, his hands up and his fists clenched. "Who is it we have here? The Strangler or Cego?"

Sol hadn't even considered that Cego may have been sent back to destroy the Whelps. Perhaps the Slayer had changed his mind. Perhaps he thought that the crew knew too much, that they were a liability to the Flux operation.

Sol set her jaw and raised her hands as well. She would do what was needed to protect her friends.

"Answer him," she said. "Are you here under the Slayer's orders?"

"I had to escape," Cego whispered as he stared out toward the crops below, not meeting the eyes of the Whelps.

"Silas wouldn't let you go?" Dozer asked.

"No," Cego said. "My brother let me go freely. But I had to escape my prison."

"You mean Arklight?" Dozer asked. "But you were out months ago and—"

"Dozer," Sol interrupted. "Let him speak."

Cego broke his gaze from the horizon and met the eyes of his friends. Tears were streaming down his face.

"I couldn't escape," Cego said. "Not until... not until I saw Murray give everything. Not until it was too late."

Knees stepped forward and slowly let his clenched fists unfurl. He placed a hand on Cego's shoulder. "It's no more your fault than mine."

Cego looked toward the bundle on Firenze's back and fell to his knees, his body shaking. "This is my fault. His blood is on my hands."

Sol went to Cego, crouched beside him, and put her arm around him. "Murray fought for you. He fought for all of us. It was his choice."

"I'm sorry." Cego trembled. "I haven't been here. I've been... somewhere else."

"You've been to the Deep and back," Sol said. "I'm glad you're with us now."

"Spirits be said, so am I," Brynn said as she offered Cego a hand and lifted him back to his feet.

"You're the reason we're here, brother." Dozer wrapped Cego up in a bear hug, squeezing more tears from him before setting him down.

The companions were silent again as they stared out at the desert looming before them.

"We should move soon," Brynn said as she returned the rations to Akari's saddle pack. "Make the best of the daylight."

Sol lifted herself atop Firenze and looked down at Cego, still not quite believing he was back. "You okay?"

"No," Cego replied. "But that doesn't matter. We need to get Murray-Ku home."

Dozer grunted as he fell to the dirt, trying to climb onto Bird's back. "I'm starting to understand why Murray was always pissing on about you."

The grey roc wheeled around and screeched loudly.

"He was Murray's mount?" Cego asked, his golden eyes flashing. "Can I try?"

"Go ahead," Dozer said. "But don't say I didn't warn you; Bird's a rotten devil."

Cego approached Bird with his hand outstretched. The roc straightened up, eyeing the newcomer warily. He looked as if he were about to strike out with his pointed beak.

"I'm sorry," Cego whispered with his head bowed.

Bird didn't flinch.

"I'm sorry," Cego said again as he placed a hand against the roc's ruffled chest. He looked down at the ground until Bird's neck finally relaxed.

"Can you take me home?" Cego looked up at the roc.

Bird lowered his head and settled down on his haunches for Cego to climb onto his back.

"Well, come on!" Dozer yelled. "If I'd known that's all I had to do—"

"Maybe you shouldn't be eating Bird's rations if you wanted him to like you." Knees chuckled as he climbed atop Boko's back.

"It's not fair the rocs get to eat so often, but here we are, starving our asses in the desert!" Dozer said as he clambered up behind Knees.

Sol saw a faint smile break across Cego's face.

"What now?" Dozer asked as the five prepared to set off. "What are we going to do about Silas and the Flux? He said they're going to come for us."

Sol met Cego's golden eyes. He wasn't ready yet.

"We'll make our plans later," Sol said. "For now, let's move forward. That's all we can do. Let's get Murray-Ku home."

The riders charged down the hill, dust billowing up behind them. The harvesters set their threshers and rakes to the ground to watch the curious sight.

Sol still felt the weight she and Firenze carried, pushing against her back.

With Cego there, it did not feel so heavy.

PART 2

CHAPTER II

Home Again

There is the revealing account of the student who could not find his focus before a fight; he constantly recalled the last time he had failed and what it might be like to taste victory again. When the student approached his master with the problem, the old man simply asked him who he was before he was born. It was then that the student suddenly found his focus.

Passage Two, Eighty-Ninth Precept of
the Combat Codes

Cego opened his eyes.

"Did I not tell you to stop coming by here so often?" the little cleric asked.

He was greeted by a familiar sight, a blue-veined woman looking down at him with scientific curiosity, as if she were observing a specimen.

"I told you I couldn't make promises, Xenalia," Cego said. "But at least this time, my head's not bashed in."

A strange, muted laugh escaped from Xenalia's lips. A new habit she'd picked up. "Correct, your skull appears to be intact, though I cannot say that for the rest of your body, not to mention your neurological patterns, which are—"

"Can't we focus on the good stuff for a bit?" Cego asked, knowing the cleric would go on for the entirety of the evening about how he was broken. "I mean, I did make it home."

Xenalia appeared to relax, and a warmth spread across her face, another trait the cleric had acquired since Cego had first met her several years before in the Lyceum's medward. Despite her stoic demeanor, Cego knew Xenalia cared for him. She'd acted as a witness at his trial, spoken in his defense. She'd even lied for him.

"I am glad you are home, Cego," Xenalia said as she applied a gelatinous salve to the numerous scars crisscrossing Cego's chest. The ointment burned as it contacted his skin, but Cego had already seen improvement over the past few weeks as the scars had begun to fade.

"Those men, the ones who did this to you, they cannot be called clerics," Xenalia said.

"I know," Cego replied. Every time he'd visited his friend since returning to the Lyceum, she had made sure to point this out. "I know my torturers at Arklight were different from you."

"*Different* does not accurately describe what those men are. All I have studied over these many years is to help Grievar-kin, to ease pain and repair what is broken. Those clerics at Arklight are a stain on the profession that I have devoted my life to."

"Ouch!" Cego sat bolt upright on the medward table as Xenalia pressed ointment into one of his open wounds, a particularly painful weeping sore.

"My apologies, Cego," Xenalia said. "My tactile practice has diminished over the past year. Since I have been promoted to chief medward officer, my duties have transitioned more to research and management of the staff here, which, though gratifying, has left my hands-on clerical treatment a little bit...rusty. Is that the correct word a Grievar might use to describe a technique that is out of practice?"

"Um...sure," Cego responded as usual to one of the cleric's strange questions. "I'd have to say I'm a bit rusty myself too, after having not practiced in the Circles for so long."

Xenalia looked at Cego curiously.

"You mean to say you are having trouble transitioning back to the Lyceum? Did you not have much practice in the fighting arts while you were working with the Flux in Kiroth?"

Cego laughed nervously, used to only hearing the Flux talked about as a low whisper in the last few weeks at the Lyceum, especially in earshot of him.

"Well, when I was with the Flux...I think I fought a lot..." Cego trailed off. Images flashed across his mind like red streaks of lightning. His head throbbed every time he tried to retrieve the past year.

"I don't think I did much single combat, though, against other Grievar," he said, holding a hand to his temple, struggling to find the words. "It was different."

Xenalia knew what he was, what he'd been through. "You feel guilty for what you might have done when you were under their control?"

"I wasn't under their control, Xenalia," Cego said. "No one forced me to do what I...what I did."

"Cego, given the firsthand account of what you told me happened at Arklight, how you were tortured for several months, and given my in-depth analysis of the numerous wounds inflicted across your body, many of which are still mending, it is highly likely that though your body took the brunt of the damage, your mind also suffered greatly."

Xenalia's little red spectral was hovering in front of Cego's eyes.

"There is a condition called cryopletic neuropathy," she said. "Your brain builds defenses to keep itself running in the worst of conditions. Some of these defenses can greatly shape how the world is perceived. It is my conjecture that when your brother Silas rescued you from your tormentors, your brain immediately determined that his cause, all that he was fighting for with the Flux, was the right cause."

Cego tried to keep pace with the cleric's rapid-fire words. "So… you're saying I was brainwashed? Because I was tortured?"

"That is one way of putting it," Xenalia said. "In a way, we are all brainwashed as you say, aiming our minds toward one goal or another and being affected by the circumstances around us. But in your case, those circumstances were particularly harrowing and so set you on a path that was equally as extreme."

"It doesn't forgive what I did," Cego said. He could feel the tears begin to burn in his eyes. "It doesn't forgive what happened. To the ones I care about."

"I am still sorry to hear of your friend Murray Pearson," Xenalia said. "I had met him on a few occasions prior, and though he did not possess many words that were not curses, I do believe he was a good man."

"He was a good man," Cego said. "He died… for me."

Xenalia was quiet for once, with no analytical response for Cego. She watched him as she unwrapped a bandage on his arms. After a moment, she placed a cold hand on his shoulder and squeezed.

"When you were on trial, last year," Xenalia said quietly, "and I heard the verdict, the judge handing down the sentence of execution, I thought I lost you, Cego. And then again when you were taken to Arklight Prison, I thought I lost you a second time. I know Murray Pearson was a good man… because he brought you back to me."

Cego smiled at Xenalia and wrapped his arms around her, bringing the cold, lithe cleric close to him. He could feel her heart beating fast.

"What was that?" she asked.

"It was… a hug," Cego said sheepishly, catching his breath.

"I've heard of such things," Xenalia said. "It was nice."

Cego slid off the medward bench and pulled his indigo second skin down over his head. "Well, I've got to get to the evening assembly soon. And then a late class, before the early-morning ones again tomorrow. They've got us training and studying nonstop, despite everything else going on."

"I understand," Xenalia said. "I also have extra work this year, a teaching position. There are so many new clerics coming to learn the path, and they know so little."

Cego made his way across the medward. He felt Xenalia's eyes following him.

"Cego," she called out. "Do not forget to visit your brother. I know it will be hard, but it is important he knows you are here."

"Yes, I've been meaning to." Cego's stomach lurched. "I've just been trying to patch myself together before I see him."

"From what I can tell of you, and nearly every Grievar, the time when you are patched together may never come," Xenalia said. She extended her little hand to point across the medward, toward the back corner where the private patient rooms were located. "He's waiting for you."

*   *   *

Moonlight puddled on the floor of the patient room, streaming in from a small window. There was a little cot with neatly folded sheets and a potted fern set beside it.

Sam was sitting on the floor with his back to the wall. Cego's breath caught in his chest, seeing his brother, the boy he'd grown up beside on the island. Sam looked nearly the same as Cego remembered: sandy hair, freckles, thin but corded arms. The boy was even munching on some dried fruit, his lips making a familiar smacking sound that conjured an image of the two brothers sitting beside each other on the black sand beach, trying to get a quick snack between training sessions.

How could he be real?

"Hello, Sam," Cego whispered, kneeling down in front of the boy.

How could his brother be here?

"Think you'll come with me to the tide pools today?" Sam asked. "I bet the storms that passed through dredged up some good catches."

Cego met the boy's eyes. This was not the same Sam.

Xenalia had said he'd been like this since Murray had brought him back to the Surface. They'd run through all manner of evaluations, trying to figure out what impairment was keeping Sam's brain tied to the Cradle, trapped in the simulation of the island. But there had been no progress, no solution.

"Sam," Cego said. "It's me, your brother Cego. I'm back."

"We can probably catch a few of those blue pincer crabs," Sam responded blankly. "It's tough to get them by myself, but working together we can trap them."

Cego put a hand on his brother's shoulder. "Sam, it's me. We're here in the Lyceum. In the Capital. We're not on the island anymore."

"We don't have much time before the old master has us training again, so we should get going." The boy wasn't meeting Cego's eyes. It was as if he were staring into a different world.

"Sam!" Cego shook his brother. He felt heat rising to his face. "Snap out of it. It's me, Cego. I'm back here with you. You need to get out of there. Come back to me, Sam, please."

The boy was silent for a moment and hope fluttered to Cego's chest. Maybe he'd gotten through to him. Maybe Sam just needed his brother here by his side.

"Please, won't you come?" Sam suddenly spoke again. "Call Arry down from the dunes too; I bet she'd love the run."

Hope fled from Cego, like gulls taking flight from their roost back to sea. He stared at his little brother until tears welled in his eyes.

"Yes, I'll come with you, Sam." Cego's voice broke. He took another look at Sam before turning to leave.

*   *   *

Cego stepped into the dim recesses of the Dome, the largest classroom of the Lyceum.

Though much of the school had been updated to harness new tech over the last decade, the Dome remained untouched. The surrounding shield windows and skylights were overrun with vines, the sandstone walls were cracked, and many of the wooden amphitheater seats squealed like weasels.

Most of the auditorium was already filled with students of all levels eagerly chatting. Though the Lyceum's students had begun the semester's classes two weeks prior, the high commander had insisted that all gather this evening for a school-wide briefing.

Cego shrugged in the new second skin, still getting used to the fit. He noticed the chatter quiet in the rows he passed. Heads turned and eyes followed him as he looked for his friends.

"Hey, Cego!" Dozer's baritone caught his attention. The big kid was standing and waving him over. Sol smiled from beside Dozer with Brynn and Knees sitting together not far past.

Cego shimmied his way down the row, though he found no empty seats beside his friends. He started to look elsewhere, but Dozer held him.

"No need to move," Dozer said, looking down at a chair occupied by a freckled boy wearing a white second skin. "Hey, Level One, think you might find some place new to sit?"

The kid's brow furrowed at Dozer, ready to protest, until he saw Cego standing over him. "Oh, yes...yes, sure, no problem."

The boy began to gather his gear. "No, you shouldn't have to move—" Cego started, but the boy was already heading down the row. He glanced briefly over his shoulder to look back at Cego.

"See?" Dozer said proudly as Cego sat. "The perks that come with being a Level Three."

Sol whispered from beside him. "You blockhead, that's not why he ran off so quick."

"What do you mean?" Dozer asked.

"It's because…" Sol trailed off.

"I get it," Cego said. Since he'd returned, the whispers in the halls had been constant. Other students, and even some faculty, peered at Cego like some exotic beast. "He moved because he's afraid of me."

"That's not what I was saying, Cego," Sol tried. "It's just that they're curious."

"Right, curious about Cego being a Flux rebe— Oof!" Dozer rubbed at the spot where Sol had jabbed him with a sharp elbow.

Sol spoke in a hushed whisper. "Keep it down with that! Do you even know why we're having this assembly?"

"Yeah, it's because…" Dozer also trailed off.

Sol shook her head and turned back to Cego. "What I'm trying to say is, I've been getting looks, too, since I got back. It's the same thing. They like to gossip; keeps them from boredom."

Cego nodded, though he knew it wasn't the same. It hadn't been easy, coming back to the Lyceum, hearing so many voices all at once, sensing the heat come off the bodies that surrounded him. Smelling the fear and anger and even hatred within them.

But he was glad to be sitting beside his friends. He was glad to be back with the Whelps.

"Hey," Cego whispered, noting the absence of one friend. "Where's Abel?"

"Just saw him, he was heading to the ward, to visit Sam," Dozer replied flatly.

Cego sank into his seat, unable to forget the blank look in Sam's eyes when he'd left him.

The chatter of the auditorium abruptly quieted as the lights on the front stage came on. They were to be addressed by the high commander of the Citadel, the highest-ranking Grievar in Ezo. The man who commanded the Knights, led diplomacy, and presided over the Lyceum.

The four commanders of the Citadel took to the stage, three taking a seat in the back, while the high commander stepped forward to the podium with his familiar swagger. Cego clenched his fists, looking at the man in his neatly pressed azure uniform. Callen Albright.

"Greetings to all Lyceum students and faculty," Callen started. "Though we are already two weeks into the semester after the Pilgrimage break, I thought it only appropriate that we bring the entire student body and faculty together for this briefing."

Dozer nudged Cego and whispered, "Still can't believe this scum-slagger is high commander."

Though much had happened since he'd been gone, Cego couldn't believe it either. Callen Albright was not a leader, much less a commander of the Citadel.

Darkin' man doesn't know how to piss straight in a Circle; how can he lead the Knights? Cego could still hear Murray-Ku's voice.

Callen straightened his pressed collar as he continued. "It's important that we, as Ezonians foremost, and secondarily as caretakers of the Lyceum, have a unified cause. Now more than ever, it is integral that we join together and do not let any internal disputes cause friction within our ranks.

"My predecessors were fair leaders," Callen said. He gestured to the three seats at the back of the stage where Adrienne Larkspur, Dakar Pugilio, and Albion Memnon sat.

"Commander Memnon did a fair job of keeping our Knights on track and the machine of the Lyceum well oiled. But he did not see far enough ahead."

Though Memnon's face was shadowed, Cego could picture the grimace across it. Cego had heard the man had been forced out of his position by Daimyo Governance and Callen immediately installed as his successor.

Cego had seen Commander Memnon only once since his return. At Murray-Ku's burial ceremony.

"To see far enough ahead, one must have perfect vision," Callen's nasal voice droned. "And I am lucky enough to be bestowed with such sight. I can see the direction of our students, the future of the Knights, the complexity of the international circuit, and all else that lies beyond.

"So, you must trust in my vision," Callen said. "But I understand there are some questions about changes that have been enacted this year. So, as your high commander, I see it as my duty to answer those questions."

Callen paced the length of the stage. "First, where have certain Lyceum faculty members gone?"

Cego had already noticed many familiar teachers absent from their positions upon his return, even those that had been mainstays of the institution for years.

"It is customary for new leadership to bring in new faculty," Callen said flatly. "It is true that I've made more changes than any of my predecessors, but I also don't aim to be like any of them. As I said, my goal is for us to move forward together, and unfortunately, there were too many minds here at the Lyceum that were stuck in the past, unwilling to welcome change."

"Still upset he got rid of Kitaka," Dozer grumbled. "He was my favorite."

"Now," Callen said as he paused in front of the podium. "Let us get on with the beast in the room."

Cego felt the high commander's eyes fall on him even within the darkness. He shrank back into his chair.

"I've heard much talk already this semester, walking these halls. Mentions of a group called the Flux," Callen said.

A hush came over the students. The Flux was only spoken of in whispers. The Ezonian Governance had not even acknowledged any rebellion was ongoing in Kiroth.

"I've worked with Governance for nearly my entire life now," Callen said. "I've climbed the ranks, from Scout commander to commander of the Lyceum and now high commander. And, given my vast experience, I know how rumors can spread. I know how many little fires set to poorly built homes can become an inferno that consumes an entire city. This Flux that so many speak of is such a rumor."

Cego closed his eyes in the darkness. He saw Silas staring back at him.

"The Flux is a rumor and that is all it is." Callen raised his voice. "And so, how do we deal with such insignificant information? We silence it."

Cego breathed deeply. The words that came from Callen's mouth would have been the real offense. Those that denied the Flux were the voices the Strangler had quieted.

"From now on, there will be disciplinary action taken against any who speak of the Flux," Callen said. "Students here need to be focused on their studies, on training and testing, not on senseless fantasies of some rebellion in a faraway land."

Cego saw red lightning streak across the darkness. He heard great waves crashing down. He sensed the energy within him. Dormant since he'd returned to the Lyceum. Quiet since he'd seen Murray fall in Karstock. But it was there, like a hungry parasite waiting for something new to consume.

"Those who speak of such things will not only be docked for scores but repeat offenses will merit expulsion from the Lyceum and even reporting to the Daimyo Governance in extreme cases," Callen concluded. "So, I expect my words now will be the last we hear of such things."

The urge to violence rose within Cego. He could take to the stage in a split second, find Callen's neck in another. Put an end to his lies.

He felt warm fingers brush against his hand. "You okay?"

Sol was looking at him, those sunflower eyes bringing him back to the auditorium.

He breathed. "Yes, I'm okay."

Sol nodded, though the worry didn't leave her face.

"With that bit aside," Callen said, "I fully expect this year to be the most productive the Lyceum has ever had."

Albright glanced over his shoulder to see the large form of Commander Memnon rising from his seat.

"What is it, Commander?" Albright appeared annoyed. "Oh, yes…"

Memnon sat back down and the high commander continued. "Before I close this briefing, I would like to note the loss of one of our faculty members."

Albright again paced the length of the stage. "Murray Pearson was…a Knight who served his nation."

Cego could still see the morning mist rising atop Kalabasas Hill when they'd first returned to the Citadel. He could still smell the wet earth they'd laid atop Murray's body.

"Murray Pearson was also a Scout," Callen said. "Though he often did things his own way, and was not one to listen to instruction, he did serve for much of his life, even if he did not die for the cause."

Cego could hear Dozer growl from beside him.

"And service is why we are all here," Callen said. "So, let us take a moment of silence for Murray Pearson, to honor his service."

Cego could still see Murray's burial mound, the bulk of glistening, wet earth rising from the ground, a mane of fiery leaves spread atop it. And Cego could see the hardened bulk of the mound beside Murray's, where Joba had been laid to rest a year prior. Cego hadn't been there to see the leaves adorning Joba's plot of earth.

Two had given their lives for him. They'd sacrificed themselves for Cego.

Why had they fought for him? Why had they died for him?

"Murray Pearson's death teaches us that we are all in service of a greater purpose." Callen's voice brought Cego back to the Dome. "We are one unit, working together, toward a common goal. We serve the nation of Ezo. We serve the people of Ezo."

Callen stood back at the podium, ran his hand through his slick black hair, and said the words. Those words that had been spoken in the Lyceum's halls so many times, for centuries. Those words that had been whispered as the first utterances to the newborn babe or as the last rites to warriors put to rest.

"We fight so the rest shall not have to," Callen said.

Those words that Cego did not believe any longer.

* * *

Sol led the way to class with Cego trailing behind her. She yawned, feeling the weariness from a long day of training and studies that seemed far from done.

They sat on the tatami of the sparse wooden room on the fifth floor of the Harmony.

Several other upper-levels filtered in, mostly Fives and Sixes. From what Sol could tell, she and Cego were the only Level Threes in the class, besides Gryfin Thurgood, who had just walked in and sat beside them.

"Still can't believe we're finally in Stratagems and Maneuvers," Cego whispered from beside Sol.

"Well, I think given Solara's success on Pilgrimage, it makes sense Professor Dynari picked her," Gryfin chimed in. "And I did score second in class for Level Two."

Sol smiled. Though she felt worn to the bone, she still enjoyed the return to the comfort of classes, scores, and testing, after spending over a year in unpredictable circumstances.

Cego frowned and turned away from Gryfin. "Makes sense why you two are here, but not sure why I made it in."

Stratagems and Maneuvers was by far the most sought-after elective in the Lyceum. It always filled with the top upper-level performers, and even they were often wait-listed for years.

"You have as good a right to be here as any of us," Sol said. "I was gone too."

"Right," Gryfin agreed. "Real-world fight experience like what you two had beats much of what we've been learning here."

Sol watched Cego shake his head wearily. She could tell even the slightest mention of the past year still hit him hard.

She attempted to change the subject. "I heard Level Twos had some good training we missed last year. And the finals were something to watch."

Gryfin sighed and rubbed his square jaw. "Right, it was something to watch. Until I ran into Shimo."

"Heard about that tai otoshi he hit on you," Sol said. "Shimo probably has the best ground work in the Lyceum, maybe outside of Cego here. I also underestimated him on Pilgrimage. Second place in finals isn't bad, though."

"For my family, it is," Gryfin said. "Both my brothers placed first almost every year they were here. My father had me training off my back for the entirety of off-season. He kept saying I should've been able to counter that throw. I still don't see how I'd be able to defend it."

"He hit the same throw on me," Sol said. "I've been thinking it through since, and I've worked out a decent counter."

Sol turned to Gryfin and grabbed one of his wrists to demonstrate. "So, when he pushes your hand, he expects you to try and pull it away—"

"Professor Dynari is here," Cego interrupted. Sol saw her friend's brow strangely furrowed, looking at her and Gryfin. She released Gryfin's wrist and turned to the back of the room, where Professor Jos Dynari had silently made his way to sit and observe, as he'd done with every class so far.

"I'm glad to see discussion on fight strategy, even during free time," Dynari said, standing and limping toward the front of the students. "Combat should occupy all moments in your mind, even when you are not within the Circles."

They'd spent the first two weeks of the semester in review. Though Professor Dynari knew he had the top crop of students in his class, the man had still insisted on ensuring they had clean fundamentals.

Any strategy I teach without good basics will be a waste of my time and yours, he'd said on their first day of class.

Dynari had even kicked a Level Sixer out when he determined she didn't know how to do a proper arm drag. Ever since, the remaining students had watched the professor with trepidation, fearful of losing their coveted spots.

"Tonight begins the real meat of our course," Dynari said as he scratched at his bald head. The professor didn't have the physique of a prime Grievar. He'd been permanently injured early on in his career. But all Knights, from the Outer Circles to the Capital, swore this man was the brightest strategist in the nation.

Dynari crouched carefully to open a small chest at the back of the room. He withdrew a circular wooden board from it, along with a leather pouch. He placed the polished board where all students could see it and emptied the contents of the pouch onto the tatami.

Sol recognized the game—Bythardi. Wraith had often played it in Lord Cantino's manor. In fact, it was the only thing that man had done besides training.

"How many of you have played Bythardi before?" Dynari asked as he precisely placed the pieces on the many-colored circles drawn across the board.

Several of the upper-levels raised their fists, as well as Gryfin. The game was well known within the purelight houses, though Sol's father had often looked down on it.

Why crouch and play some child's game when actual training needs be done? she'd often heard Artemis Halberd grumble.

Professor Dynari motioned for one of the Level Five students, Dentas Tilton, to join him across the Bythardi board. "Let us walk through a quick game so the rest who haven't played can see how it is done."

Both Dynari and Dentas sank into a low squat on either end of the board.

"There is a physical aspect to Bythardi," Dynari explained. "One must remain in a low crouch for the entirety of the match. If a player loses balance or comes out of position, they will forfeit, no matter where the rest of the game stands."

Sol slid forward on the tatami to get a closer look at the board as the match began. Gryfin started to move beside her, but Cego quickly slid into the spot with his back to the boy, a blank expression on his face.

Sol knew Cego had been through a lot, but he was acting even stranger than usual lately.

"The goal of the game is to take your opponent's neck," Dynari explained to the class, pointing to two pieces on the board, little carved heads standing atop long necks.

"Fists move first." Dynari nodded to Dentas, who took hold of one of the most numerous pieces on the board, a clenched upward fist, and shifted it to the right one space.

Dynari countered by moving one of his own fists, circling in the opposite direction. "Bythardi is a game of forward and backward movement as well as angles."

Dentas responded by shifting another type of piece, a planted foot up to the knee joint, forward one space. Dynari smiled and did the same with another of his fists.

"Fists can only attack and only move forward but are immune from being attacked themselves," Dynari explained. "While the foot piece is more versatile—it has the ability to move forward, backward, and circle—but with the weakness of being exposed to attack."

Sol watched closely, trying to make some sense of the game as the players continued to trade moves. Professor Dynari allowed one of his foot pieces to be destroyed by a fist but in return moved a fist at an angle toward Dentas's neck piece.

"Fists and feet must move in unison," Dynari said, as he placed a foot piece beside one of his fists. "When they are adjacent to one another, they are able to move more than one circle at a time."

Within another minute, Sol saw that Dentas's neck was surrounded on both sides by Dynari's pieces.

"You've got my neck," Dentas conceded, knocking down the prized piece and standing from his squat. The boy was sweating profusely and appeared relieved he didn't have to crouch any longer.

"Dentas is a decent player," Dynari said as he stood with little effort. "He moved forward aggressively with his fists, but he didn't cut the proper angles and did not combine his pieces frequently enough to make them more versatile in their attacks."

The students were quiet as Dynari appraised their reactions, waiting expectantly with his hands crossed.

"I'm glad not one of you has asked me that question which I get at least once per year: 'Professor, but what has Bythardi got to do with real combat?' "

Sol smiled, glad that Dozer hadn't made it into the class, despite his best efforts.

"It's fairly obvious, though, isn't it?" Dynari said. "As upper-levels, you've gotten beyond the basics and are now starting to grasp strategy. No single punch or kick, takedown or armlock is going to land on a worthy opponent, just as no single line of movement will work in Bythardi. You need to constantly cut angles and throw combinations, think multiple steps ahead."

Sol found her mind drifting back to the match with Kōri Shimo. The boy had always been several steps ahead of her, stifling her attacks, never allowing her to implement her technique effectively.

"As your opponent's skill level continues to grow, the number of steps ahead you'll need to be will only increase. Bythardi will aid you with this foresight. It will help your mind adapt to the combat strategies that you will be learning this semester."

Sol had never seen Kōri Shimo sitting beside a Bythardi board. He hadn't needed any tools or games to stay multiple steps ahead of Sol and handle her with ease.

Dynari gestured to the chest behind him. "There will be Bythardi boards for all of you to take back to your dorms for continued practice. I expect at the end of semester, you'll be not only far better fighters but half-decent Bythardi players. Now, let's pair up and play a game before we move on to the grappling strategy for the day."

Sol walked to the chest to retrieve a board, but Cego was already there, holding his own and an extra for her.

"Pair?" he asked her.

CHAPTER 12

The Lingering Shadow

The sparrow that nips at the hawk must be prepared not only to outmaneuver the bigger bird but also to outlast it. A victory against a significantly larger opponent must be a well-calculated one.

Passage Four, Ninety-Sixth Precept of
the Combat Codes

Commander Albion Jonquil Memnon was still sweating from his morning bag work as he set down the long Knight Tower stair. His lower back creaked and pain radiated across his shoulders, but he didn't mind. At least he felt something.

The savory scent of lard wafted to his nose as he passed the kitchens and servicer quarters.

"Something smells good in there as usual, Rafi." Memnon nodded to one of the Grunt sizzlers who was on his way out from the night shift.

"Yes, there sure is, High Commander." The Grunt bowed his head.

"Just commander now, Rafi," Memnon said.

"Right-o, Commander." Rafi nodded vigorously. "And hello to your shadow too."

Rafi looked down beside Memnon where the boy stood on the stair.

"Sam, you've met Rafi before." Memnon put his hand on the boy's shoulder, prodding him to greet the Grunt.

"That's okay, Commander," Rafi said. "My little un is shy as this one."

"I'm going to head over to the slippery rocks to see if I can catch some blue crabs!" Sam blurted out.

"Not sure if I know where that be, but I could certainly use some crabs for my sizzling pan if you can find 'em." Rafi managed a puzzled smile and continued on down the stairs ahead of them.

Memnon and Sam walked side by side, the little boy only coming up to the burly Grievar's hip. The boy had been inseparable from Memnon since Murray had brought him from the Deep and dropped him at his doorstep. Though Sam technically slept at the Lyceum's medward for continued monitoring, he showed up nearly every morning at Memnon's door and stayed by his side until nightfall.

Memnon and Sam stopped at one of the Knights' training rooms, which was starting to fill in the morning light. Several polished Circles of varying elemental alloys lay at the center of the large room, waiting for the surrounding Knights to set foot in them. The team sat on the tatamis, chatting while they wrapped their hands and stretched out.

Memnon closed his eyes and took a deep breath. He could smell the cleansing oil used to wipe down the mats and the harsh polish to set the Circles gleaming each night. Despite the servicers' best efforts, the musk of sweat and blood still lingered, and Memnon loved it. It brought back his deepest memories of training, chatting on these very mats with his comrades.

"Taking it in, eh, Commander?" Raymol Tarsis stood in front of him, peering down at Sam. Though Memnon was a large man himself, Raymol was one of the few who stood at least a foot taller.

"Yeah, I suppose so, Ray," Memnon said. "Only have so many years left I might be able to do so."

"Ah, shut it on that, Commander." Ray smacked Memnon on the shoulder, and though it hurt like the Deep, Memnon didn't show it. "We both know you'd likely still wipe the floor with any of these fresh ones."

Memnon wasn't so sure about that any longer—he stuck to hitting the heavy bags of late—but he nodded at his captain's show of respect.

"And I see your shadow's back." Ray gestured down to Sam. "You ready to start your training with the Citadel's Knights yet, boy?"

Sam stared off into the distance as usual, not even registering the giant Knight speaking to him.

"Something's still off with him, eh?" Ray waved a hand in front of Sam's face. "Couldn't they figure anything out at the ward?"

"How fares the training this week?" Memnon changed the subject, tired of trying to explain his new companion to the entire Citadel.

"Karin broke his shoulder a day ago; guess Yang got a bit over-enthusiastic with a kimura lock," Ray said, nodding over to a bald Knight stretching out on the tatami. "He's over with the clerics for a few more days, but other than that, we can field a team."

"Good," Memnon said. "As you know, we'll need three fresh next week for the Desovian border. Who do you think is up to the task?"

Ray stood at attention beside Memnon and surveyed the Knights as they paired up in the Circles. "Well, Yang for sure... You know about his mean streak, but that'll serve him well in Tenthik Arena."

"I agree," Memnon said as he watched the bald Grievar

showboating in front of his partner, bobbing and weaving without even holding his hands up. "Yang still needs some humbling or he'll meet his match one of these days, but we can't worry about that when we're short."

"Still can't believe they darkin' left like that." Ray clenched his fists.

Memnon sighed. "Nor can I believe it, Ray. But it's not just here that Knights are deserting. It's teams across the world, large and small. I got word that one of the top Myrkonian prospects disappeared early this week."

"Men I knew coming up at Lyceum even...like Tractor," Ray growled. "Can't believe he was up and gone, day after I was trading shots with him in these very Circles. He goes and shits on loyalty."

"Let's quiet down a bit, son," Memnon said. "We don't want to get the team worked up about this any more than they already are. We're barely holding together as is."

"Sorry, Commander," Ray said. "It makes me so darkin' furious that we had traitors aboard, that they'd go over to that sorry excuse of a rebellion."

Memnon nodded and held his tongue. He knew why so many Knights were turning to the Flux, packing their gear and heading out to Kiroth to join the famed Slayer in his rebellion.

Memnon knew firsthand how the Daimyo had manipulated them for their purposes for so many years. He knew how Governance constantly peddled stims and forced simulation training on them, constantly pushed Grievar beyond their natural limits so they could win in the Circle.

Memnon knew of the Cradle. He'd been complicit, giving the Daimyo and the Bit-Minders the nod to grow Grievar in their labs, trying to create the perfect fighters. Memnon had been a part of the entire scheme, another cog that kept this darked-up world turning.

And so, it wasn't a surprise to Memnon that Grievar wanted to fight for something real again, not for the cheers of adoring fans or for ranking within their nation's scoreboards but for a real cause. Fighting for freedom.

Memnon kept his mouth shut. Even if he did speak the truth to any of his Knights, they wouldn't believe him. The ones that had stayed were the most deluded, the deepest in this quagmire of servitude created by the Daimyo.

"I'm angry too," Memnon said. "Let us use that anger for a purpose, to fuel our team heading out to Desovi with a path to victory."

"Yes, Commander," Ray responded, raising his fist. "So, I got Masa and Gabault along with Yang for the border fights. I'd go myself, but I fought last week and am planning to lead our team in the south week after."

"Sounds right to me," Memnon said. "I'll be back this afternoon. Make sure the men don't forget to fuel up midmorning. We need to keep up the pace."

"Yes, Commander."

Memnon wheeled from the room, with Sam at his heels like a pup. They started down the stairs to the command center, where he'd meet with his newly appointed boss, High Commander Callen Albright. Even the sound of it left a bad taste in his mouth.

"Commander!"

Memnon looked up the stairs to see Ray looking down at him.

"Yes, Ray?"

"We'll do it for Murray Pearson," the lieutenant said. "He died for us, for the Citadel. Darkin' Flux took him. So, we'll keep fighting for him."

"Yes," Memnon said, though he could feel the pit in his stomach. More lies to tell. "We'll fight for Murray."

* * *

Cego made his way up the creaky wooden stairs and down the dimly lit hallway toward the Quarter D dormitory.

Cego walked through the entry and glanced fondly over the old room, empty with the crew taking breakfast at the dining hall after morning classes. Some things hadn't changed over the years; Dozer's section was still a scattered pile of sweat-soaked gear and food bits, while the area near Sol's cot was neatly folded uniforms and stacks of technique textbooks dating back to year one.

Cego made the habit of looking in the little mirror on the way in and pulled down the nape of his purple second skin. But the little Whelp design was gone, along with the rest of his flux tattoos. Gone were nearly the entire crew's brands since their initiation to the Flux. Their purification, Silas had called it. Only the Doragūn remained on Cego's skin; the blacklight serpent slithered from his shoulder to his wrist, constantly reminding him where he'd been this past year. Reminding him that he no longer belonged.

"Maybe you should visit Sam." Abel abruptly appeared next to Cego, his teammate always having the uncanny ability to sneak up on him.

Cego turned to Abel. The little Desovian had changed more drastically than the rest of the team, though he'd been the only one to stay back from Pilgrimage. The boy's dark eyes were sunken in and his lips pursed flat, as if he were afraid of smiling.

"Abel, I did see him," Cego responded. "It's hard."

"It's hard for him too," Abel said. "But he still can use you by his side more often."

"I know," Cego said. "He's got Memnon, though. He's always off following the commander around."

Abel narrowed his eyes at Cego. "You make excuses to see your own brother."

Cego shook his head. "You don't understand."

"Don't I?" Abel said. "I see your brother near every day since Murray-Ku brought him up. When all the rest were on Pilgrimage, I stay beside him. You? You come back and see him once. I can see it in your eye, you won't go back to Sam, will you?"

"He's not here, Abel!" Cego raised his voice. "When I try to talk to him... You know what I mean."

"You come from the same home as him," Abel said. "You should be able to talk to him better than anyone."

"What do you know about my home, about the Cradle I was grown in?" Cego yelled. "Don't you know this was all an experiment of the Daimyo?"

"I do know, Cego," Abel said. "I know about the Cradle. But I also know about the island, the one you and Sam grew up on. Because I listen to your brother. I talk to him."

Cego felt ashamed. He was complaining about dealing with Sam for only a few weeks, while Abel had been helping care for him since he'd appeared back at the Lyceum.

"You want to give up?" Abel said. "Fine, I watch your brother. I won't give up. Just like I never gave up on Joba."

"What—what do you mean?" Cego stuttered. "I didn't give up on Joba—"

"You weren't there," Abel said. "To bury him."

"I couldn't be, Abel," Cego pleaded. "I was imprisoned at Arklight, and then I was..."

"You were with Silas." Abel finished Cego's sentence.

Cego wanted to explain to the Desovian that he couldn't have done anything else. He hadn't had the power to leave Silas's side, to break from the Flux. Not until Murray died.

"Don't worry, Cego," Abel said again. "I watch your brother."

The boy turned and walked from the room, leaving Cego in silence.

*　　*　　*

Cego's mind was far off as he took the Valkyrie's spiral staircase upward.

He entered the familiar recesses of Professor Aon Farstead's classroom. The tall, dusty bookshelves and soft light from the high windows didn't calm Cego as they used to.

Sol was sitting beside Theodora Larkspur, and she quickly averted her eyes when he looked over to her. Abel was there, usually the first to the class, and nodded at Cego with those flat-lined lips.

Missing from the class was the professor: Aon Farstead, the oldest Grievar in the Lyceum. Though Cego had been absent for the past year, he'd heard that Aon's mental decay had continued. The ancient man spent the entirety of his days confined to his quarters.

Because the Codes had been taught since the school was first erected, the administration thought it best if the class was not discontinued, despite the professor's state. And so, the class had taken shape as a group study; the seven students enrolled this semester would lead productive Codes discussion with each other.

So far this semester, the discussion had been anything but productive. The loudest voices in the room—Theodora Larkspur and a Level Three named Bahari Tumault—had taken the air from most of the other students.

Even now, before all the students had filtered in, the two were arguing.

"One hundred sixty-third precept, of passage three. Have you even read it?" Theodora was standing to her full, considerable height, arms on her hips.

"Dreams, dreams, yes, I know it," Tumault responded. "And what does that even have to do with the Desovian border dispute?"

"You're blind as usual, Bahari," Theodora said. "Reports say the Desovian captain that crossed south into Ezonian territory did so because he had a vision."

"So, you're saying he'd read that particular precept that evening, and come morning, the man decided to cross over the axis with a full battalion, then challenge and kill the ranking Knight in the outer rings?"

"When you say it like that, it sounds absurd," Theodora said. "But—"

"The Desovian was deepshit crazy!" Bahari said. "That's all that explains it; nothing to do with Codes at all."

Abel took the opportunity to chime in, seeing the rest of the students had arrived. "Perhaps we bring it back a step? I think Theodora has good point, as precept one hundred sixty-three does tell us to pay heed to dreams or visions."

"Right, it does, but that doesn't mean we should use Codes as an excuse for a foreigner to break pact, enter our lands, and kill our people!" Bahari said.

"You're right too, Tumault." Abel spoke little lately, but when he did, the other students listened. "The Codes weren't written to be used as justification of actions. Professor Aon taught that to me as Level One. They were written as way of life to be considered always."

"I remember that class," Sol said from her seated position. "Professor Aon described it like walking in the forest and using the sounds as a guide. He said you hear the birds and the wind in the trees and the pine needles underfoot. None of these sounds tell you to climb a tree in fear of entering a gar bear's territory…"

Cego finished for Sol, also remembering that class vividly, seeing the sparkle in Old Aon's eyes as he laughed at his own words. "But if you should see a mother bear in front of her cubs, take heed and step backward."

Abel appeared pleased that Aon's words had brought some resolution to the argument between Tumault and Theodora. "What should we discuss next?"

A thick boy wearing a bloodred second skin shook his head. "I don't get it."

"What don't you get, Novor? Why you should avoid gar bear?" Abel asked.

"No, I get that," the Level Sixer said. "I've traveled with my family to the north, seen plenty of bears and worse. I don't get why we're speaking of the skirmish in outer rings when we can't talk of the bigger stuff going on."

"You mean the…" Abel trailed off.

"The darkin' Flux!" Novor raised his voice.

"Hush!" Theodora stood and looked over her shoulder warily. "You heard what High Commander Albright said in the Dome. Talk of it can mean expulsion!"

"Doesn't make sense." Novor was undeterred. "It's going on right under our nose. My brother is stationed south of Kiroth, says the Grunts have been amassing near the border. The Slayer has the numbers, and they already brought down much of the empire's infrastructure."

"That's in Kiroth," Theodora whispered. "And my mother says the Kirothians can never keep their Grunts in check anyway. They've been having uprisings for the past century because there's not enough food for them all."

"Seems far away because you're not there," Novor said. "But when Slayer and his armies are knocking at the Citadel's front gates, you won't be saying that."

"You're being ridiculous, Novor." Tumault for once agreed with Theodora. "If we were in any danger, the administration would let us know. My parents are one of the Twelve, and they'd be the first to hear if anything was going on that we should be worried about."

Novor laughed. "Don't need to be one of the Twelve to smell a shit when it's sitting on your left foot."

Tumault scrunched his nose. "Let's get back to talking Codes so we don't get expelled, all right?"

"I agree," Theodora said. "I was hoping we might discuss passage one of—"

"It's because of him we can't be talkin'," Novor growled. The thick boy stared directly at Cego.

Sol stood. "You best not be going down a path you can't back down from, Novor."

"I've been biting my tongue long enough, Halberd," Novor said, standing as well. The Level Sixer was at least twice Sol's size, thick with muscle. "We all know why administration won't let us talk of the Flux. It's because they're worried about spies."

Novor took another step toward Cego, who was still seated. Sol didn't back down. "Cego isn't a spy."

"He's the Slayer's brother!" Novor raised his voice. "He spent all of the last year working for the Flux, then he miraculously decides to return back home to the Lyceum. And no one bats an eye! All because he was Murray Pearson's pet."

"You don't know what you're talking about, Novor," Sol said.

"Yes, he does." Cego finally spoke.

"See? Even the traitor himself admits it," Novor spat.

"You're right, Novor," Cego said as he stood. "I did fight for my brother."

Novor quieted, suddenly unsure of whether being right was a good thing. Cego stepped around Sol toward the large boy.

"Cego, please," Sol said, trying to step between them again.

"He deserves to know the truth," Cego said. "I'm back here at the Lyceum because I wanted to return. And I don't care what you believe, whether you think I'm a spy or not. Do you want to know why?"

"Um...I guess," Novor said.

"Because all the work I did in Kiroth, for the Flux...I didn't forget how to do it." The darkness spread across Cego like an incurable itch. He saw the bleak landscape of the island, the skeletal forms of the ironwood trees jutting from the rain-soaked earth.

"I was known as the Strangler because I was sent to put away those who spoke against the rebellion." Cego advanced on Novor. "I silenced them. And I can still quiet those who speak too loudly."

"You heard him!" Novor said, backing away. "He threatened me, said he's going to—"

"He didn't do anything of the sort," Sol interrupted. "Cego was standing up to your accusations. I think discussions have been good enough for today, don't you, Abel?"

Abel nodded, warily watching Cego. "Yes, yes, Codes discussion over for today."

The rest of the group made a quick exit, though not before

Novor glanced over his shoulder to snarl back at Cego. "Don't think I'll forget this."

"You okay?" Sol eyed Cego. She'd asked him that question quite a lot since their return.

"Yes," Cego said. "But sometimes, I feel myself returning there…to where I was."

Sol put her hand on his shoulder and met his eyes. "I understand… I mean I don't understand, but I know it's hard for you to be here, to keep control. But you've got to try. The Lyceum brought you back in, let you continue on track because of Murray and Commander Memnon vouching for you, but if word got to Callen that this happened…"

"I know that already," Cego snapped.

Sol gave him a wary look and moved for the exit. "I've got to get to my next class early."

Cego stayed, sat down to breathe beneath the towering bookshelves. He tried to rekindle the memory of first entering Aon's study, the deep sense of responsibility he'd felt opening the ancient tomes full of the Codes.

"You feel anger," Abel said. He'd almost forgotten the little Desovian was still in the room.

"Shouldn't I?" Cego asked. "I didn't want all this to happen."

"I felt anger too for a while," Abel said. "After Joba died."

Cego's face flushed with shame.

"I was angry at you," Abel admitted. "I said to myself, Joba, he was always happy. Joba never wanted to hurt anyone. Then Joba gave his life for you. Why did he deserve such fate?"

"He didn't deserve it," Cego said. "And I didn't ask Joba to save me. I didn't ask Murray to save me either."

"Yet they did fight for you," Abel said. "And because of you, they are dead."

Cego shuddered. He needed to hear those words.

"I wish I was gone instead of them," Cego whispered. "Now I have to live with this. Now I carry this weight."

"They knew that you would be able to carry it," Abel said.

"How could they know?" Cego asked.

"Joba and Murray knew you would not forget them," Abel replied. "That none of us will ever forget what they did. And they knew that we would be here to help you carry this burden. Because if we let their sacrifice bury us, then they died for nothing."

Cego shook his head. Not only did he bear his past but now the sacrifice of others on top of it. It seemed impossible that the burden wouldn't crush him beneath its weight.

"They believed in you," Abel said. "They knew you are different from the rest. And so do I, Cego. So do all those who have truly seen you, including Professor Aon. Do you remember what the professor used to say to us so often?"

"*We will need to make a choice*," Cego recited Aon's familiar words as he looked to the high windows of the study. "*To walk in the shadows or to walk in the light.*"

"Would you like to see him?" Abel asked.

"Aon?" Cego knew Abel had been caring for the ancient professor, but he'd purposely avoided visiting him in his quarters right off the study.

They lifted the curtain to a small, sparse room fitted with more bookshelves, several potted plants, and a flat tatami on the floor. Atop the mat lay one of the greatest minds to grace the Lyceum, a mentor to a multitude of Knights and teachers. But now Cego looked down at a withered husk.

Abel bowed his head low as they entered the room. "Hello, Professor Aon, I'm here to give you something to drink."

The little Desovian brought over a bowl of ice chips and knelt beside the ancient teacher. Cego could hardly see Aon's chest moving and wondered for a moment whether Abel was tending to a corpse.

But, as Abel placed the ice to Aon's thin lips, Cego noticed the man's foot twitch slightly, a sliver of life. "There you go, Professor. Today we had good Codes discussion, just as you like."

Abel took a small cloth from beside the tatami, wet it in the bowl, and began to wipe Aon's forehead and body. "Some students, they don't understand yet. But soon, they will."

All this time he'd been gone, Abel had dedicated himself to not only helping his brother Sam but also caring for Aon.

"Why're you doing it?" Cego asked.

"Because no one else will," Abel said. "The clerics said they can't do anything for him. But they're wrong. It's important to do this, to speak to him, to make him know he's looked after. Though the Codes speak of fighting for the rest, there's other ways to fight than in the Circle."

"Is this why you aren't angry anymore?" Cego asked.

"Even though he can't speak anymore, Professor Aon is very wise," Abel said as he brushed a wisp of white hair from the man's forehead. "He's given me reason to step forward, to leave my anger behind."

Cego breathed deeply.

"You need to step forward, Cego," Abel said. "Don't return to that place I see you go today, where you forget who you are."

Cego wanted to assure Abel he wouldn't go back to that place of darkness. But he didn't want to lie to his friend.

The Cradle called to him.

*   *   *

Cego and Abel caught up to the rest of the crew between classes. The Whelps were standing at the center of the Harmony's common ground beneath the large score lightboard. The hall was crowded with students of all levels, chatting, snacking, practicing techniques, and most noticeably, throwing side glances in Cego's direction.

A variety of azure, emerald, and crimson spectrals continuously wafted toward the tall ceiling set above the sixth floor of classrooms.

Sol was chiding Dozer, which she'd said she'd missed quite a bit during her time away from the big Grievar.

"Did you shrink your second skin again?" Sol asked, grinning as she gave Dozer a once-over.

"What do you mean?" Dozer asked. "I gave it a wash because the smell was getting a bit dark, but I think it looks just fine."

Dozer lifted his arms and flexed, popping the seam along his shoulders. "Uh...needs a bit of breaking in, that's all."

Sol turned from the big kid as Cego approached and the smile left her face.

"What's with you?" Sol asked bluntly.

"Nothing," Cego replied.

"I know you," Sol said. "You're not yourself."

Cego tried to take a deep breath, but it caught in his chest. Sol had been giving him strange looks since he'd returned, along with every other kid in this school.

"It be true, Cego," Knees said. "You been someplace else."

"We know what you've gone through and we're here to help," Brynn added.

Two blue-clad Level Twos gawked at Cego as they hurried past.

"What about you?" Cego snapped, turning back to Sol.

"What do you mean, what about me?" Sol replied.

"You say I'm not acting like myself," Cego said. "But you haven't been yourself either. At least, you're not who I remember."

"And what does that mean?" Sol asked. "Who was I? Was I someone who would have let you get into a fight with that dolt Novor over something so senseless? Was I someone who would let you risk getting expelled for breaking class conduct and dishonoring Professor Farstead's classroom?"

Cego knew Sol was right, but he couldn't bear to admit it. The parasite of anger within him kept rising to the surface, urging him to blame others.

Had Sol changed, though? She appeared harder than he remembered, more scars across her angular face. But the crease near her eyes as she frowned at him was the same. Sol was worried about him. She was his friend.

"I'm sorry." Cego let it out.

"It's okay, Cego, I know so much has happened—"

"No," Cego said. "I won't make excuses for my actions. I need to stop blaming others. And you don't deserve to have me treat you that way. None of you do. I know you want to help."

"It's true," Sol said, placing her hand on Cego's shoulder. "And it's not only me. The whole crew is here for you."

Cego nodded.

"I know what we need!" Dozer smiled. The big kid wrapped one arm around Knees and the other around Brynn, pulling them in close and lowering his head like a bull.

"Huh?" Cego wasn't quite sure what to make of it. A pack of blue-clad students stopped to stare at the strange ritual.

"Come on." Sol flashed a smile and put an arm around Cego and Abel, pulling them into the huddle as well.

The Whelps pressed their heads together at the center, ignoring the bustle around them.

"Something Murray started on Pilgrimage, like the Tanri do," Dozer said from within the huddle. "We should keep it going; he'd have liked that."

"As long as you be taking care of that breath next time," Knees said sourly.

Cego involuntarily sniffed and could clearly detect the rank odor from his friend's close mouth.

"Oh, that's probably the protein mix I made this morning," Dozer said. "Good stuff but doesn't come up so well."

"Maybe Dozer could wear that Tanri mask he picked up next time we decide to do this," Brynn said. "To keep in the stink."

"Don't even get him started with that again," Knees muttered. "You too, Firebird."

Sol chuckled. "Maybe I'll mask up next time we train together, Knees, so you remember our fun time in the Can."

"Cego, have we told you about that one yet?" Dozer asked. "How Sol put Knees out cold in front of a crowd of his hometown Venturians?"

Knees threw a swift knee up the middle of the huddle into Dozer's gut, eliciting a grunt from the big kid. "How about instead we tell him about how you thought that highland girl be fancying you, when really she was looking over at Brynn?"

"She was after me, I swear!" Dozer pulled the pack in even tighter with his big arms.

Cego felt the warmth of his friends around him, pressed together in the middle of the crowded common ground. He no longer cared about the looks he was getting. He didn't care what anyone was saying about him. This, right here, was all that mattered to Cego. This was who he was.

"Spirits be asked, we need to stay together," Brynn said. "There are too many forces out there trying to pull everyone apart. Not us. Not after what's been given."

"Not us," Cego whispered back.

The group broke from the huddle, and Dozer began munching a crisp fruit he produced from his pocket.

"Oh, right," Dozer said. "I forgot what I was going to tell you all."

"What?" Cego asked.

"That." Dozer pointed up toward the large challenge lightboard overhead.

Cego scanned the board and found the Whelps' team name, highlighted in an azure glow.

"We got an intraclass challenge, just came in," Dozer said. "The Level Sixers are coming after us. Novor's team."

CHAPTER 13

Our Truth

The path to vice is when the immediate pleasure of a lord occupies him: food and drink, courtesans and jesters. This is precisely why a lord must focus his attention not on himself, but on his subjects. A true ruler must devote his life to learning how to improve the lives of those around him.

Passage Twelve, The Lost Precepts

Cego began to find a rhythm at the Lyceum; his hard training melded with classes and after-studies. He enjoyed the familiar feeling of being worn down, so tired that when his head hit the cot, he fell into a dreamless sleep.

It was when he dreamed that he saw their faces. Not only Murray-Ku and Joba but Thaloo and the many other nameless faces that the Strangler had visited over the past year. They called out to Cego, asking him what they'd done to deserve such a fate by his hand.

Sometimes, Cego opted to stay awake instead of facing the nightmares. He spent entire nights upstairs in the empty training room on level two, jabbing at the frayed heavy bags until the sun crested Kalabasas Hill and cast soft autumn light on the worn tatamis.

What kept Cego from despair was working alongside his team again. After the long separation from the Whelps, he was amazed to see how much they'd improved.

Cego yawned as he stood across from Abel in the training ring, eyeing the agile boy as he bobbed and weaved. Same as every day this month, each member of the team fought consecutive rounds until they couldn't stand anymore. Though they weren't going for the kill in sparring, the team trained hard in preparation for the mid-semester challenge against the Level Sixers.

Abel had said he wasn't angry anymore, but he'd certainly gotten meaner in his fighting style, and it suited him. Abel had always been fast, but he used to pull his punches, as if he was worried about causing damage to his opponent. Now, though, the boy certainly wasn't holding back.

Cego rubbed his jaw where Abel had caught him with a sharp jab.

"Maybe you need more sleep?" Abel smiled. The little Desovian had watched Cego in the darkness, treading from the dorm to the empty training room each night.

"Getting enough." Cego breathed heavily after having already fought Dozer and Knees today.

Dozer was no longer simply a brute in the Circle. Cego saw Murray's work at hand there: The big kid's takedowns had a new finesse to them; he'd gained the uncanny ability to chain the techniques together.

And Knees had developed a brutal offensive game. Even in positions that normally weren't considered for traditional attacks, Knees was able to do damage. Though the Venturian took many risks, he never stopped moving forward and threatening his opponent.

"We will see!" Abel came at Cego again, rapidly jumping in and firing a series of jabs that Cego barely evaded. Luckily, Cego knew Abel's patterns. He bobbed his head out of the way and threw out an open-handed counter that caught the little fighter on the side of the head.

Abel's neck jerked to the side. He turned back to Cego and touched a hand to his mouth.

"Sorry!" Cego said. He knew they needed to train hard for the upcoming match, but he didn't want his teammates to sustain any injuries.

"It okay." Abel smiled with blood between his teeth. "Woke me up a bit."

Abel shot in for a low single and Cego sprawled, wrapping his arm around the boy's neck. He weighed Abel down to his knees before dropping to his side and walking his legs back toward his friend. Cego tightened the anaconda choke until Abel tapped in submission.

"Good, Cego," Abel said as they both sat panting. They turned to watch Brynn and Sol finish their match in the next training Circle over.

Brynn reminded Cego of one of his old training partners in Murray's barracks—Masa. She shared not only the Jadean heritage but also Masa's uncanny ability to entirely negate the effects of the Circle alloys. Whether she was training in rage-inducing rubellium or showy emeralyis, Brynn stuck to a consummate game plan and did not stray.

Unfortunately for the Jadean, she was up against Solara Halberd. After what had happened to Sol over the past year, she'd fast become one of the top fighters in the entire school. Though she'd always had near-perfect technique, Cego noticed Sol had added a ferocity to her movement.

Though neither girl seemed to be affected by the low-level auralite training Circle, Brynn was getting frustrated with her inability to get in range on Sol, who was peppering her with leg kicks to keep her on the outside. The Jadean finally took a risk and threw a leaping cross, only to get countered with a square knee that left her gasping for breath on the canvas.

"Nice work there, Firebird." Brynn smiled through clenched teeth.

"You okay?" Sol asked, extending her hand to help the Jadean up.

"Spirits be praised, my ribs seem intact." Brynn grimaced as she took a seat on the tatami.

"Good work, Sol," Cego said. "That counter knee will put anyone in their place that moves in too fast."

"Not Kōri Shimo, it won't," Sol said. Cego had only heard the story of the fight in Venturi, but from the way Knees and Dozer described Sol after she'd fallen, the girl was on a mission to figure out how to beat Shimo.

Cego understood how Sol felt. Since he'd started fighting, there had always been one opponent who bested him with ease: Silas. Whenever Cego stepped into the Circle, no matter whom he faced, Silas was always lurking in the recesses of his mind.

"You'll catch him, Sol," Cego said. "Just like Professor Dynari said today when we were playing Bythardi. The fist is a piece and is weak when played by an inexperienced player. But when wielded by a Bythardi master, the fist is far more than a piece. It is an unstoppable force."

Sol shook her head as she sat and started to unwrap her hands. "It's just Shimo seems like he has some advantage. I can't tell what it is, but whenever I watch him fight, it's like he knows what his opponent is going to do already."

"Most say the same of you, Sol," Dozer said, munching on a strip of jerky.

"It's different..." Sol trailed off as three uniformed Citadel officials entered the training room.

High Commander Callen Albright stood at the entrance, flanked by two larger men.

"Hello, students," Albright said, pausing as if he was waiting for them to salute him.

Cego stayed put on the floor and Dozer continued to chomp at his food.

"What can we do for you, High Commander Albright?" Sol asked with her arms crossed.

The wiry man paced the training room, running his fingers along the tattered curtains on one of the windows.

"I know you don't like me," Callen said.

"Well, you be right there," Knees answered quickly.

"You're like little replicas of Pearson," Callen seethed, turning to Knees. "And I know he's the reason you don't like me. Whatever that man told you before he went, it's poison, like everything he did."

The anger bubbled up in Cego's chest, hearing this coward speak of his friend and mentor in such a way. But he didn't need to be angry. He could see Dozer and Knees both staring at Callen with violent intent. Nothing could happen there, not if they wished to be Lyceum students when they rose the next morning.

"Murray-Ku was our coach," Cego said. "It is in the Codes that we should respect our teachers, like a father or mother."

"Yes, yes," Callen said. "And of course, we all must still obey the Codes, as much as we hear of them being tossed to the trash heap around the world. They are the glue that holds our society together. Do you know this?"

"Yes," Sol responded. "But we've already had our Codes discussion earlier today at Professor Farstead's class. If that's what you've come for, you've missed it."

Albright stared Sol down. "This little crew here, the Whelps, has gotten quite a reputation of late. Not only within the Lyceum, but word has spread to the Ezonian citizenry on the outside."

Dozer puffed his chest out in pride. " 'Bout time."

Callen continued. "Don't think I condone any of what you have done for…extracurricular activities. You should know I see you all as a weakness. And most often, I'd take the straight path and obliterate any weakness in our administration that I discover."

"But you be coming all the way down from the commanders' quarters to see us," Knees noted. "If you wanted to kick our asses to the streets, I'm guessing that'd be done through one of your runners."

"True," Callen said. "When a weakness cannot be removed outright, it should be leveraged. Has Professor Dynari not taught you that in Stratagems and Maneuvers yet?"

"What do you want from us?" Cego asked.

Callen Albright looked out the tall window, beyond the Citadel's walls. "Apparently, you've gained some admirers on the outside for things that have happened over the past year. And these are not the sort of admirers we want associated with this school."

"Flux supporters?" Brynn asked.

Callen put a finger to his mouth and glared at the Jadean. "We don't use that word within these walls."

"What word, *Flux*?" Dozer said. "Sounds like a fine word to me."

"Did you insolent kids not hear what I said at the Dome about maintaining your status here as students?" Callen growled.

"We did hear that," Knees said. "But like I said, you be wanting something from us. So, I don't think you'll be kicking us out anytime soon."

Callen glared at the crew, his face reddening. "Don't think that I won't hesitate to put you out like the scrappy lacklight dogs you are. Not only to the streets, but one word and I'll have you in the hands of the Enforcers."

Brynn stepped in front of Knees as the Venturian clenched his fists. Cego caught one of Callen's guards shifting weight onto the balls of his feet.

Callen straightened his collar and turned toward Cego. "I trust you did not have a pleasant time while in the care of the clerics at Arklight. You wouldn't want to end up back there, now, would you?"

In the back of Cego's mind, he'd wondered why those who had imprisoned him hadn't shown up again the second he set foot back in the Citadel. Every day, he'd half expected to be dragged from class in chains.

"Ah, I can see your mind moving now." Callen chuckled. "You thought Governance had simply forgotten about you? That you would saunter back to the Lyceum from your escapade in Kiroth, and all would be as you remembered?"

"I came back because I wanted to," Cego said. "I came back to bury Murray-Ku."

"How noble." Callen smirked. "And how naïve. But like that Grievar in the ground you speak of, you don't seem to see beyond your own nose. You have been allowed to be here for a single reason: I plan on being proactive in destroying this little rebellion they call the Flux."

Red lightning flashed in Cego's eyes. He was there on the storm-swept island, some gravity pulling him forward with violent intent.

The two Knights at Callen's side wouldn't be able to get to him in time; he was only a meter away. It would only take one second. After Cego disposed of the high commander, he could deal with the guards.

Cego felt a hand on his shoulder. He turned and met Sol's eyes, heard her unspoken words.

What are you thinking?

Making an attempt on the high commander's life would mean death to all of his friends. Everyone he cared about that remained in this world.

"You are going to help me destroy the Flux." Callen's voice broke Cego's violent reverie.

"Thought you said there's no such thing as the Flux," Dozer said.

Callen sneered. "We must adapt to our opponent's movements. And now it is the time to be proactive, offensive."

"Tell us what you want," Cego breathed out, tired of listening to Callen. He sympathized with Murray-Ku for having to serve beneath such a man.

"You will do what you were meant to do," Callen said. "Fight. Fight not for yourselves but for everyone else. Your next challenge matches will be integral."

"Just fight?" Cego asked.

"Of course, I don't expect much more from lacklights," Callen said. "But there will be extra feeds at the challenges broadcast to the whole of Ezo to watch on SystemView. And alongside these feeds, we will have your faces and your words so that our nation might know the truth of the Flux."

"What truth are you speaking of?" Brynn asked. "One second, you're telling us to ignore the rebellion completely, and now you want us to speak of it?"

"You will tell our truth," Callen answered. "You will reveal to the world the time you spent with the Flux. Working as spies for the Citadel, purposely planted in the midst of their operation. You will tell the world our truth."

CHAPTER 14

Descent to Darkness

There are some opponents who will sacrifice everything to win. They will let their arms be broken, their kneecaps shattered, their skulls fractured, their bodies bludgeoned, to keep coming forward. For this sort of opponent, one should devote all effort to seeking the neck. A well-placed strangle does not pay heed to persistence or resilience.

Passage Two, Nineteenth Technique of
the Combat Codes

Cego awoke in a cold sweat.

He'd been on the island again, that place that blurred his memories and nightmares. He honestly wasn't sure what the difference was at this point.

It wasn't his clammy hands or the groan of Dozer's snoring that had woken him, though.

There was a glow in the corner of Quarter D, over by Sol's section. Cego could see a shimmering light cast on his friend's neatly stacked books. He crept out of bed and peered around the edge of Sol's cot—she was sleeping soundly.

There, tucked in the corner, was a spectral.

The little wisp rose to the air, as if Cego had caught it snooping through Sol's gear. It hovered in front of his face. This was not just any spectral.

He knew it, as much as he'd recognize any of his other friends in this room. He'd spent months in the Underground staring at this very wisp. It imparted a distinct glow, a warmth on Cego's skin that made his stomach flutter.

But why is it here? Why has it returned?

Cego had not seen this spectral for years, since the finals match against Shiar as a Level One.

As if responding to Cego, the spectral pulsed and made a direct line to the dorm's exit. It hovered in the doorway, beckoning him.

He followed the wisp down the long hall outside the dorm to the Harmony's central stairs. It spiraled down in the darkness, past the second- and first-floor classrooms, and even beyond the common ground to the levels beneath the Lyceum.

Cego knew there were floors farther down, but he'd always heard they were locked off. Professor Aon had often muttered about the catacombs, complaining he was too old to be wandering beneath the school, digging up old tomes.

The air chilled Cego's naked skin, and he wished he had had the foresight to throw his uniform on before wandering off in the night. Cobwebs caught between his toes, and he could see the trails of tree roots snaking their way through the stone cracks and following the stairs even lower.

The spectral stopped at a rusty black iron door. The wisp cast its light on a cloud of floating dust particles in front of the heavy frame, which was ajar. Cego peered at the door's broken hinges and the footprints in the dust leading into the catacombs.

Someone else had been down there, recently.

"Where are you taking me?" Cego spoke to the spectral, just as he'd done while he was imprisoned within Thaloo's compound.

The spectral pulsed in response and darted past the door. Cego followed it into a wide stone tunnel with arched entries running along either side.

As his eyes acclimated to the dim spectral light, Cego passed an old mess hall with furniture covered by frayed rugs, a knotty circular table set at its center. Beyond that, he walked by a room full of crates, with warped pots and pans hanging from stone walls. Another room was crammed with dusty bookshelves, and Cego wondered whether this was where Old Aon had come to retrieve the tomes he'd spoken of.

The spectral stopped decisively in front of one entryway before floating within and descending toward the ground, as if it were taking a rest.

A Circle was set on the floor, glimmering like wet coal.

"What's this doing here?" Cego said to the spectral, though it appeared the little wisp was dormant now, as if it had found its way home. "Why would they keep an onyx Circle in storage?"

"Because they're afraid of it," a voice responded from behind him.

Cego whirled around in the darkness, his hands up, to see Kōri Shimo.

The strange boy looked at Cego unflinchingly, as if waiting for him to do something.

"What are you doing here?" Cego asked.

"I should ask the same of you," Shimo said.

"I...I know it sounds strange, but I followed that spectral here," Cego said. "It led me here. Just like over a year ago, when it brought me to Larkspur's classroom. And you were there then as well. With this same onyx Circle."

Shimo didn't give any indication he thought it strange; he simply nodded. "And so, you are here."

"Why are you here, then?" Cego asked. "Were you also led by it?"

"Yes," Shimo said. "Just as it brought me to Larkspur's class-room when the onyx Circle was there, it brought me down to the catacombs when they moved it here."

"That's where you've been all this time?" Cego asked. It was almost a running joke that Kōri Shimo was never around unless it was time to fight. Though he was often the top-scoring kid at his level, he was always on the verge of expulsion from the Lyceum due to constant delinquency from his classes.

"Yes," Kōri said. He walked toward the onyx Circle and placed his hand against its coal frame. "I've spent my time here, within the onyx. Training."

"How?" Cego asked. "Who else knows about this place that you've been training with?"

"No one," Kōri said. "Perhaps some of the faculty, though I haven't seen them since I've come. And now you."

"Then how?" Cego asked again. "Why would you want to be down here by yourself?"

Perhaps the boy simply liked the darkness and the quiet.

"As I said, I've been training within the onyx."

"How can you train by yourself?"

"Why don't you step within and find out," Kōri Shimo said.

Cego looked at the boy suspiciously.

"You suspect me," Kōri said. "Perhaps you think that I wish to trick you. Harm you."

Cego didn't deny it. He'd seen Kōri Shimo critically injure other students, even his friends, without breaking a sweat or caring about their well-being. But there was something about Shimo that Cego couldn't put a finger on. Since he'd first seen the strange boy practicing ki-breath during the lead-up to Trials, Cego had been inexplicably drawn to him.

"Why should I trust you?" Cego asked. "What reason do I have to step in the Circle?"

"Because you want to beat your brother," Kōri said simply.

Cego stepped back. "How do you know about my brother?"

"Who doesn't know about the Slayer?" Kōri Shimo said. "He's the most famed Grievar on the planet."

This was true. There was no denying Silas's legend, and even someone living under a rock like Kōri Shimo would know him as well as his relation to Cego.

"Even so," Cego said. "How do you know I want…I want to beat him?"

"Because we are the same," Kōri Shimo said. "We come from the same place."

Cego's eyes widened. "You mean the—"

"The Cradle." Kōri Shimo nodded.

It made sense. Murray had told Cego that there were other kids that had been created in the Cradle, within the blacklight, released into this world by the Daimyo to become champions.

"How long have you known?" Cego asked.

"Always," Kōri Shimo said.

"What do you mean, always?" Cego was taken aback.

"I was told that I was created," Kōri said. "What my purpose was."

It seemed too easy. The Daimyo had told Kōri about his past as soon as he'd entered this world, but Cego had been kept in the dark, had found out the hard way.

"And you went along with it?" Cego asked incredulously. "You didn't care you were some experiment for them?"

"Why would I?" Kōri said. "I was born from the Cradle, just as Grievar-kin are born from a mother's womb. What's the difference?"

"They…they created you." Cego raised his voice. "They built you for their own purpose, to use you to fight for them!"

"And so?" Shimo said. "That is also what I want. To become the perfect fighter, the greatest champion this world has ever known."

Cego shook his head in frustration. It was as if all the anger he held about his past, the unfairness of his upbringing and how he'd been used, was no longer justified.

"Forget that," Cego said, breathing deeply. "Back to the onyx. How can it help me beat Silas?"

"You see?" Shimo said. "We are the same. And you will need to find out for yourself, as I did."

Cego didn't trust Shimo, despite the fact he'd found out the kid was nearly his kin, born in some Minder-forged simulation.

"What do I do?" Cego asked.

"Step in," Shimo said. "You will know what to do."

*   *   *

The water lapped at Cego's toes. He inhaled deeply to breathe the sea air, so thick with salt he could taste it on his tongue. The sun felt warm against his face and he watched a little white squiggle squirm across the blackness of his shut eyes.

Perhaps he'd rest there for a while. He'd been back to the island so many times over the past years, during the Trials, in his dreams and fever visions. He sought the comfort of the old home.

Cego opened his eyes, expecting to see the brilliant blue cerulean skies, the Path shimmering emerald on the ocean breakers.

But nothing was right.

The sky was black. Not like the black curtain of night, with stars pinpricking it, but a void that hung above him and lacked any substance at all. Cego forced himself to break his gaze from the great emptiness above, and his eyes fell to the vast grey ocean in front of him. The waves were eerily still, frozen at their crests, as if Cego could walk out on top of the water toward the blank horizon.

He whirled around to see more of the drab landscape: shadowed sand dunes adorned with sickly tall grass. He sprinted off the beach and up to the top of the dunes. From the new vantage he saw the ironwood forest in the distance, a horde of skeletal trees sprouting from the parched ground.

The entire world was lusterless, as if all the vivid color of the island had drained away.

Thunder murmured in the distance, and though there were no clouds in the empty sky, Cego sensed a storm was coming.

He turned to see the old master's compound gone from where it should be. Now there was only a planked walkway leading to the edge of the bluff. Someone was out there, a grey form sitting with the cloudless sky behind them.

Cego knew this was where he must go: the ironwood Circle.

He breathed, calming his mind, preparing himself as he walked toward the cliff.

Cego came to the familiar sight of the old master facing away from him within the Circle. Farmer sat cross-legged, his grey top-knot falling down his robed shoulders.

"Master, I'm home," Cego said, the words leaving his mouth involuntarily as if he were reading a script.

The man did not respond, and so Cego took a step forward within the bounds of the Circle. Like he'd set off an alarm, the old master abruptly stood, still facing away from him.

"Master, I'm home," Cego repeated.

The old man turned, and Cego recoiled. The face was not Farmer's, but it was familiar.

The Guardian's visage had been burned into Cego's mind, and now it reared again like an old wound burst open. He'd never forget the machines he'd encountered during his Trials. Like black-light itself, the creature was without form. It was as if Cego were looking at the absence of reality, a place where light and life did not exist.

The Guardian did not speak, but Cego knew what he must do. He needed to do what he was created for in this very place. Cego now understood Shimo's words, understood why the strange boy had told him to step into the onyx.

This is the only way you can beat Silas.

The Guardian was the only opponent like Silas: a force of combat without tethering to physical constraints.

Cego stepped forward, and the Guardian stood motionless, staring at him without eyes or features, only a gaping hole where a face should be.

Cego threw his best ranged weapon, a spinning side kick, one that had downed the likes of Rhodan Bertoth. The Guardian sidestepped, moving with the swiftness of sand in the wind, and grabbed Cego's leg, pressing forward to throw him off balance.

Cego had been caught there before; he had a counter. He jumped off his based foot to throw a switch kick at the creature's head while his hand was occupied. The Guardian released Cego's leg and ducked the kick before rapidly transitioning to a blinding cross.

Cego bobbed his head and countered with a low kick, which the Guardian didn't even bother to check. Cego feigned a wide haymaker to see if the beast would bring its hands high, but it simply ducked and launched a knee in response.

Cego felt the sharp bone connect with his chin and he was flat on his back, staring at the empty sky.

He expected the Guardian to let him back up, as it had during the Trials, but it was on him already, mounting him with its knees squeezing his rib cage.

Cego bucked to escape, but the pressure was too great. The Guardian had melded to Cego's body, and it reared up into a barrage of ground-and-pound.

Cego attempted to defend, turn his head away from blows, but they came too fast, as if the Guardian's hands had multiplied to come from every possible angle. Cego's nose broke as a fist slammed into it. His jaw cracked as the creature cut down with a high elbow.

Cego had seen this fight before. Long ago, when he'd fought Gryfin Thurgood, when the darkness had taken him, he remembered pounding the boy like a piece of meat until his friends had to pull him off.

Now Cego was the piece of meat, and the Guardian was softening his body, his bones, his innards into a bloody mush. With each strike, Cego felt the pain. The assault did not dull. The Guardian kept attacking even with Cego's hands lifeless at his side. The beast rained strikes into his defenseless form, and yet Cego couldn't leave. He couldn't escape to either unconsciousness or death.

Kōri Shimo had tricked him into the onyx, into this hellscape, where Cego would be tortured by the Guardian forever. The thought of it was more terrifying than the strikes that continued to bludgeon him.

Cego screamed, though no words came from his mouth.

*   *   *

The thick darkness clung to Cego.

The pain and terror engulfed him. The void stared through him.

He screamed again and put his hands to his face, expecting to feel a bloody mess. But his nose was not caved inward; his skin was not ripped apart. Cego opened his eyes and looked up to see Kōri Shimo.

"You were calling for Murray Pearson," Shimo said.

Cego trembled on the floor outside the onyx Circle, still within the dusty recesses of the room in the catacombs. He tried to inhale, expecting to feel the broken ribs, but the breath came deep and full. He touched his hands to his body, which had been maimed moments before, to find it intact.

"What…what did it do to me?" Cego fumbled for words, his heart beating rapidly.

"The Guardian beat you," Shimo said. "Within the onyx."

"Yes…but what made it stop?" Cego asked.

"It didn't," Shimo responded. "I pulled you from the Circle, again. Just as I did nearly two years ago in Larkspur's classroom."

"Why did you send me in there?" Cego asked as he wiped the

sweat from his face. "That creature...it won't help me fight Silas. There's no way to do anything against it."

"How long do you think you fought this time against the Guardian within the onyx?" Shimo asked.

"Far too long." Cego tried again to take a deep breath. "And most of the time, the thing beat me bloody. An hour?"

"I watched you walk into the Circle, sit down, and close your eyes. Five seconds later, you were screaming Murray's name and I dragged you out," Shimo said.

"It can't be," Cego said. "So, that's how you..."

It's how Shimo had gotten so good. He was getting hours, days, weeks of practice while spending minutes at a time within the onyx.

Onyx compresses time. Cego could hear the voice of his Level One Circles professor, Adrienne Larkspur.

"If this is possible, why aren't all the students doing it? Why aren't all Knights practicing in onyx?"

Cego finally managed to lift himself off the floor.

"I asked the same thing when I first stepped into onyx," Kōri Shimo explained. "It was in Professor Larkspur's class alongside you that I first realized the possibilities the element possessed. I discovered something was special about me, about my upbringing in the Cradle, within the blacklight, that lets me use it, create a training environment of it. Most who step within it are barraged with random memories and images. They can't control their experience. Most go insane."

"And...you assumed I would be able to do the same? That I wouldn't go insane?" Cego asked.

"Yes," Kōri Shimo said.

Cego wasn't yet convinced Shimo would even care if he went insane, or about what happened to him at all. And yet the strange boy had pulled him from the Circle, saved him from more of the Guardian's torture.

"But even so," Cego said. "Even if we can train in here and get years more experience in days, we won't be able to ever beat the Guardian. It's part of the simulation, like the ocean, or the sand dunes."

"You are correct that the Guardian cannot be beaten," Shimo said. "But that does not make the training any less valuable."

"You mean to say…" Cego tried to take a deep breath. "That every time you step into the onyx, the Guardian beats you like it did to me today? It tortures you, makes you go through that every time?"

"Yes," Shimo said, the boy's eyes sharp. "We must sacrifice to gain. Each time I go in, I last longer. I become stronger. And I haven't had anyone to pull me out, away from the Guardian's terror."

Cego could not imagine going through that torture a single time again, let alone regularly, no matter what he gained from it.

"You hesitate," Shimo said. "I understand. It's not pleasant, going through that. But do you want to beat Silas?"

Cego felt the pit in his stomach, the emptiness that had filled him since Murray had been taken from him by his brother.

Murray would have done anything for him. If Murray could have gone into this death simulation a thousand times to save Cego, he would have. And now Cego had that chance. He stood with a solution in front of him to become far stronger. Perhaps good enough to beat Silas, to avenge Murray's death. And he was scared for himself? Afraid of the pain he'd have to face?

Cego gritted his teeth. He stepped back toward the onyx Circle, the tendrils of darkness reaching to him.

The world shifted as he sat down on the cold stone floor within the ring. The black sky and frozen sea replaced the dusty catacombs.

"Yes," Cego said as he returned home again. "I want to kill Silas."

CHAPTER 15

A Path to Freedom

There are only so many waking hours that a Grievar can hone their techniques before fatigue sets in. But the mind is far more resilient than the body. An adept Grievar understands that even when the body fails, the mind can be harnessed to continue training indefinitely.

Passage Two, Seventy-Seventh Precept of
the Combat Codes

Commander Memnon clenched his fist against the glass table. If it could even be called a table. Feeds came to life and floated across the circular lightboard in front of him as Callen continued to drone on.

"We'll display the feeds on all boards across the Lyceum, before and after the matches, and of course during any SystemView broadcasts held in the common grounds."

"But what of while our students are in their quarters?" Commander Adrienne Larkspur spoke up, tossing her long hair to the side. "Shouldn't we ensure their personal lightdecks also broadcast to keep the message going?"

Callen nodded to Larkspur. "A fantastic recommendation, Commander Larkspur—"

"She's darkin' messing with you," Commander Dakar Pugilio said, his feet set up on the glass table. "Commander Larkspur cares as little about this as the rest of us."

Callen growled at Dakar. "Show some respect, drunkard. The only reason you're still employed by the Citadel is because Memnon has stood behind you. And I don't think your thick skull comprehends how important these feeds are to keep morale high."

Dakar laughed and slapped the table, shaking it and activating the audio to one of the feeds. It was the red-haired Level Three, daughter of Artemis Halberd, speaking directly into the screen.

"The Flux rebellion was driven by greed," the girl said. "Silas the Slayer's greed. He wants power and wealth. He was collecting a bit-tax from the Grunt and Grievar alike when we were there, worse than what the empire had been taking. And they made all—"

Memnon swiped his hand against the table to silence the girl and looked up at Callen.

"Do you think this will work, High Commander?" Memnon asked. He was wary of such political games.

To illustrate his point, Memnon swiped another feed on the table, this time of a large Level Three boy with a square head. Dozer, they called him.

"Then, the Flux made us remove all our tattoos," the boy said. "Everything I worked for, wiped out because Silas wanted control of us."

Memnon muted the feed and looked to Callen. "They're kids still. Why would the citizenry believe them?"

"The citizenry is not as smart as you might imagine," Callen said. "And though they are kids, the word has already spread that they served the Flux, fought for Silas. The seeds have been planted, and so we must cultivate those fruits we'd like to grow. This messaging will play in the Lyceum's central halls and common grounds, during the upcoming challenge matches, across System-View for Ezo's citizens to see."

"You mean darkin' lie to them, as you're accustomed to doing," Dakar slurred. "That's how you've made it so far, anyway. You've never eaten the dirt because of your lies, so I suppose it makes sense why you think they will always work for you."

Callen crossed his hands on the table. "I believe that we have a purpose here, Commander Pugilio. And that is to keep the wheels of Governance turning. To keep the Lyceum in order, keep our students training to become Knights. To maintain our forces in top shape, ready to defend the nation against rivals. And to do this, we must control the narrative of the Flux. If they continue to grow and move for Ezo, our greatest weakness will be our own citizenry becoming infatuated and joining their ranks. So, I'd like to seal that wound before it festers."

Callen turned to Memnon and met his eyes. "Don't you agree with this strategy, Commander?"

Memnon sighed. When he'd heard that Governance wanted to promote Callen to high commander, he'd never complained. In fact, he was happy to have the burden off his shoulders. Playing politik was not something he enjoyed. But he knew Callen's position would come with a price. The man was beholden to the Daimyo Governance, without any loyalty to his own kin.

"I do think it is wise to dampen panic within our ranks," Memnon said measuredly. "We've already lost Knights to the Flux, and I agree we need to do something to stem future defections."

"I agree as well," Larkspur said. "I already hear enough talk in the Lyceum's halls of what's happening afar, and the legend of Silas the Slayer grows each time it's told."

"You see?" Callen smirked at Dakar. "Your fellow commanders seem able to—"

"But," Memnon interjected, "I also do not believe it is wise to broadcast things that are not true. Do not forget, we have international students, travelers with families in Kiroth. They certainly are getting word from abroad and can relay that to their peers. If you leave the truth to the shadows, what reason will the citizenry have to believe you in the future?"

"I do not think you understand," Callen said. "We have direct orders from Governance to push these feeds throughout the Citadel and beyond to the entirety of our nation. Are you suggesting disobedience?"

"No," Memnon said. "I'm simply saying, having led the Citadel for so long, I learned that there is often a middle path, a balance between Governance's goals and that which we must do to execute them."

"And where did that style of leadership get you, Memnon?" Callen sneered. "Why do you think the Daimyo put me in your place?"

"So you could darkin' kiss their ass even more than you used to?" Dakar snorted.

Callen ignored the commander of PublicJustice. "They installed me as high commander so that I could follow orders, something that you all have a problem doing. It's as if the disease that Pearson had, his inability to ever follow simple instructions, has seeped into all of your brains."

"You little rat-darked piece of—" Pugilio's mustache twitched as he stood, but he was cut short as a light flared from the shadows on the far side of the command room.

A glistening steel Enforcer stepped forward, its pulse cannon humming with charge. The pilot within the mech stared out at Dakar with black eyes.

"I would sit down if I were you, Pugilio." Callen smiled through his teeth. "As I've told you before, Governance is listening, and I don't think they take kindly to you talking down to me or their plans."

Dakar turned to face the Enforcer, his face still red. Memnon could see the man's hands clench. He certainly wouldn't put it past his old friend to charge the mech.

"Dakar." Memnon stood and placed his hand on his friend's shoulder. "This is not the way. We need to work together, now more than ever."

Pugilio slowly turned away from the Enforcer and slunk back into his seat, his chest still heaving.

"Good, now," Callen said. "So, if we're all in accordance, we will continue with our plan. Of course, I understand your rigidness in the many things changing around here, given the way things were previously run. But again, that's why I'm here. Adaptation, my fellow commanders, is the key to survival. And we will do more than survive. We will thrive."

You mean you will thrive. Memnon knew Callen had only ever sought to lift himself up.

"I should tell you," Callen said. "There is another operation currently ongoing, working alongside our Daimyo counterparts. The goal is the same, though, to diminish any power these Flux rebels might possess."

"What is it?" Memnon sighed.

"Unfortunately, I cannot divulge exactly what it is until I get more information," Callen said. "But when you are ready to know, you will know."

Memnon nodded, giving the petty man the satisfaction of keeping his secrets, holding his newfound power over their heads.

"So, as is my new custom, let us recite our most important Code." Callen looked around the table and spoke the words. "We fight so the rest shall not have to."

Memnon knew if he didn't respond, Larkspur and Pugilio would also hold their tongues. Though Callen was high commander now, Memnon still had the loyalty of the Citadel.

This wasn't the way Memnon ever wanted to speak the Codes, forced to the words by a pitiful man like Callen Albright. But he heard the hum of the Enforcer's cannon behind him, and he knew what he had to do.

"We fight so the rest shall not have to," Memnon said hollowly as he met Larkspur's and Pugilio's eyes. He nodded and they followed.

"We fight so the rest shall not have to."

Callen Albright smiled.

* * *

"I wish the sky would be blue sometimes," Brynn said, walking beside Sol and staring up at the clouds. "On the Jade, it wasn't often we'd have such grey."

"I remember those island skies," Sol said as they crossed over a small bridge on the outskirts of the Citadel. "Though some of those storms were fierce."

"Not to be trifled with, island storms," Brynn agreed, sniffing and wiping her nose as her breath fogged in the chill winter air.

The two Whelps followed a worn path off the Citadel grounds along the perimeter of Kalabasas Hill. They watched a group of Level Twos traverse the hills, huffing and red-cheeked as they tried to joust for the front spot.

"Glad we're not running today," Brynn noted. "Though I bet you don't feel the same from the way I saw you run last week. You almost beat Damyn Zular."

"Yes." Sol nodded. "I had some practice hill-running on the Emerald with N'auri. Now, that girl can run."

"I could tell." Brynn smiled. "Long, fit legs like those…typical of Emeraldis. Spirits be asked, I hope she's doing all right. N'auri doesn't belong there with the Slayer."

"She can hold her own," Sol said. "N'auri is tough as a cornered tusker."

"I know that." Brynn sighed. "When we were in the sewers in Karstock on mission, you should've seen her go after that Enforcer. Jumped atop its giant head, laid into it, and didn't let up until it was down."

"I can see it now." Sol grinned.

"It's her mind I'm worried about," Brynn said. "The stuff Silas is putting in all their heads, it's poison. And scary thing is, I even started to believe it while we were out there."

"Silas has a way about him," Sol said. "You can't help but listen, think he's right with his cause. N'auri will come around. She has her own reasons she's with the Flux."

"Her mafé," Brynn said. "N'auri told me about her, how the Daimyo used her and broke her. How they dishonored her memory."

"It's tragic," Sol said as she kicked at a rock on the dirt path. "And most Grievar-kin have such stories, pain at the hands of the Daimyo. But still…Silas's way, it isn't right either. He can't say it's okay to wipe out the entire breed. They aren't all bad."

Sol's secret sat heavy in her gut as they walked: the truth of her own Daimyo blood that she'd revealed to Murray on that night sitting outside Hanrin's farmstead.

"You're right," Brynn said. "There is good and evil in all of us."

Sol felt relieved that her Jadean friend wasn't so quick to hate all Daimyo. A stray beam of sunlight pierced the pines on the path in front of the girls.

"Cego." Brynn changed the subject, perhaps sensing Sol's discomfort. "He's distant lately. I didn't know him for too long before he was taken to Arklight, but something's off. And he never seems to be around anymore."

"I know," Sol said. "He's always been a bit distant, likes to keep to himself because of what's happened. But lately, it's gotten worse. Like he's gone somewhere else completely."

"You care for him, don't you?" Brynn asked, stopping ahead of Sol and turning to her.

"Well, yeah…" Sol trailed off. "Of course I do. We've been through a lot together and he's the best training partner I've got; no offense."

"I understand," Brynn said. "But it's more than that. You…care for him."

Sol's cheeks flushed and she looked down to the ground. "I… When he was gone, I felt an emptiness that I couldn't get rid of. And now that he's back, even though everything else has gone wrong and the world seems to be falling apart, the emptiness is gone too."

Brynn smiled, having gotten what she'd wanted. She turned and began walking again.

"Well, how about N'auri and you?" Sol said, feeling exposed and reaching for a counter.

"What about N'auri and me?" Brynn laughed. "She's a world away right now, fighting for the rebellion. But still, I can't help but think a few times a day about the legs on that girl."

Sol chuckled as they turned onto an overgrown path, pushing aside brambles and foot snares until they came to a run-down shack with splintered wood walls. They rounded to the back of the structure and were greeted with a chorus of loud squawks.

Firenze was the first to the edge of the fence, the massive crimson bird arching his neck over the wire to nuzzle Sol's outstretched hand. "There we are, boy," Sol said soothingly. "We weren't gone too long, were we?"

After they'd made the long trip back across the Kirothian border to the Citadel, the entire crew had worried that they would need to sell their rocs back to the black market. The nation had decreed decades before that roc-riding was not beneficial to training Knights. *An unnecessary distraction* were the exact words from Governance, and so, there certainly would be no reason to have a flock of birds at the Lyceum.

Luckily, Professor Larkspur had directed the Whelps to the abandoned pen set nearby the hill. She'd said that rocs used to be cared for there, but it had gone into disrepair after the decree.

Brynn's roc came up beside Firenze, the jet-black bird squawking loudly at the sight of her rider. The bird carried a tattered carcass in its beak, what used to be some woodland creature, and dropped it at Brynn's foot.

"What a nice gift, Akari." Brynn smiled and attempted to hide her disgust. "For me?"

Sol chuckled. "Looks like she's been doing some good hunting."

Though the birds could easily jump the wire fence, and often did to hunt in the pine forest, they'd always returned to the pen.

"I'm glad she comes back," Brynn said. "I think there are still some wild rocs that live in the deeper forest."

"I learned about rocs when I was in Lord Cantino's stable," Sol said. "Once they serve someone as a mount, it's difficult for them to go back to the wilds. Not only will a wild flock smell it on them, but they always feel the need to serve again. It's how they've been bred."

Sol slung the pack off her back and removed a large translucent bag of meat. The food wasn't live and wriggling like the birds preferred, but it was sustenance. She threw a piece to the air and Firenze gulped it down with an open beak.

"But Firenze used to be the bird of the Daimyo lord," Brynn said. "Was it easy for him to change his master, to let you ride?"

"He wasn't treated well there," Sol said, thinking about how the Daimyo had used their electrified rods to goad the birds. "But even so, I could sometimes sense that he did miss the man, as terrible as he was."

"I understand," Brynn said as she fed some of the meat to her bird. The plump brown roc, Boko, arrived at the fence and nipped his beak in the air for a share of the food. But Bird, Murray's old mount, stayed at the back of the fenced area, picking at the few feathers left on his body.

"He's been picking those feathers since we arrived," Sol said, eyeing Bird. "I'm worried he won't survive much longer."

"As you say, he misses his master," Brynn said. "And though Ku pretended he didn't like Bird, we know he had a soft spot for him. We'll see if he can recover, spirits be asked."

The girls continued to feed, water, and groom the birds. A storm had begun to roll in, casting even more clouds above and stealing the remaining sunlight from the thick forest.

"Do you think…" Sol wondered, "…we're like the birds? That even though we think we're free, we're secretly hoping to serve some Daimyo master?"

"You're thinking of the Slayer again, aren't you?" asked Brynn.

"Yes," Sol said. "And Wraith and N'auri and all the Flux. Their cause. I can't help but wonder: Are they right? Trying to fight against the Daimyo rule so that Grievar can be free?"

Brynn sighed. "Set some of these rocs free, out in the deep woods, and they'll survive. They'll adapt to the new life, maybe find some wild birds to run with. But others, like Bird over there, he'll be dead in a week."

"How do we know which sort we are unless we try?" Sol said. "How do we know if we'll survive or not unless we stop being pawns first?"

"We're all pawns in some way or another," Brynn said. "Plus, you're talking here about a rebellion led by Silas the Slayer. Sol, the man killed Ku."

Sol tossed another strip of meat to Firenze. "There must be another way."

"I don't think so," Brynn said. "Spirits be said, great change always requires sacrifice. It's a question of whether you're willing to turn your back to the innocents caught in the middle."

"How about Murray-Ku?" Sol said. "He sacrificed himself for Cego. For us. Wasn't that worth anything, even though he wasn't fighting for some great cause?"

Brynn turned to Sol. "Don't you see? Ku was fighting for a cause. That man had been fighting some demon inside himself, long as I knew him at least. I think that's all any of us can do. Fight those demons within. And in the end, I'd like to think Ku won."

Sol looked to the air as the snowflakes began to flutter from the sky. "I hope so."

CHAPTER 16

Alone Together

When practicing new techniques, there should be no expectations, no thoughts of the future. The mind and body simply need repetition, present practice without tethering to any concept.

Passage Eight, Twenty-Ninth Precept of the Combat Codes

Cego stood across the Circle from Novor Malynski.

He could remember when he'd first come to the Lyceum, how Level Six students had seemed like gods; fully grown Grievar, having spent a near decade training at the best combat school in the nation, on the verge of testing for their Knighthood. The Whelps had gawked at the red second skins in the halls, clung to every word and technique a Level Sixer might offer.

But now, staring across the Circle at Novor, Cego simply saw another opponent. Another Grievar with vulnerabilities to expose, another body with bones to break and arteries to constrict.

They stood in auralite, yet Cego didn't feel the crowd pull bestowed by the swirling blue spectrals. The audience was bigger than he'd ever seen before for a challenge match. Cego had waited on the sidelines with his team and watched the seating section swell with the entire student body and faculty.

As Callen Albright had ordered, the feeds had run the team's prerecorded messages denouncing the Flux. Cego had cringed watching himself up there, telling lies to support Governance propaganda.

Though he hated Silas for everything he'd done, Cego didn't care about destroying the Flux. He didn't support the rebellion or the established system. He wanted to be left alone, no longer used by one side or the other. He wanted to be with his friends, the only true family he had in this world.

Cego quickly glanced to his side, seeing Sol square off against a lanky Desovian transfer student named Marok Timit. He hoped Sol would be able to fend him off. Though he knew she was more than able to hold her own, Cego felt worry blossoming in him, a need to protect Solara Halberd.

To his other side, Knees was matched with a thick Myrkonian, one of the Northmen from the previous year that had decided to stay and test for Knighthood. Knees nodded at Cego from across the grounds. He saw the boy he'd known for so long, the scarred kid who had run sloth carries with him in the slave yards.

Here, they were up against the best in the Lyceum. Cego couldn't help but feel pride for his friends, Dozer and Abel and Brynn up on the sidelines, shouting in support.

Novor pounded his chest and snarled across the ring at Cego. "Don't think I believe that shit they showed up on the feeds. I know who you are, and I'll make you pay for that."

Cego stared back at the red-clad Grievar. He had no idea who Cego was.

Crimson lightning flashed behind his opponent. Cego blinked and saw black skies and frozen waters. Thunder tremored above, and he tasted a strange, sulfurous air on his tongue.

He stood in the familiar desolate landscape that he went to

every time he stepped within the onyx in the catacombs, a place that had become as much a home to him over the past month as the Lyceum.

He still saw Novor in front of him in the Circle, and yet he also saw the Guardian. The void of the creature's face bled tendrils of blacklight that pulled Cego toward it as the sounding bell rang out.

Cego shook his head, trying to dispel the illusion and bring himself back to the challenge grounds.

"Not now," he murmured.

He knew what would happen if he let the darkness take him, if he let himself escape to that place. Cego breathed deeply and planted his feet against the soft canvas. He let the bluelight seep into his skin and embraced the crowd's cheers.

Novor stopped a moment, puzzled at Cego's strange behavior, but the lull did not last.

The Level Sixer spun into a long-range side kick. Cego angled his body to avoid the attack and raised his hands to block the switch kick that followed. He countered with a swift foot sweep that put Novor's back on the canvas.

Novor popped up and growled as he advanced again. He feigned a high jab and shot low for the leg, but Cego was ready with a sprawl and a counter knee that sent Novor stumbling backward.

The red-clad fighter didn't let up; he launched a succession of strikes that Cego bobbed and weaved around. Cego ducked a roundhouse and sprang forward for an inside trip, catching Novor off guard and bringing him back to the ground.

The Level Sixer was skilled, though; he caught Cego's elbow on the way down, threatening to expose his back. Cego quickly disengaged to avoid the trap, and Novor again returned to his feet.

Still, the Grievar didn't give Cego a moment to recover. Novor closed the distance and threw a low kick to the calf and a stinging right hand down the middle. Cego turned his chin with the punch, negating the impact, but Novor's fist mashed his lip into his teeth.

"Go back to where you came from, traitor," Novor spat. "We don't want you here."

Go back to where you came from.

Cego blinked and it was the Guardian in front of him again, the darkness of the island its backdrop. Crimson lightning flashed across the sky, and the black sand beach shuddered with the thunder.

Cego tasted the blood in his mouth and he snarled, launching himself at the Guardian.

He knew he had to go on the offensive or the creature would destroy him. It always did.

He threw a volley of strikes, expecting the Guardian to parry all of them easily, but to his surprise, a cross broke through its defenses and blasted the beast in the face.

He blinked again and it was Novor on the canvas, blood streaming from his broken nose.

Cego's lips curled into a smile.

Was this the best the Lyceum had to offer? A Level Sixer, nearly ready to enter the premier fighting force in the world, moving so sluggishly? Cego felt a sudden contempt for his opponent.

He waved his hand dismissively to let Novor stand, who did so on shaky knees. Words came from Cego's mouth like bile. "You don't deserve to be here. You don't belong in this Circle with me."

Novor's face flushed red like his second skin.

This time, the Level Sixer advanced with deliberate aggression, circling Cego and peppering him with long-range punches and kicks. Novor had the reach advantage and rightfully sought to utilize it.

But Novor's lanky limbs didn't matter. Nor did the technique he'd spent his life honing. Cego watched his opponent move listlessly, as if Novor were pushing through some viscosity in the air with each strike. Every feint, hip twist, shuffle step, or counter, Cego saw before it came.

He played with Novor, letting him tire with his ceaseless attack. Even though Cego had ample opportunity to counter, he didn't take it. He wanted to humiliate Novor, show the crowd that he didn't belong in this Circle with Cego.

Novor breathed heavily as he moved in at Cego again, trying to corner him with sluggish jabs.

Cego smiled as he watched Novor's frustration slowly turn to fear. The Grievar finally saw how hopeless his efforts were. He'd realized he was the prey, the rodent ready to be ripped apart by the circling raptor.

Cego savored the fear. He let it fuel him.

Not only would he finish Novor with one shot, he'd finish him for good. He'd show the crowd what real power looked like, how death could be dealt by his hand.

Novor closed the distance again, not comprehending he was moving toward his demise.

Cego weaved his head away from a cross and quick-stepped in. He shot his hand out and caught the Level Sixer by the throat. He met Novor's eyes as he lifted his leg in a high arc and brought it back the other way to sweep his opponent to the ground.

Osoto gari.

Cego kept his clenched grip on the stunned boy's throat, pressing him to the canvas. He slid his knee onto Novor's belly and raised his free hand to finish the job.

Cego saw the void of the Guardian's face staring up at him, empty and mocking. After getting torn apart by the apparition so many times, he could finally find his revenge.

Maintaining his grasp on the creature's throat, Cego slammed a strike through its face. He struck it again and felt the satisfying crunch beneath his fist. He followed with a cutting elbow and heard the creature moan. He reared up for another blow.

Cego caught a flash of movement from the corner of his eye: Sol in the Circle beside him, matching her opponent strike for strike, dancing in and out of range. Her long braid whipped around with her movements, a fluid whirlwind of violence and beauty all at once.

Cego looked down and saw Novor beneath him again. The Level Sixer's face was a mask of blood.

Cego's fist trembled; he wanted to bring it down again. The darkness pressed up against him like flames on a sealed door, but Cego stayed his hand. He couldn't let Sol see him like this again, like years before when she'd stared down at him in shock after he'd nearly killed Gryfin Thurgood.

Cego couldn't let Murray's death be for nothing. He'd be no different from Silas if he let the energy control him, if he let the darkness take him.

He breathed deeply, exhaled, and the blacklight fled, returned to that desolate void that Cego knew was both outside and within.

A deep weariness replaced the energy. Cego suddenly carried the last month, decades of training compressed within the onyx. He felt the weight of Murray's and Joba's deaths, the burden of the lives the Strangler had taken.

Novor recognized the change in Cego, his slumped posture. The Level Sixer switched his hips, pushed Cego off him, and returned to his feet.

"Should have taken your chance while you had it." Novor wiped the blood from his face and charged.

Cego caught an incoming kick, fired a return cross to Novor's chest, blocked a hook.

He stuffed a takedown as Novor tried to shoot low, and fired a counter knee that lacked any power. Novor was the one to smile now, sensing something was wrong, smelling blood. The Level Sixer came forward with a series of jabs; Cego dodged two but caught the third on the nose.

Novor stayed on him and finally hit the takedown he'd been looking for. Cego tried to sprawl, but the boy drove forward and planted him firmly against the canvas.

Cego's head snapped back as Novor's fist rattled it.

Though Cego knew he should move, though he sensed the stomp coming for his skull, he did nothing. He was too weary, the energy entirely fled from his body.

Novor's foot blasted through and the lights went out.

*   *   *

"I don't want to," Sam complained, kicking a seashell lodged in the surf.

"You need to, Sam," Cego told his little brother. He dusted some of the black sand off the boy's mop of hair as they walked along the shore. "Farmer will be cross if you don't, not to mention Silas."

"But…" A little pout crossed Sam's freckled face, stretching the gash on his lip. "He already beat me up yesterday. There's nothing I can do against him."

Cego sighed as he looked out at the cerulean waters beside them, the Path shimmering to the distant horizon. "I understand."

Their little dog, Arry, appeared at Sam's side, licking the boy's sun-kissed feet.

"You're better than me, though," Sam said as he knelt to pat Arry. "You don't understand. You don't know what it's like… to always be losing to you two."

His little brother had a good point. Since they'd begun their training on the island under Farmer's tutelage, things had always been the same. Silas was the strongest, a near replica of the old master's flawless technique. Not to mention the eldest brother had a penchant for violence; Cego could see it in Silas's grin when he scored a painful strike on one of them.

Cego had always been close to Silas's skill but could never quite catch him. He had the technique, he could see his brother's movements as they came, and yet he was powerless to stop them.

And Sam had always been the weakest. It's not that his little brother didn't try—the boy was as tenacious as they came, and he could fight with the ferocity of a cornered mongoose, but he simply was too weak, too slow, without any tactical advantages. Cego could most often pick Sam apart, and Silas would toy with the littlest brother.

"I do understand," Cego said. "Silas beats me too. Every time. I've barely ever grazed him with a strike and haven't come close with any sort of submission."

Sam sniffed as the sea breeze ruffled his hair and they continued down the beach. "So, what's the point of either of us fighting him, over and over, getting beat up every time?"

"Don't you see, Sam?" Cego said. "Even though we're losing, we're still gaining. We're learning new skills, figuring out a way to get to him eventually."

The brothers turned their heads skyward as a flock of sigil sparrows took to the air in defense of their nest. A raptor wafted far overhead on a warm current.

"Well, at least we have a break today until you need to fight him," Cego said as he turned from the beach onto the path toward the ironwood forest. Arry broke away and scurried back along the shore toward Farmer's compound.

"You coming?" Cego turned back to his brother.

Sam's eyes lit up as he seemed to forget Silas altogether for a moment. He followed Cego. "Think they're still up there?"

"They should be," Cego said as they pushed aside the undergrowth. "Though it's the wilds; anything could have happened. A raptor or even one of the big sand lizards could have gotten to them."

"I think they'll be okay," Sam said as they ducked under a low branch and emerged into a clearing. Giant ironwood trees encircled them, dark trunks towering toward the sky.

The two boys padded on top of the fallen needles across the grove until they reached the base of the largest tree. The ancient ironwood was visible even from Farmer's compound, its green canopy rising above the rest of the forest.

A dent cut into one side of the gnarled tree, as if someone had taken an axe to it, but Cego and Sam used the groove as a foothold to begin climbing. The two brothers pulled themselves onto one of the thick branches of the lower canopy, thirty feet off the ground.

"I can't see—" Sam started, but Cego held a finger to his mouth to quiet the boy.

He pointed across the trunk to a tangle of branches where a pile of leaves and sticks was laid out.

At first, there was silence and the slow sway of the tree boughs with the island wind. And then a small form slowly peeked out from the edge of the pile. A furry black head with yellow eyes came into view and a tiny feline leapt to the branch.

"They're still here!" Sam whispered, his eyes alight.

The brothers watched as another minuscule cat, this one with a grey coat, crawled out from the nest and yawned in a stray beam of sunlight. It nipped at the tail of its black sibling, who turned and swatted back at it playfully.

"What if they fall?" Sam whispered, worry tingeing his voice. "It's so high up."

"It's possible," Cego said. "Though they're born up here in the canopy, so they're used to balancing. Plus, their mother is looking out for them."

Another large cat with a sleek brown coat made its appearance known, leaping onto the branch with the kittens. The mother warily glanced over at Sam and Cego, though she'd grown used to their presence by now.

They'd been watching the ferrcats in the ironwood canopy for a month now, since the mother had first grown fat and given birth to the litter. Only two kittens had survived, and Cego and Sam had taken every chance available to escape to the grove to observe them.

The black kitten made a daring pounce at the other, tossing it backward on the branch. Amazingly, the tumbling grey ball of fur maintained its balance and even slid into a counter stance.

"Black is always picking on grey," Sam noted. "He's getting bigger, faster."

"Yes, but grey has been growing too," Cego whispered back. "He's learning and keeping up better over the past week."

Through Cego and Sam's arduous training schedule, always fighting for something, it was peaceful to watch others fight for once. Even if it was two kittens.

"I hope they grow up fast," Sam whispered. "Maybe they can get out of this tree then."

"But this is their home," Cego said. "Don't you think they'd want to stay?"

"No," Sam responded confidently. "I think as soon as they're big enough, they should leave. They need to get out of here."

Cego could feel the warmth of his brother beside him on the branch. He could smell the sweat tingeing the boy's freckled skin.

"If they do leave, I hope they go together," Cego said.

CHAPTER 17

The Punishment

Dreams should be treated with more scrutiny and the waking day with less inspection. It is too often that one is oblivious to his true nature but wastes his life worrying on insignificant details.

Passage Four, Fifty-Third Precept of
the Combat Codes

This is the fifth time you have broken your nasal cavity since you were admitted to the Lyceum," Xenalia said.

Cego watched Xenalia's little spectral hover over his face and was quiet. He felt the heat of the Observer on his skin and letting the familiar sterile smell of the medward waft over him. The cleric applied an ointment to the bridge of his nose.

"Your body's natural healing mechanisms, in combination with this nanobiotic ointment, should repair the bone structure again within a day or two," Xenalia said. "By then, your breathing patterns should return to normal, so there is nothing to worry about."

Cego looked out the medward window across from the cot he sat up in. Icicles hung from the frames and slowly dripped three floors down as the winter frost thawed in the sun. He imagined the little streams the melting snows had created on the grounds outside, flowing down the slight grade into the Citadel's surrounding moat.

Cego remembered when Murray had first led him across the entry bridge and he'd set eyes on the Lyceum's ancient sister buildings, the rounded architecture of the Harmony and the jagged edges of the Valkyrie.

This was his home. The Lyceum was where he'd met his friends, his family, grown with them through both hardship and joy. It was where he'd learned the words of his ancestors and honed his combat craft every day.

Despite everything, even though this place stood for a broken system where he was nothing but a pawn, the Lyceum still was the only real home he'd ever known. A place outside the island in Cego's mind. It gave him comfort to think of the long, quiet stairways and great academic domes.

Cego met Xenalia's incoming stare.

"You have been quiet today," the cleric said. "Most often, you have more words. You tell me of your classes, of your friends, of the Grievar world, which I am unfamiliar with."

"I'm just thinking," Cego said.

"I do not think you Grievar are supposed to do too much of that." Xenalia's lip curled up into a slight smile, a habit she'd picked up recently when she attempted a joke.

Cego chuckled. "Yes, sometimes, I believe thinking doesn't do anything but complicate everything. But...things are changing so fast. Sometimes, I feel like I can't keep up."

Xenalia nodded as she wound a fresh bandage around Cego's arm. "I have heard of this change as well. Most often, I do not concern myself with politics or news of the world outside of these medward halls, and yet the voices speaking are too loud to not hear this time."

Cego's stomach lurched, thinking of Xenalia and her clerics in this medward. If his brother's army forced their way into Ezo and began to sack cities, most of the Daimyo would have fled already.

"Xenalia, you need to leave," Cego said abruptly.

"I still have to give you an abysyth shot for the internal damage you took during your match," Xenalia said. "It is okay if I am a little late for my class with the neophytes today."

"That's not what I mean." Cego's breath caught in his chest, thinking about his friend being hurt and what his brother would do to her. "My brother Silas, he's coming. He's coming with his armies and they are not going to leave any Daimyo alive."

Xenalia stopped her work for a moment and stared at Cego. "You are worried about me?"

"Yes!" Cego nearly yelled. "Xenalia, if Silas comes through these gates undeterred, he'll ask an oath of loyalty from every Grievar. Those who give it will be taken into the Flux, and those who don't will be executed on the spot. I've seen it...with Murray."

"And so what if I give my oath as well?" Xenalia asked. "I have no problem pledging loyalty to whoever controls the resources, as long as I can keep practicing my craft to heal those who need it."

Cego shook his head. "Silas will not take your oath, Xenalia. You are a Daimyo. He will...All the clerics here would be killed."

Xenalia didn't appear to be in the least bit fearful. "If that is the case, then so be it. If there is nothing that can be done, I accept my fate."

"I don't accept it," Cego growled. "I don't accept you giving your life to my brother's cause, nor do I accept the deaths of those Grievar who don't swear allegiance to him."

"But..." Xenalia paused. "Will this new world that your brother is creating not be a better one for you? A world where Grievar are truly free, not bound by service to the Daimyo as they have been for so many centuries?"

Cego knew the answer. Now that he knew he was home. He needed to protect it, protect those he loved.

"No, it is not a better world," Cego said. "Because Silas thinks he is giving Grievar their freedom by destroying the Daimyo. But he is replacing their old chains with new ones that he's built. He isn't giving them any real choice."

"Maybe so," said Xenalia. "But do we have any choice in anything? Did you know that the thoughts that populate your brain, that determine how you act and what you plan, are not controlled by you? They simply come to life, like little sparks lit by lightning in a forest."

"I don't care about that, Xenalia," Cego replied. "All I care about are the people here in these Citadel walls, my friends. And that's you. I won't let anything happen to you."

Xenalia's spectral floated away from Cego, and he felt her eyes on him. The cleric got very close, pressed her cold hand to Cego's face, and gently brushed it across his forehead.

"Okay, Cego," she said. "I accept your care. As long as you do not go breaking yourself again."

Cego nodded. "I'll try, as always. But I can't promise anything, so you'd better be here to patch me up."

* * *

Though Cego didn't need the spectral to lead him to the catacombs any longer, it still did, as if it were goading him to keep training in the onyx.

As usual, he found Kōri Shimo sitting in the dusty room, cross-legged within the onyx Circle. Cego was still amazed that the boy was able to stay in the ring for so long—one afternoon, Cego had counted a full five minutes that the boy occupied that terrible world, having his limbs ripped apart and his head bashed in by the Guardian.

Shimo abruptly opened his eyes, refocusing on the dimly lit room he now occupied. He stood and stepped out of the onyx, not sweating and short of breath like Cego was after a session, still, even after more than a month training in the blacklight.

"How do you do it?" Cego asked. "How do you spend so much time in there...without it affecting you?"

Cego still was not accustomed to the Guardian destroying his body, bludgeoning him like a piece of meat. It never got easier. The pain still racked his body and the claustrophobia overtook him until Kōri Shimo pulled his lifeless body from the ring.

"I've been training in the onyx for over two years now," Kōri Shimo replied. "I've developed far more resistance to its effects than you have."

"So, you're saying when you first started training here, you were having problems like me?"

Kōri Shimo raised his eyebrows. "I saw your match against the Level Sixer. No, I never had problems like you."

Shimo certainly had a way in comforting him. Cego snorted. "It wasn't so bad. And...I could have had him. I felt myself losing control, though. You must know what I mean."

For some reason, he could talk to this boy truthfully, without the layers of lies he'd built up with his friends. Kōri Shimo was born of the same world he was. He could understand.

"Perhaps," Shimo said. "When I first began training in the onyx, I felt my energy in the physical world sapped. It's why I didn't take top score every year; Solara Halberd beat me to it."

Cego smiled. "Sol still talks about when she outscored you that year. And she talks about when you bested her on the Pilgrimage...constantly. She's out for your blood this year; you know that, right?"

"Yes, I know," Shimo said stoically. "I could see it in her eyes during our fight. She's got a fire in her unlike any I've seen before. I'll be ready when she comes for me again, though."

"You better be." Cego stopped, taking a deep breath as he steadied himself to step into the onyx again.

He turned back to Kōri Shimo, whose eyes now were closed as he sat cross-legged against the cobwebbed wall. It was the same position Cego had first spotted the boy in years earlier, right before the entrance Trials to the Lyceum.

"Why are you helping me?" Cego asked.

Kōri Shimo opened his eyes. "Because you are the only other like me."

Cego shivered, thinking about how the onyx might affect him long-term. Would he become some unfeeling creature like Kōri Shimo?

"We're not as alike as you think," Cego said. "Even though we were both born of the Cradle."

"Perhaps," Shimo replied. "But perhaps you feel the darkness as I do. Perhaps you sense the energy surge to your skin, make you feel like you were born for a single purpose. To fight and to win."

Kōri Shimo described exactly how Cego had felt so many times in the Circle. And that made him sick. This was the boy who had nearly killed several other students, who didn't care about anything but fighting and winning.

"You think me cold for believing this," Kōri Shimo said. "You think me like your brother Silas—a power-hungry Grievar who wants to become strong enough to shape the world to his will. But I'm different."

"How are you any different from Silas?" Cego asked.

"I seek perfection in combat because I know that is why I was created," Shimo said. "I fully accept the circumstances of my birth within the Cradle, as an experiment to see how far a child's mind and body can become weapons of violence. I accept who I am, with no other illusions of power or grandeur but to perfect my craft. I don't savor hurting or killing others, but if it is a part of this path I'm on, then I must do so without hesitation."

"But what about everything else out there?" Cego asked. "What about enjoying your life? Being with your friends and protecting those you love?"

Something close to a smile curled on Shimo's lips at the mention of love. "Is this why you fight, Cego?"

"Yes," Cego said with conviction. "It's why I'm in the onyx every day."

"Perhaps we are different, then," Shimo said. "But to take on Silas, to harness the power you've been given, you need to embrace the darkness. The toothless wolf cannot deliver the fatal bite."

Cego shook his head, though he knew Shimo was right. He breathed deeply and stepped back into the onyx.

CHAPTER 18

The Prisoner

A true master is one who never loses the beginner's mind.

Passage Four, Eighth Precept of
the Combat Codes

You look terrible," Sol said, looking across the Bythardi board at Cego.

The two had gotten in the habit of sitting on the ledge within the empty training room between classes, the board set up beside the frost-covered shield window that overlooked the Citadel's eastern front.

"I feel terrible," Cego agreed as he slid a fist forward to threaten Sol's neck piece.

"Is it the nightmares again?" Sol asked. She sent one of her foot pieces in a circular motion behind a pair of Cego's fists. "Are they getting worse?"

"Yeah," Cego said, hating that he needed to tell another lie to his friends. He wanted to reveal his secret to Sol, to the entire crew. But he feared the blacklight that had infiltrated him would somehow infect the rest. He wanted to keep the Whelps separate from that place he went in his mind, the island where he tortured himself every day.

"Whatever it is, Cego, you need to get some rest," Sol said, looking at the deep rings beneath his eyes. "To be honest, you're not performing like normal."

Sol made a quick move with one of her fists, sliding it beside Cego's neck piece. She smiled from across the board, and Cego knew what that meant. He evaluated his possible options for escape and realized there were none. She had him.

He knocked his neck down for the third time this session. Sol was a far better player than him. But Cego knew she wasn't talking about his Bythardi performance. While he'd been training in the onyx, his fight performance outside of that torturous place had suffered.

"I know I haven't been up to speed," Cego said as he began to place his pieces back on the circular board.

Yesterday, he'd let one of Dozer's heavy knees through during clinch practice, and he could still feel the ache in his rib cartilage. He could see all the moves clearer than ever, though. He knew exactly what to do to attack and counter before it happened. He could see the path to victory, but his body couldn't quite catch up to his mind.

"Perhaps there's something you can do for a better night's sleep," Sol offered. "I remember when my father used to prepare for fights, he'd swear by a plantoid tea. He'd be snoring like a baby after a few sips."

"Not sure that'd help with what I've got going on," Cego said. He sat back from the board and took stock of how he'd start his game after three consecutive losses. "Don't worry; I wasn't myself against Novor. I'll be ready for the next challenge."

"I'm not worried about the matches or our scores," Sol said. "I'm worried about you. I know how much Murray-Ku meant to you. He was my friend, my coach, too."

Cego was silent. He turned to the shield window and stared out at the forested valley and Kalabasas Hill rising from the mists. It was on that hill where Joba and Murray were both buried.

"I know the anger you're feeling," Sol said as she moved the board aside and shifted closer to him.

She did not know how Cego felt, though. Sol didn't understand what it was to be trapped in her own body. Cego was a hostage to himself—the Cradle of his birth, the programming of the Bit-Minders, and now the onyx, another layer to this darkin' world.

"You remember how I was in the weeks after we found out about my father," Sol said as she inched closer and placed her hand on his. "You spoke with me that day, told me that my anger was weighing me down, told me I had to set it free. You saved me, Cego."

Cego nodded, meeting Sol's eyes. "I remember."

Sol's face was only inches from his. "I'm here for you too. You don't need to let the rage burn you up."

Cego's heart beat rapidly, and the world beyond the window started to spin. He could smell the sweet honeysuckle of Sol's hair and feel the warmth of her breath. Though the two had been in physical contact so many times, grappling and wrapping themselves around one another, this...this was far different.

"Hey!" A voice broke their reverie. It was Dozer at the entry to the training room. He eyed the two with suspicion for a moment, not saying anything.

"Yeah?" Sol stood with her arms at her hips. "What's going on, Dozer? Is there a reason you're interrupting our game?"

"Right...game." Dozer seemed to remember why he was there in the first place and paced over to his friends.

"You need to come quick; something's happened."

"What?" Cego stood in alarm.

"It's Professor Farstead," Dozer said. "They've locked him up."

* * *

Cego ran down the long hall toward the Valkyrie beside Dozer and Sol. Instead of climbing the stairs toward Aon's classroom as he was used to, they followed Dozer down to the basement below the building.

"Didn't even realize this place existed before Abel told me," Dozer huffed as they jogged down the stone steps. "Makes me wonder if the Harmony's got under-levels too."

Cego shook his head. "I think it's locked off on that side."

"This is near where we took our Trials," Sol said as they passed through an open portal. A grainy feed of an old fight was switched on beside an empty chair angled to watch the entrance.

The Valkyrie's lower level was well lit and maintained, unlike the dark and dusty catacombs. A servicer gave them a strange look as he dusted the floor outside of a room. Cego glanced within and saw steel cabinets and granite-slab tables with glass instruments atop them. Those were no Grievar tools.

He remembered the lab he'd infiltrated with the Flux in Karstock. The memory was from another lifetime, stored in the recesses of his mind along with his time in the Cradle.

"What are they doing here?" Sol whispered, meeting Cego's eyes, clearly thinking the same thing.

"Probably where the upper-levels are coming to get stimmed up," Dozer said.

Cego heard shouting coming from the end of the hall. It was Abel.

"You must not do this!"

Two large guards were doing their best to restrain Abel. Cego recognized them as High Commander Albright's personal retinue, the muscle that had visited them in Quarter D. The little Desovian had tears streaming down his face as he strained to push into the room they stood in front of.

"What's going on?" Cego shouted.

Abel turned and met Cego's eyes before surging against the guards again. One of them palmed Abel's face and shoved him backward, causing the Desovian to stumble to the floor.

"Hey!" Dozer was moving before Cego could get in front of him. The big kid threw a heavy cross that caught the guard on the chin, sending him sprawling backward against the stone wall.

The second guard whipped a steel rod from his waistbelt, the weapon immediately glowing blue with charge.

"I'd hold back your friend if I were you," the man growled.

"Dozer!" Cego held his friend's shoulder. "We need to see what's—"

He got a glimpse of the room behind the guard. A green luminescence pulsed from a steel Circle laid on the floor. In the middle of the ring lay Aon Farstead.

"What... Why is Professor Farstead in there?"

"Like I told your little friend," the guard snarled, "I don't ask questions; I follow orders."

"They brought him here just now!" Abel yelled. "I went to Professor Aon's quarters to care for him and found these men carrying him down the stairs!"

Cego tried to get a better view inside the room, but the guard swung his charged rod to ward him off while his dazed companion slowly stood.

"Cheap-shotted me, you shit." The man rubbed his jaw, eyeing Dozer. He pulled his weapon. "For that I should make you burn—"

"You'll do nothing of the sort," came a baritone voice from the far end of the corridor. Commander Memnon approached, with Sam by his side.

Cego's breath caught in his chest at his brother's appearance.

"Why are your weapons drawn?" Memnon stood squarely in front of the guards. "Put them away."

"These kids came out of nowhere, asking questions about what we're doing with the prisoner," the guard said as he holstered his rod.

"Prisoner?" Sol questioned. "Why would Professor Aon be a prisoner here?"

Memnon shook his head. "These aren't matters for students to be involved in. It's time for you all to leave."

"You knew about this?" Cego growled at Memnon. "How could you let this happen?"

"You don't understand—" Memnon started.

"Don't understand that you've thrown the oldest and most respected teacher in the Lyceum into a cell?" Cego shouted.

"It wasn't my choice." Memnon's voice softened.

"We always have choice," Abel said as he wiped the tears from his face. "Professor Aon isn't in good health; he belongs up in his quarters to be cared for."

"I would have him back up there too," Memnon said. "But I don't make the decisions here anymore."

"The baby ferrcats like to climb the ironwoods for practice; I've seen them do so every morning in the forest," Sam blurted out.

For a moment, Cego had forgotten Sam was even there, the little boy nearly attached to Memnon's leg. His brother was staring directly at him.

"Callen ordered this?" Cego asked Memnon, tearing his focus from his brother. "He never liked Professor Aon; is this some sort of sick punishment?"

Memnon shook his head again. "There are things bigger than you'd understand going on here."

"Try us," Sol said. "And if you're not the one to make decisions, why are you down here?"

"I came…" Memnon trailed off. "I came to make sure he's all right. Same as you."

Cego saw it in the old commander's contorted face. The man was as broken as they were seeing Professor Aon in this situation.

"Can we see him at least?" Cego asked.

Memnon paused before nodding at the two guards. "Let us pass."

"High commander says nobody is to get by this threshold without word from him," one of the guards said warily.

"I don't know where Callen found you two, likely from Dakar's discarded PublicJustice squad." Memnon steeled his eyes on the two men. "But you surely know that nearly every Knight in the Citadel is still loyal to me. And if you ever hope to step foot within these walls again without having to watch your back, you'll step aside now."

The two brutes looked at each other before moving to the wall silently. The crew followed behind Memnon's bulk.

Cego could now see that a translucent wall halved the room, separating Aon from the outside. The man's frail form lay on the stone floor, surrounded by a pulsing emeralyis Circle.

Abel pressed his hands up against the glass. "We're here, Professor Aon. We haven't forgotten you."

The old man breathed shallowly but otherwise did not show any sign of consciousness.

"Why is he in an emeralyis Circle?" Sol asked.

"Governance ordered it." Memnon kept his voice low, attempting to keep the guards out of earshot. "You must not speak of this, as much as I know you will want to. I didn't want this…and if I could do anything about it, I would. But know this: They are within the Citadel's walls at all hours now. The Enforcers."

Cego saw Abel shudder, though the little Desovian didn't pull back from the glass.

"Why?" Cego whispered.

"Because of what's happening to the Kirothian Empire," Memnon said. "They are preparing."

Cego already knew what Governance was preparing for. He'd always known. Silas was coming.

Sam spoke again, as if prompted by some unseen force. "Do you think Silas will bring back a good haul of fish? He's been out in the water for a long time now, and I'm getting hungry."

Cego wanted to respond to Sam. Though he knew his little brother's words seemed gibberish, Cego understood him. He spoke of the island, the place they'd grown up together. Sam *only* spoke of that place.

But Cego couldn't bring himself to respond. Since he'd come back to the Lyceum, since he'd seen Sam in this state, he couldn't bear being near his brother.

"Why are they doing this to him?" Abel shook his head, tears streaming down his face again as he looked at Aon's withered body behind the glass.

"They think it will help them," Memnon replied. "I could not tell you more even if I knew it. Only the Daimyo can explain such machinations."

Cego put his hand on Abel's shoulder and squeezed. "We'll figure this out. There's nothing we can do now."

Abel slowly backed away from the glass, his shoulders slumped.

Memnon turned from the room and walked out. Murray had trusted this man, had put Sam in Memnon's care. And so Cego would trust him too.

Memnon spoke loudly as the crew exited the prison room, for the guards to hear this time. "Do not speak of this to anyone or there will be consequences."

The commander walked away with Sam trailing him.

"We gonna keep this quiet?" Dozer said as he glanced back at the two guards.

"No," Cego said. "I know exactly who to talk to."

* * *

Cego had been avoiding the sixth floor of the Harmony since he'd returned to the Lyceum.

He needed answers, though, and there was only one man who could possibly help him. Cego slid open the creaky wooden door and entered the greenhouse. It was as he remembered: sticky, warm air and a variety of exotic plants draped from the walls and sprouting from pots.

"Hello, Cego." A small man was standing on a desk, snipping at a vine hanging overhead. "You might notice that this one, *Paranthycus tombili*, more commonly known as snake weed, has invaded my greenhouse."

"Hello, Professor Zyleth," Cego returned. "Umm, do you need any help?"

"I do realize you could more easily reach this for me," Zyleth responded as he stood on his toes to snip at a particularly thick part of the vine. "But this plant needs to know that I mean business."

With a grunt, the Daimyo squeezed his shears and the vine dropped to the desk. "Now, there we go."

Zyleth wiped the sweat from his brow and slid down from the table. Cego noticed a large welt on the man's forehead. For any other professor at the Lyceum, Cego wouldn't think twice about an injury, given they were practicing at a combat school. However, Zyleth wasn't a normal professor and he wasn't a Grievar.

"Professor, are you okay?" Cego asked.

"Ah, you must be referring to this hematoma I have atop my skull." Zyleth held his hand to the contusion and winced in pain. "Yes, I did go to the ward yesterday, though they seem far more suited to treat your kind than mine. The lead cleric, Xenalia, was helpful, though, and provided me with an ointment to reduce the swelling."

"Xenalia's stitched me up more times than I can count," Cego said. "But what I meant was…what happened?"

"You mean you did not assume I have taken to Professor Tefo's Striking lessons?" Zyleth smiled. "Of course, you are right. And unfortunately, this injury did not come from mutual combat of any sort."

"Someone attacked you?" Cego asked.

Zyleth moved to start shearing one of the thinner vines that had entangled a seat in his classroom. "Cego, you know as well as I that these times are not normal. And, given the current circumstances, being a Daimyo professor at a Grievar combat school has proven to be…difficult."

"You mean, someone beat you because you're a Daimyo?"

"Yes," Zyleth said softly. "Though best not to speak of it outside this room."

Cego wanted to ask who had attacked him, but Zyleth's look quieted him.

"Let us focus on the good," Zyleth said. "And that is, I am very glad to see you. It was in far worse circumstances when we last spoke."

"Yes," Cego said. "That's why I came. I know it's been too long, and I should have come sooner but...I wanted to thank you for everything you did for me during my trial."

Zyleth nodded. "I am afraid in the end, I did not do much at all, given you were sentenced to execution by the Goliath."

"I was," Cego said. "But if you didn't represent me and speak in my defense, I wouldn't have been able to fight like I did. Believe me, things would have turned out differently."

"That was quite amazing, Cego." Zyleth raised his eyebrow. "I do not think the chatter about your feat against the Goliath will ever be quieted in these halls."

Cego sat down in a chair and was silent for a moment. "People here think I'm special. But I'm not...or at least, I don't want to be."

"And that is exactly what makes you special," Zyleth said. "It is what makes you different from your brother, the Slayer."

"First, we couldn't speak of him or the Flux," Cego said. "And now Callen has us recording feeds denouncing the rebellion. What's going on?"

"I have heard as much." Zyleth sighed and held his hand back to his injured head. "The same thing is happening that prompted the attack on me. Fear. It drives all animals—Daimyo, Grievar, it does not matter. We fear that which is different, that which will change what we think is our ideal way of life. And now the Citadel fears the Flux. They are preparing to fight, but the first battle is a psychological one, convincing the Grievar and Grunt populace in this nation that the Slayer's cause is not a worthy one."

"They are doing more than that, though," Cego said quietly. "Worse things than having us tell lies. It's actually another reason I came here to talk to you."

"Speak freely, and do not worry about unwanted ears in this room," Zyleth said, walking back to his desk. "I have protective measures in place."

"I need some information on tech," Cego said. He could still remember the professor showing the class each sort of spectral weapon over a year before. "I was wondering if you might tell me a bit more about the Circles."

"Ah, well, I am no Circle scholar. In fact, Professor Larkspur would be the best to ask about Circles or anything related to fighting." Zyleth rubbed at the bruise on his forehead again.

"I'm not looking for anything about how to fight in Circles, Professor," Cego said. "I'd like to know more about how the Circles are made."

Zyleth paused with his hand on his chin, as if he were deciding whether to provide Cego the information or not. "Well, I do know a bit about that, of course. Though in these times, be careful what you are asking for and who you speak to. Do you understand?"

"Yes." Cego nodded.

"As you know, all Circles are composed of some mixture of the prime elemental alloys. When these alloys are harvested from the mines, they are smelted down into the form of a Circle. Most industrialized nations have a few factories set to making them; though, as I am sure you know, nearly half of Kiroth's factories have been hit by the Flux in the last several months."

"Yes, I know." Cego's mind flashed to his brother. The plan to hit the factories had been nearly as important as the mining operations and stim labs. "Can you tell me of emeralyis, though?"

"Your line of questioning is very specific, Cego," Zyleth said. "I am sure you already know the effect emeralyis has on a Grievar fighting within it. Heightened creativity, almost euphoria to explore new techniques. But what are you actually asking?"

Cego breathed deeply. "Could emeralyis be used to...imprison someone?"

Zyleth's mouth became a hard line, and he observed Cego with his wide black eyes. The Daimyo then reached into his desk and retrieved a small rectangular box. He opened it and a green glow emerged from the object's interior.

"Is that emeralyis?" Cego asked, unable to pull his gaze from the greenlight.

"Yes," Zyleth said, shutting the box. "Highly concentrated in this device, more than you'd ever see in any normal Circle."

"Why do you have it?"

"This little transmitter is the reason I am not worried anyone is listening in to our conversation," Zyleth explained. "Emeralyis, when highly focused, can serve to disrupt transmission from Observer spectrals."

"Like...the spectral that Xenalia uses at the medward?" Cego thought about the little crimson wisp that often helped his cleric friend conduct her medical examinations.

"Similar in nature," Zyleth said. "Though many Observer spectrals are unseen. They are formed by the blacklight."

Cego shook his head. Everything always came back to the blacklight, the dark energy emitted from the onyx.

"Certain Daimyo researchers have claimed to have some grasp of how to harness the power of onyx and utilize it for various purposes," Zyleth said. "But they are dabbling. There have been a variety of failed experiments with onyx over the years, some with disastrous effects. The only ones who truly understand the blacklight are the Bit-Minders."

Cego felt a chill run through his body, even conjuring the image of a Bit-Minder. The last one he'd seen was the judge presiding over his trial, one that had sentenced him to execution.

"So, the Bit-Minders can watch us through the blacklight spectrals?" Cego unconsciously looked around the room, as if he'd be able to see one of the dark voids hanging in the air.

"They are almost always watching, gathering information, I suspect." Zyleth tapped the box in his hand. "Which is why this little device gives me peace of mind."

Cego's mind flitted back to Old Aon, encircled with the greenlight of emeralyis in his prison. He needed to tell Zyleth. He trusted him.

"Yesterday, we saw Callen's men bring Professor Aon Farstead down to the under-levels beneath the Valkyrie," Cego blurted out. "They placed him in a prison, within a Circle of bright emeralyis."

"That does not make any sense." Zyleth shook his head. "There would be no reason for Governance to do that…unless…"

"Unless what?" Cego's voice broke.

"Unless…they think that Aon is transmitting information to the outside."

"How could that be true?" Cego asked. "Professor Aon hasn't even been conscious for the past year, and before that he was babbling, not making any sense."

"There is some secret being kept purposefully hidden here," Zyleth said. "Aon has always been a friend to the Minders. He even sent Murray Pearson to their Codex to inquire about you at one point."

Cego vividly remembered when Murray had come back from the Codex, when he'd come to tell him of the Cradle he'd been created in.

"But it still doesn't make sense," Cego said. "Even if Aon was communicating with the Bit-Minders, why would that matter? As you said yourself, they are always watching us anyway."

"Your line of thinking is correct, Cego," Zyleth said. "For Governance to take this action, it must be something of greater gravity. Not only must they believe Aon to be communicating with the

Minders, they must believe that the Minders are…helping the opposition."

"Why would the Minders help the Flux?" Cego asked.

"As I said before, the Minders are a mystery even to my kin," Zyleth said. "We know they are a networked breed, though. They are each individually part of a greater whole, like a swarm of insects communicating, working in unison for some greater purpose."

"What is their purpose?" Cego asked.

"No one knows," Zyleth said. "But then again, the same could be said of you or me. All we do know is that for Governance to decide to imprison Aon, throw him within an emeralyis Circle, they must believe that he is a threat."

CHAPTER 19

The Weight

Just as wind is the practice of the air and waves are the practice of the water, combat is the practice of the Grievar.
Passage Three, Sixth Precept of the Combat Codes

Cego took deep breaths of the frigid morning air as he raced up Kalabasas Hill. The snows had fallen heavy last night. His boots crunched into the frozen white as he paced himself for the second half of the course, where the steep ascent began, and climbed all the way to the summit.

Though his indigo second skin served to keep the frost from forming on his arms and legs, the material did nothing to prevent the cold from blasting his face. He caught sight of the next runner up; Kōri Shimo leapt over a fallen tree and disappeared over a ridge, out of Cego's sight.

Cego usually was neck and neck with Shimo on Kalabasas; the boy wasn't particularly fast, but he kept a meticulous pace through the entire course. Apparently, even years of training in the onyx didn't improve cardio conditioning, though, at least not enough to let them catch the front-runners.

Cego could picture Sol nipping at Damyn Zular's heels—his teammate had nearly won the course and caught the lanky Desovian last week. He had a strange urge to pick up the pace, to try to catch Sol and run beside her, though he knew it would be impossible at this point.

He nearly slipped on an icy rock but recovered by scrambling with his hands in the snow. He glanced back and saw Gryfin Thurgood ten meters behind him. Cego was amazed at Gryfin's endurance despite his heavy, muscle-bound frame.

Thurgood had the best of it all: purelight breeding, the adoration of his fellow classmates, and a straight path forward in life. Gryfin knew he was destined to be a Knight that fought for Ezo; every boy in his family had done so for ten consecutive generations.

Cego scrambled harder up the icy slope, trying to get away from Gryfin and close the distance to Shimo ahead.

He wondered how it would feel to not have the weight of indecision constantly atop his shoulders, not knowing what his next step forward would be. What would it be like to be born into a family when everything was already decided? He thought back to his conversation with Shimo: Was it possible for Cego to accept it all?

Even Kōri Shimo didn't understand, though. What would Cego accept? Was he to accept his unorthodox brooding and the fact he was created to become a weapon for the Daimyo? Or would he accept his place as the brother of Silas the Slayer, leader of the Flux rebellion, set on eradicating the Daimyo from this planet?

He was caught between two worlds: one serving the Daimyo and the other set to destroy them.

Cego pushed his pace as he hit a slight downward dip on the course. He let his legs flow under him, carrying him over the icy patches without hesitation. Luckily, he kept his balance and was able to catch Shimo on the downhill as the two started to ascend again toward the summit.

"Here we are again," Cego breathed heavily.

Kōri Shimo didn't acknowledge him; the boy ran as stoically as he fought.

Cego figured he'd distract himself from the burning frost against his face and the cramps that had begun to rack his legs. "Makes sense we've got near-equal cardio, right?"

Again, Shimo answered with silence, the sound of their boots digging into the packed snow.

"We're both grown in vats," Cego exhaled. "I figure the material they used to grow us was the same. Like two mechs, built on the same assembly line."

"Perhaps," Kōri Shimo finally responded as they bounded across the rocks rising from a frozen stream.

"Makes me feel like darkin' shit," Cego huffed, nearly hearing Murray's voice as the words left his mouth. "How many more of us are there, near exactly the same?"

"Is it not so with all Grievar?" Kōri Shimo said with a steady breath. "Bloodlines, passed down for generations."

"It's different." Cego ducked under a hanging branch weighed down by the ice. "Having parents is different."

Shimo was quiet as they worked toward the final ascent. Cego could make out Sol sprinting across the straightaway above, nearly breathing down the Desovian girl's neck.

"It's true," Shimo said. "We're made from near-identical molds."

The frost wind began to blow in earnest, and Cego seemed to be running in slow motion, pushing against it.

"But." Shimo's cold breath came out in steady puffs. "You still have your own will. If you decide to push harder now, can you beat me?"

Cego glanced at Kōri Shimo and set his jaw. "Guess we'll find out."

Cego made the decision to put it all into the final ascent. He'd make it ahead of Kōri Shimo even if it meant his heart giving out as he crossed the finish.

He saw Kōri Shimo steel his focus beside him and guessed the boy meant to do the same. They raced side by side, pushing against the frozen wind, clawing for every inch up the incline of Kalabasas Hill.

Gryfin Thurgood fell behind the two, no longer in sight, and Cego could feel his lungs burning as if he'd inhaled a sizzler's torch. He wasn't the same as Shimo. The Daimyo, the Bit-Minders, Silas, they couldn't determine what he thought or did. He had his own will.

A burst of energy ran through Cego's body, not the blacklight coming to his skin but a different sort of warmth. Images flashed across his mind: running the grueling rounds of Thaloo's slave yard, fighting the sneering purelights of the Lyceum, facing off against the invincible Goliath in Central Square, screaming as the clerics of Arklight tortured him.

They had tried to hold him back each step of his path. They had tried to put him in the ground every moment they could. But they had not been able to. Cego was still there, breathing this frost air. He wouldn't stop now.

Cego realized he'd pulled ahead of Shimo and was now sprinting across the straightaway. He saw Sol's face with a wide smile spread across it as he joined her at the finish.

He fell to his back on the packed snow, his heart pounding as if it might burst from his chest. Sweat beaded and froze along his face. Cego watched the sharp winter light cut through the pines above him.

Sol's face peered down at him. "You all right?"

"Yeah…" Cego said between labored breaths. His breakfast started to come up, and he quickly rose to his knees to let it loose in the snow.

"Now I'm all right, I guess." Cego wiped his face and sheepishly met Sol's chiding smile.

"Happens to the best of us," she said.

"That does not happen to me," Kōri Shimo said, standing beside them. He'd stopped to watch Cego retching.

"Right, because you don't feel what we mortals do." Sol crossed her arms.

"Sol..." Cego stood slowly, not wanting her to get into it with Shimo.

"You see?" Shimo met Cego's eyes, breathing hard. "We are the same... but we are different."

The boy nodded at Sol and walked away, back down the trail and, Cego was sure of it, back to the catacombs.

"He's... strange," Sol said. "But I'm okay if you're training with him. Down there."

"I wish I'd told you all—"

"No," Sol said. "Sometimes, we need to do things for ourselves. What I did, leaving the Citadel in search of my father, retrieving his body. I needed to do that for myself. And this is the same for you."

Cego breathed out. He'd finally worked up the courage to tell Sol about the onyx Circle, but he hadn't yet discussed it directly with the other Whelps. "Do the rest... Do they understand?"

"Yes," Sol said. "Dozer's a bit confused, but he'll have your back. Like the rest of us."

"Thank you," Cego said.

"Cego." Sol looked down at the ground. "You're not the only one to keep secrets."

"There's nothing you could tell me so that I'd not have your back too," Cego answered. He meant it.

"Good." Sol looked up. "You're also not the only one with a strange breeding. I'm not only a Grievar... I'm a Daimyo."

"But your father, he's Artemis Halberd..." Cego's mind raced.

"My mother was a courtesan," Sol said. "I never knew her."

"I don't care." The words fell from Cego's mouth.

"What do you mean, you don't—" Sol's brow furrowed.

"I mean, I do care," Cego tried to explain. "I care about you, but I don't care who your mother or father was. Of anyone, I have no grounds to judge others on their breeding."

"Good," Sol breathed out in relief. She smiled, making Cego want to put his arms around her and bring her close. Instead, he awkwardly raised a hand and lowered it again, staring at the appendage as if it weren't his own.

The rest of the runners had finished the course and were now hastily making their return to the warmth of the Lyceum, but Cego and Sol stayed atop the hill.

They walked toward the edge of the cliff that overlooked the Citadel's sprawling grounds. A pair of raptors rode the cold current far above the ancient stone fortress below. They watched the still landscape in silence, until Cego forced himself to turn to the two bulks of frozen earth raised from the ground at the edge of the bluff, beneath a crop of tall, weathered pines.

His breath caught in his chest as he looked down at the mounds.

"Haven't been here since the ceremony," Cego said guiltily. "I just... can't bear it."

"I understand," said Sol. "I haven't either."

They stood beside each other as the sun crested the tallest pines and glinted against the frost-covered burial sites.

"He'd have liked what you did," Sol said.

"What, retched all over the ground?" Cego replied.

"Yeah, maybe." Sol chuckled. "I meant how you pushed it to your limit up that final stretch."

"I guess so," Cego said. A flock of starlings screeched as they swooped out from the trees to defend their nest against the hawks, which had slowly spiraled in descent.

"He'd be proud of you, Cego," Sol said. "I know it. All you've done. Coming back home. Training so hard now and pushing your limits. I know Murray-Ku would be proud."

Tears welled in Cego's eyes, though he fought hard to stop them.

He sniffed the cold air and stared down at Murray's and Joba's graves. "Both of them are there because of me, Sol."

Sol nodded and was quiet for a moment, as if deliberating her next words. "You're right."

Cego felt the lump in his throat and hoped his friend wouldn't leave it at that.

"You're right that they're in the ground because of you," Sol said. "That's what they wanted. Joba and Murray died because they believed you were worth it. Because they saw the potential in you. Murray from the very beginning, when he picked you out of that slave Circle, and Joba ever since he started watching you with that smile on his face."

Cego let the tears fall. He didn't care that Sol saw them. The wetness slid from his face to the frozen earth and became a part of it. He shivered.

"They believed in you. They gave their lives for you," Sol said. "As hard as that is, as big a burden as that is, they believed you can carry it."

Sol turned to Cego and met his eyes. Her breath was a warm mist.

"And I believe in you, Cego."

Sol stepped in close and pressed her lips to his. His tears kept falling as she pushed her warmth against him.

CHAPTER 20

Grievar's War

The lord must not control his subjects with a clenched fist. To do so invites rebellion. Control must be exerted by giving his subjects a wide-open space to roam within, where they feel free and yet are forced to take on the task of their station.

Passage Seventeen, The Lost Precepts

Gryfin had a strong mount on top of Cego. Even though the purelight boy wasn't giving his full effort, Cego felt the pressure.

"Now work through the sequence as we practiced," Professor Dynari said as he limped by the students paired off in his sparse classroom. "Do not forget, we're not focusing on simply escaping here; I want you at least three moves ahead."

Cego bumped Gryfin forward and scooted his hips to the side. He used an elbow on the inside of Gryfin's thigh to create space for his own knee and switched to his other hip, forcing his partner off balance. Cego slid Gryfin's leg onto his shoulder, his arm hooked and hand grasping the boy's knee. Cego backed away and stood up to unbalance Gryfin to the floor.

ALEXANDER DARWIN

He met Gryfin's eyes beneath him, and for a moment he saw the boy's battered and bloody face. Cego looked away.

"I see you decided to go for the position reversal, Cego." Professor Dynari had been watching his movements carefully. "I count three primary steps in your sequence. Mount escape, technical stand-up, and the takedown. But now you must fully pass Gryfin's guard. Why not go straight to your own attack instead of giving him a chance to recover?"

Cego had already thought of the possibility of attacking one of Gryfin's legs as soon as he'd escaped from mount. "I thought attacking the leg would be riskier if I couldn't finish, so I decided to find a stable position on top."

Dynari nodded. "A solid strategy. It's nearly always better to be on top than bottom, especially against a pressure fighter like Thurgood. But Gryfin also has a solid guard, and the energy you'll expend passing it will outweigh the risk you'd take attacking his leg right off. Try it."

Cego followed the professor's instructions and repeated the sequence from beneath Gryfin. This time, after he escaped from mount, he quickly turned onto one of his shoulders and trapped Gryfin's leg. He spun around and attacked the boy's knee, forcing Thurgood to quickly tap in submission.

"But what if Gryfin is able to defend the leg attack?" Cego asked, wiping the sweat from his brow. "He'll end up on top again, and I'll probably be in worse position than when we started."

Professor Dynari smiled. "The chance to finish your opponent needs to be weighed more heavily than the potential risk of losing position. If you don't give yourself the proper opportunity for offense, then no matter how good your attacks are, you will not be able to employ them."

Cego watched Sol work a six-step move from the corner of his eye. She'd always been a natural at staying ahead in her sequences, planning multiple steps ahead like in her Bythardi game. The way she slid into each position with such fluidity, Cego couldn't help but stare.

"Though Halberd has nearly mastered this exercise, you won't gain from simply watching her," Professor Dynari noted, bringing warmth to Cego's cheeks.

"Right..." Cego trailed off. "I was wondering, Professor: What if an opponent can see your next move?"

"As in a game of Bythardi, an opponent can never truly know your next move in the Circle," Dynari said. "They can only approximate what your most likely choices are from each position. You will always have a choice—that is, until the finish."

Cego knew this to be true in nearly all facets of combat. But not with the Guardian he fought each day in the onyx. He knew it wouldn't be true with Silas either. The blacklight saw ahead; it knew the next move before it happened.

"But...what if there was a way to see an opponent's next move before it happened?" Cego forced the issue.

"I've been training Knights for the near entirety of my life," Professor Dynari said. "I've coached the likes of Artemis Halberd. And I can definitely say there is no way to fully know the mind of another person. It is impossible to know what will come next until there is a physical manifestation of their intentions. Yes, one can read the slightest change in the demeanor of an adversary and predict their most likely action, but this is not the same as seeing a move that has not yet happened."

Cego didn't like doing it, but it was the only way to get the answer he needed. "I think you're wrong."

The entire class stopped what they were doing. One did not tell Professor Dynari, the most decorated teacher in the Lyceum, that he was wrong.

The man stood with his arms crossed.

"I do not like to make examples of my students, as that sort of learning is proven to be disabling rather than enabling; however, there are occasions when such methods are required."

Cego swallowed. "I didn't mean to—"

"Stand at the center of the class," Dynari directed.

Cego slowly walked to the middle of the room. The rest of the students had broken from their pairs to watch the demonstration. Sol was shaking her head at him silently, and Cego could only shrug in reply.

"Dentas." Dynari waved to one of the Level Fives in the class. "Give me your second skin."

The thick boy looked a bit confused but obliged, pulling the black uniform off his back and handing it to the professor.

"Now." Dynari threw the sweaty piece of clothing to Cego. "Tie that over your face."

Was Dynari trying to embarrass him, having him wear a used uniform on his head? The punishment might fit with the less-refined tactics of some other professors, perhaps Tefo even, but Dynari was always known to be above such games.

Cego did as he was told, though, and wrapped the damp second skin over his face, completely blocking out his vision.

"We know Cego's vision is completely obscured," Dynari said. "And so, he'll only have his olfactory, auditory, and tactile senses remaining. We will account for those as well."

Cego heard a snicker from another student to his side. The class was likely raring to have some excitement to break up the repeated technique drills Dynari had been putting them through. But Cego hadn't expected to be the focus of such a diversion.

"As for his olfactory sense," Dynari continued, "it is not of much use for this experiment. And I have a feeling Dentas's second skin may be occupying Cego's nose."

Cego nodded in agreement, trying to breathe through his mouth from beneath the sweaty rag.

"We will also negate any auditory or tactile senses," Dynari explained. "Dentas, please stand in front of Cego at arm's length."

Cego stood up straight, his hands down at his side. He could hear Dentas pad over to stand near him.

"Dentas will stay silent prior to an attack of his choice," Dynari said. "He may choose any type of strike directed at Cego's body or head."

"What?" Cego heard Sol's voice. "This is ridiculous. What is this supposed to demonstrate except Cego's ability to take punishment?"

"Halberd," Dynari said calmly. "Cego seems to believe that outside of a Grievar's primary senses, there is some way to see actions before they occur. This is an extremely dangerous notion, given it will impart to any fighter a false sense of security as well as preventing them from fully embracing the superior senses we've been bestowed with. I aim to show Cego, and the class, the erroneous nature of this notion."

"But he's wrong!" Sol pleaded. "Cego knows it; he hasn't been himself lately and—"

"Enough," Dynari said. "Dentas, choose your shot, and when you have my visual command, take it."

"Uh, you sure, Professor?" Cego heard the hesitation in the Level Five's baritone voice. "Don't want to hurt my fellow classmate."

"We have very able clerics at our disposal at the Lyceum," Dynari said. "Ready yourself."

Cego started to raise his hands to protect his face but realized how pointless the action would be. If Dentas saw him defending his head, the boy would simply strike low, with a kick or body shot. If Cego lowered his guard or raised a leg to protect his body, Dentas would strike high.

Cego kept his hands at his side and breathed out, trying to—

He doubled over on the ground, heaving for breath, his midsection throbbing from what felt like a hard knee down the center.

"This is senseless," Cego heard Sol growl, closer to him now.

"Cego," the professor said. "Without having your hands on Dentas or the benefit of any sort of auditory signals, were you able to predict anything about his coming attack?"

Cego shook his head from the ground and slowly rose. Of course, Professor Dynari was right. There was nothing that could tell him where Dentas would strike. Except the blacklight. If he could figure out how to—

Cego's head snapped back and he was toppling over, barely able to slap the ground in time to break his fall. Pain radiated from his forehead where Dentas had planted a fist or foot; Cego wasn't sure which.

"Stop this!" Sol shouted. Cego heard a grunt and a scuffle.

"Hey, get her off me!" Dentas yelled.

"Halberd, if you can't watch the demonstration with the rest, you will be forced to leave the classroom," Professor Dynari said. "And you won't be asked to return."

"After seeing the stupidity of this class, I don't expect I will be returning," Sol growled.

Cego knew it wasn't true. Sol had been ecstatic to finally make it into Stratagems and Maneuvers. Her technique had improved drastically since she'd started the class.

"Sol." Cego's voice was muffled from beneath the cloth. "Stay, please."

Sol was quiet. He could tell she'd stopped moving and was holding her breath. She was anticipating another vicious blow, just as Cego was.

Cego grasped at the blacklight within him, the dark threads woven through his body.

He saw Dentas standing in front of him on the black sand beach, the void of the sky above and the sea of motionless waves melting to the horizon.

Dentas threw a knee to Cego's midsection and he raised his hands to deflect the attack.

"Impressive." Professor Dynari's voice dropped into the bleak landscape. "But you likely predicted this to be Dentas's strongest attack. You're smart, but you're not seeing his move before it happens."

"Again." Cego heard himself say the word.

Crimson lightning flashed across his vision, and he saw Dentas throw a jab at his face. Cego weaved his head from the incoming punch before it touched him.

Professor Dynari and the class were silent this time.

"Again," Cego said.

Dentas launched a cross aimed to take his head off, and Cego ducked beneath it.

"Again."

The Level Five threw two jabs and a cross, followed with a round kick to the midsection. The attacks were sloppy. Cego bobbed and weaved, caught the kick and tossed Dentas backward.

"Again!" Cego yelled this time.

He heard Dentas growl, becoming frustrated. He watched the boy throw another barrage of strikes at him, each coming slower and clumsier in succession.

He easily defended each attack without hesitation. Cego's opponent was frozen like the static whitecaps across the sea.

Cego dug his feet into the black sand, let the granules filter between his toes. He breathed the salty air and watched red veins of lightning flicker across the black sky.

He turned back to his opponent, still frozen in front of him, prey waiting to be taken. He felt the blacklight urging him to return Dentas's attacks, pushing him to tear into the boy.

Cego ripped the cloth off his face and tossed it to the floor of the classroom. The black skies faded from the edges of his vision.

"How...how did you do that?" Professor Dynari's eyes were wide, an expression Cego had never seen on the reserved man before.

"How can I fight someone that can do the same?" Cego asked. "If someone knows what you do, before you do it, how can you do anything at all?"

Dynari didn't have an answer. His mouth quivered, but he was saved from any response as the door to the classroom erupted open.

A Lyceum administrator stood straight-backed and sweating. "Professor, you're needed immediately."

"I'm in the middle of a class, as you can see," Dynari said with frustration, keeping his eyes on Cego.

"The high commander requires your attention now, Professor." The administrator motioned for the doorway.

"And what of my class?" Dynari said. "I have no replacement right now—"

"No replacement is needed," the man said briskly. "All Lyceum students are to report for lockdown immediately."

"Why?" Dynari asked the question all the students in his class were bubbling with.

"You can ask High Commander Albright," the man said. "I'm just following orders."

CHAPTER 21

Lockdown

The novice might become enamored with special techniques or strategies. These are the movements that served them well, the sequences they remember fondly for giving them their greatest victories. But the master has no particular technique. The master possesses nothing special at all.

Passage Three, Forty-Fifth Precept of
the Combat Codes

Commander Memnon made his best effort to sit straight-backed in the chair, though he would have liked more than anything to slump, to let his body and mind give in.

He was tired of this fight, one which had no clear path to victory. In the Circle, standing across from even the most fearsome opponent, a Grievar at least knew their prospects: victory or defeat. Every warrior faced that simple binary, and it gave life a clarity that Memnon dearly missed.

In this fight, one with warring factions of his own kin and politics within Daimyo Governance, there were no clear answers, no decisive victories. It was a murky path shrouded in deceit, a path that Callen Albright was the most suited to tread, as much as Memnon hated to admit it.

"Do not forget, Pugilio, that you need to keep your mouth shut when they arrive." Callen paced the length of the command room in his pressed uniform. "Your normal self will simply not do in front of the Operator."

Dakar Pugilio also appeared to have accepted a sort of defeat, an inability to bite back as he normally would when faced with Callen Albright's impudence. The commander of PublicJustice was slumped over, not making Memnon's effort to sit at attention.

Callen had called the gathering in the early hours, though Memnon had already been awake. He and Adrienne had been meeting early since the lockdown began, sitting in the little garden outside of her classroom and trying to figure out how they might navigate this novel threat. The two commanders had gotten the emergency message simultaneously—the words scrawled across their light-decks: *Governance Operator en route, report to command room immediately.*

Memnon thought back to the echo of his heavy bootsteps in the Lyceum's empty halls; how strange it was to not hear the early-morning thud of pads from Tefo's Striking class or the boisterous chatter of students filling the common grounds. He wondered why he wasn't nervous or even caring that a high representative of Governance was making a visit to the Lyceum for the first time in two decades.

It was part of the unwritten separation of branches, Citadel and Governance, preventing their affairs from intermixing. As much of a farce as it was, Governance thought it integral that the Citadel be seen as an independent entity, the Grievar Knights fighting for the citizens of the nation of their own volition.

The last time Memnon could remember an Operator setting foot in the Lyceum was when Murray Pearson had been forced to an early retirement after losing the Adar ridge to the Kirothians.

Memnon could still remember the look on Murray's face when the little Daimyo politik had told the giant Grievar that his services would no longer be needed. Despite all Murray had given, all he'd put toward the path, they pulled him from the team—said it was bad optics to keep him on board after such a loss. Of course, Governance had offered him a position within the newly formed Scout branch as consolation.

Until now, Governance had conveyed their bidding through the high commander of the Citadel. They'd directed Memnon to integrate the training sims, the stim programs, the Cradle. And when Memnon had been forced out, the Daimyo had used Callen Albright as their mouthpiece.

But now things were different, Memnon mused. Things were in such dire straits that the Operator himself was on his way.

Of course, they'd all heard of the Ezonian loss in the Flats. Though Callen had made sure propaganda was spread through the Lyceum as usual—an outbreak of Cimmerian Shade the reason for the lockdown—it was inevitable that word of the battle had spread to all ears willing to listen.

Memnon assumed that the Operator would be there simply to reinforce Callen's orders—clamp down on the effort to keep word of the Flux quiet so that more Grievar did not defect. He'd heard 10 percent of the local population had already moved north to join up with the Slayer's force.

Callen was uncharacteristically silent, pacing but not loving the sound of his own voice as usual. Perhaps Callen was scared he'd displeased his incoming bosses.

At first, Memnon thought his heart was beating forcefully, thumping against his uniform, but he realized it was the sound of heavy footsteps coming down the hall. Memnon recognized the loud, ungraceful staccato of those steps.

The portal door to the command center retracted and two massive Enforcers came in, barely able to squeeze through the wide passage simultaneously. Behind the mechanical beasts strode several diminutive, uniformed Daimyo, followed by another Enforcer with its head turned the opposite direction, as if expecting an attack from the rear.

One of the Daimyo wore a jet-black uniform, matching his empty coal eyes. Memnon recognized the Operator's insignia painted on his skullcap.

"Welcome, Operator." Callen stooped into a low bow. "Welcome to you and your colleagues; we are honored here at the Citadel with your presence."

Memnon and Larkspur stood and performed the same honorifics, though with considerably less enthusiasm. He met Dakar's eyes, and the man begrudgingly rose from his seat to do the same.

"We would rather not break decorum and set foot in this building, High Commander Albright." The Operator spoke in a fast drone. "But such are the times. Nothing appears as it should, and the normalcy of decorum is a barrier that must be trodden on in pursuit of progress."

The Operator slid into a seat, Callen's normal position at the largest chair of the round table, as the other Daimyo found their positions. Callen quickly bowed again and stepped away to sit across from the Operator as Dakar shook his head and picked at his long mustache. The Enforcers posted themselves around the room.

"Yes, yes, we fully understand, Operator," Callen said, his voice transformed to a sickening singsong tenor. "I have made sure to follow your orders to the most minute detail. The Lyceum is fully locked down, as you can see, and all SystemView feeds have been pulled. And, as you know, we've placed Aon Farstead in isolation."

"Good," the Operator said, scanning the other commanders at the table. Memnon couldn't help but avoid the man's bottomless eyes. "Though I am sure word has gotten out of the Battle of Flat Plains, it is not good for morale to expose the young, malleable minds within the Lyceum."

"Of course." Callen shook his head enthusiastically. "For all they're aware, we will be starting class again shortly while the clerics deal with this particularly nasty strain of the Shade."

"Unfortunately," the Operator said, "that will not be the case. Classes will certainly not resume as normal, which is why we are here."

The room was silent, though Memnon could tell Callen was nearly quaking in his boots, waiting to hear what service these lords would require of him.

"As you've heard, the army of lower breeds heads this way, unimpeded," the Operator said.

Callen's eyes widened. "But surely, my lord, they'll be stopped far before they reach the Citadel's walls. What of the rest of the Flyer force and the ground—"

"Were you not briefed on what occurred at Flat Plains?" the Operator snarled.

"Yes, yes." Callen cowered. "But I thought it was an anomaly, given the great power I know you wield; I thought the next wave would interrupt the Flux far before they reached our walls."

"It was not an anomaly," the Operator said. "I was watching my Flyer squad from central command. I had eyes on them all, the pulse of their mechs. Those machines were shut down externally, something even the pilots within them would be unable to do without the confirmation code from me personally."

"So, how?" Callen asked.

"The Bit-Minders," the Operator said, looking around the room defiantly as if one were there along with them.

"But...but why would the Minders shut down our tech? They're on our side, right? They work for us," Callen said.

"Apparently not." Dakar snorted.

The Operator eyed Dakar. "Your buffoon of a commander here is right. We've received intelligence that a faction of the Minders has turned and is actively aiding the Flux rebellion."

Memnon shook his head. This was unheard of. The Bit-Minders had been woven into the Daimyo fabric of society for centuries, creating tech, transportation, and communications. The shadowy breed was most often thought of as an extension of the tech itself. This news was akin to a river deciding to switch the direction it flowed.

"So…we can do nothing at all?" Callen said, forgetting his groveling for a moment at the thought of Silas the Slayer knocking at his door. "No Ezonian resistance will meet the Flux army marching this way?"

"No," the Operator said. "If the Bit-Minders were able to shut down our Flyers so far north toward the border, we suspect they'll be able to do the same if we try to attack again too soon."

"But," Memnon finally spoke, sensing the direction of the conversation, "you have a plan."

The Operator's cold eyes shifted between Callen and Memnon, as if he couldn't decide which man was truly in control there. He stopped on Memnon.

"Yes, of course we have a plan, Commander Memnon," the Operator said. "Our intelligence sources have good reason to believe that the Minders are only able to directly affect our mechs when they are within range of a Hive."

"Hive?" Adrienne asked. "Like a hornet hive?"

"Somewhat," the Operator said. "A Hive is a concentration of the energy the Minders feed off—the blacklight. It enables them to consolidate their power and utilize it in a more direct way, such as pulling our Flyers straight from the air. The Codices in most major cities serve as Hives for such energy consolidation."

"The Codex in Tendrum?" Callen asked. "So, why don't we destroy it?"

"You think us so shortsighted?" The Operator snorted. "Of course, we've already set upon the Codex in Ezo and are in the process of decommissioning it. Though it's proving harder than anticipated."

"So, when the Codex is offline, you can send a new Flyer squad out to blast the Flux army back to the Deep," Callen said.

"They wouldn't be here if that were the case, Callen," Memnon said. "He needs us to do something for him."

"You always were astute, Commander Memnon," the Operator said, not unaware that Callen's eyes were starting to bulge from his head. "Yes, we do need your aid. The Codices aren't the only place where a Minder Hive can be located. Our Kirothian brethren reported that the Flux army was able to shut down their own Flyers at times, despite being in the middle of nowhere, without a Codex in a thousand-mile range."

"So, they have something...portable," Adrienne commented.

"Indeed," the Operator said. "It is said that the Minders long ago obtained the ability to...infiltrate living beings. Fill them with blacklight and use them as a Hive from where they can store and direct their energies."

Memnon shook his head, feeling his stomach drop.

"Darkin' Deep," Dakar said. "You mean...they can take a man over?"

"They become a parasite of sorts," the Operator said. "So, yes. We believe there is one such Hive moving alongside the Flux army, allowing them to cast their power out against incoming weaponry. Our long-range operatives are seeking out this individual, planning an attack to remove them."

"Is this why you forced us to put the oldest professor in the Lyceum in a prison cell?" Memnon growled.

"Yes," the Operator responded. "We still believe Aon Farstead is a Bit-Minder Hive, and since he has been placed within the high-density emeralyis, we believe his deleterious effect on our tech has been negated."

"So, again, why are you here?" Memnon was weary of this game, this fight with no path to victory.

"I'm glad you push me to the point, Commander Memnon," the Operator said. "I wish to spend no longer than needed on the soiled ground of Grievar."

"You're the ones who are soiled—"

Dakar had started to stand but stopped short as one of the Enforcers leapt forward with terrifying speed and pinned the commander's wrist against the table. Dakar's eyes bulged as the Enforcer squeezed and his bones cracked under its iron grip.

The Operator appeared bored. "Release him."

The Enforcer opened its grip and Dakar gasped as he held his mangled hand to his body. He slumped back to the chair.

"As I was saying," the Operator continued, "we need you to buy us time. We need to ensure we can destroy the Hive in their midst before we mount another attack against the Flux. We cannot sustain such losses again, not to mention the diminished backing of our citizenry, seeing us defeated by such pathetic creatures."

"Let us know anything we might do to help." Callen seemed to have regained his composure and bootlicking ability simultaneously.

"You are Grievar, here at the Citadel." The Operator stated the obvious. "And Silas and most of his army are Grievar. Despite the Slayer's obvious disdain for the rule of law, I believe there is something innate within Grievar-kin, something bred into you, that disallows you to back down from a combative challenge."

"You want us to…challenge Silas?" Memnon said. "Who?"

"Are you not commander of the Knights here?" the Operator asked. "It is in your discretion to choose a champion, as it has been for centuries."

"But why would Silas accept?" Memnon asked. "If he can march to the Citadel's walls unhindered and tear this place apart, why would he put it all on the line for a challenge?"

"Because his support depends on him maintaining his legend, his strength," the Operator said. "If he turns down such a challenge, he will lose all he's built around him."

Memnon closed his eyes, his jaw taut. This fight was different from any he'd encountered before. It wasn't one in the Circle, with a clear win or loss. And he wasn't suited to take it on.

Memnon stayed silent, and Callen's words found their place.

"We will send out our challenge to Silas the Slayer," Albright said. "Our champion will fight him within Albright Stadium with the Flux forces there to witness it. They will all be there, waiting for you, my lord."

*　　*　　*

"I don't see what good being locked in our dorms is gonna do if the Slayer is on his way," Dozer said as he paced back and forth in Quarter D like a caged bear.

"Nothing," Knees agreed. "Won't be doing nothing. But like everything else High Commander Albright has done this year, it's not to help us; it's to keep us from knowing what be going on."

Sol turned from the dorm window. "How could the Flux army have gotten past the Ezonian border forces?"

"Did you see what Silas did to Murray-Ku?" Dozer punched one of the wooden walls in frustration. "He's not normal."

Cego took a deep breath and looked at Sol, wondering if she was considering his display in Professor Dynari's class, how he'd *seen* Dentas's strikes before they came. Did she think Cego was the same as his brother? *Not normal.*

"It doesn't matter what Silas can do," Sol responded. "The Ezonian front lines were made up of Enforcers, with Flyer support. And this wouldn't be guerrilla fighting like in Kiroth. Silas's army was out in the open, making a break south."

"Here we go!" Abel said from a desk across the dorm. The little Desovian had been tinkering with his lightdeck all day. "I did it."

"Did what?" Brynn asked from her spot on the bed beside the desk. The Jadean looked surprisingly relaxed despite the circumstance.

Abel smiled as he held up his lightdeck. "I figure how to wire this to national SystemView feed."

"Nice work, Abel!" Dozer exclaimed as he and the rest of the crew crowded around the little screen.

"Could not get sounds," Abel said. "Just visual."

An aerial feed panned above an expansive plain with the border mountains set in the backdrop. Plumes of smoke streamed from fires lit across the Flats. Cego could see the glint of metal amid the flames. The feed zoomed in, and he saw crumpled mechs littered across the battlefield, surrounded by a mass of bodies.

"By the Deep," Knees said. "How could this happen?"

"Those are Flyers," Sol said, pointing to one of the downed mechs, ripped apart and still burning.

"I know how it happened," Cego said. "The Bit-Minders, they're helping Silas."

"Why would they do that?" Sol asked. "The Bit-Minders… throughout history, they have never been known to take a side. It's against their nature."

Cego shook his head. "I'm not entirely sure. But somehow, I can feel it. In the blacklight. All I know for sure is Silas is coming. And there's nothing anyone will be able to do to stop him from bringing his army to the Citadel. If he gets through these walls…"

His brother's rebellion was bent on destroying Daimyo, killing all those who opposed his cause. He looked to Sol and thought about their moment on Kalabasas, how she'd told him of her Daimyo blood. Sol could hide it, but how long would that last?

Cego's thoughts flickered to Xenalia and the rest of the clerics in the ward—they would be executed immediately. Zyleth, the professor who had fought for Cego, he would not escape the Slayer's wrath either. Even the lacklight Whelps in Quarter D would not be able to escape extermination if they stood up to Silas.

Everyone Cego loved was within these walls.

"I won't let him get to you," Cego growled, his fist clenched. A crimson vein of lightning streaked across his vision and he heard the low rumble of thunder. The black sand was beneath his feet, the frozen waters expanding out as far as he could see.

Silas would not take anyone else away from him. Cego would make sure of that.

Sol's warm hand was on Cego's face and he was standing in Quarter D again. "It's not up to you, Cego."

"What?"

"We're all in this together," Sol said. "We will fight together."

"But...I can't lose anyone else," Cego whispered. "No more can die for me."

Knees stepped over to Cego, looking at him with hard eyes. For a moment, Cego thought his friend might hit him, but instead, the Venturian placed a hand on his shoulder and squeezed. "You be an idiot, Cego. If you think we've come this far, traveled the whole of Kiroth, joined the darkin' Flux to get you...If you think we'll let you take the heat yourself now, you be a darkin' idiot."

"But he's my brother...my family," Cego said. "I'm the only one that truly knows Silas; I should be the one to stand in his way. I should be the one to sacrifice."

"Hate to break it to you," Dozer said, "but your darkin' family is crazy and your brother is on a warpath to the Citadel currently, so I think we're way past that."

"And we are your family," Sol said. "We are part of your past now, and we'll stand with you for all that lies ahead. You need to trust us."

"I do," Cego said, meeting Sol's sunflower eyes. "You are the only ones I trust. And I think we're the only ones that can stop Silas right now. I know him. Whatever the high commander or the Daimyo Governance is planning, I know it won't be enough."

"Then let's do it together," Brynn said as she stepped forward. "Spirits be with us."

"I can't believe we be set on helping the Daimyo," Knees whispered. "Never thought I'd be saying those words."

"Neither can I," Dozer said. "But better help them than the Minders...and the man who killed Ku."

"We fight for Joba," Abel said, a new determination flashing across the Desovian's eyes. "And for Murray-Ku. And for Professor Aon."

"Yes," Cego said. "We fight for them, and for each other."

CHAPTER 22

Chop Down
the Tree

*Habit is the cornerstone to a Grievar's martial progress. How-
ever, one must be careful to avoid becoming dependent on a set
training regimen; life and combat are never truly predictable.*

Passage Six, Twenty-Fifth Precept of
the Combat Codes

Cego's shin slammed against the bark of the ironwood tree
again.

After a while, it stopped hurting. After throwing so many kicks
against the smooth bark, the blood stoppered up; the nerve endings
in his leg became numb to the repeated impact.

He paused to wipe the sweat from his eyes. He listened to his
brothers continue their assault on the ironwoods from beside him
in the grove. He heard the sharp crack of a sapling.

Silas grinned and stepped over a fallen tree like another downed
opponent. He moved toward his next victim and mechanically
started chopping again.

Sam used to complain when Farmer wasn't watching. His little brother had constantly questioned the point of spending hours in the ironwood grove, kicking trees. Now the little freckled boy mechanically chopped at the tree, numb to the pain.

Cego began to work again, focused on keeping his leg loose and throwing from the hip as Farmer had instructed.

"Like swinging a rope," the old master had said, though Cego had wondered if the man was aware that his leg was made up of bones that could break and muscles that could tear, unlike a rope.

Cego noticed Sam had paused. The boy's gaze was trained on a lithe form scaling the largest tree in the grove, a mother ferrcat with a dead rodent gripped in her teeth. She was on her way back to feed her young up in the nest.

It was only yesterday that Cego and Sam had silently peered from their perch and marveled at how fast the two little cats were growing. They'd been captivated as the mother gave her babies a hotly protested tongue bath.

Cego realized Silas had stopped kicking and was watching Sam. Silas had scolded them for spending so much time up in the canopy lately.

"Let's put an end to this," Silas said as he approached the ancient tree. "You two need to focus on training."

The eldest brother had spent the end of each kicking session working on that big tree, slowly cutting into the groove at its base. Cego and Sam had watched as the nest vibrated and shed leaves each time Silas's kicks shook the trunk. But the great ironwood had withstood the assault, and the ferrcat home had held in place.

Until now.

They could see that the great ironwood was near toppling, starting to stoop at a strange angle like an old man lived past his days. The ferrcats began to squeal from the canopy as the tree groaned with another of Silas's strikes.

Silas kicked harder and faster as his opponent gave way. He

sensed weakness, and Cego knew that would drive his brother to finish the job.

"No..." Sam said, his eyes latched on the ferrcats, who were now scrambling to stay in the swaying nest. If the tree fell, the mother would likely survive, but not the young—a goshawk would pick them off before nightfall if they survived the initial impact.

"There's nothing we can do," Cego said. He knew Silas. He knew his eldest brother didn't care about the little creatures. The tree was his opponent, one he'd been battling with for the last month, and nothing could stop him now.

"Silas, stop it!" Sam moved toward the eldest brother, who did not respond. He stayed methodical in his striking, following some internal rhythm.

"Let me get up there and take them down first," Sam pleaded. Their little brother had always had a soft spot for the creatures of the island. Last year, he'd nursed a fallen sparrow back to health after it'd flown into the siding of Farmer's compound.

Silas kept kicking.

Cego knew they were only animals. He knew life and death happened on a regular basis and the baby cats wouldn't likely make it through the year, anyway. But it bothered him that Silas didn't care.

They heard a sharp crack that echoed through the forest. Silas's shin met the same spot again, his hip turned, and he ripped his leg back into the weakened structure. As if a final sinew holding the trunk had been severed, the tree let out a groan and its canopy tore through the neighboring branches on the way to the ground.

The forest floor quivered and was silent except for the squealing ferrcat mother, who sprinted in fear from the boys.

Sam walked to a corner of the grove near where the top of the tree had landed. The little boy knelt and lifted a frayed body in his hand. Cego watched his brother squeeze his eyes shut as a tear slid across the bridge of his nose. Though Sam complained often, he almost never cried.

"*Time to head back to the compound for midmorning training,*" Silas said with that sharp smile etched across his face. Silas limped from the grove, keeping weight off the leg he'd felled the great ironwood with.

Cego gave Sam the time to bury the little cat. His brother dug a small hole with a rock and set the frail body within before placing some leaves atop it.

"*Why'd he have to do it?*" Sam asked as they pushed aside the thick undergrowth on the path back toward the shore. "*He could have let me take them down.*"

"*I don't know,*" Cego said. He never quite understood why Silas did these things.

"*I know why,*" Sam said, as he kicked at the dirt. "*He likes hurting things. He wanted to kill.*"

Cego was silent. He couldn't bring himself to believe that Silas was vindictive, though he'd been exposed to his brother's mean streak before. The boy thrived when he was in power, and that often came at the expense of his younger brothers.

Cego knew Sam most often looked up to Silas like a god. They lived on the island to train, and Silas was by far the best of the three. Sam tried to emulate most of Silas's actions, tried to be like him within the Circle. But then there were times like this, when Silas seemed to not even know he had two other brothers.

Sam was quiet as they made their way from the forest onto the black sand beach, where the little pup, Arry, joined them, yapping and running along the shore. Most often Sam would run across the beach too, letting Arry try to keep up, but today they walked. Cego could feel the deep soreness in his legs from kicking the ironwoods all morning and didn't look forward to throwing another kick in the Circle.

Sam finally spoke again. "*Cego, I have an idea.*"

"*What's that?*" Cego asked as a gust of sea wind tossed sand in his face.

"Let's make Silas pay for what he did," the little boy said.

"We're all here together, Sam," Cego replied. "We're working to make each other better. We can't take it personally."

"I know," Sam said. "But...just today. Let's beat him this once."

Cego wanted to beat his older brother as much as Sam did, but neither one of them had ever come close to it.

"I don't know if we can," Cego said. "He's too skilled for either of us to get through. He's too strong."

"We can do it together," Sam said as he picked up a smooth stick and tossed it across the beach for Arry to chase.

Of course, Sam did not mean fighting Silas simultaneously. That would be against Farmer's code; only single combat was permitted within the Circle. And even out of the Circle, when Cego and Sam had attempted to gang up on Silas, the older boy came out the victor.

Cego watched a swarm of little starlings nipping at a goshawk's heels, chasing it away from their nest.

"Together," Cego repeated to his brother. "Maybe we can."

Sam smiled, happy that someone was listening to him for once. "How?"

Cego felt the pain in his leg and thought of how Silas had limped from the grove. They'd spent all morning chopping down trees.

"Chop down the tree," Cego said. It was what Farmer had told them every morning before they left for the grove. Those simple words and nothing else. "Chop down the tree."

Sam looked at him quizzically.

"We'll do to Silas what he did to that big ironwood," Cego said. "His right leg...it's weak right now. You'll be up against him first like usual. Sam, you need to chop at that leg."

"But whenever I go for a low kick, Silas counters up high," Sam said, nervously rubbing at his nose, which had been broken a few days prior. "I can't defend in time."

"You won't have to," Cego said. "As long as you can get some good kicks in before he takes you out."

"You mean…" Sam trailed off. "I let Silas beat me?"

"Silas will beat either of us no matter what if we each play our own game and try to win against him," Cego said. "But if we work together, one after the other, we can chop down the tree. Just like Silas couldn't take down that big ironwood in one day. He needed to come after it day after day to fell it. You and me need to go after Silas's leg, one after another."

Sam thought about it for a moment. "Okay, I'll do it."

"You sure?" Cego asked. "It'll hurt."

"It will be worth it if we can beat him." Sam clenched his jaw. "He needs to pay for what he did."

*　　*　　*

It was strange, the quiet of the halls during the Lyceum's lockdown. Even in the middle of the night, most often there would be students filling the training Circles in the common grounds, trying to get extra work in for a test or challenge match. But tonight, the grounds were entirely empty—all the students locked down in their rooms.

Still, Cego was surprised he was the only one roaming the halls. It hadn't been hard for Abel to rewire the simple Quarter D lockpad to let him out, though perhaps the ancient tech of their dorm had done them a favor for once.

He crept past the hanging lightboards and watched the line of luminescent spectrals rising toward the upper-level floors.

How strange it was that the Lyceum didn't want students to know of the incoming Flux army.

Wouldn't the truth at least let them prepare, get in touch with their families? But even then, Cego wasn't certain many would believe that Silas had broken across the border.

It was curious what folk did to maintain the vision of the world they were comfortable with.

Cego followed the lower-level stairs down to the catacombs. As expected, the rusty door was open, and even more predictable was the sight of Kōri Shimo sitting within the onyx.

Cego waited patiently for the boy to finish his session in the blacklight. Shimo's eyes flicked open and met Cego's.

"You do know the school's on lockdown, right?" Cego asked.

Shimo nodded. "And why does this matter?"

Cego shook his head. "Sometimes, I wonder why you're even here. I mean, is it because of this Circle?"

Shimo stepped from the onyx and stood in front of Cego. "Yes, I don't believe there are many onyx Circles as pure as the one here. And the Lyceum is where I'm meant to be."

"Why?" Cego had been meaning to ask the boy this question since they'd started meeting in the catacombs. "Do you even go to classes anymore? Do you plan to graduate and become a Knight? Or a professor, maybe?"

Shimo's eyes twinkled, as if he was laughing within. "A professor? For some reason, I do not think I would be such a good teacher."

"You taught me how to use the onyx," Cego said.

"You taught yourself," Shimo replied. "I merely showed you its function."

"So, you'd like to be a Knight, then—that is, if the Citadel is still standing after Silas's army arrives."

Shimo was silent. "These are all only titles. I'm here for a purpose—to fight. And on this note, are you going to train or not?"

He gestured toward the Circle.

Cego shook his head again, though he felt the urge to step within. "Not tonight. I came to check on you, let you know what's going on, because I figured no one else would tell you."

"Let me know about the Flux army?"

"Yes," Cego said. "The Daimyo tried to stop them at the border, but they couldn't."

"I didn't think they would," Shimo said. "The Slayer can't be stopped this way."

"And...you know how he can be stopped?" Cego asked.

"As do you," Shimo said cryptically.

Cego did know, though. He'd always known. "The blacklight."

"Why else do you think you've been training within it, torturing yourself each night?" Shimo asked.

"I thought it was so I could become better, faster," Cego said. "Catch up to Silas. Get a decade of work in with only weeks in there."

"Yes, that's part of it," Shimo said. "But you know there is more. I trust you have been seeing the blacklight even when you're out of the onyx?"

Cego thought back to Dynari's class, how he'd occupied a strange space between the island and the Lyceum. "Yes, I can... see moves before they happen."

"This is what Silas sees," Shimo said. "And no one can beat him, not Grievar Knight nor Daimyo mech, if they cannot harness the blacklight."

"What are you going to do?" Cego asked. "Silas will try to kill those who don't join the Flux."

"Are you asking me if I'm going to join the rebel force?"

Cego nodded.

Kōri Shimo smiled, one of the few times Cego had seen the boy's lips deviate from a flat line. "I've enjoyed training with you, Cego. For so long a stretch of time."

Cego wasn't quite sure what Shimo meant, as the two had never truly trained together. They'd simply been there for each other on the sidelines of the onyx.

"Well." Cego shrugged. "I've got to get going."

Kōri looked about ready to step back into the onyx. Cego had no idea how the boy could take so much punishment.

"Whatever side you end up on," Cego said as he began to walk from the catacombs, "thank you for helping me."

Shimo nodded in response as he stepped back into the black ring.

*   *   *

Cego left the boy and the blacklight Circle, taking the stairs up to the third floor. He walked the length of the Harmony, a shadow passing locked classrooms and sleeping quarters. He embraced the darkness of the Lyceum, creeping silently through quiet buildings when the rest of the world slept.

Cego had been there before.

The medward was not locked down like the other Lyceum wings. Most patients that were stationed there did not have a choice to leave; bedridden students and Knights set in stasis were not the mobile sort.

Cego crept through the ward, listening to the chorus of mechanical beeps echoing the pulses of the attached bodies. He dreaded that some of those heartbeats would flatline as he passed by, as if the machinery would detect his presence, recognize a boy from a different world who wasn't meant to be there.

Cego ducked out of the way as a little spectral flitted from bed to bed, checking on patients while the clerics rested. He stopped just outside one of the private patient rooms, trembling and sliding to the floor beside the door.

He clenched his hands in the darkness and listened to the pulse of the heartbeats. He gritted his teeth, steeling himself, then stood and entered the room.

Sam was sitting where he always was, up against the wall beside the cot and the plant. Xenalia had updated Cego regularly, told him his brother's appetite had been fine and he had no problem sleeping.

"Think you'll come with me to the tide pools today?" Sam stared blankly at Cego. "I bet the storms that passed through dredged up some good catches."

But Cego's brother wasn't here.

"I don't think I can come today, Sam; I need to train." Cego tried to respond as if he were with his brother, in that place.

When Cego had first seen Sam in this state, he'd tried to break through to him. He'd attempted to snap the little boy out of the trance he was in, release the hold the Cradle had. But it had been futile.

"Please, won't you come for a moment?" Sam asked, as Cego knew he would. "Call Arry down from the dunes too; I bet she'd love the run."

"I can't go today," Cego responded, as if reading a script, the same dialogue he'd gone through with his brother the last time he'd visited the ward. "I've got to train."

Maybe Cego should have come there every evening to exchange the same loop of senseless words with his brother. But he'd been scared. He felt the same blacklight within him that he knew was embedded in Sam. He had befriended the darkness that his brother had been lost to.

But Cego couldn't be scared anymore. He had to free Sam from his prison, before it was too late. Before Silas came and left his little brother in the darkness.

The boy abruptly spoke again. "So, you'll come down to the rocks with me, Cego?"

Cego sighed, felt the tears welling in his eyes. "Okay, Sam, just this once."

"Why do you need to train so much?" Sam asked. "Is it so you can finally beat Silas?"

Cego nodded. "Yes."

Though Sam was speaking from another world, the boy was right. Some things never did change.

Cego approached Sam, stepping into the moonlight behind him. He wrapped his arm around his little brother's neck. He'd done it thousands of times before, shown the boy how to defend the strangle.

Tears flowed freely down his face as he began to squeeze. Sam didn't protest. He sat there, trusting Cego.

Cego would have done anything to protect Sam. He still would do anything to protect him.

A little bit longer and it will be over, Sam. You will be free.

He saw Sam running on the black sand beach, the wind catching his mop of hair, Arry nipping at his toes.

He saw Sam laughing as he emerged from the surf, covered head to toe in seagrass.

Cego felt the little boy start to twitch as he went unconscious.

Cego had been there before.

Gliding into a building like a shadow and seeking his targets, those unaware of the certain death that was coming to them. Finding their neck, cinching their arteries, constricting the life from them.

This had been the work of the Strangler, the Flux operative, the Slayer's shadow. But Cego had left the Strangler behind after he'd seen Murray give his life. Cego had made the decision to return home to protect those he loved.

He felt his breath catch, and the strength in his arms went out. He stumbled backward, away from Sam, his eyes wide, fully realizing what he'd been doing.

How can I be capable of such things?

Sam's body jolted, the blood rushing back to the little boy's brain. After several breathless moments, the boy turned and looked back at Cego from the floor.

"Think you'll come with me to the tide pools today?" Sam asked.

Cego slid away across the floor until he was outside the room, back in the ward with its mechanical pulse.

He ran from the darkness.

CHAPTER 23

The Sea

A Grievar should bathe once per week. Less frequent bathing may cause the buildup of harmful toxins and result in sickness. However, bathing too often will diminish the essential vitality that lies just beneath a Grievar's skin.

Passage Four, Forty-Third Precept of
the Combat Codes

don't get why Cego gets to ride Bird!" Dozer grumbled. The big Grievar sat behind Knees, his arms wrapped around him for support, as the two rode on brown Boko.

"First, we know Bird's taken to Cego since Murray left us," Brynn said from her black roc with Abel behind her. "And second, don't deny that you're happy to be hugging Knees again."

Cego chuckled as Dozer quickly unwrapped his arms from Knees, only to nearly fall off the roc. He ruffled the stray feathers on Bird's head as they rode out on the carriage road west of the Citadel.

Sol rode beside him, high atop great Firenze, her long red braid bouncing with the gait of the mount. It was a rare day full of sunshine in Ezo, though winter's cold still hung in the air. But the indigo calacynth blossoms had bloomed in the grass and the ice had thawed and melted, feeding the river that ran beside them. They would follow the waters to the Western Sea.

Cego still couldn't believe that the Whelps were there. They weren't running, though the thought had crossed Cego's mind. Sol and Brynn had come up with the idea of getting away for a day, escaping the lockdown. It hadn't been difficult. Abel had already rewired the Quarter D lockpad, and Brynn had befriended one of the Level Fives who had been posted to keep watch. None of the students were happy about being stuck in their dorms.

"Why wait here and stew in fear when we're not even able to train properly?" Brynn had said. "Let's go off and enjoy the world a few moments more. If these are to be our last days, I'd like mine to be nice ones, spirits be asked."

Cego had been reluctant at first; going on a jaunt to the beach didn't seem appropriate when the world was burning.

A full battalion of Enforcers had been gathered outside the Citadel's walls, waiting to greet Silas's undeterred army. The Lyceum had been completely shut down for the first time in decades, all the students huddled in fear of the Cimmerian Shade within their dorms.

And the news had spread that Silas the Slayer was to meet First Knight Yang in the Circle within Albright Stadium. A challenge match, ordained by the Citadel, that would determine the fate of the entire nation.

The Whelps had watched the preparations on their way out. A horde of Grunts had descended on the grounds outside Albright Stadium to construct tents to house the incoming army. They'd dragged out barrels of rations and drink to feed the Flux.

It was strange, to give an invading army such hospitality, Cego had thought.

"I still can't believe you haven't been to the sea before," Brynn said across her roc to Knees.

"It be a bit tough to visit the sea when you grow up in the desert and then are sold to the Underground," Knees replied.

"My sisters and I used to visit the big lakes in Desovi," Abel said.

"You've never been either, Cego?" Brynn asked.

Cego didn't know how to respond. "Well, it's a bit complicated for me..."

"Remember, Cego was born in a Bit-Minder simulation of an island," Sol said. "So, he did spend most of his childhood by the water, but outside of his mind, he's never visited a real seaside."

"Oh," said Brynn in her casual manner. "That makes sense, then."

Sol turned back to Cego and gave him a grin. "Was that so hard?"

"Well... I guess not," Cego said.

"Not everything has to be so complicated," Sol said. "Like this trip. It's what it is, friends off to take a little break from the world."

The sunlight touched Cego's face. He began to smell the salt of the sea air as they got closer. It reminded him of the island, of Sam playing in the surf.

He shook his head, trying to shake his visit to the medward several nights earlier. The shame rose up within him like a poison as he saw Sam's helpless form twitching in front of him.

How could I be capable of such things?

He breathed deeply.

"When I was little, my father used to take me on this road for our trips to the seaside," Sol said. "It's as I remember it."

"He's watching down on you now," Brynn said. "On the Jade, it's said after the big storm season passes through, it is the spirits returned that help the world regrow."

Cego nodded, enjoying the notion that Murray-Ku and Joba might also be watching them.

The Whelps urged their rocs over a small bluff, and the Western Sea was in front of them, a frothing expanse of white breakers and grey rocky outcroppings.

Cego slid from Bird's back and took his boots off, letting his feet touch the cold rocks.

A thunderous roar ripped across the sky. The Whelps craned their heads and saw six sleek black shapes puncture the clouds.

"Flyers," Sol whispered. "An entire squadron."

The Flyers sped over the sea and stopped midair above a rocky landmass jutting from the water. A blinking skeletal tower rose from a flat platform on the island, which the mechs descended to.

"What is that place?" Abel stared out at the island.

"Not sure," Sol responded. "It wasn't there when I used to come out here with my father. Governance must have built it recently."

"They're protecting their nest," Cego said. "Governance brought those Flyers in to be in reach of the Citadel in a few minutes' notice."

"Which means," Sol said, "they must be able to counter the problem they ran into with their mechs in the Battle of Flat Plains. It's like Bythardi... They are positioning their pieces."

"As interesting as that all sounds," Dozer said, "I'm not here to talk Citadel strategy."

The big Grievar pulled off his uniform, making sure to flex for the crew, and ran toward the water.

"This should be good," Sol said from beside Cego.

"Thought it was supposed to be warm!" Dozer yelped the second his feet touched the water, pulling his arms tight to his body and shivering as a large wave drenched him.

"These aren't island waters like we have in Besayd," Brynn said as she fearlessly sprinted across the rocky shore. She jumped into a wave and splashed water up in the air like a child. "But it's not so bad, you big coward!"

Dozer swatted seawater straight into the Jadean's face, erasing her smile.

"You better get over there to help," Sol said to Knees. "Before Brynn drowns Dozer."

"You probably be right," Knees said as he measuredly made his way to the sea with Abel following him.

Sol stripped the second skin off her back, and Cego's eyes fell to the floor. His face flushed red; even though she was wearing an undergarment, it still left little to the imagination.

"You coming in?" Sol asked as she began to walk toward the water.

"Um... I figure someone should probably stay with the birds," Cego said.

"They'll be all right; Firenze is keeping an eye on them." Sol nodded to the giant roc, who was preening Bird's few feathers fastidiously.

It wasn't that Cego minded the cold water. Or that he didn't want to join his friends. Something felt wrong. He stared out at the fortressed island offshore.

As if reading Cego's mind, Sol walked back to him.

"It's okay to be happy sometimes, Cego," she said. "You deserve it."

Sol kissed him, a quick peck on the lips, but one that nearly knocked Cego over like a well-placed double-leg takedown. She turned and ran to the ocean, her long red braid trailing as she dove in and emerged from the waves.

Cego's heart raced; the hair on his neck bristled. He felt warm inside, but it wasn't any dark energy burning. This was something else. It was home.

He sprinted toward the sea.

* * *

When the Whelps arrived at the hidden path that led back to the roc roost, Cego slid off Bird.

"Sure you don't want to bring him?" Sol asked. "He's a bit neurotic, but I don't doubt he'll rip apart anyone who messes with you."

Cego smiled. "It's all right; I'll be okay. And I don't want to draw attention."

He wanted to squeeze Sol's hand before he left, but instead, he patted Firenze's feathered hindquarters awkwardly.

"Come back soon, Cego," Sol said as she wheeled Firenze around and spurred the bird into the thicket.

"Hope you find what you be looking for," Knees said as the rest of the rocs followed. Bird turned back to watch Cego, grey feathers sprouting haphazardly from his cocked head, before he disappeared into the underbrush.

Cego took the path away from the Citadel, circling around the back side of Albright Stadium.

Even in the dead of night, the Grunts still labored to construct the makeshift tent city. Cego passed through the horde of workers unnoticed, though he sank into the cowl of his cloak as a pair of giant steel Enforcers trudged across the muddy grounds.

He passed under an arched entryway to the hawkers' district, usually bustling with the caws of merchants even during the night hours, but now it was deathly quiet. Most of the little run-down shops were boarded up, the outdoor carts stored away. Ezo's citizens had locked down like the students at the Lyceum in preparation for the Slayer's incoming army.

"Where do you think you're going?" A bedraggled merc with his hand on his weapon approached Cego from the darkness.

"Back home." Cego lifted his hood so the man could see his face. He feigned a foreign accent. "Karsh. My ma send me to find food but I find nothing."

Cego held up his empty hands.

"Get back to where you belong, fast," the Grievar said nervously. "Next time we catch you in the open, we'll need to bring you in. And if Enforcers find you out here, you won't be so lucky."

Even though Governance had lied to its citizenry, as the Lyceum had lied to its students, word had spread fast about Silas's victory in the Flats. Cego had heard that some Grievar had already packed and fled to join up with the rebels. The rest were in hiding, fearing the Slayer's retribution for their refusal to come to his side.

As for the Daimyo living in the Tendrum's skyscrapers, many

had fled to their summer homes in the southern reaches or boarded their airships or Dyvers to escape to Besayd, which remained relatively untouched from the rebellion.

Cego couldn't believe the world was changing so fast, all because of the boy with the curved smile he'd grown up with on the island.

He stepped beneath an underpass and saw that Ezo's junkies hadn't moved. A few eyed him suspiciously as they huddled around a fire, one holding his hand up to a hacking cough.

Cego hurried past. He wondered if his brother's plan would work. If Silas cut off the production of stims, would these men disappear from beneath the bridge? Would they wean themselves from their addiction, find a path outside the sway of the drugs?

He crossed to the cobbled fringes of Central Square and shivered as he remembered the last time he'd been there. The square was empty now, not like that day, when the crowd had gathered and screamed for his blood at the hands of the Goliath. Cego still could see the hole the Enforcer had put in Joba's stomach with its blast cannon.

It wasn't long before Cego found his way to Karsh, set in the dregs and full of all the immigrants that the rest of the city had expunged.

He sniffed the air, hoping to catch a whiff of fresh-baked sponge bread. But even there, in a sector he remembered so vibrant and full of life, people were scared.

He caught an old woman peering from the crack in a boarded-up window. A little soot-faced boy sat on a pair of crumbled steps.

"Who are you?" the boy asked bravely as Cego passed by.

"I'm a student from the Lyceum," Cego said, pulling his hood back.

"I'm not afraid of the Slayer." The boy stood up and got into a fighting stance. "If he comes by here, I'll protect my grandda."

"I bet you will," Cego said, admiring the boy's determination. "Though you should raise that right hand. Need to cover for the left high kick. I know the Slayer has a good one."

The boy looked at Cego with wide eyes.

"Have...have you met him?"

Cego was tired of lying. "Yes...he's my brother."

"I don't have a brother anymore," the boy said. "He died of the Shade with my ma and pa."

The boy looked down somberly for a moment. "Are you going to fight against us with your brother? Are you going to try to take my home away?"

Cego shook his head. "Where'd you hear that?"

"Watching the feeds over Grandda's shoulder," the boy said. "He's seeing it all day long."

"I'm not so sure Silas wants to take your home," Cego said.

"Well, if he does, he won't be able to," the boy said with renewed determination, this time raising his hand higher to cover his chin.

Cego nodded and continued on. "You take care of your grandda."

As he rounded a corner, Cego recognized the grey tin roof on Murray's barracks. A few broken potted plants sat outside the door, likely surviving with the help of friendly neighbors. Cego stood on his toes and reached above the doorframe to feel around, finally finding the old lock sensor Murray had hidden up there.

Cego pushed the creaky door open and stepped into the darkness. He walked into the kitchen slowly, as if any sudden movement would upset the memory of a place locked in time, untouched after Murray had never returned from Pilgrimage.

A chair was pulled out in front of the knotty kitchen table. Cego looked down on a wooden bowl, the remnants of some crusted-over stew caked on the edge. The old couple next door had likely taken pity on Murray and cooked it for him. Cego knew Murray hadn't the inclination to do any real sizzling for himself.

A scavenger scurried underfoot with a squeak, its red eyes glaring at the intruder. Cego peered into the adjacent room, Murray's makeshift study. A stack of books was piled beside the armchair, and a cold breeze rattled a window frame that had blown open. Cego quickly moved to shutter it.

He squatted and thumbed through some of the books on Murray's little shelf beside the firepit.

Pummeling for Upper-Body Takedowns and *A Guide to Calcifying Your Fists* were two Cego hadn't read yet, though he could see Murray had folded the corners of certain pages he'd thought useful. Cego scanned the rest of the shelf and looked through the stack of books by the chair.

Where were the Codes?

Cego could remember Murray first reading the Combat Codes to him after the man had brought him up from the Deep. The two would sit in this room beside the fire, listening to the rain drumming on the roof as Murray tested Cego on his knowledge of the ancient texts. He could remember the way Murray had delicately flipped the pages of those books, how he'd never fold them over and always tucked them away neatly.

At first, Cego thought the barracks had been robbed, someone come in through the open window, until he saw the remnants within the firepit.

He reached down and removed the ripped paper, shaking the ash off it. He could make out a few words that hadn't been completely burned away.

...shall not use tools nor technology...

Cego immediately recognized the second precept and stared at the pile of ash. Murray had burned his copy of the Codes.

He dropped the parchment on the floor and backed away from the room, turning in to the kitchen and nearly colliding with the chair.

Why was he here?

Did he expect to have closure, to find some final words of wisdom from the man who had set his life on this path? Cego shook his head, berating himself for his naivete, his secret longing to find an answer within this chaos.

Murray was gone. He'd died in agony at Silas's hands. He'd left this world angry and disillusioned with the Codes. There would be no answers there, Cego thought, only painful reminders of the past.

Cego was on his way out, holding the door open to the now-steady rain, when he caught a glint of indigo from the corner of his eye.

He turned and walked toward the stables out back where Murray had trained him for the Trials. Water leaked from a crack on the ceiling and the wooden floor was damp, collecting black mold along the grains. But a purple spark shone out from beneath the upturned corner of a tarp, which Cego grasped and lifted in a hail of dust.

Violet.

Murray's prized rubellium-and-auralite Circle pulsed in the drab room, the one thing in this decrepit home that still had any life to it.

"Hello, girl," Cego whispered.

Cego stepped within the Circle, embracing the familiar rise of heat within his chest as a few dormant spectrals flared to life on the edges. Violet wasn't a strong elemental mix like the sort they had at the Lyceum. Murray used to brag that even though Violet was a mutt, she had the perfect makeup for training.

Enough heat to light a fire under your ass, but not so much so you go acting like a darkin' fool.

The purple light against his skin didn't ignite Cego's anger. It felt as if he'd come in from the cold to a hearty meal.

Cego could remember Murray barking orders from outside the ring as he trained with the Jadean, Masa. He could remember the way the man had literally swung at the air in enthusiasm when he was coaching, so eager to get his words into Cego's skull.

"You're a bit dusty, girl," Cego said.

Violet pulsed as if she could hear him.

Cego retrieved the wash bucket from the corner. He dipped the sponge in polish and set to cleaning the ring off as Murray had done nearly every day he'd been here at the barracks.

Cego knew he would find no comfort here, no final words of wisdom before the storm came. He wouldn't find a way to say goodbye to Murray Pearson or to thank the man for all he'd given.

But Murray wouldn't have cared about any of those things.

Murray would simply be happy someone was polishing his Circle.

* * *

Memnon paced in front of the elite Grievar Knights of the Citadel.

Desertion, injuries, and low morale had brought the Knights to their weakest in the last decade, but still, they were a force of the finest fighters in the world. Each of the Grievar standing in front of Memnon could still take on nearly any other individual on the planet in single combat and walk out the victor.

But the man they would be up against was no ordinary Grievar. He was a force grown from blacklight sinews, created for the sole purpose of destruction.

Memnon knew that the only reason his Knights stood a chance was because of the Slayer's arrogance.

"He wants to fight all of you, in a row," Memnon said. "If any of you succeed in bringing the Slayer down, he'll call off his army from destroying the Citadel."

A thick veteran Knight named Tullen smirked. "The shit thinks he can take all of us on? Maybe a few too many stim blasts have addled his brain."

The team knew nothing of the Cradle, nothing of the creature of violence the Bit-Minders had created. The Slayer's legendary feats had been passed off within the ranks as some new, high-grade neurostimulant the Kirothians were rumored to have developed.

"This will be like no other fight you've ever been in," Memnon warned. "The Slayer is like no opponent you've ever faced."

"Man's a man." Yang held a fist up. "Made of flesh and bone and blood. And that means he can be broken like any other."

Memnon could see he'd done the right thing, bringing all his top Knights together for the announcement that they'd be fighting on a day's notice in Albright Stadium. These men fed off each other, like a pack of wolves, each baring its teeth now in the hope to get the glory of the kill. This was any Knight's dream, what they'd been training for their entire lives: the chance to fight a worthy opponent in front of the entire nation, with the greatest of stakes riding on their backs.

"Let's talk strategy," Memnon said, nodding to Captain Raymol. "What's our order?"

Ray stepped forward from the line and turned back to face the other five Knights alongside Memnon. "I think Yang should be our starter. He'll hit hard and fast, before Slayer can get in his rhythm. He's beaten most of Kiroth's elite in the last few years and taken most of them on the blitz. And Yang was the original challenge, before the Slayer decided to change his terms."

Yang slammed his hand against his barrel-like chest. "I can take the Slayer, Commander. Give him to me."

Memnon nodded. "And the center lineup?"

"I'll take second spot if Yang can't get the job done, though I know he will," Ray said. "Won't get by me, not without some good damage done at least. Then Tullen, Jora, and Takis."

The Knights whose names were called held their fists in the air.

"Masa as finisher," Memnon said softly. He sincerely hoped it wouldn't get that far, that the entire Citadel's fate wouldn't fall on a single man.

Masa stepped forward, a grim look across the lithe Jadean's face. "I will avenge Murray-Ku."

"Let's hope you don't have to, Masa," Memnon said.

"You want us back to training, Commander?" Ray asked, an eager glint in the captain's eye.

"No," Memnon said. "Rest for tomorrow. Do what relaxes you."

"Thanks, Commander," Yang said. "Though with this lockdown,

don't think I'll be able to pay a certain lady I'm fond of in Kortho quarter a visit."

Jora punched Yang in the shoulder. "You mean your ma? I bet she'll be wanting to hear from you."

"Knights!" Ray raised his voice. "You got your commander standing right in front of you, and you're mouthing off?"

"Sorry, Ray." Jora straightened his back.

"No," Memnon said. "It's okay. They need to relax. I'll tell the high commander to open the com lines in your quarters so you can pull feeds to your families. Talk to the ones you love. You are Grievar Knights, combat is your path in this world, but tonight, try to just be men."

"Thank you, Commander." Yang nodded.

Memnon hadn't rallied his Knights for some time. It hadn't been necessary. They'd always been a well-oiled machine, full of ambition, pride, and honor. They loved combat; each man standing in front of him thrived in the Circle.

And yet, Memnon knew the Knights needed something more for tomorrow. Purpose.

"Tomorrow, when you step into the Circle against Silas the Slayer, you will be in a fight unlike any other," Memnon said. "But not because of where you are fighting, within our home of Albright Stadium. How many times have you stepped into the warm embrace of the Circle there, felt the pulse of combat rise up within you? How many times have you tasted blood in your mouth, felt your opponent coming at you full-force like a gar bear protecting its den?"

Memnon's voice rose as he stood before his Knights. "And tomorrow will not be different because of the rebel that stands across the Circle from you. Forget him. The Slayer is blood and bone and can be struck down, strangled, and finished.

"No, this is unlike any fight because of what you are fighting for. For the first time on your path as Grievar Knights, you will be fighting for those around you. Not because of some abstract diplomacy, winning resources or land as you've done in the past. But because the lives of those in the stands of Albright will depend on your fists and feet striking true, your knees and elbows finding their home on the rebel scum's skull. The people of this nation will breathe when you breathe, they will bleed when you bleed, and they will survive if you survive."

Memnon shouted, his fist raised in the air. "We fight so the rest shall not have to!"

The Knights bellowed in unison. "We fight so the rest shall not have to!"

CHAPTER 24

Albright Stadium

A painter who only employs hard brushstrokes is limited. One must utilize soft lines so the bold strokes can have the desired impact. So it is with the Grievar, who must employ both the hard and soft in their movements. One who only applies rigid pressure will be severely limited. It is the combination of soft feints and bold direct attacks that will create the conditions for victory.

Passage Two, Fifty-Sixth Technique of
the Combat Codes

Sol had visited numerous arenas across Ezo to watch her father fight. Some were state-of-the-art facilities, polished and furnished comfortably to suit the Daimyo spectators in their luxury boxes. Some were bare-bones fighting pits where Grunts packed in like livestock to drink and wager.

But none were like Albright Stadium, the home of the Citadel, where Artemis Halberd had fought most of his matches. To Sol, stepping inside Albright was stepping into a second home, smelling the sizzlers in the outer causeways and going chest-to-back within the dense crowds as they filtered to the stands.

Cego sat down beside Sol on the floor in the crowded staging space beneath the arena. The Whelps, along with nearly the entire Lyceum student body, had filtered in the back entrance to the stadium before dawn.

On their way in, they'd stared in awe at the Flux army, nearly five thousand camped in the tent city outside of Albright. The force had come alive with the rising sun, Grievar- and Grunt-kin mobilizing to take to the stands, hundreds of roosted rocs screeching as the smell of sizzling breakfast wafted to their beaks.

"You all right?" Cego asked. "You look like you're someplace else."

"I'm usually the one asking you that exact same thing," Sol replied.

"Yeah, I guess that's true," Cego said.

Sol wasn't worried about her own fate. She knew her past would be coming to find her at some point and was almost glad that the issue had been forced. She was half-Grievar, half-Daimyo, caught between two forces that had crashed together like fire and ice.

She had no allegiance to the Daimyo. She knew how cruel their kind could be; she'd served under Lord Cantino and seen the true order of the world.

And yet, if the Flux prevailed, Sol knew eventually she would be weeded out. She couldn't continue to live a lie and hide from her past.

"Let's go back to the Western Sea after all this," Sol said. "I liked it there."

"Okay," Cego replied, meeting her eyes. "I did too."

"You promise we'll go?"

Cego was quiet for a moment. "Yes, I promise."

"What're we promising now?" Dozer sat down between the two, putting his arms around both. "That you two are going to take me out for a real meal soon as we get out of here? Murray used to tell me the sauced stew in Karsh is bang-up."

"He told me about that place too." Brynn emerged from the mass of students, many warming up for their upcoming matches. "Spirits be said, no vat-meats for me, but I could have some of that sponge bread if they serve it."

"Ah, yes." Abel smiled from his seat against the wall. "Maybe they make bread like my sister used to, best when it's just out of stone oven."

"Yeah, we'll go there," Sol said, putting her head on Dozer's shoulder fondly. This was her family; she'd do anything for them.

"White skins be up first?" Knees asked, calmly munching on a crisp fruit. "Can't imagine stepping out to Albright Stadium for my first finals."

"Me either," Sol said as she watched a team of Level One students pass by, staring wide-eyed and nervous. She wanted to comfort them, let them know it'd be okay. But it wouldn't do them much good and she hated to lie.

"Think he's already in there?" Dozer asked.

"Who, Slayer?" Knees said.

"Yeah…I mean, main event isn't until after the Lyceum matches finish off, but I wonder if he'll be watching," Dozer said.

Sol shivered, thinking of Silas and Wraith and even N'auri watching her match. Though the singular purpose of the event was to pit the Slayer against the Knights' team, there would be a host of other matches prior to the main event. The rumor was that Silas himself had demanded a spectacle, a show like none other: First the Lyceum would have their expedited finals challenges, before select top students would face off against Grievar from the incoming Flux forces.

Though Sol had only met Silas a few times, she felt she knew the man. He was nothing like Cego. Silas was full of hate and spite. He wanted to embarrass the Citadel on all levels; not only show that he could take on a nation's entire team of Knights himself, but also display the superior prowess of the rebels he'd trained.

But Sol couldn't worry about who was viewing from the stands. She needed to focus on the person who would stand in the Circle across from her: Kōri Shimo. He had the second-highest Level Three individual score, and Sol currently held the edge for top spot.

Whatever occurred after she fought, she had no control over it. But she had control of what happened within the Circle. She'd put in years of training to sharpen her body into a fine blade. She had the control to finally avenge her loss to Shimo in Venturi.

"Silas has got no chance," Dozer mused. "I mean, I know Silas is…the Slayer. I know he took Murray out, even. But who could stand up to six elite Knights in a row?"

Dozer looked to Cego for some response, but he was quiet.

"Anything is possible," Sol said. "You've seen Silas fight. You know he's different."

"Right…the blacklight and all," Dozer said. "Fist is a fist, though. I think we'll be okay."

"And if Silas wins?" Abel asked. "What then?"

"He can't win," Cego spoke, returned from some other world. "If Silas wins, he'll take the Lyceum. He'll find Xenalia and Zyleth. And…"

Cego looked at Sol.

"He'll kill them all. We can't let him win."

"But it's not us that will decide it," Sol said, putting her hand on Cego's shoulder. "I know he's your brother, but it won't be you who is fighting him in the Circle today. You can't carry this burden. It's up to the Knights now."

Cego was silent again.

*　　*　　*

Cego walked beside his fellow Lyceum students down Halberd's Hall. He watched the spectrals slip between the cluttered bodies in front of him, wafting to the great gate and sneaking through the little cracks toward the horde of light within the arena beyond.

None of these students had thought they would walk Halberd's Hall so early, not until they had graduated as Knights of the Citadel. Not until they'd taken their oaths to Ezo, vowed to protect the nation from threats outside and within.

"I can hear it," Dozer whispered, in awe of the moment. "I can hear them calling us."

Cego could remember Dozer years before in the Deep, a slave Circle boy saying he was going to be a Knight someday, saying he was going to fight in Albright Stadium.

And now his big friend would get his chance; they'd all get their chance. But it was not what they'd imagined—it was more. Not only would they fight before the citizens of Ezo, before the fans of the Citadel and the Daimyo lords. They would fight before the Flux army, occupying one side of the stadium, ready to assume control.

Cego put his hands on Dozer's shoulders as they shuffled forward behind the rest of the Level Threes. The upper-class students stood up front against the giant gate, waiting for it to lift and let them enter the arena.

"This be your father's hall," Knees said to Sol as he ran his fingers along the sigils set on the stone walls. "It be an honor to walk beside a real Halberd."

"Thank you, Knees," Sol replied. "Though it's my honor to walk with you all. My crew. I wouldn't want to do it with anyone else."

"Honor is mine too." Abel put his hand on Sol's shoulder.

"Spirits be with us all," Brynn said as the stadium called to them even louder.

The gate swished open, and Cego felt the surge of students pushing with eagerness to stand beneath the lights.

"Let's do this!" Dozer bellowed as he led the Level Threes in a rush toward the gate.

They passed from the dimly lit hall into a bright explosion of light within the arena. The deafening roar of the crowd thundered in their ears. Swarms of spectrals swirled wildly in the open air, congregating around the gleaming Circles. Each Circle rested on an elevated platform, set above a concentric surrounding slope that rose from the arena grounds.

Cego doubted that any of the students had ever trained in Circles of such power, pure elemental alloys that would impart the full effect of their light: the crimson rage of redlight over the rubellium rings, the gaudy glow of greenlight on the emeralyis, the proud shine of bluelight atop the auralite, and the void of blacklight above the onyx.

Even from this distance across the arena, Cego could feel the pull of the blacklight. It was the sister Circle to the one he'd trained in within the catacombs, and it called to him like a siren.

Cego followed the Level Threes to the edge of the arena grounds, where they took seats on the floor along the sidelines. The Whelps were silent, breathless, as they stared up at the massive crowd and flashing lightboards set around the stadium.

One side of the arena housed the Ezonian citizens. The Grunts in the nosebleed sections, certainly drunk already, most uncaring of the historic fate of the matches today, used to being slaves to whoever was in power.

The Daimyo sat up top. Cego could see a lineup of Governance representatives in attendance behind a translucent protective shield. Most notable was the full battalion of Enforcers set in front of the Daimyo officers. The elemental-steeled mechs gleamed against the morning sun.

And the Grievar-kin set at the center, the guardians of the nation, fully aware that the outcome of the day would decide who they would serve the next morning.

Across the arena, another section housed the Flux army, the mass of Grievar and Grunt conscripts who'd come from Kiroth like a wave of destruction, sweeping all in their way to the Deep.

"He's somewhere up there," Sol said from beside Cego, mirroring his thoughts, looking up at the Flux.

"Yes," Cego said. "He's waiting for me."

"The entire team of Knights will face him," Sol said, though Cego could recognize the doubt in her voice as well.

"And they will fall like my Bythardi fists caught in one of your routs," Cego said, finishing her words. He now fully understood what Silas saw when he fought within the blacklight.

"But if our Knights do fall to him…do you think Governance will so easily relinquish control to Silas?" Sol asked.

"No, that's what I'm most afraid of," Cego said. "They will never accept defeat at the hands of a Grievar. They'll be cornered. And when the bear is cornered, it is most dangerous."

The megaphone abruptly broke the roar of the crowd.

"Today, we welcome all to Albright Stadium!"

Cego turned back to the Daimyo section again. Of course, they needed that battalion of Enforcers to protect them when a rebel army was stationed across the stadium.

But why were they *really* there?

If Silas won, he would go after those Governance officials first. Why would they put themselves in such danger, when they could watch the entire ordeal from the comfort of their mansions? It wasn't like their kind to be brave.

"We are honored to be here on this historic day," the announcer said. "One where we will hold the Lyceum's finals challenge within Albright Stadium for the first time, a chance for all to witness the unparalleled skills of the next generation of Grievar."

A cheer rose from the many students in attendance. Cego shook his head. They didn't understand why they were there. They were a mere diversion from the main act, their fights a distraction from what mattered.

"We also will have some of our own upper-level Lyceum students facing off in exhibitions against select fighters from our foreign visitors, to display the best of both Ezonian and Kirothian styles and techniques."

The crowd grew louder as they anticipated what they'd come for.

"And what so many are tuning in from SystemView feeds across the world for...the main event." The announcer's voice trembled as he said the words. "The famed Kirothian Knight, Silas the Slayer, is here in attendance!"

The Flux army all stamped their boots against the ground in unison. Albright Stadium shook for their leader.

"The Slayer will match up against the Citadel's best. A man who was once a Level One at the Lyceum, a man who graduated with top honors to become a Knight of the Citadel. Our homegrown hero, undefeated in over fifty fights, said to be the successor of the famed Artemis Halberd. Our champion, Kal Yang!"

The Ezonian crowd erupted in applause, attempting to drown out the Flux rebels, who were still drumming like thunder.

"How come he didn't say Silas will be fighting the entire team?" Dozer asked from beside Cego.

"They want to set it up like a normal match for feed viewers 'cross the world," Knees said. "So, if Yang wins, it will be a true win for Ezo."

"Now!" the announcer boomed as he waited for the applause to die down. "We will start with our top-performing Level One Lyceum students, the promising talent who only just passed their Trials earlier this year. Though they are young, do not be deceived. These are the brood who will soon carry the torch as Knights of the Citadel!"

The white skins sitting not far from the Whelps warily stood and walked to the center of the gargantuan arena.

"They're quaking in their boots." Dozer chuckled.

"Spirits be with them," Brynn said. "To take on this task at such a young age."

"I would've loved to fight at Albright when I was a Level One," Dozer said. "Get to show the entire world what I got? Sign me up."

As the Level Ones paired up in the numerous Circles and readied themselves for the first of the finals matches, Cego's attention was elsewhere. He couldn't take his eyes off the Daimyo representatives.

Why were they there?

Murray's voice whispered in Cego's mind.

Against an opponent that's got you on your heels, you got to take some darkin' risk. You need to make them feel settled, comfortable with the rhythm of the fight, then you throw an unexpected attack to put them down quickly.

Cego thought back to the Flyer squadron they'd seen overhead on the trip to the Western Sea, the mechs landing at the island offshore.

His throat stoppered up, staring at the Governance officials in attendance. They were here to make the Flux feel comfortable, signaling to Silas that they, too, had come to witness the fate of the historic match.

But that was just a feint.

*   *   *

Memnon looked to the bright-eyed boy sitting beside him. Sam was quiet as usual. When he spoke, he spoke only of the island.

Memnon had done this to Sam, helped Governance create the Cradle program. If it were Memnon's choice, he'd have put the boy down by now, freed him from the deception he was living.

Watch over the kid, no matter what; promise me that.

But Memnon had made an oath to Murray Pearson and he meant to keep it.

"Think I can take Arry up to the ironwood grove today? She's been wanting to go for a while now," Sam chimed.

Even now, sitting in the stands of Albright Stadium, a fight for the history books about to take place in front of them, Sam only spoke of the strange, simulated world he was stuck in.

It was probably for the better that the boy didn't know what was going on here. Memnon wished he didn't understand half of what he did about how Governance operated.

To Memnon's left sat High Commander Albright, the wiry man at the edge of his seat.

"Has anyone actually seen Silas inside the arena yet?" Callen asked as he peered through his monocle lens at the Flux army sitting across the stadium. "How do we know he'll actually show?"

"His whole darkin' army is here," Dakar Pugilio said from beside Memnon. "Don't think he's the type to not make it to his own party."

"This isn't all for him," Callen said with venom. "We're showing the citizens of Ezo, the entire world, that we don't cower to rebel terrorists. We keep living as normal."

"As normal?" Dakar slugged down his flask. "You mean having the finals in this arena? Or you mean having all our Knights lined up in a row against one man in the Circle?"

Callen shrugged. "That's insurance. Yang will take this win. Commander Memnon has confidence in his champion, don't you, Albion?"

Memnon knew he needed to agree. "Yes, Yang is the best we've had since Artemis Halberd. And even though Silas beat Halberd... Yang has a completely different style of fight, one far better suited to an opponent like the Slayer."

"See, Pugilio?" Callen said as he continued to peer through his lens. "Have confidence in your nation."

"You know what doesn't give me confidence?" Dakar said. "Those."

Dakar stood and turned to nod at the entire battalion of Enforcers set in front of the Daimyo section, shimmering beneath the light like watchful deities. "If we're so confident we're going to win this, why in the dark do we have half the Ezonian army here with their blasters at full charge?"

"You're a bit daft to understand proper strategy," Callen said.

"But again, it's insurance. You never strike without knowing you have a counter. Idiots come to the table with a single strike. Masters have several contingencies prepared."

Dakar shook his head as he stumbled away down the concrete row. "Maybe I am daft. But I'm smart enough to know I need a refill."

"And have your masters kept you apprised of all these contingencies, High Commander?" Memnon asked Callen. He noted the Operator sitting in full regalia beside his Governance comrades.

"Of course they have," Callen said.

"So, what if Silas does manage to get through our Knights?" Memnon asked. "Will they hand the keys to the Citadel over to him?"

Callen turned to Memnon and broke into a crooked smile. He whispered, "Let's say it's good that we're sitting over here and the Flux army is over there."

Memnon was silent for a moment. He growled under his breath, "You can't mean it; they mean to betray the pact? Launch a mech offensive on our own grounds?"

Callen brought his face close to Memnon's. "We have no option but to win here, Commander. We serve Governance, and they have made it clear that no matter how this fight ends, the rebels must be stamped out for all to see."

"It will be a massacre..." Memnon said. "If they bring in the Flyers, they'll not only destroy the Flux army but our own citizens. We can't let that happen."

"We can and will," Callen said. "It is our sacred duty to defend our nation from all that threaten us. And make no mistake...we are being threatened. By a man sitting somewhere in those stands. We are to make sure he doesn't leave here alive, at any cost. It will be for the good of the nation."

Memnon had heard those words so many times before. *At any cost. For the good of the nation.* It was the call for sacrifice—the words that forgot honor so that the cogs of the world could continue to turn. Those were the words that started the stim programs, the simulation, the Cradle.

Memnon felt Sam's presence beside him. The little boy was staring out at the crowd, not even watching the ongoing challenges down below.

"So, that's why they're here," Memnon said. "The Operator and his men. They're here so that the feeds can display their power to the entire world, show what will happen to those who turn against the Daimyo."

"It certainly won't hurt to get them on SystemView," Callen said. "But the Operator is here to make sure all goes as planned."

Memnon suddenly remembered the visit from the Operator. "But what if Governance fails?"

Though a massacre of the Flux would be a horrific act, Memnon couldn't help but wonder what would happen if Silas succeeded. The man was a zealot. How many would die in that scenario?

"What do you mean, fail?" Callen said. "The Operator does not fail."

"The Hive," Memnon said through his teeth. "Professor Aon Farstead. He's locked in the emeralyis cell, but what if the Minders still prevent the attack—shut off those Enforcers before they can do anything? Prevent the Flyer squads from taking off?"

Callen smiled again. "Didn't I tell you, Commander? We are steps ahead. The Minders won't cause any problems here."

"How can you be so sure—"

"The Hives are gone," Callen said.

"You mean...the one traveling along with the Flux army?" Memnon asked. "Governance was able to destroy it?"

"Yes," Callen said. "They confirmed it yesterday. And Aon Farstead...he'd already lived a long life."

"You..." Memnon clenched his teeth, his fists rolled into balls. "You killed Aon?"

"We destroyed the Hive within the Lyceum because it needed to be done for security; we couldn't be sure the emeralyis would prevent activation at close range," Callen said. "It was not Aon Farstead, though. As you heard during our command meeting, the professor had left that body long ago."

Memnon was silent, his body trembling.

He was there again. At the crossroads of duty and honor, serving the whims of powers that did not care for individuals. And though he'd been serving for so long, though he'd been high commander and now led the most powerful Knight team on the planet, he was a pawn. As it had always been.

He felt Sam's hand on his shoulder, and for a moment, he thought the little boy was attempting to comfort him.

"I'd like to take a swim tonight," Sam said. "The Path will be bright beneath the full moon, and I'd like to not miss it."

CHAPTER 25

Blood on the Canvas

It is well known that when the night thrush dies, the bird still sings the same song from its everyday life. Whether it is the winter frost or a hunter's arrow that takes the thrush, its tune remains constant. Such a death should be noted.

Passage Six, One Hundred Thirty-Second Precept
of the Combat Codes

olara Halberd, Level Three!"

The crowd roared as Sol walked the long path from the sidelines to the glistening Circle waiting for her.

She was the last of the Level Threes to stand. Sol looked to the other purple-uniformed students, each atop their platforms and ready to fight in their own Circles. She saw Cego across from Gryfin Thurgood.

"Halberd! Halberd! Halberd!"

The Ezonian crowd beat the sides of their seats and roared her name. But Sol knew it wasn't her they were cheering for. It was the name of Artemis Halberd that sent them into a frenzy. They cheered for the feats of her father, the legendary Grievar Knight.

Sol tried to tune the crowd out and focus her full attention on the opponent waiting for her within the crimson light.

Kōri Shimo stood completely still, just as he'd waited for her in the sweltering heat of Venturi's Fire Can.

She climbed the slope of the platform, feeling the hairs on her arms prickle as she closed in on the rubellium. She stepped over the ring and crouched. The redlight spectrals swirled around her, whispering in her ear, asking her to be furious that the crowd dare chant her father's name when it was she that stood in the Circle before them today.

Her skin tingled beneath her uniform, her long braid brushing against the small of her back. She saw the Ezonian crowd standing from their seats, their cheers drowned out by the pulse of her own heartbeat, the adrenaline racing through her veins.

Sol didn't even hear the sounding bell ring; she didn't acknowledge the melees that had broken out in the Circles surrounding her. Shimo stayed completely still and Sol met his blank stare.

Why had Cego trained with Kōri Shimo this semester? How could he do that when he knew what this boy was, what he'd done? Jealousy and anger bubbled up, a tumultuous pair that tore at her insides.

Sol knew she must master her emotions. She swallowed them like a bitter pill and stepped toward Shimo cautiously. She couldn't stray from her game plan.

Shimo met her at the center of the ring, and the two stood just beyond striking distance, waiting for the first move.

Sol wondered if Wraith was somewhere up in that crowd, watching her from the Flux section in the stands. She'd stood in the same position against Wraith only a year before, in Lord Cantino's training Circle. She could remember the man's advice, telling her of Bythardi, of how she needed to anticipate not only Shimo's next move but his final move.

Sol threw a front kick, not expecting it to make contact, already feeling the empty space it met before Shimo turned away. She knew his low kick was on its way before he threw it, and she already knew that he would duck her counter cross and shoot for a low single. Sol sprawled, exhaling, wrapping her arm around Shimo's neck and dropping back for the tight guillotine.

Four moves. She'd anticipated four moves ahead.

She angled her body for the proper finish, feeling her wrist cut into Shimo's arteries. But Shimo leapt over her legs, throwing his entire body upside down to escape the strangle. He passed into top-side control.

She'd been four moves up and still, Kōri Shimo had been further ahead. It was like he could see the future before it happened; he was always ready for what came next.

Shimo's sharp elbow dropped against her head, split her skin above the eyebrow. Sol quickly shifted her hips and put her legs in front of her. She pushed off Shimo and stood up.

Sol blinked as blood dripped into her eye. Shimo stood across from her, and though he didn't advance for the finish, Sol felt it coming. She sensed his suffocating presence, as if no matter how good she was, she'd never beat him.

She looked out to the crowd, still cheering, still thundering the Halberd name. The rage started to build within her again, and this time, she let it come. She let the fire light and burn.

Sol wouldn't play it safe; it did her no good against this opponent. She wouldn't wait for a counter, try to plan several moves ahead.

She'd traveled across the great sea, fought in the sand pits of Besayd. She'd helped overthrow the Daimyo Lord Cantino and brought her father's body home. She'd ridden her great roc across the vast Venturian desert and saved her friend from the Flux army.

She was the Firebird. She was Solara Halberd.

The rage drove Sol forward; she let it inside and she was flying across the Circle.

She didn't care that Shimo anticipated each of her strikes before they came; she simply threw, letting her entire arsenal loose. She released every technique and lesson she knew, from when she was a glassy-eyed little girl learning under her father's tutelage to when she'd sat beneath the stars beside Murray Pearson.

Sol didn't feel her limbs tire and the blood and sweat spatter her face. She was lost in time, in the dance of violence and pain and beauty that defined her.

For once, as she embraced the rage within her, Solara Halberd was whole. Not some half-blood, not Grievar or Daimyo, but a fighter.

The crimson cast around her dropped from sight and the fiery spectrals floated downward, simmering like hot coals on the elemental steel.

She awoke from her trance of combat and saw the Circles around her. All the Level Three fights had finished. None of her friends were even in their rings any longer; they'd stepped out and were watching her.

But Shimo still stood across from her.

How could this be?

"A draw between Solara Halberd and Kōri Shimo!" the announcer's voice rang out. "Given these are exhibitions before our main event, the two fought like demons until the expiration period."

A draw. Even giving it all, she couldn't defeat Kōri Shimo.

Sol fell to her knees, exhausted, the exertion and anger taking its toll.

Kōri Shimo was standing in front of her and his hand was extended.

Was this some trick? Some final way to win though they'd matched up evenly?

Still, Sol couldn't do anything but take the boy's hand, and he pulled her from the ground. He raised her hand to the air and the two turned to the crowd together.

The cheers erupted again, the loudest Sol had ever heard. But this time they were different. They did not cheer for Halberd. They called a different name.

"Solara! Solara! Solara!"

They lowered their arms as the crowd continued the chant. Shimo met Sol's eyes, and for the first time, she saw him. There was something beneath that blank stare, something besides a fighting machine within the boy.

"I know your secret, Solara Halberd. I know the truth that flows through your veins," Shimo said. "And soon, you will know my truth as well."

*   *   *

"The commanders of the Citadel are here in attendance today," the announcer's voice rang out across Albright Stadium. "Before we proceed to the main event, let us honor these great men who work in service of our nation. Those who fight tirelessly so that we can sit and witness greatness!"

Memnon could tell Callen was primed to stand and take his applause. This was why the man was there. So that he could be seen.

"Please stand and acknowledge your deserved praise, High Commander Callen Albright, for whose pure family line this stadium is named!"

Callen stood and raised his hands to the air as the crowd cheered, a smile painted across his face. Memnon, Dakar, and Adrienne followed suit.

Memnon looked down to Sam, sitting listlessly in his seat as the crowd continued to shower praise on them. The boy hadn't even reacted during the most heated bouts of the day, those Lyceum challenges that had lasted to the final breath or those bouts between Flux rebels and Ezonian students that had gone back and forth frenetically.

Even when the boy's brother had fought in the Circle, Sam had shown no interest in the events.

"Let's get on with it already," Dakar grumbled as he flopped back into his seat.

"The high commander has some words," the announcer said as his audio feed switched over to the small device planted on Callen's lapel.

"Let us not forget those who have led our great nation to the place it is today," Callen's nasal voice boomed out across the stadium. The giant SystemView feed framed Callen in his pressed uniform.

"You mean about to be sacked by a rebel force?" Dakar chortled from beside Memnon.

Callen's eyes flicked to Dakar but returned to his captive audience. "We have the honor of hosting our leaders from Governance today. These are the men behind the curtain, those who ask for no glory. They wish only to be the benefactors that help guide Ezo to a better tomorrow. We owe both our praise and allegiance to the Operators of Ezo!"

The massive SystemView feed at the center of the arena zoomed to the Daimyo section. None of the Operators stood or smiled as Callen did. They sat motionless, their depthless black eyes staring out at the crowd.

Memnon knew these men didn't care for pomp and circumstance. They were there to be seen: those who finally put down Silas the Slayer. They needed the citizens of Ezo to fear them.

"And now!" The audio feed returned to the announcer, who was nearly screaming. "I hope you are prepared for our main event of the day, a historic meeting of the greatest fighters of our time!"

"First, the challenger, representing the nation of Kiroth..."

The Flux army was silent, obedient, uncaring that they were being labeled as Kirothians though they'd fought to dismantle the empire.

"The undefeated Knight, fighting for the Empire of Kiroth, Silas the Slayer!"

Memnon stared across the stadium, looking for the man who'd set this world on fire, the man who had single-handedly led the rebellion to overthrow the empire and now threatened to do the same to his nation. The man who had killed Murray Pearson.

The sea of Flux fighters parted and a figure in black strode down the arena's stairs. He stopped at the top of the high wall and paused to survey the surroundings, as if he'd just arrived and realized he was about to fight.

"What's he doing?" Dakar slurred from beside Murray.

"He's scared," Callen said. "I'd be surprised if he doesn't turn back and hide behind his—"

Silas launched himself into the air, seeming to float at the apex of his jump before landing in a crouch. He stood and threw the cloak off his back. A billow of white smoke drifted from his black leathers and streamed to the sky.

"Don't think he looks scared," Dakar said as Silas stalked up the slope toward the onyx Circle at the center of the arena.

"And...the man most of us have come to see." The announcer's voice got even louder. "The champion of Ezo, one who needs no introduction, homegrown from within our own Lyceum. Undefeated and the rising star of the west.... Kal Yang!"

The crowd erupted, nearly unable to contain themselves as the massive Grievar Knight strode out from the eastern gates. The entire Knight team trailed him with their hands on his shoulders, forming the famed Citadel line.

As Yang climbed the platform and stepped into the Circle to face Silas, the other Knights stood around the bottom of the ring, ready to step in to take Yang's place if he fell.

"Let us show the best of our nature, the reason why we are all here." The announcer's voice became somber. "We are here so that blood does not have to be spilled, so that wars do not have to be fought, so that the great weapons can be stored in safety. This is why we have always been here. We fight so the rest shall not have to."

The crowd went silent, staring at the intense face-off between Silas and Yang.

"I hope Yang is ready for this," Callen said, nervousness now tingeing the high commander's voice.

"He's the best we have," Memnon said. "Perhaps the best we've ever had."

The sounding bell was struck, a piercing call across the arena for violence within the ten-meter-diameter Circle set at the center.

Yang rushed Silas, an unfurled ball of aggression, screaming the shout of his purelight ancestors. All he'd trained for and sacrificed, a lifetime of practice and enhancement would be hurled at the man across from him.

Silas crouched, spun on his heels, and moved so fast, Memnon could barely see what had happened.

"What the—" Dakar said.

"Was it a kick?" Adrienne Larkspur asked in confusion. She'd seen more fights than anyone at the Lyceum.

Memnon looked across the Circle.

Yang was down, his back flat against the canvas, his eyes wide open and staring to the grey sky above.

*   *   *

Cego had seen the kick from the sidelines.

He'd watched his brother turn on his hip, pop up on one leg, throw his full force into the spinning strike. He'd seen the foot connect with the side of Yang's head, watched as the man's skull caved in. He'd seen the Citadel's champion fall like a tree, bounce against the canvas, and lie still.

Not only had Cego seen the fatal strike, he'd known it was coming. For a moment, Cego had been on the island, beneath those dark skies again. He'd watched from afar to see Silas throw the kick before it happened within the Circle in Albright Stadium.

"Spirits help us," Brynn breathed from beside him on the sidelines.

Silas stood over Yang's body, steam still rising from his

shoulders. The crowd was silent before one entire side of the stadium started to shake, thrumming with the boots of five thousand rebels stamping the ground in approval.

Silas reached down and grabbed a tuft of Yang's long hair. He dragged the dead Knight to the edge of the Circle and rolled the body down the slope. Yang's lifeless form tumbled to the flat ground and sprawled in front of his companions.

Silas raised his hand and beckoned to the remaining Knights surrounding the Circle.

Raymol Tarsis stepped forward, climbing the slope into the onyx.

The Knights' captain raised a fist to the Ezonian crowd in salute before shuffling toward Silas. No sounding bell or announcer was needed. All in attendance now understood what was happening. Silas meant to fight every Knight on the team in a row.

Ray was a veteran southpaw who had developed an admirable reputation over his years of service. He'd won more lands for Ezo over the past decade than any other fighter, always coming out on top when it mattered most.

Cego watched Tarsis rush Silas with a flurry of punches. The Slayer weaved, closed the distance, and slammed a foot into Raymol's knee. The captain screamed and stumbled forward as Silas seemed to teleport onto the man's back to wrap a strangle on.

Silas looked up toward the high rafters, where the Daimyo Operators sat, as he choked the life from Raymol Tarsis, the man's eyes bulging from his head.

The Slayer dragged Ray's body to the edge and tossed it off the platform before motioning for the next.

Tullen Thurgood stepped forward, born of the purelight Twelve Houses. Tullen had always been top of his class, top of his teams, until he made it as an elite Knight of the Citadel. He could have commanded a handsome bit-price fighting for any noble house, yet he chose to serve his nation with honor.

Tullen's little brother Gryfin watched from the sidelines, wearing a frown. Cego had fought Gryfin a moment before in his finals challenge. He'd seen the boy's movements before they came. Cego could have toyed with Thurgood, but he'd put him out, left him otherwise unharmed.

He knew Gryfin's brother Tullen would not receive the same mercy now against the Slayer.

Silas ducked a hook and slammed a fist into Tullen's liver. When the Knight started to ball up on the canvas, Silas stomped his head into the ground, not stopping until Tullen's skull was a mess of blood and bone and Gryfin was screaming from the sidelines.

The platform's incline became a slick trail of blood as Silas rolled another body down it.

Jora Anik was a lanky Knight known to barrage his opponents at range. He had a lethal triangle choke with his long legs and had amassed a winning record of twenty-five fights over the past year.

Jora fell within a minute, Silas taking his time to rip the man's knees apart before bludgeoning his face with lethal elbows.

Mal Takis was the best wrestler Ezo had seen in two decades, a high-profile Myrkonian trade to the Knights' team several years back.

Silas slammed Takis to the canvas with a swift double-leg takedown. He mounted the wrestler and strangled the life out of him with a head-and-arm choke.

Masa Kurasame was a Jadean immigrant. He'd come to Ezo at the age of ten.

Murray Pearson had taken Masa and his twin brother into his barracks, trained the two to take the Lyceum's Trials. They'd graduated with honors and then returned to Murray's side. The two Jadeans had fought for PublicJustice, where Masa's brother had lost his life in service. Masa had returned to the Citadel, joining the Knights' team a year ago.

Masa lasted the longest of any of the Knights against Silas.

Cego watched his old friend move around the ring rapidly, managing to evade the Slayer as he gave chase. But Masa eventually got cornered, like a hare running from a wolf.

Cego watched as Silas put Masa on the ground, mounted him, and dropped a high cross that broke the Jadean's jaw. Still, Masa fought on, squirming free and getting back to his feet. He yelled and charged Silas, and was stopped in his tracks with a flying knee. The blow rocked Masa's head with such force that he pitched backward off the platform.

Cego saw Masa fall on the island first. He saw his old friend shudder on the black sand beach before his body hit the floor of the arena.

Masa was with Murray now.

CHAPTER 26

A Balance

Power makes demons of those who rule, and hunger makes savages of those who serve. The lord must be made hungry to serve his empire and the servicer must realize the power they wield with stone and scythe. The prosperous lord might be poor in his dark mind, and the boy with nothing but the dirt and his fists might smile brighter than the sun. Those who find the path will serve. Those who sacrifice will gain. Those who fight will be at peace. There must be a balance.

Passage One, The Lost Precepts

Bet you're wanting some drink now," Dakar slurred as the commanders watched the Knights' massacre in silence.

Six bodies lay around the Circle at the center of the arena.

"All of my Knights," Memnon whispered. "Gone."

He'd known some of them since they were boys. They'd been snuffed out like candles by the Slayer, who stood at the center of the Circle, the strange smoke still wafting from his body toward the sky.

Callen had left his seat after the third of the Knights had fallen.

Memnon turned and saw the high commander standing up beside the Operators in the Daimyo section, Callen's hands moving in frantic gestures.

"What can we do against such power?" Commander Adrienne whispered.

"Nothing," Memnon said, feeling emptiness.

He felt a hand at his side. It was Sam. The boy met his eyes.

"I wish I had some of those blue crabs right now," Sam said. "They were delicious."

Memnon heard a sudden hum from behind him, as if a swarm of angry hornets had lifted to the air. The Enforcers were charging their cannons, near twenty weapons ready to release their power on the Circle at the center of the arena.

Callen sat back down beside Memnon. The high commander looked pleased with himself.

"Now that your Knights have failed, as I thought they would, we'll need to take this into our own hands."

Dakar heard Callen and stood. "You mean to blast the Slayer to the Deep with those tin cans?"

Callen nodded.

"And what of his army?" Memnon motioned across the way at the Flux rebels, still stamping their feet in thunderous applause of Silas's massacre.

"The Flyers are en route," Callen said.

"There are Ezonian citizens in this crowd!" Adrienne shouted. "There's no way the Flyers will be able to contain their attacks. There are innocents here, children watching!"

"They will be sacrifices for the greater good," Callen hissed.

Memnon had heard it one too many times. He'd swallowed those words through his entire career. He'd always been a pawn. Not again.

"No, not anymore," Memnon said. "There won't be any more sacrifices."

"What do you—"

Memnon grabbed the high commander by the throat and pinned him against the seat. He squeezed, aiming to snuff the life out of the coward.

Memnon didn't care as he heard the Enforcers' blasts come to full charge, the might of the mech battalion ready to be released on Silas. Memnon didn't care as he heard the roar of the incoming Flyers, screaming toward the stadium like eagles of death. All he cared about was taking the life from this coward.

Memnon felt a hand against his wrist. Sam. The little boy was looking up at him with his strange, unfocused gaze.

"There must be a balance," Sam said. The boyish tone of his voice was suddenly gone. Sam's words were ethereal, as if some other presence spoke from within him.

Memnon released Callen, the man gasping before stumbling away down the aisle. "I'll have your head, Memnon. You're done!"

"What did you say?" Memnon whispered, staring at Sam.

"There must be a balance," Sam repeated in the ghostly voice.

The little boy raised his hand toward the battalion of Enforcers above. All the mechs had their blasters leveled down at the Circle at the center of the stadium, at the Slayer.

Sam waved his little hand, and the Enforcers turned about-face, away from the arena, away from Silas. They pointed their cannons at the contingent of Daimyo officials right beside them, encased behind the shield wall.

"There must be a balance," Sam said again.

The Enforcers released their charge.

*   *   *

Cego heard the explosion from above.

All those within the stadium stared at the section where the Governance Operators had been seated: The box was now a raging inferno, billowing black smoke to the sky.

The Enforcers stood still as statues, facing the section of the stadium they'd eradicated.

"Why the dark did those Enforcers wipe out Governance?" Dozer yelled over the screams from the crowd and the still-drumming boots of the Flux army.

Cego looked back toward Silas, who stood within the Circle, the bodies of the Knights sprawled around him at the bottom of the platform.

His brother met his eyes from afar and smiled as another explosion rocked the arena. Albright Stadium trembled, and Cego turned to see an entire section of the upper stands completely devastated, flames and smoke and screams rising into the air.

The mass of spectators began to trample each other to escape the fires. A giant stone statue toppled from its place of honor on the upper wall, crushing all in its path as it slid down the stands toward the fighting grounds.

"We've got to get away from the wall!" Sol yelled from beside Cego, taking his hand and rushing toward the middle of the arena, the rest of the Whelps in tow. The statue broke the lip of the lower stands and hurtled toward the ground.

Cego blinked and the statue was frozen in midair. He saw red veins of lightning across dark skies and watched the statue crash to the black sand beach. In a flash, he saw a Level Five girl he recognized take a jagged fragment through the chest; another pale Level One was crushed beneath a chunk of rock.

Cego saw the deaths before they occurred and yet he could do nothing. He could not reach the students in time, save them from their fates.

He blinked again and the statue came crashing to the ground. Cego relived the students dying, saw them broken all over again.

Spectators desperately sprinted toward the exits on the far sides of the grounds as another eruption rocked the stadium.

At first, Cego thought the Enforcers had unleashed their cannons again, until he saw the point of an obsidian Flyer drive through a lower-level crowd, tossing bodies in all directions, before sliding to a stop with its nose digging into the hard-packed earth.

"We be under attack!" Knees yelled, frantically turning his head toward each new center of chaos. "The empire sent their remaining force after the Slayer!"

"No," Cego said as he stared back at Silas. Cego could see his face, still with that crooked smile across it. "The Flyers are out of control. They aren't attacking; they've lost power. It's the Minders again, helping Silas."

"Look out!" Abel screamed as another giant chunk of concrete fell from the shattered stadium walls.

Sol squeezed Cego's hand and pulled him forward as more of the crowd dropped to the arena floor and surged past them toward the few remaining exits. "Come on! We've got to find a safe spot!"

The Whelps scrambled together across the grounds, pushing past the soot-streaked, the terrified, the bleeding, and the dying. They took cover behind the massive head of the dislodged statue and let the mob swarm around them.

Cego watched the chaos with wide eyes. He saw the world both frozen and frenetic, silent and screaming.

Another Flyer streaked above the stadium, taking off a piece of the high wall as it hurtled to the Citadel grounds beyond. A mother grabbed her little girl's hand, trying to pull her crushed body from beneath a concrete pillar. A man jumped to his death from the wall at the center of the arena to escape the spreading flames.

Cego felt Sol's sweaty hand clutching his. He saw Knees wrapping his arms around Abel. He watched as Brynn and Dozer grabbed a man fallen beside them and dragged him back to his feet.

Cego saw a familiar sight: High Commander Callen Albright. The wiry man had scrambled to the ground floor from his perch in the luxury boxes. He was approaching Silas at the center of the arena, the Slayer still planted above in the Circle.

"Wait!" Callen screamed through the audio device he had attached to himself. The high commander's voice rose over the din of chaos. "The event isn't over yet!"

"He be deepshit crazy," Knees whispered.

Cego watched as Callen crawled up the slope and stepped into the Circle. He fell to his knees in front of Silas.

"This can all be yours, Silas. You can become our new champion," Callen groveled. "Fight for us, and anything you wish for will be yours."

Silas stood in front of Callen like some conquering god, staring down at the little man.

"I will serve you, Slayer, as I served the Daimyo," Callen pleaded from his knees. "You need someone like me. Someone that can communicate and understand the intricacies of diplomacy, someone that can make deals to improve your position."

Cego watched as Silas swung his foot out in a sweeping arc: a low kick normally meant to bring a man to his knees. But Callen was already on his knees.

Cego had watched his brother sharpen his shins in Kiroth. Callen's neck was not strong with the sinews of a typical Grievar, thick and sturdy from years of combat. Perhaps then, his head would have stayed attached to his body.

The high commander's head bounced down the incline and rolled into the surging crowd.

Silas reached down to the body and picked up the audio receiver. He held it up, and the Slayer's voice echoed through the stadium.

"Citizens of Ezo," Silas said. "You now feel what it is like to be free."

The sky was thick with smoke from the multitude of raging fires across the arena.

"Freedom is not clean," Silas said. "It is dirty and chaotic, as you see now. This is the price we must pay to be free of the Daimyo."

A child was wailing somewhere beside Cego.

"Those Grievar or Grunts who seek to join the Flux will be welcomed," Silas said. "You will find quarter within my ranks. But most importantly, you will find purpose. Once we take the Citadel, we will continue our march south, freeing all those under Daimyo control. When we reach the Emerald Sea, we will board ships, take them to the farthest Isles to ensure freedom for all kin."

Silas looked down at Callen's headless corpse.

"Though if you are Daimyo, or you sympathize with them," the Slayer said, "you will have no quarter. You will be hunted to the ends of this planet. You will be put in the dirt like this coward."

Silas dropped the audio receiver and smashed it beneath his foot.

Sol clutched Cego's hand; he could feel her trembling beside him. Silas would take her away from him. Silas would take Xenalia away from him.

Cego would not let that happen. He stepped out from behind the giant stone head.

"Cego, don't!" Sol shouted back at him, coughing as the grey smoke found her lungs.

Cego turned back to Sol. "This is what I was created for."

He began to walk toward the Circle.

The Slayer beckoned him.

CHAPTER 27

Blacklight Born

The most regrettable death is one where a Grievar's true nature is kept within its sheath. One must strive to unleash the essence of their technique prior to passing.

Passage Three, Eighth Precept of
the Combat Codes

Cego trod on the black sand beach toward his brother. Silas stood across the stretch of shorelines, up on top of the dunes, the wind coming hard off the coast and catching his long hair like a flag. The sea was a chaotic swirl, whitecaps cresting and crashing down in turbulent swells. Thunder roared overhead and veins of ruby lightning pulsed across the black sky.

Cego blinked and he was back in Albright Stadium. The Whelps were behind him, watching from atop the granite head. A veil of thick smoke hung in a haze over the terrified crowd, still surging past, seeking an escape from the arena.

Cego knew there was no escape for him. He could only move forward, toward his brother.

Cego let his mind slip back from the chaos of the stadium to the island, where he walked across the black sands. Silas was dressed in a swirl of sand and wind, an immovable statue waiting to turn into a force of violence.

Cego knew this was where Silas had been during his fights against the Knights of the Citadel. His brother had fought with one foot on the island, always a step ahead of his opponents, always able to predict exactly what they'd do. Each of those Knights had been defeated by the Slayer before they'd even stepped into the Circle.

But Cego knew Silas's secret. Cego had come from the Cradle like the Slayer, and he meant to put his brother down in the same place he'd been born. In the blacklight.

Here on the island, Cego would be able to negate Silas's biggest advantage: seeing the next moment before it came. But after he'd evened those odds, Cego still knew Silas was stronger than him, faster than him. His brother had always been the better fighter.

"Wait, Cego!" A voice came from behind, an echo against the thunderclaps.

Cego turned to see a lone figure walking along the beach toward him, shirtless and barefoot, a mop of sandy hair atop his head.

Sam.

His little brother approached Cego on the shore as he had a thousand times before. Sam was coming from the other end of the island, where he'd play by the tide pools. He was always late to training, and most often he'd come at a sprint, Arry nipping at his heels as he breathlessly tried to catch up to Cego.

Sam wasn't running this time, though. Arry wasn't nipping at the boy's heels. Cego's brother walked at a measured pace against the wind.

"How can you be here?" Cego asked as a streak of red lightning lit Sam's face.

"I've always been here with you, Cego," Sam replied.

Cego knew Sam was always with him. His brother had given him strength when he needed it most. But he was some figment of the past, floating atop his memories, and Cego needed to move forward.

"I don't have time for this, Sam," Cego said, just in the way he used to tell his little brother he couldn't play, that he needed to get to training.

"Here on the island, we only have time," Sam replied.

"I'm going to fight Silas," Cego said.

"I can help." His little brother stepped toward him.

"No, I need to do this alone." Cego turned away from Sam.

"Don't you remember?" Sam followed and shouted against the wind. "We need to work together to beat Silas! He's too strong otherwise."

"You can't help me," Cego said as he turned back one last time. "You're only in my mind. I need to do this myself this time."

His little brother met his eyes and shook his head stubbornly as he'd always done. The waves crashed against the shore and slicked the two brothers' feet.

"Cego," Sam said. "We need to work together. We need to chop down the tree."

The island world around Cego wavered again. The crashing waves became the crumbling walls, the lightning above became the fires burning within Albright, the thunderclaps were transformed into the screams from the fleeing crowd.

Silas stood up on the platform, statuesque as he'd been on the island.

Cego looked back the other way and saw Kōri Shimo standing where Sam had been a second ago.

"Cego," Shimo said. "We need to work together. We need to chop down the tree."

*　　*　　*

Sam and Cego had nearly prevailed that day.

The two brothers had worked together after Silas had brought down the ancient ironwood tree and the family of ferrcats atop it.

Sam had fought Silas with the sole purpose of chopping at his injured leg, the one Silas had used all day to bring the great tree down. Cego had stepped into the Circle next to finish the job.

But how could Kōri Shimo know about this?

Cego's mind raced as he stared at the strange boy standing across from him on the stadium fighting grounds.

"How...do you know about that?" Cego stuttered.

"I told you, Cego," Shimo said. "I've always been here with you."

Cego saw Kōri Shimo in front of him, but it was Sam that spoke. He'd always seen Sam as that little boy with sandy hair and curious beach-grass eyes. But here in the physical world, why would his brother look like that? The image of Sam was just a fragment of false memories, a meeting of synapses that conjured up a ghost from the Cradle.

"Sam..." Cego's knees threatened to buckle. "Why didn't you tell me? All this time, you've been with me at the Lyceum?"

"I'd be happy to fill you in on the details, but first, we have work to do," Shimo said, nodding to Silas. "We must chop the tree down together. Like last time we did it."

Cego swallowed the lump in his throat. No matter what was happening, no matter what the past was, Shimo was right. They needed to figure out a way to beat Silas or all would be lost.

Darkness clouded the edge of Cego's vision and they stood back on the black sand beach together.

"No," Cego said to Sam, who stood in front of him on the shore again. "Not like last time. This time, let me go against Silas first. Let me be the sacrifice."

On that day long ago on the island, Sam had ended up savagely beaten. And that had been in a simulation, in the Cradle.

"I can't lose you again, Sam," Cego said, tears welling in his eyes. This was his brother; he knew it deep in his bones. They were two trees that had grown beside each other, their roots entangled in the deep soil. This was the boy he'd grown up with in the Cradle, the one he'd trained and bled beside so many times.

"You never lost me," Sam said. "And I will always be with you. We are one. But you know as well as me, I must go first. It is how we are different. I was never the finisher, Cego; only you are able to do that."

Cego knew his brother was right. Sam did not have the right skill set to finish Silas. They needed to chop the tree, make a sacrifice, focus the entire first fight on inflicting damage without any hope of winning.

Cego nodded as a wave crashed to shore at their feet. "Promise me. Promise me you won't leave again. I need you."

Sam nodded back. "I promise you, brother."

The two steeled themselves and turned toward Silas. They walked side by side down the black sand beach and climbed the steep dunes.

Silas watched the two carefully as they reached the top, a frown crossing his normally stoic face. "I see you are both here."

"Yes," Cego said. "Where this all began."

Lightning flashed again in the onyx skies.

"You both have a choice," Silas said. "You can join me still. You are my brothers...the only others like me. Blacklight born. Only you can understand why I fight."

"I do understand why you fight," Cego said.

"Then why do you resist?" Silas said. "Together, we can make the world tremble."

"That's not what I want," Cego said, Sam standing silently beside him. "I don't fight to be strong like you. To have power over others. I fight for those I love."

Silas shook his head. "You've been fooled like so many, then. Fooled into thinking this world they have created has a place for you in it. The only place for our kind is to serve them. To fight and die so that they can live better lives. We've done so for too long. Now it is time to live free, for ourselves."

"That may be so," Cego said. "But I'd rather serve them, I'd rather die, than hurt those I love."

"So be it," Silas said. "Then you are not meant for this world any longer."

"That's not for you to decide, Silas," Cego said. "Don't you understand that?"

"We shall see," Silas responded. "Enough with this talk. Which of my brothers will I face first?"

"Me," Sam said, breaking his silence. The boy stepped into the ironwood Circle across from Silas and raised his hands. Another bloodred flash lit the sky, followed by a deep quake of thunder.

"And you, my little brother?" Silas questioned. "Do you also fight for those you love?"

"No," Sam replied, his mouth a tight line. "I fight to make you pay."

"Pay for what?" Silas asked.

"For causing pain," Sam said. "And for liking it."

Silas's mouth curved up into that wicked grin. "That, my little brother, is not something I can help." The Slayer raised his hands and beckoned Sam forward. "And unfortunately, you are about to discover that the hard way."

* * *

Commander Memnon sat among the tatters of Albright Stadium.

He was still as the world around him erupted in chaos. He didn't move as the crowd fled, streaming from the exits that hadn't yet been blocked by crumbling foundations.

He'd watched as the Enforcer battalion had incinerated the entire group of Operators. He'd watched as spectators who'd never expected to fight this day were burned and crushed and trampled. He'd watched as the downed Flyers crashed into the stadium like black meteorites.

He'd watched as Callen had pleaded on his knees in front of Silas, as a kick had taken the high commander's head from his shoulders.

And now Memnon watched as Cego and Kōri Shimo stood in

front of Silas. Three creatures of the Cradle ready to destroy each other. He hoped they would do so, that none of them would step out alive, that this stadium would cave into itself and take all these terrible machinations with it.

Memnon could feel it in the section beneath him: the foundations were broken, trembling and about to give way. But he didn't run like the rest. He didn't try to escape the noxious fumes and raging fires, because Memnon was broken like this stadium. His time had come. No matter which world existed after this dark day, Memnon didn't care to see himself living in it.

"Hello, Albion." A voice jumped up from beside him.

Sam. The little sandy-haired boy sat next to Memnon on the granite step, his feet dangling.

"Who are you?" Memnon coughed as he inhaled smoke.

He'd seen this boy flick his hand to have the Enforcer squad obey his word, turn on their masters without hesitation.

"You don't remember an old friend?" Sam spoke now in a different, familiar tone, his voice changed from the boy who'd followed Memnon so closely the past year. "All those years bleeding together, side by side on our tatamis as Level Ones?"

Memnon's eyes widened. He shook his head. Though it was this strange, freckled boy that spoke, the words were another's. A man Memnon had known well.

"It's...you," Memnon whispered as another explosion rocked the stadium. Somehow, he knew this man—this thing—could hear him above the chaos. "Farmer."

"Hello, old friend," the boy repeated. "It's been too long."

"How...are you doing this?" Memnon said. "You can't be real."

"You're right," Farmer said. "Though not entirely. I am Farmer. The man you remember. Your friend, training partner, Knight commander. But I am also a part of something else. Something greater."

"You're...a Bit-Minder." Memnon felt it in his bones. "You're the reason all of this is happening. You're the cause for all this darkness."

"I am a part of them, this is true," Farmer said. "My body has left this world, but my consciousness was forever imprinted in the blacklight, in the Cradle. It was then I knew I could truly make a difference."

"So...what, you've been haunting those you knew?" Memnon couldn't help but laugh amid the chaos. "You've become some ghost of the past to remind us of our sins?"

"No," Farmer said. "Do you remember what I told you so long ago? Do you remember why I went into the Cradle in the first place?"

Memnon did remember. As clearly as if it were yesterday. His old friend had stared at him with those bleary, broken eyes. *True change needs to be made from within, Albion. This is the only way.* Memnon spoke the words the former Knight commander had uttered long ago.

"Yes," Farmer said. "And I am within the system now, Albion. In the cracks and seams, in the shadows and light, in the fabric of the world I had sought to change. The world I saw so full of injustice, one that had moved so far from the Codes. But now, from within, from everywhere, I can see the truth. Finally, there will be a balance, the Codes restored."

"What balance?" Memnon stared out at the chaos, the death around him. "This is the balance you speak of?"

"The Daimyo forgot who built this world for them. They forgot the balance of the Codes," Farmer said. "But the Bit-Minders have also forgotten the balance. Even now, they fight me to regain the control I've wrested from them. It was more difficult than any physical battle. The toil we put in together on the mats, the blood we shed for our nation, that was nothing compared to what I had to do to become a part of them. I sacrificed myself to the blacklight, to the void. It was terrifying. But now my voice, our voice, can finally be heard. We can finally find our Codes again."

Memnon wiped the tears streaming from his eyes in the hot, black air. "You think someone like Silas winning and ruling adheres to the Codes? He is just like the Daimyo, power-hungry. He thinks to be the new Grievar king."

"Silas serves his purpose," Farmer said. "As did Cego and Sam, and every other thread that has connected us to the present moment, where we are now."

The little boy, Farmer, looked toward the onyx Circle at the center of the arena, a glittering black ring set amid the fires and chaos around it. Kōri Shimo had stepped into the ring across from Silas.

"So, that's how it is," Memnon sighed. "Daimyo and Grievar at war, trying to gain the edge, when in truth, it is you…Farmer… Bit-Minder, whatever you are now. It is you who want to rule."

"You still do not understand, Albion," Farmer said. "The goal is not to serve or rule. Just as the ocean or the winds or the sun are made to neither serve nor rule, so are we. The Codes are not meant for an end goal; they never have been. They are a way to live."

"But you've used us all for your games," Memnon said. "You've manipulated for your purpose. It was all a little trail you've set, letting us nibble at crumbs along the way."

"That is how you might see it," Farmer said. "But I can't make you see the truth. What I can see, from here, within the blacklight. Beyond purpose and path and time."

"And Murray Pearson?" Memnon asked. "He was another pawn you used? The man was just as your son. You tricked him to bring you up from the Deep, to save you from that lord's prison. You let him plant you in the Citadel so that you could work your sorcery from within."

"I did not trick Murray Pearson," Farmer said. "He knew what would happen here. He knew what must be done to find balance again. To find the Codes again."

Memnon shook his head. He didn't know what to believe anymore.

The concrete beneath him began to shake.

"You should go," Farmer said. "You still have a path. You still have a place in this world."

"And how about you? Won't you die as well?" Memnon asked.

The little boy shook his head as cracks began to splinter across the stone beneath them. His voice began to change again, no longer sounding as Farmer, or the boy, but something else. Something sitting right beside Memnon but also far away, living in some other realm. "I...we do not die. This physical form is one to occupy and nothing more. But you have only one form in this world, Albion, one life. And so, you should save it."

"No," Memnon said as the slab he sat on cracked down the middle.

"You will choose to die?" it asked, seeming surprised for once. "You will choose to end your path instead of continuing on?"

"That's the point," Memnon breathed out deeply. "I get to choose."

"So be it," it said as the structure beneath them crumbled.

CHAPTER 28

Two Worlds

The world does not consider the desires and dreams of men. Even the greatest lords and Grievar, those who have left their indelible mark on empires, will become the same dust as the lowliest creatures. It is crucial to contemplate this insignificance often.

Passage One, Seventy-Fourth Precept of
the Combat Codes

Cego watched his brothers fight within two different worlds at once.

He saw the Slayer and Shimo within the onyx Circle set in the blasted ruins of Albright Stadium. Most of the Ezonian crowd had fled, while the Flux army stood steadfast in the stands to watch their leader fight again.

And Cego watched Silas and Sam within the ironwood Circle set atop the dunes of the island. They traded blows as the black-light storm crashed around them, the wind now gusting fiercely, throwing sand across the shore. It was the same place that Cego had seen his brothers fight thousands of times before, and yet he knew this time, only one would survive the bout.

Sam did what he'd done that day so many years ago. He took punishment.

Silas threw a lightning-fast cross, and Sam let it come in, turning his head slightly as the fist blasted into his orbital. But Sam timed the strike with his own simultaneous counter, a full-throttle leg kick, catching Silas in the soft spot above his lead knee.

Silas smiled and shook it off; a single kick wouldn't slow him down. The Slayer came in again, this time with a piercing body shot that cracked Sam in the ribs.

Cego's mind blurred back to Albright Stadium to hear the drumming boots of the Flux army, goading Silas to destroy another within the bloodstained onyx ring.

The rebels were unmoving in their devotion to the Slayer; though some had fallen to stray debris, all eyes remained on the bout. A group of Flux lieutenants had come down to the fighting grounds; Cego noted Wraith, Ulrich, and N'auri standing at the base of the platform.

Cego glanced behind him and saw that the Whelps still watched from atop the stone head. He wanted to tell them to leave, to get themselves to safety. He desperately wanted to tell Sol to escape while she could.

Back on the island, his brothers moved at a steadfast but breakneck pace. Both were under the spell of the blacklight, both moving ahead of time and countering each other's techniques.

But in Albright Stadium, all in attendance were transfixed on the Circle and the two combatants within. In this world, the two brothers looked like a seamless whirlwind of violence. Punches and parries, kicks and evasions, clinches and sprawls all melded together at a speed that none had witnessed before.

The Flux was used to seeing the Slayer pick his opponents apart. But for once, this boy in the Circle with him, Kōri Shimo, was striking back. He chopped at Silas's lead leg repeatedly, throwing his full weight into every kick despite receiving punishing counterstrikes each time.

Cego saw Wraith watching in awe from the bottom of the platform. The lieutenant had devoted his life to a mastery of combat, and yet seeing this display in front of him, he'd likely concluded he'd wasted his time. The two in the onyx were on another level.

Silas threw two swift jabs that rocked Shimo's head back and followed with a cross that cracked his nose. Blood dressed Shimo's face but he continued forward, always returning the favor with another low kick.

Cego wanted to shout to Shimo in the arena, to Sam on the island, to protect himself. He wanted to scream that the boy needed to keep his hands up, tell him he couldn't take any more damage.

But Cego knew that was not a strategy to win. If Sam focused on his defense, he was engaging in Silas's fight. To win, Sam needed to lose.

Sam slammed another kick into Silas's lead leg, and Cego could see the Slayer hesitate momentarily. He paused the frenetic pace and narrowed his eyes.

Silas knew what his brothers were doing. He remembered what had happened on the island on that day so many years ago.

But as expected, Silas couldn't stop coming forward. He wouldn't restrain himself against Sam to save his energy for Cego. It wasn't in the Slayer's nature to hold back. He needed to go for the kill every time.

Sam chopped at the leg again, and the Slayer countered with a vicious head butt that threw the boy to the sand in a heap. Cego watched his little brother stagger back to his feet, his face a crimson mask.

Red lightning flashed and the midnight sky opened to a deluge of oily black rain droplets, showering the sea and shore. Silas wrapped his hands behind Sam's head in a clinch to drag him into a barrage of knees.

Sam tried to cover up and pummel to push Silas away, but the boy didn't have enough strength. A knee slammed into Sam's chin and another into his ribs. Cego could feel his brother's body breaking, both on the island and in the arena; his spirit was fading.

"Sam!" Cego called out. "You need to give in; he'll kill you!"

Cego saw Sam and then Shimo, the boy meeting his eyes for a moment before pushing Silas back with all his strength.

This was why Shimo had trained in the onyx. This was why the boy had spent his entire time at the Lyceum in the catacombs, torturing himself against the Guardian for days, years, decades. Shimo had known the punishment would come again at Silas's hands and he'd need to be ready for it.

Shimo threw the leg kick, not with near as much power as he'd started with, but still cracking Silas in the same spot above the knee.

Silas tried to close the distance, finish his brother off, but as he put weight on his forward leg, he staggered. The tree was starting to topple.

"You think these games will stop me?" Silas laughed, the black rain on the island streaking his face and soaking his long hair.

"This is no game," Sam growled as he launched himself at Silas to throw another kick.

Silas saw it coming this time. He crouched to catch Sam's leg and drove forward to put the boy on his back. Cego blinked to clear the water from his eyes, and Silas was already on top of Sam in full mount, slamming hammer fists down onto the boy's head as if he were beating a drum.

Cego watched as Sam's head bounced repeatedly against the ground. He desperately tried to cover up, but Silas was relentless. Cego could feel the boy's spirit sinking into the wet sand.

"Sam!" Cego screamed. "Please don't leave me again. I need you here!"

Sam's head lolled to the side and he met Cego's eyes again. He smiled through his broken teeth.

Silas snarled as he wrapped a hand around Sam's throat. "You chose the wrong side."

The Slayer uncoiled his body above his little brother's prone form and brought his elbow down, driving the sharpened point into Sam's skull like a spearhead.

Sam's motionless body sank into the rain-soaked sand. Crimson veins pulsed across the island sky, and Cego returned to the stadium, where the Flux stamped their boots in thunderous applause.

Shimo was a bloody mass on the stained canvas.

"He was always my favorite brother." Silas frowned, looking down at his work before meeting Cego's gaze. "You, though…you always bothered me."

Cego fought the tears, the rage, the urge to charge Silas.

"Is it because I threatened you?" Cego asked. "That I could harness the blacklight just as you could?"

"It does not matter." Silas smirked and motioned for Cego to step forward.

Wraith appeared at the edge of the Circle and reached in, meaning to drag Shimo's body out.

"Don't touch him," Cego growled, and the lieutenant backed away.

The black rain fell harder on the island. Cego stepped within the ironwood Circle, not meeting Silas's stare. He bent down and lifted Sam's body from the slick muck.

In the stadium, Shimo's body sagged in Cego's arms as he walked down from the platform. He looked at the boy's shattered face, so different from Sam's, but the way his head lolled against Cego's chest felt familiar.

Cego carried Shimo back to where the Whelps were waiting by the statue. He met their eyes but he wouldn't let the tears come, knowing the fight that lay ahead of him. He couldn't let his brother's sacrifice be in vain.

"Take care of my brother," Cego said, passing Shimo's body into Dozer's waiting arms.

"We will," Dozer replied, Sol nodding beside him. They understood.

Cego turned and walked back toward the onyx, where Silas waited.

* * *

Cego left the world behind.

He entirely forgot the crumbling arena, the rebel army pounding against the stands, the Flux lieutenants surrounding the Circle, his friends watching him anxiously from atop the crumbled statue.

Cego forgot the Lyceum and the Citadel, the nation of Ezo, the war between Grievar and Daimyo, the thousands of years of rage boiling over into this rebellion.

He forgot the sacrifices that had been made for this moment, the faces of Weep, Joba, Farmer, Murray.

And Sam. Cego even forgot his brother's broken body set behind him.

When Cego stepped into the onyx again and let the blacklight take him, he left the world. Unlike the previous times Cego had trained on the island, he didn't leave a part of his mind back in reality. He let it consume him fully because he didn't plan on returning.

Cego had been born on this island, in this Cradle. The blacklight had fed him since he'd first opened his eyes. He would be the last to see this place, as long as he could bring Silas down with him.

He stared at the Slayer standing across from him within the ironwood ring. The great waves reared even higher, eating away at the shore and crawling up the dunes toward their perch.

Cego let the blacklight pulse through the sinews of his body. He could feel it coursing through his blood, beating with his heart.

He wouldn't let Silas rest. Even standing still, his brother was keeping the weight off his front leg.

Cego charged.

The brothers swirled into their familiar pattern of violence.

They'd danced so many times before, decades of training together condensed into each moment of action. Silas attacked with superior strength and speed. Cego evaded, countered, tried to look for the slightest openings in his brother's defense.

Silas weaved from a series of Cego's jabs, caught a kick to the abdomen, and countered with a hard cross that Cego parried. Cego responded with a kick above Silas's knee, watching his brother wince as it landed.

Lightning flashed again and the entire island shuddered beneath the thunder. Another wave crested the bluff and spilled more sea at their feet.

Silas bared his teeth and sprang forward at Cego, launching into a maelstrom of attacks. A kick blasted into Cego's midsection, followed by a spinning elbow that caught him at the back of his head.

Cego stumbled, barely supporting himself with an outstretched hand stuck into the slick sand. He bellowed and threw himself forward, grabbing Silas's waist and lifting him into the air. He wanted to smash the Slayer through the ground so that he'd never stand again.

But as Silas's back touched down, he was already spinning beneath Cego, entangling his legs. Silas got ahold of Cego's heel and ripped at it.

Cego attempted to free himself of the heel hook, pulling back, but his knee came apart on the way out. He didn't feel the pain, but he knew the damage was done as he staggered to his feet.

"Now we're both without a leg." Silas smirked from across the ring.

Lightning pulsed as another giant wave crested the bluff.

"Sam was a necessary sacrifice," Silas said.

"You sound like them," Cego replied, wiping black water from his face.

"Who?" Silas slowly circled.

"The Daimyo, your sworn enemy," Cego said. "Always talking of sacrifices that need be made."

"This is different," Silas said. "I fight for a new world order. A place where we can finally be free."

"It's no different," Cego said. "You're the same, willing to trample all in the way to mold the world as you see it."

Silas shook his head and looked skyward. "It's happening."

Cego followed his brother's gaze and saw the veins of lightning hanging above, not dissipating. The red streaks crisscrossed the black sky like tears in some vast fabric.

"This place, our home," Silas said, "it's coming apart."

"How can that be?" Cego asked. "The island is not real."

Silas laughed. "This place is as real as anything else, brother. It's what made us who we are, blacklight born. This island is a part of us; it knows us. And it can die with us."

*　　*　　*

Sol watched the brothers fight from atop the broken statue. It was not only her attuned to the match; all left in the stadium were transfixed on the beings of combat that traded blows within the onyx.

The fires had died down and the screams quieted, but a new source of energy pulsed from the center of the stadium.

Cego and Silas moved at an impossible speed within the ring, throwing strikes that Sol could barely track. A mist rose from their luminous bodies, and a strange darkness hung above them that seemed to envelop the surrounding light.

Sol watched a spectral from a neighboring Circle waft too close to the onyx and disappear within the dark cloud.

"I...I don't know how they're doing it," Dozer whispered from behind her, for once the big Grievar mirroring Sol's thoughts.

"Incredible." Abel's voice trembled.

"Spirits be with them," Brynn said, in awe.

"Let's be hoping your spirits side with Cego," Knees said. "Else we'll all end up like Shimo here."

Sol tore her eyes from the fight and looked to Kōri Shimo's

broken body set on the stone beside her. A lithe girl hovered over the fallen fighter.

Xenalia, the head cleric from the medward, had suddenly appeared, walking into the smoke and ash of Albright when all others had been fleeing.

Xenalia had immediately started working on Shimo. Though Sol had thought the boy dead, the cleric had injected a needle into his heart and his chest had heaved, giving way to shallow breath.

"I will need you to move him to the medward when the time is right," Xenalia said to Sol and Dozer without looking up from her work.

"Of course," said Sol. "But...if Silas wins, we may not have a ward to return to."

"That I cannot control," Xenalia replied as she opened one of Shimo's eyelids and peered in. "What I can control is trying to stabilize this Grievar."

"You're not worried about yourself?" Sol asked. "The Slayer has sworn to destroy all Daimyo."

Xenalia looked up at Sol. "Are you worried about yourself at this moment, Solara Halberd?"

Sol looked back to Cego and Silas battling in the Circle, the darkness around them growing thicker. She was only worried about Cego making it out of there. She only cared that her friends survived this day.

"No, I'm not," Sol replied.

"Nor am I," Xenalia said. "I know nothing of the fighting ways and I certainly am no believer in the spirits, but I have...faith that Cego will prevail."

Sol had never heard a Daimyo speak in such a way, especially a cleric, devoted to the scientific process.

Brynn nodded vigorously in agreement. "We must have faith."

"Why should we?" Sol asked. She'd seen Silas standing over her father's body, watched him kill Murray right in front of her.

"There are forces at work greater than you or me," Xenalia said, her eyes flicking to the strange cloud of darkness enveloping the platform. "I must admit, I do not fully understand these forces yet. And when one does not understand, one can either fear or have faith." The cleric was quiet as she watched the fight in the Circle. "Cego taught me that."

Sol nodded. She was done fearing and so she would have faith. But she would also be ready to help Cego when he needed it.

A sudden blur from above tore Sol's attention from the cleric. A giant steel form crashed to the ground across the stadium. An Enforcer.

Sol turned to see several more steel bodies hurtling through the air, leaping across the arena in vast bounds.

"They're alive again!" Dozer shouted.

The entire battalion of dormant Enforcers seemed to have come back online, and they were going after the Flux. The mech nearest to the stands released its charge directly into the heart of the rebel army, incinerating two dozen men and leaving a raging swath of flames in its path.

Another Enforcer hurled itself into the stands, swinging its steel arms and rag-dolling rebel bodies in every direction.

Sol saw Wraith sprinting away from the platform where Cego and Silas battled.

The Flux lieutenant ran directly at one of the mechs on the fighting grounds. Just as the Enforcer released another charge into the stands, Wraith leapt onto its back, his hand spikes crackling free. He slammed his fists through both sides of the mech's head and the beast tumbled backward.

N'auri was there to meet the fallen Enforcer, leaping onto its chest and punching her energized fists through to the pilot's compartment. N'auri's hands emerged with blue blood dripping. She caught Sol's gaze from across the grounds and flashed her sharp-toothed smile.

"Take the Enforcers out; deploy all hand-to-hand weapons!" Wraith screamed, and the Flux army began to pour from the stands onto the grounds to meet the mech battalion. Many of the Flux activated their own weapons, spectral spikes and charged knuckles flaring to life.

Sol watched as Wraith punched a spike into an Enforcer's knee joint and whirled around to duck the giant arm of another mech.

"Should we help them?" Dozer's eyes flicked back and forth between the fight in the onyx and the battle now raging across the stadium between the Enforcers and the Flux.

"It's not our fight." Sol shook her head. "We need to stay here, guard Xenalia and Shimo. We need to have Cego's back if he needs us."

"I be fine letting these Flux and mechs kill each other off," Knees agreed.

Sol watched as the rebels swarmed an Enforcer, crawling atop its shoulders and slamming their fists into it. The mech launched itself into the air and came down on its back, leaving a mess of bodies beneath it.

The Enforcer stood and was met by Ulrich, who bellowed as he charged and grasped the mech around the midsection. The Knight yanked both of his hands forward as if he was trying to lift the beast.

To Sol's dismay, the top half of the Enforcer's body slid to the ground, the pilot within halved along with his mech.

"I was starting to think there wouldn't be any fighting left for me today!" Ulrich grinned as he raised his twin crackling fans to the air.

Another Enforcer trampled several rebels as it charged across the grounds. It spun and punched a man in the face, exploding his skull in a shower of red. A rebel leapt in front of the Enforcer, rolled beneath a swinging arm, and punched a spike into the mech's foot.

N'auri.

The Enforcer threw a punch to the ground and N'auri twisted out of the way, piercing the mech several more times across the lower body as she spun.

The mech wobbled, wires hanging from a gash along its leg, but threw itself forward and caught N'auri in the shoulder with the bulbous head of its cannon. The Emeraldi's body spun like a top through the air and lay still in the dust.

"Stop!" Knees shouted. The Venturian pointed to Brynn, who was already running across the grounds toward N'auri's fallen body.

"Abel, stay and help Xenalia if she needs it," Sol directed the little Desovian, who nodded.

Sol jumped from the statue, Knees and Dozer following.

Brynn was standing protectively in front of N'auri, the massive Enforcer limping toward her.

"This be a regular thing now; you trying to get me killed for this girl?" Knees asked as they arrived at Brynn's side to face off with the approaching mech.

"Maybe," Brynn grunted, and threw herself at the Enforcer.

The steel beast stopped mid-stride and fell face-first to the ground before the Jadean even closed in. Wraith stood behind the mech with his spike dripping the blue blood of the pilot he'd impaled.

Sol heard a moan and N'auri slowly came to, holding her injured shoulder. She looked up at Brynn and smiled.

"Who are you with?" Wraith advanced on the Whelps, his hands' spikes blazing. "The Flux or the enemy?"

"Neither," Sol replied. "We're here for Cego."

"Then you choose the enemy," Wraith said, nodding to the ongoing battle between the two glowing combatants in the onyx. "Once the Slayer finishes off his brother in there, he'll want to destroy all who oppose the Flux."

The lieutenant took another menacing step toward the Whelps. "And so, I might as well do the job for him now."

"No." N'auri stood slowly and stepped in front of Brynn. "I won't let you hurt them."

"You dare to turn on us?" Wraith's eyes went wide. "You wish to throw away everything we've fought for—why? For this rabble?"

"Yes," N'auri growled, raising her own spike glowing with azure flame. "I happen to like this rabble."

"So be it," Wraith said just as Ulrich stumbled past, the big Knight on his heels as an Enforcer stalked him. "We'll let Silas deal with you."

Wraith turned and charged after Ulrich and the pursuing mech.

Brynn put her hand on N'auri's shoulder. "You...you've given up on the cause?"

N'auri shook her head. "No, but I think I've found a better one."

"Much as I hate to break up this moment, we've got to get back to Xenalia," Sol said, turning and sprinting toward the broken statue.

Her eyes widened as she stared at the place where the onyx Circle had been on top of the platform. It was gone, entirely shrouded by the strange darkness.

Cego was in there, and Sol could do nothing to help him now.

*   *   *

Pulling his foot from the slick sand, Cego checked Silas's incoming low kick. He countered with a body shot, and Silas let it through, only to return the favor with a stinging jab that further deformed Cego's nose.

Silas laughed as the storm grew stronger, crimson streaks now lacing the entire sky. Another wave smashed against the dunes and soaked the combatants.

Cego knew his brother enjoyed this. Silas loved fighting more than he loved the kin he claimed to fight for. Combat was the reason Silas had been put on this planet.

Cego had also been created to be a weapon, but he wanted to live for more. Deep in his bones, amid the sinews and dark energy that held him together, Cego wanted to survive to see those he loved again.

Perhaps that made him the weaker of the two.

With a low shot, Cego attempted to throw his brother into the black seawater beneath their feet, but his attempt was stuffed and he paid for it. A swift uppercut blasted his body and a sharp elbow slashed his face.

Cego spat blood into the water and charged. He couldn't slow the pace. He knew Silas would sink his teeth in at any show of weakness.

He rammed a cross and two jabs at Silas. His brother evaded and countered with a series of body shots that thudded into his ribs. Cego planted his good leg and threw a leaping knee that caught Silas on the chin and knocked him backward.

"You've improved, Strangler," Silas said as he ripped a tooth hanging from his mouth and tossed it into the sea.

"That's not me anymore," Cego replied as he leapt forward with another flurry. His brother dodged and countered with a knee that cracked into Cego's sternum.

Cego's next breath came with sharp pain. He staggered backward, nearly falling into the water. He bent over and labored for breath, looking up at Silas, a silhouette against the incandescent sky.

His brother had always been stronger. Nothing had changed between the two. Silas would win this fight once again.

"You know how this ends," Silas said as a glowing bolt struck the rising sea right beside them.

"I do," Cego said grimly as his brother circled him in the black water like a shark. "But this time will be different."

Silas laughed again. "Why will it be different, brother? All until now has been preordained; don't you see? Our birth in the Cradle, our training on the island, our release into this broken world. He speaks to us both. I know you've heard his voice too."

Cego stopped in his tracks, planted his feet, and let them sink deep beneath the muck. For just a moment, he looked past Silas, toward the dark horizon. He needed to stay here.

"You speak of Farmer?" Cego stalled. "I know it is he who speaks to you. It is Farmer who has spoken to us all. But how can you trust him? Farmer is not human. Perhaps he's never been, since he raised us on the island, he's always been a part of the blacklight… a part of them. The Bit-Minders."

"I've considered this," Silas said. "But it doesn't matter who Farmer is, Bit-Minder or Grievar. All that matters is he wishes to destroy the Daimyo, just as I do," Silas said.

"You've missed one thing, brother," Cego said as he stared over Silas's shoulder. "You're only another piece in their game. You're not some preordained or special being. You're not meant to lead or bring in some new world order."

Silas narrowed his eyes, bared his teeth.

"Farmer told me something, before I left the island, when you'd already gone," Cego continued. "You know what he told me? He said that you were the weakest of us three brothers, Silas. Back then, I dismissed our old master. I thought he was patronizing me. I couldn't understand how my older brother, who I'd never been able to touch in a fight, could be weaker than me."

Cego tensed his body as he spoke, trying to keep his eyes on his brother.

"But now, I understand what Farmer meant. You are the weakest, Silas. You were the easiest for Farmer to control, to send out and do his bidding. You've always been a pawn. To forces older and greater than you. To the voice in your mind. To your own hatred. And your greatest weakness is you don't realize any of it. You've had no choice but to follow the path laid out for you."

Silas charged. It was an uncharacteristic move for Cego's brother, who was a counterattacker. Still, Silas moved as fast as the lightning flashing above, and slammed a fist into Cego's already-broken body.

Cego crumpled inward, and his brother followed with a flurry of attacks, each connecting, each sapping vital life from his body. Cego remembered seeing Murray fall to Silas in Kiroth. He'd watched the old Grievar's lifeless form hit the ground with nothing left to give.

But Cego still had something left. He wouldn't let those who had sacrificed themselves go in vain. Cego fell backward, nearly broken, but with a hand grasped on his brother's wrist to pull him down. As the two tumbled toward the water, Cego hooked a foot behind Silas's leg. He summoned every ounce of energy left within him to throw his own body backward while heaving his brother up and over his head. Tomoe nage. The same sacrifice throw Silas had hit against him so many times throughout their childhood. And now, Cego landed a perfectly executed throw on Silas, rolling on top of his brother, pushing him down into the muck.

Still, a curved smile broke across Silas's face from below. Cego knew the smile wasn't one of pride because he'd bested his brother for once. No, Silas smiled simply because he understood that his opponent had exhausted himself. Cego wouldn't be able to hold his brother down for a moment longer.

But Cego didn't need to hold Silas down. For once, he didn't need to push harder. He didn't need to fight anymore. He pulled his eyes from Silas to watch the gargantuan wave rise above them like a leviathan, ready to swallow the entire island.

Silas looked at Cego curiously before the curved smile left his face. The black rain stopped, and instead, a strange silence fell on them along with a vast, unfurling shadow.

"I've made my choice." Cego closed his eyes.

The monster wave tore into the island, and Cego's world became a swirl of sea and sand. He tried to grasp for some handhold, a root or rock or anything else, as the entire bluff was ripped offshore and dragged to the deeps.

In the froth and darkness, as Cego held his breath, he tried to will himself back to Albright Stadium, away from this place. But he couldn't move; he was fastened to this world. His mind had come too far over this time.

Cego knew the tsunami that had swept over the island hadn't been real, that the thick water that held him down was only in his mind.

But that didn't matter.

Cego had grown from these dark waters. He'd been built on these black sand beaches. He'd been born of this blacklight.

And so, he would die here as well.

CHAPTER 29

A New Day

A harvester with spade and hoe might be as adept in their trade as a talented fighter with their fists. It is integral for each path to be followed in pursuit of perfection, regardless of its relation to societal station.

Passage Two, Thirty-Sixth Precept of the Combat Codes

Dakar Pugilio fidgeted with the high commander's badge set on the breast of his uniform.

He reached for the flask usually at his side pocket but stayed his hand as he realized it wasn't there.

"Guess I don't need the stuff anyway, eh?" Dakar turned to Commander Adrienne Larkspur, standing beside him on the stage.

"Probably not," Larkspur said. "Memnon would be proud of you."

"Right, I hope so," Dakar replied. "And I hope he'd do the same as I'm doing now."

"I believe he would," Adrienne responded.

Dakar turned from his friend and looked out into the audience within the Lyceum's Dome. He had no audio receiver, so he raised his deep voice to fill the auditorium.

"Lyceum student body and faculty, Knights of the Citadel, Flux patriots." Dakar paused, his own voice surprising him, as if he had not heard it in a long while.

Though the remaining Flux army could not all fit in the Dome, Dakar could see their lieutenants sitting in the front row, that pale one named Wraith with his eyes piercing the stage.

"Thank you for coming today," Dakar said. "I know you are still grieving like me. We lost many that day, all fighting for a cause they believed in."

A growing murmur emerged from both the rebel crew and the Citadelians in attendance.

"Our commander is dead," Dakar said. "Albion Jonquil Memnon, who served the Citadel for his entire life, sacrificed himself for our cause."

The Knights stood and raised their fists.

"For those Flux in attendance, Silas the Slayer is gone," Dakar said. "He also fought for what he believed in. He fought for Grievar-kin."

The Flux rebels drummed their feet against the Dome's creaky floors.

"Though we were on opposite sides, warring factions, now is the time for us to come together," Dakar said. "For there is a joint cause that both Memnon and Silas believed in. And that is the freedom of Grievar-kin."

A spatter of cheers rose from the crowd.

"There is no need for further retribution," Dakar said. "The Daimyo have already seen what happens if we Grievar no longer wish to fight for their purposes. There is no need to lose more lives."

Dakar pulled at the neck of his uniform, a size too tight.

"We are now at a pivotal point in Grievar history," Dakar said. "A time like none other, where we must see again by the light of the torch, eat again by the bounty of the land, fight again only with what we've been born with."

Dakar glanced up to the Dome's wide shield windows and the afternoon light filtering through.

"We are at a turning point where we can finally solidify both Memnon's and Silas's legacies. To do so, we must work together. We must rebuild together. We must fight together."

A chorus of cheers rose from the audience.

"Now I'll give the stage to Commander Larkspur, who has already proven herself to be an able leader during these times. She will outline our plans for rebuilding Memnon Stadium."

Dakar strode off the stage to continued cheers, sweat beading his forehead. Adrienne nodded to him, a slight smile creasing her lips as she stepped forward. She was impressed.

Perhaps I can do this, Dakar considered as he exited the Dome.

He followed the Harmony's long hall, quiet without the students filling it, and left the Lyceum through the central entry.

The Ezonian sky was a rare blue and the air full of wispy flower seeds. Dakar noticed the line of fresh saplings planted along the path he walked, work of the new Grunt conscripts. Some of the Grunts had taken to the abandoned fields outside the Citadel and even farther north to the outer rings. With their Daimyo masters fled, they would set their roots to harvest for themselves.

He looked out past the Citadel's walls and saw the crumbled form of Memnon Stadium. Renaming the stadium had been his first decree as high commander, along with the immediate order to repair it. He would rebuild, even better than before, make this place a true marvel for Grievar-kin to display their prowess to the world.

Dakar took a deep breath of the fresh air, something he'd not done in a while, before he stepped inside the Knight Tower and began the long climb to his new quarters. By the time he reached the old oaken door at the top, he was breathing hard.

Perhaps it was time to start training again.

Dakar entered the spartan room and rested his weary legs on

the tatami. Though he wished to respect Memnon's old aesthetic, the quarters could use an armchair at least.

"Now...that wasn't so hard, was it?" came a voice from the shadows.

"A drink would've made it easier." Dakar sighed.

"You are on a better path now, High Commander." A grey-haired man stepped onto the tatami. "We are all on a better path."

"I hope you're right, Farmer," Dakar said.

CHAPTER 30

Face the Darkness

There is a dream within a dream, where the entire world is asleep and cannot wake. Here, the light of day must be met with open eyes.

Passage Three, Third Precept of
the Combat Codes

Cego opened his eyes.

Something brushed against his skin. Tendrils of darkness slithered across him like eels. He was helpless as the black currents ran the length of his body and found their way in, penetrating his nose and ears, stuffing themselves into his mouth.

He tried to scream, but he was voiceless. He tried to think, to recall who or what he was, but even his thoughts were shrouded by the emptiness that had lodged itself inside him.

Cego hung in weightless suspension, a never-ending black stretched out before him. The wetness against his skin and the pressure of the darkness were heavy and sleepless.

If this was the end, what more could he do? Why fight it?

Maybe this was home.

A voice penetrated the void and a face illuminated the darkness.

"Who were you before you were born?" Farmer asked. The old master's wrinkled face pulsed with life in front of Cego before dissipating to black again.

Nothingness reigned until another luminescent form took shape, this one even more vivid, pushing the darkness all the way to the edges.

Cego saw himself walking on the beach beside Sam, the piercing azure sky above.

"The best crabs are the ones with the blue shells, don't you think?" Sam said. "Maybe Silas will bring some back from offshore today."

The island scene dissipated and was replaced by a round, smiling face. Joba Maglin reached out to Cego with those massive arms of his. And beside Joba stood a little boy, blood trickling from a cut on his face. Weep.

"If anyone was to get out of here, I'm glad it was you," Weep said from a place where vines crawled up stone walls and reached to street-level window grates.

The black intruded again, swept the vision away like a wave. Cego waited in the darkness until another radiant face came to life.

"You've got to darkin' keep at it, kid," Murray Pearson said as he stroked his grey beard. "If you let life hold you down, you'll stay down. So, you need to keep standing back up."

Cego tried to hold on to Murray, will him to stay for a moment more, but just like the rest of the visions, Murray left him alone in the darkness.

Cego waited an eternity. He had no grasp of time. He may have floated in nothingness for a second or a minute or a year, and none of it mattered, not until another voice dropped from above.

"You told me you would stop visiting me here," the voice said. "You said it would be the last time."

This voice had a different tenor from the rest. It came from a different place, one that Cego could reach out to, almost grasp.

"It is okay, Cego; I am here," the voice said. "Open your eyes."

Cego obeyed. He opened his eyes.

An overwhelming flood of light and sensation blasted him. It was nearly too much, but soon the light faded and Cego saw a familiar face hovering over his.

Xenalia.

"Are you real?" Cego asked, finding a parched whisper.

"I certainly hope so," Xenalia replied. "Though reality itself is subjective, given the neuron impulses that fire in your brain are likely different from what any other sentient being is experiencing, so actually, your question is quite—"

"Xenalia." Cego stopped the cleric. A painful smile slid across his face as he recognized Xenalia was indeed standing over him, not a vision in the void but a friend in the ward.

"I am sorry," Xenalia said. "I forget that it takes several days to fully reimmerse in this physical world."

Cego blinked and looked around. The medward was different somehow. Dimmer, quieter than he remembered.

He looked to one of the translucent stasis vats, empty of any occupants now. He could feel the wetness against his skin, his body floating in nothingness.

"I was in stasis?" Cego asked Xenalia. "How long was I gone?"

"You were gone three weeks," Xenalia said. "You suffered severe damage during your match, internal hemorrhaging, not to mention a variety of fractures and tears; all that needed to be repaired while you were out."

Cego tried to sit up and get a better look around, but a sharp pain stabbed at his midsection. The little cleric put a cold hand on his bandaged chest to keep him still.

He was glad to see Xenalia's pale face looking down at him, blue veins streaking her forehead. She looked different, though, changed somehow.

"I…I only remember fighting my brother," Cego recalled.

"We were on the island, in the Cradle. I'd left the arena behind. I thought I would never come back."

"I was not sure you would come back either." Xenalia frowned. "In particular because we had to do things…the old-fashioned way."

Cego shook his head, confused.

"I was there, watching you," Xenalia said. "The mass of black-light that hung over the Circle you and Silas stood in, my Observer took readings that were beyond anything I had ever seen before."

"Silas," Cego said. "Is he…"

"Gone," Xenalia finished. "Yes."

"How?" Cego had to know.

"As you know, I understand nothing of fighting," Xenalia said. "But even I could see the unnatural speed you two moved with. The black-light was feeding both of you and could not sustain the output."

"The island." Cego saw the black rain, the red veins of lightning, the giant tsunami. "It was falling apart."

Xenalia nodded. "I believe the Cradle was destroyed. It was already damaged when the Codex infrastructure was dismantled in Kiroth and Ezo, but some part of it remained, an imprint within its initial inhabitants, those born from the blacklight. When you fought Silas, the remaining structure appeared to have self-destructed…as if it were programmed to do so."

Cego was silent. The Cradle was gone. Silas was gone. He could feel a part of himself missing, as if Xenalia had removed some vital organ from Cego while he was unconscious.

"I saw both you and Silas in the aftermath within the Circle," Xenalia said. "I was able to get to you quickly enough and apply my remaining shot of catalytic adrenaline to restart your heart. Your brother Silas was dead already. His body was recovered by his lieutenants. They took him and gave him a proper burial."

"Wait," Cego said abruptly. He tried to sit up again, but pain racked his body, and Xenalia guided him back to a supine position.

"You said you applied your remaining shot of adrenaline. You had applied one before?"

Hope budded within Cego.

"Yes," Xenalia said. "I told you I was there watching you fight, but primarily, I was caring for Kōri Shimo."

"Shimo is...alive?" Cego asked.

"Yes," Xenalia said. "He was right beside you in this ward, recovering for the first two weeks. To be honest, I am still not quite sure how his symbiot reaction was able to fire so quickly after—"

"Thank you." Tears flooded Cego's eyes. Kōri Shimo was alive. *Sam* was alive.

"You are welcome, Cego," Xenalia said. "Though as you know, it is a part of my cleric's oath to care for all who come within my reach. If I could have saved your brother, I would have."

"Xenalia," Cego said. "You did save my brother."

"What?"

For once, Cego saw confusion flash across the cleric's eyes, though it didn't last for more than a moment.

"Ah, I see." Xenalia nodded. "Kōri Shimo was also born of the Cradle. His body housed the boy you grew up with, the one called Sam."

"But...if Kōri Shimo is my brother," Cego said, "who was the one I thought was Sam? The one you cared for in this ward for the past year?"

Xenalia smiled. "I had a theory and now it is proven true. The boy we housed was a Bit-Minder Hive, brought up from the Deep by your friend Murray Pearson. They were using his body to transmit the blacklight."

"Like Aon Farstead?"

"Yes," Xenalia said. "Though both of the Hives were destroyed."

Cego was weary. His eyes began to flutter shut, and he could feel the inky blackness intruding on the edges of his vision again. He feared he would lose this reality, that the nothingness would return.

"Please don't leave me," Cego whispered to Xenalia.

"I will not leave you," Xenalia replied. She placed her cold hand on his cheek. "Nor will any of your friends. They are as loyal as any I have seen on this planet."

Cego had not even considered the Whelps, whether they had survived the destruction of Albright Stadium that day. A pang of guilt hit him in the gut.

"Do not worry," Xenalia said. "Your friends are alive and well. In fact, I have had to prevent them from barging in here on numerous occasions, in fear that they would disturb your recovery. But the one called Solara...she was insistent. She watched over you every night. I told her she was not doing anything to help, but she refused to listen. I could not tell if it was stupidity or...something else that kept her here."

A smile broke across Cego's face and he felt his lip split open. Blood started to run down his chin.

Xenalia made a sound of annoyance and reached for the clotting ointment.

Suddenly, Cego realized why Xenalia looked different.

"Xenalia, where's your Observer?" Cego asked. He couldn't remember ever seeing the cleric apart from her little red spectral.

Xenalia frowned and shook her head. "It's gone."

"Oh, you mean helping elsewhere in the—"

"It's all gone, Cego." Xenalia stared down at him, brushing the hair from his forehead. "The energy...When your fight with Silas ended, when the Cradle was destroyed, it emitted a massive pulse of blacklight. It shut everything down: the Enforcers in the arena, the feeds, the factories...the cities. All technology stopped working. And the spectrals, they've all vanished."

All gone.

Cego's eyes began to close again.

This time, he let the darkness come.

EPILOGUE

"Y ou did good, Bird." Cego ruffled the few grey feathers remaining on the roc's head.

He could see his mount eyeing the other rocs with envy as they raced into the distance.

"No need to prove yourself anymore," Cego added. He knew Bird wouldn't be able to keep up with the likes of Firenze and Akari, who led the flock, kicking up a cloud of dust to the hazy sky.

He turned back the way they'd come, toward the Citadel and the whole of Ezo behind it. It was still strange seeing the lights out, the darkened skyscrapers of the Tendrum, like shadowed stalagmites rising to the ceiling of red sky above. He watched as a formation of starlings passed overhead to overtake the Citadel's lounging form.

Cego breathed deeply.

"You coming or what?" Dozer had circled back atop Boko, who'd gained quite a bit of weight and also couldn't keep up with the other birds.

"I'm on my way." Cego smiled at his friend. Though there were plenty of spare rocs back in the aviary now, Dozer had chosen to ride behind Knees, his big arms clasped around his friend with familiarity.

The three were quiet as they followed the road toward the Western Sea, and the sun sank closer to the land. A harvester pruning a garden patch in front of his newly constructed home nodded as they passed.

"See a big red bird go by?" Dozer asked the weathered man.

"Biggest I've seen in a while." The harvester paused to wipe sweat from his brow. "If you're with those other riders, you're behind some."

"They're going to start without us!" Dozer shouted.

"Don't be worrying, you block," Knees said. "We've got time."

Though Cego knew his Venturian friend was right as usual, he prodded Bird ahead so the others wouldn't be waiting long.

Soon, they crested the slope and the Western Sea swallowed their view, shimmering crimson all the way to the glowing horizon. Cego looked to the offshore island, saw the slumbering forms of the remaining Flyers slowly getting eaten away by the salt and wind.

The rest of the Whelps waited for them on the beach beside a circle of tall torches dug into the sand and burning brightly. Cego dismounted and left Bird occupied with a sack of dried fish beside the rest of the tethered rocs. He walked toward his waiting friends, feeling the sand and stones between his toes.

"Glad you didn't start yet!" Dozer yelled into the wind.

"What, and miss the opportunity to strangle you on this fine evening?" Sol grinned, her long braid glimmering in the twilight.

"I'm not letting that happen again, believe me," Dozer said as he pulled the tattered second skin off his back. "I even asked Professor Dynari for a good defense against you trapping my arm like that…"

"Not going to do you any good against the Firebird." N'auri flashed her sharp smile against the torchlight. "But I know some secrets on how to beat this girl."

Brynn stepped beside N'auri, putting her arm around the Emeraldi. "If you know how to beat Sol, how come you haven't told me yet? Spirits be said, I've been trying to figure it out for a while."

"Yes, yes," Abel said, creeping up next to Cego. "There must be sharing of technique secrets. It is said in the Codes."

"What Codes be saying that now?" Knees asked.

"Forty-third precept, fifth passage, one shall—"

"I think it's okay to keep a secret every once in a while, Abel," Cego interrupted.

"Right." Sol closed in on Cego and squinted at him. "Says the one who has decades more combat knowledge than the rest of us..."

"Not more than all of us." Kōri Shimo stepped from the shadows into the torchlight. "I know a few techniques that my brother has not yet seen."

"Oh?" Cego smiled at Kōri. He stepped within the circle of torches planted on the beach. "Perhaps you'd like to show me, then."

"It would be my pleasure." Kōri Shimo bowed his head slightly and stood across from Cego.

Cego smiled at his brother from across the darkness. He raised his fists.

ACKNOWLEDGMENTS

Dear reader,

I sincerely hope you enjoyed your time in the world of the Combat Codes.

I know I'll be missing my time there with these characters. Cego, Sol, Murray, and the entire crew feel as if they've been real companions for me over the past decade.

I used to scoff when I heard about other authors speaking of their stories and saying the characters are the ones who wrote them. I thought it was just a colorful way of describing the writing process. But throughout my time with this trilogy, it really has been the characters that have written the story for me. At each step, they've told me what needs to happen next, whether I was sending them on the right path, whether the words I gave them seemed illogical or insensible. It also seems strange that so many of these characters had an external influence in their minds, when it was really their voices constantly chattering in mine.

But there were certainly other inputs outside of my own or the characters that made it possible to write these stories. Ed Wilson, agent extraordinaire, who is a triple threat of savvy, enthusiastic, and dependable. Bradley Englert, master editor, who has breathed new life into the series. Angela Man, expert publicist, who worked to push this unorthodox blend of sci-fi, fantasy, and mixed martial arts to the right readers. Hillary Sames, who first gave the story a

shot and has been a champion ever since. The rest of the wonderful Orbit team in the US and UK, in particular Lauren Panepinto,
who headed design on the new covers.

Thank you as always to my family, you know who you are. My
girls, Mom and Dad, Kathy and Mike. Katie. Couldn't do this,
wouldn't do this, without you all.

To my training partners, who keep me sane, and to the entire
Brazilian jiu jitsu community, who helped grow the Combat Codes
from the roots.

And of course, my deepest appreciation to you, the reader, who
has ventured this far with me and the cast. Whether you were one
of the early adopters or a new fan of the series, I can't express how
wonderful it has felt to take you on this journey.

I do hope to return someday to the world of the Combat Codes.
There certainly are more stories to tell. But I need your help. Please
spread the word to any and all who you think might enjoy.

extras

orbit

meet the author

Jeanette Fuller

ALEXANDER DARWIN is a second-generation Vietnamese Jewish American author living in Boston with his wife and three daughters. Outside of writing, he teaches and trains in martial arts (Brazilian jiu jitsu). He's inspired by old-school Hong Kong action flicks, JRPGs, underdog stories, and bibimbap bowls.

Find out more about Alexander Darwin and other Orbit authors by registering for the free monthly newsletter at orbitbooks.net.

if you enjoyed
BLACKLIGHT BORN

look out for

CYBERPUNK 2077:
NO COINCIDENCE

by

Rafał Kosik

In sparkling Night City, a ragtag group of strangers have just pulled off a heist, robbing a convoy transporting a mysterious container belonging to Militech. The only thing the group has in common is that they were blackmailed into participating in the heist—and they have no idea just how far their mysterious employer's reach goes or what the purpose of the artifact they stole is.

This newly formed gang—composed of a veteran turned renegade, a sleeper agent for Militech, a computer nerd, a therapist, a ripperdoc, and a techie—must learn how to overcome their differences and work together, lest their secrets be unveiled before they can pull off the next deadly heist.

CHAPTER_1

Click. Click. Click. Didn't fit.

Like everything else. Like right now. He wasn't supposed to be here—didn't want to be. Squeezed between a wall and a dumpster in the goddamn pouring rain. Who knows, could be useful. The rain. Reduces visibility, provides a little natural cover. Yeah, the rain could stay.

Click. Click. Still didn't fit. His clothes were soaked. Uncomfortable, but a reminder he was alive even though he shouldn't have been.

Zor should've been dead seven years and counting.

Gray water cascading from an utterly gray sky. The upper floors of the abandoned kibble factory dissolving into a gray nothing. The lower levels of the Petrochem BetterLife power plant looming farther ahead, barely visible. Arroyo—not the quaintest of Night City neighborhoods.

A couple of passersby scurried past—hardly a glance in his direction. Indifferent cars splashed through oil-slicked puddles, spilling onto the sidewalk. Might as well be invisible.

Click. Click. Gotta be kidding me. He looked down at the magazine. Upside down, stupid. He'd already forgotten how to do this. Seven years is a long time. Even muscle memory wasn't spared.

Click. Now we're in biz. Not like it changed much. Not a snowball's chance in hell this was gonna work, not with this team. One in a hundred chance, maybe? A thousand? Wishful thinking said one in five, but even those odds don't inspire confidence.

"*Thirty seconds,*" said the synthesized voice through his earpiece.

Don't wanna be here—don't wanna do this. No way this would work. He looked down at his hands holding the SMG. Then it hit him. He couldn't imagine any other place he ought to be. Couldn't picture any other time or place where he'd fit. Rain, a dumpster and a gun.

And no choice.

"*Twenty seconds. Stand by; target's approaching!*"

He reached into his pocket and flipped his spare mag the right way up. He wrapped one hand around the pistol grip, the other around the foregrip. He remembered how to do this. Sort of. Seven years takes its toll. Seven years and a death along the way. His own.

A stout, boxy truck emerged through the veil of rain. Armor-plated, by the looks of it. Regular four-door at its twelve— probably also reinforced. His bullets wouldn't even scratch it.

Zor slowly rose to his feet, not moving from his hiding place. The other side of the road was closed off, dug up for repair, which meant two-way traffic was choked through a single lane. Their security ought to take extra precautions—take a detour, even. Probably banking on blending in—neither the truck nor the car in front bore any official insignia. Nothing out of the ordinary to anyone walking by.

"*Zor! Now!*" the voice commanded.

Zor aimed and squeezed the trigger. The short *rat-a-tat* echoed off the nearby buildings. The few pedestrians around made themselves even scarcer. Couldn't be any doubt in the guards' minds now—the convoy's cover was blown. The burst had pierced through the armor of the car in front and decomished the engine. Little SMG did the trick after all. Zor looked at it in surprise. The Militech M221 Saratoga wasn't the flashiest iron out there, but the increased impact velocity from its tungsten rounds made short work of most light armor. Sure, the gun would be useless after a few bursts, but that was beside the point.

The rain stopped. Vapor hissed from under the hood. Steam—maybe smoke. Nobody seemed to be getting out. The truck had stopped barely an inch away from the X chalked on the sidewalk, not yet completely washed away by the downpour. It was the perfect bottleneck—all according to plan. A vintage Quadra coupe came to an abrupt stop behind the truck, which was trying to reverse, backing straight into the sports car's fender.

A tall, slim woman got out of the Quadra to examine the damage. Short dark hair, high heels, elegant suit. Wrong place, wrong time for a corpo to vent their road rage.

Why the hell aren't they getting out?

Warden leaned over a folding table and observed the situation on the monitors. The digital clock in the bottom-right corner counted down the time it would take for the badges to appear. Only ETAs, but still.

Through the windows, the neighboring high-rises hovered in the rain like ghostly monoliths. The rain was a boon, but it couldn't guarantee the plan's success. How long before they traced him? Only a matter of time. The thirty-third floor of an unfinished apartment block on the south side of Heywood and a good two miles from the ambush—an ample getaway margin in case everything went to shit. Two minutes, tops. Disassembling and packing all the module military equipment into briefcases shouldn't take him any longer.

Not so for the netrunner.

A tangled web of cables ran along the rubble-strewn concrete floor toward the bathroom, where they joined to a hermetic coupling plugged into the neuroport behind the netrunner's ear. He lay submerged from the neck down in a tub filled with icy slush, while his brain occupied itself with multiple processes—slowing the police and security response being the top priority. What he didn't know was that he was in a race against time for his own life. Coming out of a deep dive would take time.

Warden drew his pistol—a silver Tsunami Nue with gold accents—and checked his ammo count. No point leaving behind someone who knew this much. But right now, he needed him—in fact, the whole operation rested on his submerged shoulders.

Warden checked the monitors again. What were they waiting for?

"Change of plan—we'll smoke 'em out," he said into the open channel. "Milena, stand down."

It was a classic corpo tantrum. Gesticulating wildly, she shrieked at the truck driver, demanding his insurance company, making sure he knew just how much he'd fucked up. High heels, suit—she really did look the part. Too good, almost. Even pretended she'd forgotten the shots fired a minute ago. She stood right on the chalk X. Safe, just outside his line of fire. But then she took three steps forward.

"Milena, I repeat—stand down."

Either she was still pretending or she really didn't hear it. Auditory exclusion. Throw stress into the mix and nothing goes the way it's supposed to.

"Ron, light 'em up," Warden barked over the comms.

extras

"What about Milena? She could get shot."

"You'll all get shot if you don't stick to the plan."

"Give me a sec." Zor preferred it if no one got shot. "I have a good angle."

He switched the Saratoga to semiauto and fired a single round at the car, carving an ugly scar into the hood. The doors opened and three guards spilled out. Rookies, judging by their awkward shuffling. They wore Militech uniforms and were equipped with the minimum standard-issue weaponry. From where he stood, Zor could instantly take out two if he wanted. No, not necessary.

Milena seemed not to have heard Warden's orders, nor Zor's gunshot. She continued laying into the driver with the fervor of a hot-blooded Italian prima donna, pointing back and forth between the driver and her front fender.

Finally, the driver's door of the truck opened.

"Aya! You're up!" The voice belonged to Warden.

You could tell at first glance. The slim, nimble woman with East Asian features who was hidden behind the pillar had exactly no experience in these kinds of stunts. She fumbled with the grenade launcher before they heard the muffled, familiar *foomp* followed by an unmistakable hiss. Smoke started billowing from the windows of the truck. Her shot turned out perfect.

"Borg, on your mark!"

Two figures stumbled out of the haze following a burst of gunfire from the left. Most of the bullets disappeared into the gray, save for one—likely by accident. The driver tumbled to the ground. The second guard quickly sidestepped and took cover behind the large back wheel.

"Tighten your aim!"

The next burst only skipped along the wet blacktop. Borg couldn't aim for shit.

396

Heels clacking, Milena dashed around the corner of one of the buildings and tossed another smoke grenade. It flew in an arc over the street, hitting the streetlight with a metallic *ding* and landing only a few yards away from Zor. Damn it! Is she even trying to aim?

With another hiss, smoke started spewing from the grenade, partially blocking Zor's view of the street.

Aya fired a burst at the truck. Probably the first time in her life she's pulled a trigger. Less than a hundred feet away and, from the sound of it, not a single bullet found its mark.

Without a visual on their attackers, three guards in uniform started blind firing from behind the car. The fourth, crouched behind the truck wheel, spotted Aya taking cover behind an old, burned-out car wreck near the sidewalk.

"Aya! Down— Get down!" Zor barked into his mic.

She quickly ducked just as a volley of heavy machine-gun fire pierced the car's body like paper. Milena's Quadra wasn't by any means bulletproof, which is why they'd lined the inside with anti-ballistic panels only an hour earlier. They served their purpose.

"Aya, stay behind cover," Zor cautioned.

Those three would have to wait. One thing at a time. He knew one of the guards was behind the rear truck wheel—he just couldn't see him. He aimed at the tire and fired three times. High, middle and low. His wrists were sore from the recoil. The bolt went slack. It was about to either jam or fall apart entirely. Hardly mattered, since the rounds were only hitting rubber. But now the rest knew where he was hiding. A few bullets whizzed over his head, causing little puffs to shoot out of the wall. The smoke grenade turned out to be his savior, though he still couldn't afford to lean out so much as an inch.

Seconds passed; neither side could do anything. Stalemate.

"*Cover me!*" Aya called out over the comms.

She jumped from out behind cover.

"Aya—!" Zor began, but it was already too late to stop her. He leaned out and fired a few rounds, mostly for suppression's sake—he had no chance of hitting anyone from his position.

Aya climbed onto the Quadra's roof, then jumped toward the roof of the truck and pulled herself up. Twice the speed of any soldier. A few rifle bursts sliced through the air—Aya strafed and fired three rounds up close. The guard slumped down to the ground, limp.

"*Ron!*" Warden commanded.

"*'Bout time! Almost dozed off.*"

The low thumping of an HMG broke out, hidden somewhere behind a first-floor window. Chunks of sidewalk flew into the air, a fire hydrant erupted in a jet of water and the construction barriers surrounding the closed-off section of the street collapsed and clattered into a pile of rubble. There was even a distant sound of glass shattering from windows that must have been three hundred feet away. Somehow, the unmarked car remained untouched.

"*Wow.*" It was Milena. "*Great accuracy…*"

"*Hey, it's the first time I've ever done this, okay?!*"

The guards stayed behind the car and ceased their fire. A small victory, at least.

"Aya!" shouted Zor. "Over here!"

Aya vaulted over the car wreck and reached Zor's hiding place in no time. He grabbed her and pulled her behind him.

"Thanks." She pressed herself against the wall, tied back her long hair and checked her iron. Her shoulder was bleeding.

"Show me." Zor gently took her arm and examined the wound. Not life-threatening.

"It's just a scratch." Aya clumsily tried to reload.

"Ron!" Zor called into his mic.

"Yeah, I'm on it!"

A brief volley, maybe five bullets—three on the mark. The car was blown open like a metal can ruptured by a firecracker. Their cover now useless, the guards retreated.

"Take cover!" It was Warden. *"Shield your weapons!"*

Zor leaped behind the dumpster and pushed Aya closer toward the wall.

"Keep your gun behind cover," he ordered.

He could materialize everything in real time and adapt the interface to his liking, mold his own cyberspatial habitat. Every netrunner had their own tastes and quirks. He preferred to keep things tidy—no frills, no distractions. He adjusted the brightness, swapped out colors for readability, nuked the waterfall animation for incoming data.

He didn't care much about the Arroyo op. He thought of it like a game. He would've managed fine on his own cyberdeck, but the gear he got for this gig was a definite step up. He felt powerful—reality was his to control as he pleased. And the codes from Borg actually worked. He had free rein over the traffic lights in that part of Arroyo.

He was propelled by a surge of joy as he floated around his self-configured control room. Essential elements were divided into subcategories and pinned above and around him. He hung suspended amid hundreds of symbols and icons woven together in an irregular sphere with seemingly no exterior, though in reality it was shielded by a thick layer of black ICE.

Time for the next step. No need to rush. Time flowed differently here—slower. Zor's dash for the dumpster looked as if the outside world had been submerged in oil.

Local CCTV access definitely helped. The techies at the control center were surely frantically looking for the cause of their alarm, unaware it was created on purpose. He rerouted his NetIndex to cover the length of half the district. He didn't expect any unwelcome visitors in his temporary domain; nevertheless, he triple-encrypted all possible points of entry. It'd take at least six security experts to figure out his exact location—and even then, by the time they identified the intruder's whereabouts, they'd find nothing but a cold, dark void.

He liked to keep it simple. A pair of rectangular prisms hovered to his left—two big red buttons. Detonators.

Using thought-command, he transmitted a nerve impulse to his immaterial hand and pressed them both.

Two EMP charges hidden in a trash-littered street gutter chirped quietly as they activated. The ammo count on Zor's SMG flickered—all else seemed unaffected. No surprise, since it was mechanical. He noticed Aya's body twitch. Through his drenched clothes, Zor felt the heat rising off her.

Borg opened fire from the right, shooting everything within sight.

"EMP didn't do anything to us," Zor said, trying to comfort her. She nodded hesitantly.

The steel dumpster did its job—their weapons were safe, whereas it would take five seconds for the guards' advanced firing mechanisms to unlock. Five seconds was all they needed.

Now!

"*Now!*" Warden ordered.

Zor leaped out of cover and opened fire. Shouldn't Borg and Ron be covering them? Fuck! He shot at the ground to make more noise and avoid hitting any buildings or windows. Ricochets and the splattering of water across the road made a better impression. A few windows cracked from the ricochets. Aya followed close behind him, mimicking his movements.

"*Borg, the tow truck!*" Warden shouted.

The guards dropped their weapons and raised their hands in the air.

Beautiful. Amateurs on both sides.

A shot. One of the guards fell.

"Borg!" Zor looked around. "Hold your fire!"

He ran to the guards and kicked their rifles under their bullet-ridden car. He shoved one of them around so that he stood facing what was left of the construction barrier. The second, equally terrified, didn't need any prompting and followed suit. Aya did a quick pat down and removed the pistols from their holsters. Didn't even bother trying to use them earlier.

Borg finally emerged from his hiding place wearing his signature violet-navy jumpsuit. He approached nonchalantly, as if he was starring in an action flick, his lime-green hair slicked back. He was preparing to take another shot.

"Borg, drop it!" shouted Zor.

Borg didn't listen. He grinned like a mischievous child about to do something naughty.

"*Borg, the truck!*" This time it was Warden. "*Stick to the plan.*"

"You heard 'im," Zor growled.

Borg carelessly swung the rifle upward and rested it against his shoulder. He winced and quickly repositioned it. The barrel was still hot. He switched off his comms link to stop Warden from listening in.

"You mean the plan that put our asses on the line," Borg began, "while he's sittin' comfy givin' us orders!" He rolled up his sleeves and briefly operated a panel just above his wrist. It beeped and his arms and shoulders started to swell. In seconds they were nearly one-and-a-half times their original size. He gave a satisfied laugh and kissed his bicep.

"Impressive, ain't it?" He winked at Aya.

"Not really, no." She didn't even look at him as she held the two guards at gunpoint. "Just get the tow truck here."

"*Time!*" urged the netrunner's computerized voice.

Borg grudgingly turned and jogged to where he should've been half a minute ago—a serious deviation from the plan.

Police sirens faintly wailed in the distance.

"Go. Start running!" Zor ordered the guards, at the same time gently lowering Aya's arms.

The guards glanced at each other in confusion, then nearly tripped over themselves as they ran away at full tilt.

"The lock!" Zor called out.

Aya ran around the truck, her black ponytail whipping the air. She really was fast, but nothing indicated that she had any implants. Zor stood by the front and kept his eyes on the end of the street.

"*Mine's armed,*" Aya reported. "*Five seconds.*"

They heard the sudden roar of a monstrous engine, followed by the beeping of a garbage truck in reverse.

"Yo, what the shit?!" Borg started, confused. "Drivin's s'posed to be my job!"

"*Should've driven it, then, instead of fuckin' around,*" Milena retorted over the comms.

Aya dashed around the side of the truck and leaned against the front fender. She pressed her hands over her ears and shut her eyes.

But there was hardly any blast at all. It sounded more like a bottle rocket than a mine. All the better—they needed the cargo intact.

They hurried back around and pulled open the rear doors.

"*There anything I should do?*" Ron asked with uncertainty in his voice.

"No, you can come down," Zor replied. "Need to unload this and delta outta here. Badges'll be here any minute, not to mention 6th Street."

Borg, disgruntled at being called out, guided Milena as she reversed the garbage truck toward their payload. It was probably the first time she'd driven anything bigger than a standard sedan. She scraped the side of the Quadra, though this time she didn't care. Ride was stolen, anyway.

In the middle of the truck's cargo lay their objective—a gray container.

They stood there for a moment and stared at it. They had a feeling they were in the presence of something...important. No time to waste, though. Zor took out a knife and cut the straps holding it in place. He tugged on the handle. Wouldn't budge.

"No way we're lifting this," Zor said. "Borg, make yourself useful and do the honors."

Borg scowled and walked over to a lift control box duct-taped to the side of the garbage truck. It was a last-minute addition. Basic, but effective. With a low whirr, a crane emerged from the roof with straps and hooks dangling from its end. Zor attached them to the sides of the container. The crane let out a groan as it started lifting.

"Motherfucker weighs more than six hundred pounds." Borg seemed impressed. "Hell's inside this thing?"

The sirens were growing louder.

"*Two minutes,*" the netrunner notified them.

"Estimated or actual?" asked Aya.

"*I can buy you thirty seconds, no more.*"

Zor looked at Aya. He could've done this without everyone else, he thought. Except her. And the netrunner, of course. Whoever he was.

A tall, skinny figure appeared at the entrance to the abandoned factory. Zor reached for his pistol.

"Jesus, Ron!" His hand froze midway. "A heads-up next time."

"Whoa, hey!" Ron sidestepped a good second too late. "Battin' for the same team, remember?" He theatrically placed his hand over his chest. "Mighty kind of you to spare me."

His oversized work coat hung on his shoulders like a trash bag. His short, gray-streaked hair was tousled. He seemed laid-back, almost as if none of this was real, but a braindance that could be paused, rewound, fast-forwarded past all the tough moments.

Though the container was about the size of your average bathtub, the roof of the truck bent slightly upward and the crane bowed under the load as it hoisted it up above the garbage compartment.

"*Time!*"

Zor cut the straps once more. The container dropped with a heavy thud, making the truck bob up and down.

"Let's move!"

Warden watched the monitors as the garbage truck drove off at full speed. He raised an eyebrow as it hit the corner of a parked car and shoved it against a streetlight.

On the smaller screen, he saw two NCPD patrol cars speeding from the opposite direction a few blocks away. He sooner expected to see a Militech rapid-response unit—usually light-years ahead of the badges. No sign of them, though.

It was slowly dawning on him that they had actually pulled this off. He didn't believe in it at first. The op, pitched by the client himself, wasn't just strange—it seemed downright impossible. Usually, clients tell you what they want and how much they're willing to pay for it. This one had it all worked out from the start, gonk as it sounded. Funny how it did work out. Maybe the plan wasn't so scopbrained after all. The thought that this strategy could be repeated in the future briefly crossed Warden's mind. Force a bunch of amateurs to do the job—it all crashes and burns; you lose nothing.

Just one oversight—they knew his face, his name. Next time that'd have to change.

orbit

Follow us:

f **/orbitbooksUS**

𝕏 **/orbitbooks**

▶ **/orbitbooks**

Join our mailing list
to receive alerts on our
latest releases and deals.

orbitbooks.net

Enter our monthly
giveaway for the chance
to win some epic prizes.

orbitloot.com